SERPEN

"Oh, God," Dave said, his hair rising on end and his knees giving. "It's got two heads."

Annabelle took the flashlight quickly from Dave's hand. She knelt by her car's open door, peering in at the animal on the floor.

The snake was about two feet long, and it did have two heads. Her throat constricted, and she could not swallow. She recognized it. It was a cottonmouth, a juvenile about as thick around as her middle finger, its skin a smooth weave of black diamonds. But she had never seen one with two heads—four eyes and two lightning tongues, flicking in and out from the white, cottony linings of the two small open mouths. The little mouths were among the most venomous in existence. . . .

THE Alligator's Farewell

HIALEAH JACKSON

A DELL BOOK

Published by
Dell Publishing
a division of
Bantam Doubleday Dell Publishing Group, Inc.
1540 Broadway
New York, New York 10036

ISBN: 0-440-22660-0

Printed in the United States of America

Published simultaneously in Canada

January 1999

10 9 8 7 6 5 4 3 2 1
WCD

This book is for Florida, my spiritual home, and for the Mikosukee Indians, who saved their lives by becoming ghosts who live in a land where there is no land

ACKNOWLEDGMENTS

I am grateful for conversations with Dr. Gary Ehrhardt, Senior Research Scientist at the University of Missouri–Columbia Research Reactor Facility, especially because he showed me that scientists have a sense of humor about science; to James Schockett of Miami, for pharmaceutical information; to Dr. Raymond Kimsey of Miami, for counsel on things that numb; to Russell Culp, Manager of Research and Development at Ansell, Inc., Dothan, Alabama, manufacturers of Lifestyles Condoms; and to Eileen DeCora, Miami Metro-Dade Police, for a tough talk about guns.

MONDAY

It is important to remember that all knowledge
is a piece and that any observation can have
an unexpected and surprising connection to something
that apparently has nothing to do with it.

ISAAC ASIMOV
The Atom

ONE

THE LAST CONDOM WAS THE WORST.

Working in the dark lab by the diffuse glow of a halogen flashlight, Rolando Ruiz de Castillo had already filled twenty of the oily latex bags with a fortune in blue topaz, now sparkling coldly on the desk through the thin beige rubbers. His fingers were cramped from nerves and haste, and they tingled with sparks of hot pain. The burning pains did not surprise him, but the messy, slippery business of the lubricant was unexpected and had added precious minutes to his handling of the gems.

And he found the topazes themselves distracting. They were "London Blues," emerald-cut and flashing pale fires up into his thick spectacles. Their potential value to his buyers was half a million dollars, but that price would only be a lovely speculation until he got the gems past the nuclear reactor's computerized detector system and alarm. *In theory*, he knew how to do it: His own body would provide the shield against sensor detection of the massive and perilous radioactive signature of the Blues—these jewels were "hot," spewing out streams of beta particles and gamma rays.

Rolly pushed his glasses up on his nose, leaving smears of the lubricant on the lenses. He pinched a few more radioactive gems out of the gray plastic box and into his oily grasp. Their cut surfaces were so smooth that he did not worry about ripping the ribbed latex as they clinked dully into the last condom.

Leaning heavily against the wall, Rolly pulled the tail of his black knit shirt out of his tight jeans, gently rubbed his stinging fingers—there were hundreds of tiny red burns on the tips—and breathed, away from the stones.

The luminous orange numbers on his watch told him that it was 11:14. The security guard would not pass by this lab until one minute past midnight. Rolly now had maybe forty-five minutes for the difficult part.

Here, in the silent basement of the Ring Building surrounding the reactor, Rolly's solitude seemed to stretch and bubble outward around him, an almost palpable protective skin, and he straightened quickly to shake off the sensation. He leaned over the desk and wiped its surface with the tail of his shirt, swirling it through the pool of halogen light. The motion was reflected brokenly on the smeared lenses of his spectacles.

He fished in the pocket of his jeans for a tiny aluminum bottle, uncapped it, and sprayed the cold mists of lidocaine into his throat, knowing that within a minute his neck would be numb.

From a paper bag on the floor he took a six-pack of bottled Evian water; from the desk, a large pair of scissors. He poured a couple of ounces of water into one of the sparkling, bulging condoms, holding it toward the flashlight to confirm his guess about the rightness of the proportion. With the scissors he cut off the hard ring of rubber at the open end and dropped it into the paper bag. He twisted the ragged latex end of the condom, tied a knot in it, and forced the whole thing into his small mouth, popping his jaw audibly. Then he drank from the bottle.

This time the first condom was the worst. Rolly thought briefly that he would die as the bagged stones lodged first in his throat and then seemed to explode under his Adam's apple while a latex flap licked the back of his mouth and the sweet taste of his own vomit went up his nose. Gagging, but frantically fighting the wretching instinct, he chugged the water remaining in the bottle and jerkily opened another. Now the topaz burned behind his sternum, and he touched himself, feeling for a bulge. There was no bulge. His watch said 11:17.

He nearly panicked. Not enough water, not enough time. Maybe the rubbers would not protect his guts against this much radiation. Maybe the lidocaine was not working. He sprayed his throat again.

He swallowed convulsively, and there it was—a blessed if partial numbness. He snatched the next condom, ripped off the ring with the scissors, tied the knot, and shoved the thing into his mouth. This time he worked while he endured the decreasing agony in his throat: pouring, snipping, tying, drinking; pouring, snipping, tying, drinking. The agony of the rhythm, or the rhythmic agony, or the adrenaline surge induced by his panic—something obliterated the passage of time, and when, exhausted and sick and sweaty, he next looked at his luminous watch, it was 11:49.

His throat was both raw and numb. His jaws ached.

Tears stung his eyes, but Rolly counted everything carefully, turning his head and peering owlishly through clean patches on the thick, smeared lenses of his glasses: twenty-one condom wrappers, twenty-one rings, seven boxes that had each held three condoms, six bottles, six tops, cardboard basket from the bottles, pair of scissors, the gem box with lid, a paper bag, the flashlight. His radiation badge lay on the far corner of the desk, and he reached jerkily for it, shoving it into his pants pocket. The trash he jammed into the paper bag, stepping on it to compress the stuff. The sudden sharp noise terrified him, and he jumped. 11:50.

He swore softly, and was absently aware that no sound came out; he must have overdosed with the lidocaine, inhibiting his vocal cords. He rolled the paper bag in his hands and, as one of the heavy condoms dropped suddenly, somewhere under his ribs, he opened the small door in the wall marked "contaminated and radioactive waste." He consigned the paper bag and its contents to the pneumatic tube behind the door, imagining the garbage riding a cushion of the gas argon-40 on its way to low-level nuclear waste storage, where trash with minor amounts of radiation was held, to be buried or burned when it measured safe on a Geiger counter. 11:51.

He crossed the lab to the vault room, with the plastic box in his hands and the flashlight under his arm. The condoms and water sloshed as he walked; he heard them as a sort of guilty accompaniment to his silent steps, and they seemed preternaturally loud, a clarion in his swollen belly.

Inserting his card key, Rolly typed in the Topaz Project code on the keypad. The door swung open. He stepped inside. The room was half full of identical boxes in floor-to-ceiling slots. He awkwardly shoved his box under two boxes in slots to the left of the door and lined them up together carefully. He stepped back into the lab, swung the door shut, and removed his card key. 11:54.

Rolly returned to the desk. Despite the rolling misery in his guts, he smiled grimly. He had forgotten nothing. 11:55.

He was going to get away with it. He pulled open the waste chute and dropped the flashlight into the pneumatic tube.

The heavy door to the lab opened with its characteristic *pouf,* like air expelled from a boat cushion. His stomach lurched, shifting the bags of topaz painfully.

"Good evening, Dr. Castillo. Working late?"

When he turned at the sound of the voice, a wave of nausea slapping against his ribs, Rolly suddenly spotted the scissors. He sat hastily on the edge of the desk, placing his left hand slightly behind him and turning to face the newcomer.

He automatically framed a reply, some conventional greeting, but what came out when he opened his mouth was a belch of such startling magnitude that it felt to him like an act of aggression.

Standing in the open doorway, outlined in the spill of light from the hall, was someone wearing a full yellow radiation suit and hood, and Rolly heard the distorted voice issue from the small microphone inside the hood:

"That's not very polite, Dr. Castillo."

He raised his eyebrows in what he hoped was a look of enlightened inquiry aimed at the radiation suit, but which was more likely a ghastly smirk. His left hand closed over the cold blades of the scissors behind him on the desk. His inability to speak was going to give him away, was going to shout out his guilt, was going to brand him like an obscene stain.

He glanced furtively at his watch. 11:56.

He looked back at the yellow suit. The natural thing to do would be to ask what was wrong, why this person was wearing full radiation protection, and to ask quickly. He opened his mouth and another belch rumbled out from the depths of his assaulted digestive tract.

"Stand up, Dr. Castillo."

There was a flat snarl in the voice that Rolly strained to understand only at the periphery of his mind, so intent was he on gathering his senses somehow to communicate, to meet whatever urgency had brought this person to the lab in a radiation suit, to get out of the room without arousing suspicion. He stood, cramming the scissors into the back pocket of his jeans. He stuck them in, awkwardly but firmly, handles first.

And he suddenly noticed, with a cold and horrible clarity through the fog of his lenses, the other's yellow gloves and what they were holding. And he saw how close they were now standing to each other. And then he felt the infinitesimal prick of the huge syringe on the skin of his tingling neck, just over his jugular.

"If you do exactly what I tell you, Dr. Castillo, I may not shoot this shit into your neck. At least not on purpose."

Now Rolly knew what the radiation suit was for. He forgot all about his watch and his timetable and his guilt. Even the bags of topaz in the tight and protesting labyrinth of his digestive tract faded to a distant and manageable discomfort. Still incapable of normal speech, fascinated by the syringe, he half mouthed, half whispered, "What is that?"

"This, my very dear Dr. Ruiz de Castillo, is a little radio-isotope called cobalt-sixty."

Oh, God. The topaz was nothing, *nothing*, compared to this.

The lidocaine was wearing off, but Rolly was not certain if the thin, cold point on his neck was all he should be feeling there.

The pressure on his neck remained steady and precise, and so did the gloved hand, but his assailant moved around Rolly to glance at the desk. Dim yellow light filtered into the lab at the height of Rolly's stomach through a low, narrow window looking onto the corridor.

"What were you doing in here in the dark, Dr. Castillo?"

Rolly opened his mouth to attempt a reply, but the metal point on his neck jumped, and he froze.

"Don't bother to answer, Dr. Castillo. It could kill you. Now, you're going to lead the way into the reactor tower. And you do one weird thing, you can kiss your bone marrow good-bye. Instantly." Rolly heard the folds of the suit crinkle beside him. "Hold it a minute."

Distorted through the microphone, the voice softened. But Rolly did not dare turn his head to peer through the plastic shield covering the face inside the suit. For a brief halcyon moment, Rolly thought he would be spared when the needle was withdrawn from his neck. Then he felt the prick deep inside his right ear.

"Move. Carefully. Cobalt-sixty does not take prisoners."

Oh, God, he thought. *Cobalt-sixty has a lethal time of forty-eight hours maximum.* But he'd be a dead man the second it entered his neck. Nothing could wash that stuff out. Nothing. He concentrated on putting his foot forward without a squeak on the shiny linoleum floor. The needle in his ear was held steady.

When he reached the lab door, he pushed it open slowly but not all the way, edging into the dimly lit hall. His eyes adjusted slowly, and he blinked rapidly. Through the white film on his glasses, he could just make out the digital clock halfway down the corridor. The blurred white numbers seemed to say 12:00:02.

If he could walk slowly enough until they reached the elevator, the guard would see them when he came to make his rounds at 12:01.

"Move, Dr. Castillo." The words were hissed through the microphone and into his ear along the length of the syringe.

He walked, estimating fifteen yards to the elevator.

They stopped by the doors, and he reached for the button automatically. His hand was nudged away. A yellow-gloved finger poked the button.

Rolly silently willed the guard to appear down the corridor. The elevator doors opened. They walked in, and, as the doors closed, Rolly saw the clock: 12:00:44.

He closed his eyes in despair, trying to think.

They rode in silence to the next floor, Rolly furiously unable to make his usually reliable mind do anything. His neck was now stiff from the effort not to kill himself by rocking into the needle. The doors opened. Together they stepped out, beside another door.

"Open the airlock, Dr. Castillo."

Rolly mindlessly dug out his plastic key case from his jeans and inserted his card key into the slot. The huge door whooshed open. They stepped into what looked and felt like a monster elevator car but was actually just a space going nowhere—the floor twelve feet by thirty feet, the walls nine feet high.

They could not feel the exchange of gases that provided a barrier of air between the outer ring structure and the reactor containment tower. In fewer than ten seconds the green light came on over the opposite door. They walked to the far end of the airlock. Rolly reached to the wall to insert his key again.

"Business as usual, Dr. Castillo, or I'll jam this radioactive soup so far inside your skull, you'll wish it was a nice, clean bullet."

His hands were so sweaty and oily that he worried he'd drop the plastic key. His captor caught Rolly's hesitation and a yellow glove took the key from his nerveless hand and shoved the plastic into the slot. They waited for the operators upstairs in the control room to respond.

Getting into the reactor building was difficult, nobody could get in without a security key and the reactor operators releasing the airlock's second door. Getting out required nothing special—if anyone ever really needed to get out of the reactor tower in a hurry, there would be no unnecessary obstacles. Fast evacuation was designed into the entire architecture of the reactor, including the operation of all doors.

The voice from the second-floor control room of nuclear containment came over the speaker: "Hello, hello, airlock, and a very good morning to you. Friend or foe?"

Rolly cleared his throat, almost as a reflex. He swallowed stiffly, convulsively. He moved his mouth close to the wall microphone and whispered, "It's Rolly Castillo."

Suddenly the other's gloved left hand covered Rolly's mouth and the whisper came: "We're going to the top, Dr. Castillo."

The glove was removed from his mouth. He tried to swallow again. "It's Rolly. Uh, good morning. I'm going upstairs. Open up, guys."

The control room came back on: "You sound like a ten-cent whore, Rolly. Spit it out and welcome aboard."

The airlock door was released, his key was returned to him, and they walked into the inner building containing the reactor.

They boarded the interior elevator, riding again without any words, and stopped at the second floor. The elevator only went to the second floor; to get to the top floor, they would have to use the stairs.

"I'm going to move the needle to the base of your spine now, Dr. Castillo, so I can walk behind you. When the door opens, I think you'll feel like walking very slowly. Wave to the boys and let them get back to their work."

Almost before Rolly heard all the words, the needle's point had been transferred to his tailbone, and his companion stepped to the side, away from the door, still holding the needle—steady and intimate—at the base of his spinal cord. The door opened. Rolly hesitated in the doorway, and an operator he knew only slightly gestured to him in greeting from behind the dense glass walls of the control room and quickly turned back to reading his instrument board. There were two other operators in the control room, both with their backs to the elevator. They were facing the reactor over long instrument panels.

"Quickly, Dr. Castillo. But watch your step or this little cannon will kill you dead."

Rolly stepped onto the dimpled metal floor. They were at the level of the surface of the pool, the three-story tower of light water that was the primary cooling system for the uranium core sunk deep in the earth. He turned to the dark stairs that ran in a spiral about the elevator shaft and climbed, the prick of the needle having gone through the denim of his pants. He stumbled once, catching himself by grabbing the edge of the stairs, and the needle was withdrawn. Behind him he heard "Fuck," but the needle once again entered his pants and somehow he made it to the top floor, his burned fingertips now cold from contact with the metal stairs.

They stood on a narrow metal walkway, an observation bridge overlooking the deep, glowing pool. Behind them was a glass wall separating them from the reactor's inner administrative offices. Heavy steel chains hung from the ceiling, dangling over the still water in the pool. The distinctive pale blue glow from the water cast faint shadows under Rolly's thick glasses. The ghostly blue was the "Cherenkov Effect," produced by gamma rays from the uranium fuel rods knocking electrons off the water molecules and causing them to travel faster than light does in water, in blue shock waves.

Suddenly Rolly knew what was going to happen to him.

And in his cold panic, he lost control of his bladder. The trickle running down his leg was oddly warm, the only comfort left in the world.

A thick black plastic bag, with a chloroformed rag inside, was pulled quickly and tightly over his head and he felt the long needle push against his eardrum. Before he blacked out, Rolly heard quiet words from the microphone: "I hope you're sorry."

Indeed, the last sensation Rolly experienced consciously was a jangled and distant remorse that even he knew was pathetic and too late.

The bag was removed from his head and pocketed. Rolly's limp body slumped from the waist over the railing. His legs were lifted by the thick yellow gloves gripping the wet denim, and Rolly was flung into the glowing blue pool of water.

The tip of the syringe in the gloved hand held high above the pool threw out a brief blue spark, a reflection of the water's ghostly, throbbing glow.

Rolly's murderer crept down the dark spiral of stairs to the airlock, the padded yellow boots soundless on the metal.

TUESDAY

What is it that breathes fire into
the equations and makes a universe
for them to describe?

STEPHEN HAWKING
A Brief History of Time

TWO

THE SLIM FORM OF DAVE THE MONKEYMAN SEPARATED itself from the colorful stream of bicyclists flowing along South Bayshore Drive across from Miami's city hall. His wide yellow wheels veered up and over the curb, across the sidewalk, and bounced up the broad marble steps of "the Pink Building." His handlebars made popping noises, protesting this form of abuse as Dave yanked them deftly, cresting the top step and coasting to a stop at the Art Deco revolving door of the building.

The Coconut Grove offices of Hardy Security and Electronics, where Dave worked, were located in the top two floors of the rosy glass-and-steel structure everyone called the Pink Building. The official name of the skyscraper, in public documents and on the understated cornerstone, was the Dorothy R. Krutulis Commerce and Technology Tower, but the more familiar name had long since replaced in the popular imagination that testimonial to a woman nobody remembered.

The passing scene reflected itself in the pink glass surrounding the revolving door: The traffic on South Bayshore was heavy—and splashed with vibrant hues at ten on a Tuesday morning, at this hour filled with tourists dressed in shorts, tropical shirts, suntans, and their clean line of expensive European cars flashing in and out of the Grove.

Dave the Monkeyman stepped off his creaky bike and tucked it against his hip as he considered the revolving door with a frown. Marcel—a miniature green parrot that continually frustrated his owner's life through a refusal to speak "the language of the seas" promised by the enterprising conman who had sold the bird to Dave for twenty-five dollars in a local bar called Señor Frog's—squawked inarticulately from his master's thin shoulder as frigid air rushed out at them through the open brass panel of a tall portal beside the revolving door. The brass door was held by the good-looking doorman who was an integral part of the Pink Building's image in the mind of Dade County. All the doormen here looked alike—tan, tall, perfect anaerobic bodies, chiseled impassive faces. In addition to looking alike, the doormen also seemed to react alike, and insofar as they ever professionally expressed emotion, they all despised Dave.

The problem, as Dave saw it now, was diplomatic rather than tactical: He could not get his bike through the revolving door. Dave could not simply avoid the he-man who was standing by the brass door with a challenging smirk on his handsome face, and a burning message in his deep-set eyes. He was waiting to clip Dave's back tire as he went through the door and send him stumbling into the building. This was a brand of rudeness the doormen had developed lately in a united burst of childish but unassailable maneuvering in their ongoing conflict with Dave.

"You've got bird shit on your shoulder, Shorty," the uncompromisingly handsome doorman said.

"Not on your life, Toots," Dave said. "This bird shits only on expensive carpets and South Beach Mafia hairpieces. Help me out by supplying the name of your optician, will you?"

"Maybe I can help you out by taking a nice shot at your shoulder. I'd like to see how you'd look as a crack in the sidewalk."

Hmmm, Dave thought, rudeness was a matter of degree and skill, and he tapped the brass of the open door with the silver tip of his lavender parasol.

"There was a rude doorman from Dade," Dave began, as he prepared to wheel his bike into the pink Cuban-tile lobby, "Who knew he was way overpaid.

"But his face was too pretty

"To deny to the city,

"So he shrugged his steroids and stayed."

Dave smiled sweetly. "I just made that up. While you think up one of your own, stop waving this brass contraption around like a cheap straw hat. You're fanning all the air-conditioning out onto the bay."

Dave nipped into the building.

The doorman, trained and paid to do nothing but look good and hold the door open when called for, was momentarily stymied by Dave's speed and his use of the back tire as a moving shield.

It probably would have been a bad idea, considering Dave's job, to take an actual punch at him, but the doorman had been planning to engineer a nasty fall into the lobby. Now he regretted Dave's superior alertness, and vowed to himself to get Dave next time.

Dave the Monkeyman, never one to croon over triumphs or dwell on misfortunes, promptly forgot the skirmish and wheeled his bike across the lobby. The well-shined and expensive women's black flats he nearly always wore swished over the slick tiles as he strolled beside his noisy bike to the elevator. He pushed the up button with the silver tip of his parasol and studied his reflection in the brass door. In response to whatever vision of himself Dave obtained in the metallic indistinctness of the door, he tugged at his blue cotton paisley bow tie, patted his high-waisted white Bermuda shorts, and smoothed the collarless lavender shirt; the parrot took a few steps on the fabric. The door opened, and Dave, with his ancient bike and his bargain bird, entered the car, which looked like an expensive jukebox, all neon tubes and mellow gold. The car rose to the eighteenth floor, the penthouse, where Dave had his office down the hall from the president's suite.

Annabelle Hardy-Maratos had moved into the white and gold suite two summers previously when her father, Jacob Michael Hardy, had retired after a profitable quarter century as head of Miami's most respected and complete private-security outfit, with offices in six other cities around the country.

Dave, for his part, had almost instantly worshiped Annabelle, the tall, beautiful woman who was now paying Dave's salary, but he never allowed her to see the extent of his admiration, on occasion even treating her with a softer, more intimate, version of the deliberate rudeness that had earned him a few colorful moments downstairs in the lobby of headquarters.

When Annabelle took over the penthouse suite, Dave had broken even his own records for staying late and attending to every job and every detail. He worked hard and sacrificed himself in order to make the transition smooth and the new president comfortable, for, in addition to the tide of his feelings for Annabelle, Hardy Security had given Dave what he had never expected from his adopted country, or from this gaudy new subtropical city that often genuflected at the altar of old influence and old prejudices. Dave had been given the chance to advance based on his eclectic abilities, the opportunity to use his decidedly eccentric brain to solve problems, a generous salary, and whatever respect he earned.

That Annabelle was deaf, Dave thought, was not a factor in his strongly protective feelings for this woman who was turning out to be an executive genius, despite her highfalutin artsy background.

Meeting Annabelle had opened Dave's eyes—not just to the emotionally complex world of the deaf but to his own inner world, for she had been, as far as he knew, the only person who had ever really liked him. His ambitious immigrant Cuban parents, thrusting him into the English-speaking world of Miami in the early 1970s, had never understood his retreat from his peers, his panicked response as a child to the language barrier. Dave had interpreted the shouted English of his peers as rudeness, and rudeness had become his way of keeping the loud world at bay, even after he had more than mastered the idiosyncrasies of English. Learning American Sign Language in order to communicate with Annabelle had finally given Dave a language to be nice in.

Annabelle had taught him to sign. He had only known her since her deafness had become total, knew only the accomplished signer and lip-reader, whose reading efficiency was often as high as 93 percent. All hope for surgical correction had been abandoned a couple of years before she took over the company, and so Dave had never been aware of that nightmare period in her life when she had lived with both a desperate hope and a desperate need to relearn the art of communication. Now, without hope, she had come to some sort of acceptance of the absolute nature of her loss and, Dave thought, a measure of peace.

Because Annabelle had lost her hearing during her twenties, she spoke without displaying a hint of her handicap, the only problem being modulation, a problem she had largely overcome through classes in monitoring her own vocal feedback in her jaw and mouth. Her soft voice was the first thing Dave heard as he stepped off the elevator.

The door to her suite was open, and Dave, parking his bike just outside, noticed with a slight start that Jacob Hardy himself was seated across from her white marble desk in one of the gold Morrocan leather chairs he had installed shortly before turning the company over to his daughter.

Annabelle, wearing a lemon yellow suit whose long jacket reached almost to the hem of her short skirt, sat on the desk with her long legs crossed, facing her father, a notebook in her lap and a Miami Hurricanes coffee mug in her left hand. She wore no jewelry, except for a slim gold watch and a wedding band, and Dave nodded at her approvingly; signers almost never wore jewelry, and on such a decorative woman as Annabelle, Dave thought, any baubles would be a distraction.

Annabelle returned his nod, smiled, and said in that soft voice, "Hi, Dave. We're having a family powwow—big kids only."

"Well, I hope you called a good caterer," Dave said. "I'm starving."

He shook hands with Jacob Hardy and served himself coffee from the copper urn on Annabelle's desk. He sat in the other gold chair, and Marcel leaped to the chair's arm. The older man was certainly accustomed to Dave, but even so, he winced at the new lavender parasol and leaned forward to study Dave's pale cheeks.

"What have you done to your face?" he demanded.

"Don't get so excited," Dave said. "It washes off. I just wanted to see if foundation makeup will prevent wrinkles." And he sat back in the chair, sipping the hot coffee. "I'm out in the sun a lot, you know."

"Haven't you ever heard of sunscreen?" Hardy snapped. "You look like a Cuban ghost." He waved a hand impatiently. "Never mind that. We've got a problem."

Hardy, his shiny bald head tanned from years of sailing the waters around Miami, wore jeans, a white shirt, and a sport jacket, his usual working attire since he had left the New York City Police Department to found his security empire in Miami. Whatever had brought him off his boat and into the city, Dave knew, was probably a big problem. When Jacob butted into Annabelle's new territory, he wasn't usually this obvious about it, preferring more subtle ways of attempting to tinker with his creation.

"I've been here since nine o'clock with the boss," Hardy said, glancing fondly up at his daughter, "and up since four o'clock thinking. Annabelle, you tell him what we've got."

Annabelle sat quietly, regarding Dave's face for a moment. Yes, he was wearing foundation. But he had applied it delicately, with a light hand, and the effect was hardly noticeable. It could scarcely compare to his experiment with a fierce-looking black eyepatch that, mercifully, had lasted only a few days after he bought Marcel from the sailor. Annabelle was only briefly curious, and she glanced down at her notes before describing the problem to Dave.

"Last night, at the University of the Keys Nuclear Research Reactor down in Naranja, a man, a scientist, apparently fell into what they call the pool. As I understand it, that's the three-story water tank that surrounds and contains the uranium core of the nuclear reactor. It's the primary cooling system. The man, name of"—here she consulted the notebook in her lap—"Rolando Ruiz de Castillo, Ph.D., age forty-two, is dead."

"What a careless man," Dave said, tracing a pattern on the white carpet with the tip of his parasol, but always careful to look at her when he spoke. "I hope they don't make a lot of sloppy mistakes like that in a nuclear shop this close to Miami."

Annabelle frowned slightly. "Makes you wonder, doesn't it?"

Hardy tapped his fist on the desk. "Let's not get sidetracked by scaring each other. The media are already doing that just fine." He passed a hand over his smooth head. "The university and I go back a long way, back to when Myron Theobald was president of the school. They were the first people in Miami to take me seriously when all of this"—he waved his hand around the room—"was just a little office on Calle Ocho with a sign that said Hardy Men and everybody called us rent-a-cops. Hardy Security still has the contract to provide guards and an alarm system down at the reactor, of course, and our man was on duty last night."

"Jeez," Dave said, "this is almost as bad as my nightmare about free guns at a Dolphins game. Does the dead man glow?"

Hardy Security now contracted with ProPlayer Stadium in Fort Lauderdale, the home of the Dolphins, to supply security guards for all events at the arena, from organized sports to rock concerts, and the familiar sky-blue uniform shirts of the Hardy Security people were a fixture at airports and shopping malls. The company's major energies were now invested in security systems and electronics, but the blue shirts were the oldest part of the business, though they counted for very little of the bottom line these days.

"The dead man may very well glow, for all we know," Annabelle said. "The university seems to be having trouble deciding what to do with the body, and not even the widow has been allowed to see it. Dad wants us to go down there and hold their hands—glowing or not—through the crisis."

"Well," Hardy said, "I've tackled a few crises for the school over the past twenty-five years, including that testing scandal in the History Department in 1982—that was before your time. Now Eugene Beckworth, the president of the university, has asked me to take a hand in this personally. Called me on my boat at four this morning."

Hardy rubbed a hand over his smooth head. "It's not like it was when Myron Theobald was running the place. I'm not sure what to make of Beckworth. He strikes me as a pompous bureaucratic ass, smug and self-satisfied, a highly finished article of would-be humanity. In fact he . . ." Hardy's words trailed off as he caught Dave's expression of surprise.

"I guess you *do* know what to make of him," Dave said, standing the parasol between his legs and twirling it on its end, absently making a deep indentation in the carpet.

"All I know about that," Hardy said, with a sad shake of his head, "is that times have changed in this business. I used to go fishing with Myron Theobald, but I wouldn't allow his replacement, this Beckworth fellow, to set foot on my boat. He's just not the right kind of man for fishing. That's the best I can explain it." He thought a moment. "Why, Dave, I've even taken *you* on my boat."

Dave was thunderstruck by the comparison, his parasol arrested in its twirling motion, his mouth open.

"My first lurid guess was that the problematic Beckworth was the real reason Dad has dumped this in my lap," Annabelle offered. She turned to face her father. "Dad, do you imagine that the family cachet is strong enough to satisfy Beckworth if you substitute me? He pretty much demanded you personally." She narrowed her eyes at her father. "You know what I think? You're going bonefishing, aren't you?"

Hardy looked as sheepish as was possible for a man who stood six feet six inches in his bare feet and whose pectorals strained his shirt. But his answer came readily: "Annabelle, nobody at the school thinks Castillo's death was anything but an accident. You can't have any foul play with that setup. I don't think what the university has here is a criminal matter. What it definitely has is a colossal public relations problem. There's hell to pay explaining how such a thing could happen. All that nuclear stuff, a body they don't know what to do with, government contracts, the media hopping around and yelling about meltdowns, that sort of thing. We just need to give the reactor an honest clean bill, that's all. Beckworth wants us to make it clear that Hardy Security did a more than able investigation—which you'll do. Show that they don't make a habit of finding bodies in their gamma ray soup, look into getting the body buried, and so on. It'll be a piece of cake for you and Dave. Besides," he added gruffly, "it's not just any bonefishing. It's the Islamorada Redfish/Bonefish Celebrity Tournament. To benefit cystic fibrosis." He paused significantly. "The tournament I finished *second* in last year."

Marcel hopped onto Annabelle's desk, waddling around in that awkward way birds have of using their legs on man-made surfaces.

"How come that goddamn bird's always jumping around like a kangaroo?" Hardy demanded. "Why doesn't he fly like a normal bird?"

"Because I keep his wings clipped," Dave explained, with a pregnant look in the bird's direction. "I've promised him his freedom when he can say a complete sentence. It doesn't even have to be dirty. I can't believe I let that sailor rip me off."

Annabelle reached behind her on the marble desk, sliding a two-page typed report from under the bird, who squawked, jumped onto the white carpet, and waddled under Dave's chair and onto his black shoe.

"According to our security," she said, handing Dave the report, "Dr. Castillo arrived at the reactor and picked up his badge from reception at ten-oh-two p.m. Dad?"

"Anyone going into the building has to wear a badge called a dosimeter. The scientists' dosimeters are numbered, and they always wear the same one. Castillo's was number three-seventeen, and that's the one he received. It measures whatever radiation you happen to pick up, and you return the badge when you leave. I guess that's never really a snag—Beckworth says nobody picks up dangerous amounts of radiation out there."

Dave snorted, sketching in the air the sign for "liar."

Annabelle laughed and resumed her synopsis of the report.

"Castillo fell into the pool at twelve-oh-seven a.m.; he fell from some sort of walkway a floor above the pool, as reported by three technicians who were on duty at pool level. They say they had let him into the reactor a few minutes earlier, he was alone, and that's all they know. Oh, yeah, and they said he sounded funny, like he had a bad cold."

"Pardon my gross appetite for sensational detail," Dave said, "but how do they handle a grown man clumsy enough to stumble into a nuclear reactor? I'll bet you a hundred bucks they didn't go in after him."

Hardy looked down at the coffee mug in his hands with a slight grin, but Annabelle answered the question, having already gone over this point with her father in detail. "He was in pretty deep, almost three stories down at the core, and although they say they acted quickly, they did have to use a hooked pole, which apparently requires some skill. They have these long poles of different lengths that they use routinely to retrieve materials that have been irradiated in the reactor pool."

"Poles? It sounds like a bunch of warlocks stirring their bubbling cauldron of eye-of-newt, toe-of-scientist," Dave said indignantly, crossing his thin legs and carrying Marcel into the air on his shoe. "Is this procedure, this pole hockey, spelled out in their emergency manual or anything? What I'm getting at is, it seems that a nuclear reactor would have all sorts of safety baloney in place, way above and beyond Hardy Security."

"I guess they never expected anyone to just fall in," Hardy said, "so they really don't have a plan for such cases. But in their defense I'd say I don't know that they could have handled Castillo any better."

"Where's the body now?" Dave asked.

"I don't know."

Annabelle and Dave both looked at Hardy as he stood, placed his empty mug on the desk, and walked over to the windows, stretching his long arms over his head. He looked out across City Hall, across Dinner Key Marina, across the limpid blue waters of Biscayne Bay. "I mean, the body is still down there at the reactor, but I don't know where they're storing it. Where can they store it? I don't know anything about atoms and radiation and that kind of thing."

"If the body really does glow and they tried to sneak it out to a mortician, they'd have trouble even under cover of darkness," Dave said. "It might be worth watching them try."

"There isn't a mortician in this town who'd touch that

body." Hardy's abruptness caused Dave to wonder suddenly if the older man was being completely candid regarding his ignorance of radiation.

"And that's part of our job," Annabelle said. "We're supposed to help them discover both the practical and the humane means of disposal. God, that sounds so heartless, just as though Dr. Castillo's corpse were a live bomb or something."

"Heartlessness is the only way to fake out Señor Death, my dear," Dave signed tenderly, taking her smooth hand in his and patting it maternally. He released her hand and continued. "Heartless burial customs are the best kind, as far as I'm concerned—they let us pretend we have some control."

Annabelle reclaimed his hand and squeezed it briefly, exchanging a look with him, and then jerked hers back when Marcel climbed Dave's leg and hopped onto their linked hands.

"I wish he wouldn't startle me like that," she snapped.

"You're a bad bird, Marcel." Dave spoke softly to the parrot on his knuckles. "Not even I would dare to hop onto the president of the company."

Annabelle concealed a smile.

"Dave, don't be mad at Marcel."

"Of course I'm mad at him. He's such a lecher. That's the only social skill he has. Next thing you know he'll be trying to move in with you. And Annabelle, I wouldn't recommend it. I've discovered that he's got several crude mannerisms, including strolling and shitting on the dinner table. He has strangely liberal ideas, especially for a Gingrich Republican."

An arrested look crossed Annabelle's face.

"What makes you think Marcel's a Republican?" she asked. "I thought you got him from a drunken sailor. What's political about that?"

"You can go into Dave's always interesting zoological speculations later," Hardy interrupted. "Beckworth has told his people to stand by for you. Full cooperation and all that."

"Beckworth doesn't sound so bad." Dave grasped the parasol's handle as though it were the hilt of a sword and extended it as a perch for the parrot, who stepped daintily onto the furled fabric, stretched his small wings, and elevated his left foot. "Look at this, Annabelle. Marcel's been watching my ballet workout video."

Annabelle glanced at the bird's antics.

"Dad, what do the police say?"

"Paul Diaz is handling this for Metro-Dade. I'm sure he'll cooperate with you, too, and there's no reason why he shouldn't," he said; then he sauntered, hands in jacket pockets, to the door, where he turned to face his daughter. "It's all yours."

"Okay, Dad. I hope you catch more fish than the other philanthropists."

"Take care, Annie." He bent a stern gaze on Dave. "And see if you're paying Dave enough. It sure looks like he's buying his clothes from the Coconut Grove Playhouse wardrobe department."

Hardy pulled the door shut behind him.

"Of course you're not paying me enough," Dave signed. "But, as chief financial officer of this corporation, I must tell you that we can't afford to give me a raise without cutting into my profit sharing. So I'll just suffer."

"Ah, the lot of man, to suffer, and to die."

"What's that from?"

"Pope's translation of *The Odyssey*, I forget exactly where." Annabelle shook her head ruefully, the heels of her hands resting on the edge of her desk, her abundant almost-black hair falling over her shoulders. "I used to know that stuff cold."

"Regrets, Annabelle?"

She looked dreamily into the middle distance, locating a time and a place and a discipline that had once been a sensible cosmos to her, a time and a place and a husband that had been more than a world—they'd been a reason for a world.

"No," she said, still focused on something Dave could not see, in the middle of that gold and white room, in that pink building, in that green and new city. "No, not regrets. Just an ill-defined sense of deficiency. You know, muscles not used. I feel kind of flabby, Dave."

She laughed when he ogled her trim, tall body with clownish skepticism.

"Not that kind of flabby, Dave."

Dave knew.

He knew the story from her own telling, but he also knew better than to probe the old wound. Her two-year honeymoon marriage to Nikki Maratos had ended on the Merritt Parkway in Connecticut seven years earlier when his car had hit an icy patch near Greenwich. Nikki had been on his way to visit her for the weekend at Yale, where she was technically in residence, writing her dissertation and teaching English. He had been fresh out of Yale Law, a hotshot contract attorney on Wall Street, and since it was midterm week, she had been away from their New York apartment, staying in the little room she had rented in New Haven to maintain her status as a resident of the university.

She had stayed in New Haven, after the funeral, to finish her degree, but she had lost steam, sometimes sitting in the Sterling Library for hours, staring into shadows.

Then, one day that summer, Dr. Annabelle Cristina Hardy-Maratos had come home to South Florida, still serenely lovely, still creatively intelligent, still convinced that English poets were smarter and better than the rest of mankind, but missing some emotional part of herself that had once made teaching the only profession for her. Dave thought it was trust. She had begun to see the students as "the enemy"; maybe she blamed them for Nikki's tragedy. Certainly the classroom no longer held any allure for her.

She had come home, to write the book that she and Nikki had planned together, *The Gender Contract: Common Law, Sexual Difference, and the Battle for the Pen.* It was a solid piece of scholarship, but Annabelle had absolutely no interest in it after she completed it. It was as if the book belonged to someone else, and her only reference to it was an occasional malicious reference to her publisher, Princeton University Press, who, she said, "will do anything not to sell a book."

Dave had read his signed copy twice.

He tapped Annabelle's shapely calf with his parasol to get her attention, so lost she seemed in a sea of lonely memories, and Marcel leaped in surprise at the motion. She looked up at once.

"Well, Dave. Let's get the car and go see the latest in scientific developments."

"Can Marcel stay in here? Or shall I go put him in his little copper jail cell?"

"Will he poop on the carpet while we're gone?"

"Certainly he'll poop," Dave said righteously. "He's not *completely* lazy." He turned the parasol upside down, and Marcel was dumped to the carpet.

Annabelle paused only to grab her key ring from the corner of the marble desk, and her jade green handbag from the top of a rattan hutch beside the door. They left the office together, closing the door as Marcel squawked in surprised belligerence behind them, and headed for the service elevator at the rear of the building.

"I'm glad we're going out the back way," Dave signed cheerfully.

"Why?"

"Oh, I just like the variety."

There were twenty smaller offices and three electronics labs arranged at intervals along the cross-shaped corridor of the penthouse, of which Annabelle's office formed the crown. Her secretary, Arantxa Ramos, was gluing the spine of a blue file folder when they entered her office, and Dave made a face at her sticky hands.

"That's an awesome suit, Dr. Annabelle," Arantxa said, her round face beaming admiration. "A really hot color."

"Thanks, Arantxa. We'll be gone for a few hours. Hold the fort, my dear. Dave will call in."

They stopped outside Dave's small office, where colorful miscellaneousness stamped its owner's belongings, including a six-foot doll with a china face, glittering black tap shoes, and the spangled chorine attire of a Radio City Rockette. The doll was seated on Dave's blue tartan loveseat—which was covered with a soft woolen throw featuring a black and white map of the earth, polar projection—her beribboned ankles crossed demurely. He dropped his parasol next to the doll, moved to his cherrywood desk, and opened the top drawer, reaching to the back for a small leather bag.

Annabelle sidestepped into the photo lab to pick up her favorite still camera, a Canon EOS 620; Dave returned to the hall with a black linen jacket, a polyester shoulder holster, and his gun, a .45 Colt MK IV, officer model.

He shrugged himself into the holster.

"Dave, I guess you don't think our scientist tripped blithely over his own feet and stumbled into that radioactive pool either, do you?"

"No, and neither does your father. Your dad wouldn't leave his fishing poles dangling in the water like this on the opening day of a tournament and come to your office for anything short of murder." Dave slipped into his jacket.

"Oh yeah? Then how come he tried to pass it off as a PR problem for the university?"

"Because, fathead, it is a PR problem for the university." Dave buttoned the jacket. "And your father never admits to your face that he worries overtime because you're deaf. But he is worried, Annabelle, and not just because his darling daughter can't hear. Jacob doesn't miss much, and this nuclear bath sounds like a particularly nasty way to die."

"Well, Dave, if you can think of a nice way to die, let me know, will you?" Annabelle summoned the elevator with one of the keys on her ring.

They descended to the parking garage.

Annabelle's red Chrysler LeBaron convertible always

struck Dave as a poor grooming choice for a woman with long hair, but he opened the door for her without comment and climbed over the back to the passenger's seat.

She drove down the garage ramps and into the burst of bright sunshine on South Bayshore. She leaned across Dave to rummage in the cluttered glove box for her sunglasses. Her car was the only part of Annabelle's life that did not seem to fit her fastidious self, Dave thought, as he often did when he rode with her, and he drew a fingertip through gray dust on the dashboard. And it never bothered her when even Jacob referred to the car as Annabelle's "Dumpster."

She took a couple of right turns, skirting the Grove on her way to U.S. 1.

At Tiger Tail and Twenty-seventh, she stopped for a red light and turned to Dave, who was leaning out over the side of the car and scowling at a woman dragging her skittish white poodle savagely into the Mayfair Hotel on the end of a rhinestone leash, the dog's sharp nails chattering shrilly on the sidewalk. Dave found poodles oddly disturbing, and he was silently exhorting the dog's owner to tug harder, to test the animal's tensile strength.

"Dave, what makes you think Marcel is a Republican?"

He swiveled in the seat, drawing his limber legs under him, facing her, and blinking in the bright sun.

"You can tell by looking at him," he signed smoothly, his face bland. "Haven't you ever noticed how he favors his right wing?"

The light changed. Annabelle shook her head and smiled, stepping on the accelerator. As they headed south, Dave leaned back against the seat and closed his eyes.

There would be no more conversation on the way to the reactor. Annabelle's concentration on traffic tended to be total, and she could not read his lips or his hands while driving.

While Dave was no coward, closing his eyes was in part a reaction to the way Annabelle drove, which was fast and fearless. Since Nikki's death some demon had arisen in her, and she courted physical danger. Dave had too often seen that hardness in her eyes when some daredevil opportunity presented itself. Dave wondered, but did not ask, if she had a death wish.

THREE

ON THE WAY TO THE REACTOR, DAVE SORTED THE PApers in Annabelle's glove box, bringing some token order to the prevailing chaos in her car. He shook his head and sighed from time to time, knowing that this new arrangement would not last beyond her next search for a pair of sunglasses, but he took cynical pleasure in disproving the maxims of his youth, in this case the one foisted on him by Cuban nuns who insisted that example was the best teacher. *"Eso es pura paja,"* he muttered.

He was tempted to expand his tidying into a clean sweep and toss the garbage in the car onto the shoulder of U.S. 1, which, as far as he was concerned, was the sorriest highway in the United States, but the grip of environmental responsibility was too strong to allow him to yield to that impulse, so he gathered the trash into a ball and stuffed it under his seat. He gazed silently at the passing landscape.

U.S. 1 bisected Miami on a diagonal and then ran south through the Florida Keys to Key West, the southernmost point in the continental United States, about one hundred fifty miles out of Miami. As it passed through the featureless topography south of Miami, the road dwindled to a four-lane stretch of crowded tedium with a speed limit of 45. It departed the salsa rhythms and bold elegance of Miami, to become a straight utilitarian slash of concrete through some scattered small towns whose names were not even posted on the side of the road, an omission that drew Dave's silent disapproval: All towns should be accorded the fleeting dignity of a readable label, he thought, even squalid and transient little centers of lost aspiration like Perrine, Goulds, Princeton, Leisure City, and Naranja.

The town of Naranja, Spanish for "orange," was about thirty minutes south of Coconut Grove, was not posted on U.S. 1, and struck Dave as a particular misnomer for a farming community that planted its cash crops in palm trees and tomatoes and harvested them with brown migrant hands. The Naranja section of U.S. 1 bore garish testimony to the transient and impoverished nature of the community, as well as to its mishmash of zoning laws. A pity, Dave thought, but a town that was so bereft of economic choices that it would sanction a nuclear reactor would apparently also allow almost any incursion against community safety: Along the highway were dilapidated "cash inns" and "cash domes," storefront operations that traded instant cash for jewelry and guns; RV parks; packing houses with titanic tomatoes painted on their peeling walls and teenagers taking refuge inside the walls to screw and smoke; pawnshops and Goodwill outlets, the one holding on to discarded goods, the other letting them go; closed strip malls, with boarded and graffitied windows; tarot and palm readers, offering palatable alternatives and attractive lies; liquor stores and saloons; and nude revues galore, with a bewildering heterogeneity of names—Piggy's, El Nopal, King of Paradise, Redneck Carl's.

The highway was punctuated sporadically by tall, faded billboards for the Alligator Hole Cafe. The billboards featured a large pink-breasted cartoon woman announcing in a word-balloon that "We Dare to Bare in the Everglades." Foot-high and flamboyant, woolly-looking eyelashes had partially blown loose from the paper face and dangled fitfully over the giant blue eyes, driven by the desultory light breezes blowing across U.S. 1 from the west. A faded pair of black snakes twined around the pendulous cartoon breasts, and the tip of an alligator tail seemed to sprout from between the swollen, blowsy red lips—Dave could not decide if the tail's remnant was a clue to the cafe's menu or an unintentional reference to the predatory hierarchy now operating in the Everglades.

Dave counted the Alligator Hole Cafe billboards between Perrine and Naranja: There were six, all in the same dispirited state of eroded showmanship.

Annabelle turned off the highway, left on Naranja Lakes Drive. For nearly two miles the convertible took them through the depressed rural landscape of Naranja, which was dotted with occasional coconut palms, rusted water towers, a jungle of high weeds, mondo grass, and small farms. Then she turned right on Broad Creek Channel Cut, a recently repaved road cutting through the flat barrens of Naranja and smelling of tar. And there was the reactor.

She stopped the car on the road.

"To paraphrase Voltaire," she said, "if Naranja didn't

already have a nuclear reactor, it would be necessary to invent one."

"Yeah, no kidding. This place is really Crotch Gulch, U.S.A." Dave wrinkled his nose. "Are your field glasses in this junk heap?"

Annabelle nodded and reached under her seat, extracting binoculars and a red-and-white-striped straw. She shoved the straw back where it came from and handed the glasses to Dave, who sniffed fastidiously and dusted the lenses on his jacket sleeve.

From their distance, the nuclear reactor facility looked like a child's mistake, a tall blue cylindrical block crammed into a short, flat yellow rectangular block. The central tower, with plain windowless walls of midnight blue, shot three stories above the level ground. The fourth and deepest level was out of sight and buried underground in the rock-hard cochina, the area's tough coral residue.

Dave studied the buildings and the flat, flat countryside through the binoculars. The Ring Building, constructed of one story of blond brick, completely surrounded the blue tower and was organized on a human scale, with doors, windows, and seasonal decorations, this particular season being represented on the main door by a smiling paper witch and her paper broom, and Indian corn imported from Pennsylvania.

"What do you see?" Annabelle asked.

He lowered the glasses to his lap and looked at her, speaking to her in sign language; Dave was predominantly a right-handed signer, but, with the field glasses in his lap, he created the grammar, the spatial relationships, and the eloquence of rapid, expert signing—with graceful balance and a flair for dramatic inflection:

"There's no fence, as far as the eye can see, and no other outside security of any kind. Maybe there's something hidden, but this place looks incredibly open. You know, there really ought to be vicious dogs tearing us intruders to bloody shreds and guards armed to the teeth with Uzis, threatening to shoot our cans off." He blinked in the hot sun. "Annabelle, this is not exactly the jewel in the crown of Hardy Security. They ought to sue us for this pathetic security layout."

Dave gripped the windshield as Annabelle started the car and drove toward the reactor, a quarter of a mile down the dusty road. She pulled into the parking lot, which had spaces for two hundred cars and today held about one hundred fifty, and drove slowly past the main entrance, parking the convertible a few feet beyond the door. From the lot she was watched by a couple of television crews standing by their vans and by several other people in open cars. Cameras were raised at her, and several journalists started forward when she stopped the car.

She stepped out of the convertible, slamming the door, and Dave marveled at her: Beyond running her hand through her hair, she had not even checked her appearance in the rearview mirror. He checked his, in the side mirror, smoothed the windblown wisps of his brown hair, and caught up with her as she entered the building, ignoring the approaching newspeople. The paper witch was not taped securely to the door, and she flapped in the slight breeze, her white yarn hair blown across her bumpy nose. Dave flicked the hair out of her face with a gentle finger.

Together Annabelle and Dave passed into the facility through the glass door, and together they stopped abruptly just inside, facing a circular portal, a tall doughnut of steel standing free about two feet into the building. A rubber-matted ramp led up and through the center of the cold tubular circle and down the other side. The whole thing looked like a giant engagement ring, standing on its rubber setting. A blue-shirted guard stood by the circle. Dave showed his company ID to the guard and raised an eyebrow at the wheel of space enclosed by the standing circle.

"It's a portal monitor, sir," the guard said. "It's supposed to pick up any trace particles of radiation you might get on your clothes or your hands or anything like that."

Dave craned his neck to study the portal monitor.

"What happens if I go through it and I've got radioactive particles on my clothes?" he asked.

"Well, it's supposed to make this big beeping-type noise," the guard explained. "Also, the operators in the control room inside the reactor would see an alarm signal on their instruments. The portal's attached to their computers—smart computers that can screen for background stuff and pass you through if you're okay."

"Let's see if it can pick up the softshell crab I had last night," Dave said, with casual authority and no hint of hesitation.

Dave stepped onto the rubber ramp and strolled through the middle of the ring, his hands in his pockets, a noncommittal smile on his face. Annabelle followed, frankly studying the gleaming silver portal as she went through. Her reflection in the metal reminded her of funhouse mirrors, and the rubber mat of hospital emergency-room entrances.

In the center of the large, cool lobby stood a huge oval desk, the iron-haired receptionist ensconced in the center, speaking into a white telephone that, along with baskets filled with papers, clipboards, industry magazines, was part of the institutional clutter on the desk. As Annabelle and Dave would shortly learn, the clutter was characteristic of the facility; offices, labs, and storage places all had a cramped feel, stemming from a simple oversupply of material things. The exception was the central building, the vital core of the place, where not so much as an eraser was out of place and no dust was allowed to accumulate. In many ways, the reactor plant was two worlds, separated from each other by a cushion of air, the outer world both servant to and—it was hoped—master of the inner.

The receptionist nervously hurried to end her conversation. She grabbed a press release from a stack on the desk and quickly shoved it at Annabelle.

"The university has prepared this statement. If you want any interviews, I'm afraid I can't help you." The receptionist took in Annabelle's smooth elegance and assumed her to be a television reporter; Dave's appearance she took to be a brand of show-business affectation and him to be one of those all-purpose individuals known as producers.

"Good morning. I'm Annabelle Hardy-Maratos, and this is my associate." Annabelle smiled at the harassed receptionist. "I believe we're expected."

"Oh, good heavens. Do you have any ID, Miss Hardy? I'm afraid it's been a terrible morning." The receptionist looked miserable.

Annabelle and Dave handed over their sky-blue plastic Hardy employee ID cards. They were examined carefully, the photos compared with their faces. The receptionist returned the plastic cards and held out two gray plastic triangles.

"Ah, dosimeters," Dave said knowledgeably, taking one. "We used red ones at Chernobyl."

The receptionist smiled sourly, and Annabelle took her badge.

"Pin them on and wear them at all times in the building. We'll check your badges for radiation levels when you leave." The receptionist picked up the telephone receiver and spoke into it, just as the university's president walked into the lobby.

"Oh, Dr. Beckworth," she said. "Here's Miss Hardy."

Beckworth was a man of medium height, brown hair, and a very active pair of gray eyes. He was wearing a white lab coat over his gray suit. He shook hands heartily with Annabelle, pumping her arm and gouging a dent in her palm with a heavy gold ring.

"Thank you for coming on such short notice, Annabelle. Your dad was bragging about you this morning, and I can see why," he said in an overloud voice and gazing knowingly at her short skirt.

His use of her first name threw Annabelle off stride as much as his decidedly improper attention to her skirt.

Beckworth glanced curiously at Dave.

"This is my associate, Jorge Enamorado," Annabelle said, giving Dave's real name a full Spanish lilt, rolling the *r*s and pronouncing every vowel generously.

"You can call me Dave," he said to Beckworth, putting

out his hand. Dave the Monkeyman smiled seraphically, revealing even white teeth, but did not elaborate.

Beckworth shot a cautious look at him, but gave his hand a good pumping.

Annabelle and Dave followed Beckworth through the only door leading into the building from the lobby, pinning on the dosimeter badges as they walked. They turned right almost immediately, into the first office in a long corridor. The office was cluttered like the lobby, and while Beckworth took a seat at the metal desk, they found seats on a plastic-covered couch, moving a couple of stacks of periodicals before they sat.

Beckworth started talking as they were still moving the magazines, while Annabelle was turned away from him, and Dave's sensitively adjusted Idiot Barometer began sending him internal signals. Beckworth obviously knew that Annabelle was deaf, from the way he was yelling at her. Why talk to her back?

"As you know, we face a peculiar dilemma this morning." Beckworth spread his hands expansively, and Dave signed the opening words for Annabelle.

"The university, while of course honoring its human obligation to the dead man, nevertheless cannot overlook its wider obligations. Frankly, that's where we want your help, with the wider obligations. We're very satisfied that our incident is a tragic accident, and now we want to smooth the waters, if you'll pardon the unfortunate choice of words, and get on with our scientific work. You understand, don't you?"

Dave, knowing that Annabelle could now read Beckworth's lips, signed, "Let's just start hating him now, without wasting valuable lead time. Jacob was right."

Annabelle compressed her lips for a moment.

"Dr. Beckworth, we appreciate your concerns," she said, "and we'll do everything we can to help you. I know my father has a fondness for this place, but I've never been down here before. It isn't quite what I expected."

"You were probably expecting a lot of science fiction, a lot of Captain Kirk hooey. A crock of baloney like electric bolts zapping around and demented scientists with bubbling beakers and bulging eyes. With what the university budgets just for public relations on this place, it's frankly shocking to me how ignorant the general public is. And"—Beckworth paused to give Dave the benefit of a suspicious, hard stare—"the level of joking since Castillo's accident is terribly inappropriate. We're going to get this mess straightened out and put a stop to all that noise."

Dave signed, "What's he got against Captain Kirk?"

Annabelle preserved an expressionless countenance, avoiding Dave's wide-eyed gaze.

"Dr. Beckworth," she began, "we certainly don't want to add to your annoyance, but some of our questions will necessarily be ignorant ones. The fact is, we know very little about what happened here last night."

"Ask him if he likes Mr. Spock," Dave signed, touching his ears.

"Ask anything you like, my dear," Beckworth said. "I'm sorry I can't participate in that delightful sign language with you, although I quite enjoy watching it—but your partner seems to be keeping up quite nicely for me. He's translating what I say *exactly*, isn't he?" When Annabelle nodded mendaciously, Beckworth shifted in the chair, pulling the lab coat away from his hips. "Now,

Annabelle, we'd like to get this over with as quickly as possible."

Annabelle nodded her agreement. "I think the logical place to begin is with some clarity about Dr. Castillo's body. Certainly a candid statement from the university would do much toward lining up the press on your side, or at least dispelling any rancorous confusion. Dad said the body is still here at the reactor. Have you been able to make any arrangements yet? The less we treat this like a sticky question, the better. Where is the body?"

Dave saw that Annabelle was uncomfortable; Beckworth was a rapid speaker, and she was having difficulty keeping up with him. Dave signaled her, indicating he would sign the full conversation, leaving the jokes out, and she flashed him a grateful look while Beckworth hastened into speech.

"That seems to be what everyone wants to know, especially those reporters outside. God almighty, they want to know if the body glows, and if so what color. Will the body have to be buried in a nuclear dump? Is there going to be a meltdown? Has there already been a meltdown? Is it safe to have a dead man in the core of a nuclear reactor? Or—and this is my favorite—is there a body at all or did he just dissolve in the pool?" Beckworth laughed stiffly. "Well, I'll tell you, Annabelle, it's just a dead body like any dead body—except for the burns, that is. We have Dr. Castillo's body safely stored downstairs in a room where we often hold radioactive materials. Not that we think the body is dangerously radioactive at all."

Here Dave put in a question, a gleam of disdain in his brown eyes: "Does that mean you consider it *safely* radioactive? Just a little hot around the edges?"

Dave thought Beckworth's cheeks would explode. Certainly they expanded, and he sputtered before launching again into rapid speech.

"I realize that to the layperson all of this nuclear business may seem pretty goddamned hilarious. Just fair game to you people who get your ideas about nuclear energy out of comic books and movies. The reactor's some sort of Spook Central, isn't it? But, believe you me, you're exposed to radiation every day of your lives, all kinds of radiation. It's just part of real civilization. Why, you fly in an airplane or sit next to a brick building and you're getting at least twice the radiation you'd ever get in this office. Or standing right next to the pool."

"But what if I jumped into the pool, Dr. Beckworth?" Dave asked, and he raised a hand when the university president opened his mouth to interrupt. "That's a serious question, not a joke. Castillo's body isn't just a dead body, is it? Isn't that the problem? Isn't his body a normal everyday hot-as-hell radioactive body? I didn't get that out of a comic book. I got that from Jacob Hardy."

Annabelle sat forward on the couch, its plastic cover pulling at her skirt. "Yes, Dr. Beckworth. If you don't tell us the extent of this catastrophe, there's no way we can be effective. At a minimum you'll have to be open with us about the body."

Beckworth looked at her as if she had pulled an eel from her sleeve, wet.

"We don't know what to do with the body," he admitted reluctantly. "The trace-mineral elements—sodium, for example—are radioactive, but we're talking about very short half-lives here. In a few days or so the body should be completely safe to dispose of. If it were a rabbit or something, an experimental animal, we could just burn it right here in this facility, no questions asked."

Dave allowed his distaste to show on his face and on his rapidly gesturing hands. Annabelle read the tone of his hands as she read the words. Among the many signers she had encountered in the past few years, even at world-renowned centers for the deaf like Gallaudet University, she'd never met anyone who could rival Dave's ability to weave a tone of voice into his gestures.

"But Dr. Beckworth, it is a human body," she said softly. "And the whole county, maybe the whole state, will be asking questions. We'll try to help you with the body's ultimate disposal, but we'll know more about your dilemma if we can see it—him. We'll need scientific as well as humane input from you and your staff. Whatever you're wary of, you shouldn't keep us in the dark." She studied the still-intransigent set of the university president's tight-lipped expression. "Will you show us Dr. Castillo's body?" she persisted.

Beckworth nodded woodenly.

"When?" she asked.

"Before you leave. I'll take you myself after you've had a chance to get your bearings and see the people your father and I thought might help us wrap this up. I mean to expedite this unfortunate, uh, problem." He cleared his throat. "I've told my people that you're deaf, and I've put together a little schedule for you."

"How thoughtful," Annabelle muttered.

"I'll bet it's a tight schedule," Dave said. "Tight."

Beckworth glared at him.

Annabelle glanced at Dave's face and noted an alarming hint of real hatred beginning to take shape around the edges of his mouth. She hoped and suspected that Beckworth was too insulated to read that look, but she acted quickly to draw the president's attention away from Dave. She raised her hand from the stack of magazines at her side.

"There's something else from our point of view," she said. "I don't know just how restricted you are by regulations, but we can at least start talking to morticians for you, and for the widow. We'll give you our best research on that in a day or so, but for now I suppose the autopsy should be the first logistical matter. Have you been able to deal with that yet? Have the police asked you about moving the body for the pathologists? Questions about medical attention to the body will probably be uppermost in the minds of the journalistic community when they get to the second stage of reporting this tragedy."

"Autopsy?" Beckworth looked stunned. "Surely you can't think one is necessary, or even very realistic? The body is badly burned—erythema is the medical term. He was very close to the core. Whole-body radiation. And there were three witnesses. It's that simple. An autopsy would be a useless desecration of an already damaged body."

Annabelle pursed her lips. "Dr. Beckworth, we can't negotiate for you with morticians until somebody supplies us with a death certificate, and nobody can sign a death certificate until the cause of death is official, with somebody taking responsibility for a signature on that document."

"Annabelle, I know all that; and the cause of death is determined. Castillo, God rest him, died of radiation poisoning. And probably brain edema. And"—here he hesitated briefly—"I have already signed the death certificate." Beckworth folded his hands together on the desk and studied his thumbs. "I signed it almost an hour ago after viewing the body."

"You signed it?"

Beckworth eyed Annabelle's knees steadily while a silence grew in the room, then transferred his regard to her vivid green eyes. "Annabelle, I am the president of this university, but I'm also an M.D., a member of the medical faculty. The police are satisfied with my conclusions."

"I see."

"I hope you do."

FOUR

"DR. BECKWORTH," ANNABELLE SAID AFTER A MOMENT, A slight frown creasing her forehead, "doesn't the reactor have a separate management, separate from you I mean? Someone else I could talk to about this? Perhaps an outside pathologist? For your own sake and for the university's?"

Beckworth's face was flushed, and his hand twitched on the desk. His heavy ring thumped against a loose pen, which skidded across the desk and onto the floor at Annabelle's feet.

"Billy Elmore manages this place, but he was up all night. I sent him home a couple of hours ago."

Dave pushed his foot next to Annabelle's, tapping her soft yellow shoe with his black flat. Quickly, and almost imperceptibly, he signed, "*Fidelito*—he runs the school like a little Cuba."

Beckworth stood suddenly.

"I'll get you started," he said, stalking out of the office.

Annabelle and Dave glanced at each other, Dave shaking his head, and followed the president down the long corridor and into another office. His face still red, Beckworth told them to wait there for Castillo's secretary, and departed with an impatient jolt of a nod, his ring scraping the door as he turned away.

They sat down in the small room's two chairs. A plaque above a large desk said ATTACK SECRETARY. On the desk, a dirty coffee mug decorated with painted bullet holes bore the legend "Sorry I missed you."

Annabelle sent her gaze around the messy office, and Dave plucked idly at objects on the desk.

"I never expected quite so much loving cooperation from the university," Dave said, fiddling with the spray tip of a can of Arm and Hammer air freshener. "Or at least not quite this kind of cooperation. Imagine having your own in-house autopsy man. I wonder what he thinks he needs us for? We're not even expected to supply the paint for this whitewash." He opened a tube of red lipstick and brushed the color across the top of his hand, rubbing it in with his thumb. He replaced the lipstick and picked up a datebook, flipping through its pages. "Our friend Beckworth's a pretty smooth article. He's so smooth, you wouldn't even have to oil him to use him as a suppository." Dave stirred a finger through a pile of paper clips.

Annabelle closed her eyes briefly. "That's disgusting." She touched Dave's bony knee. "Do you realize Beckworth has no doubt at all that we want to play this game with him, with him making up the rules? No doubt at all. He has put an entirely new spin on ruthless arrogance. I begin to see my dad's infinite wisdom here. No wonder he went fishing. Come down and hold their hands during the crisis indeed—we can't even see what their hands are doing."

A tiny woman with spiked purple hair came noisily

into the office. Dave blinked at her hair. She could impale raccoons on that coif. He'd have to discuss this eye-catching phenomenon with his own stylist. Really, that color was *grape*.

"Are you the people who are here about Rolly?"

"Yes. I'm Annabelle Hardy-Maratos, and this is Jorge Enamorado. I hope you don't mind that we've made ourselves at home. We really weren't given much choice."

"As long as you didn't touch my mouse. People are always breaking my mouse. Beckworth says you're deaf." The woman boomed her words. "I'm Bertha Puffo—Bertha S. Puffo." She turned to Dave and said. "Get out of my goddamn chair."

Dave flinched at the sound, stood, and signed, "She yelled that you're deaf."

Annabelle heaved a sigh.

The secretary slumped beside her desk in the swivel chair Dave had vacated, her short legs stretched out before her. She was wearing blue jeans, a white silk shirt, red jacket, and red heels. On her shapely and perfectly manicured right hand she wore a topaz ring.

Annabelle leaned forward in her chair.

"Bertha. May I call you Bertha?" At the purple affirmative nod, Annabelle went on. "It's true that I'm deaf, but if you face me and speak clearly, I can read lips very well. And my interpreter will render everything you say into sign language for me. Fair enough?" When the secretary nodded glumly, Annabelle asked, "What time did you get to work this morning?"

"Eight o'clock on the dot. Same as usual." Puffo folded her arms across her chest and seemed to be weighing the merits of a Spice Girls poster on the wall over Annabelle's chair.

"Was Dr. Beckworth here when you arrived?" Annabelle asked.

"Yeah."

"Was Billy Elmore here?"

"Yeah. But Beckworth told him to go home."

"Do you know why?"

"Yeah."

"Will you tell me why?"

"He didn't want him here." She straightened in the swivel chair. "What do you want from me? I'm not Beckworth's goddamn shrink."

Annabelle and Dave looked at each other.

"Ask her if she has another goddamn chair," Dave signed in frustration.

Annabelle tried a different approach. "That's a lovely ring, Bertha. Is it topaz?"

"Yeah, all the secretaries get discounts on the stones we process. Don't go getting any ideas that they overpay me here."

Annabelle decided to start over from yet another angle, convinced she was wasting her time. Clearly she would get nothing from this strangely aggressive woman. "Dr. Beckworth has satisfied himself on behalf of the university that Dr. Castillo's death was accidental. How do you feel about that? Do you think Dr. Castillo's death was an accident?"

"No fuckin' way."

Both Annabelle and Dave were startled by the vehemence of Puffo's reply. Here apparently was a subject she liked, and Dave looked at her with a dawning clinical interest.

"No fuck-in way," she repeated, hammering each syllable.

"You seem very sure," Dave said.

"Is a frog's ass watertight?"

Dave's eyes widened and he leaned forward, showing by the growing size of his signs that he was extemporizing with his American sign vocabulary to approximate the secretary's verbal scope and idiosyncrasies.

"What makes you so sure?" Dave asked. "Take your time. Dr. Beckworth said we could stay all day."

The secretary turned to look squarely at Dave. "Beckworth never said that. Well, lemme show you how I'm sure, funny man." Puffo gestured to her computer screen and her mouse. She scowled at Dave, who had bumped her mouse, which she grabbed, making a show of sniffing loudly. She typed in her password and with rapid keystrokes called up an electronic file. Dave kept his eyes on her fingers.

"See this?" she said, pointing to a short text. "Add this to the fact that Rolly couldn't possibly just fall like a goddamn ripe apple into the goddamn reactor. He wasn't *that* blind." She jabbed a manicured finger at the screen, the sparkle of her large topaz reflected on the electronic letters. "This is how I'm sure."

Dave and Annabelle rose to stand behind Puffo, looking over her shoulder. They read the words on the screen: *I'm free at last, I'm free at last, Oh, God, I'm free at last. rrc.*

"That's Rolly's last letter," Puffo said. "You can tell by the numbers at the top that he mailed it to my computer last night."

At the top of the letter they read the date: *102298.*

"And he mailed it to everyone else in the reactor," Puffo said. "We all got a copy in the electronic mail. And everybody's talking about it."

Dave signed her words to Annabelle behind Puffo's back as the secretary considered the screen with grave satisfaction.

Annabelle looked at the words again. "What does it mean, Bertha?"

"Well, it's a suicide note, naturally. I mean, what else can it mean? The business about God, for one thing. That's very theological. Sounds like old Rolly was practicing talking to his goddamn Maker."

Annabelle asked Puffo to make a hard copy of the note, and while the secretary printed it, Dave stood beside her to receive the document.

"You know, Bertha, if your boss killed himself, he chose a fairly dramatic and painful way to go," Annabelle said. "Did Dr. Castillo act like a man with suicide on his mind?"

"As far as I'm concerned, Rolly had two minds: one with sex and one with suicide. He was either up or he was down, get it? What a dick."

There is only one sign for "dick," and Dave had never used it before with Annabelle.

"How long were you Dr. Castillo's secretary?" Annabelle asked.

Dave eyed Puffo with obvious fascination, as though she were a rare specimen that had just popped up under the lens of his microscope.

"Eight long years. I'm free at last."

"Sounds like you were not especially fond of the dear departed." Annabelle was unable to resist a quick smile.

"No fuckin' way. I'm glad he's dead. I wish he could kill himself twice. Lousy son of a bitch."

That wiped the smile from Annabelle's face. "What'd he do to you, Bertha?"

"Nothing less than the royal screw. I don't happen to care if you repeat any of this, or if your funny man makes busy with his hands over it. See, I was applying for a job at the Stony Brook reactor on Long Island. You know, in New York? Well, Rolly'd been spreading a story about me, and last week it got back to the girl who interviewed me there that I sleep around with the department heads. I'm still furious."

Annabelle hesitated, exchanging a quick glance with a goggle-eyed Dave.

"Do you, Bertha?" Annabelle finally asked. "Uh, sleep around, I mean?"

"What the hell? You think I'd tell you?"

"Did you confront Dr. Castillo about it?"

A sudden light blazed in the secretary's blue eyes. She smacked her fist on the computer's keyboard, causing a spray of gibberish to explode across the screen.

And then, as her response, Puffo invoked Miami's favorite Anglo stereotype about the majority population and their cars.

She said, "Do Cubans drive IROCs?"

FIVE

PUFFO ESCORTED THEM TO THE LAST DOOR IN THE LONG corridor. It opened pneumatically into a lab.

"This is the Topaz Project," she boomed. "And that's Lon Berlin, Rolly's research partner. If you need anything else, call me later. I always take an early lunch. Lon's an ass-kisser. Always has been, always will be." She stomped down the hall, aggressively whistling some song Dave thought might be a weirdly hybrid rap version of Jimmy Buffett's "Margaritaville."

Seated at a high and narrow table in the center of the laboratory, Lon Berlin looked up in a leisurely way from the screen of a large calculator and nodded at the couple standing in the doorway, apparently untroubled by Puffo's matter-of-fact denouncement of him.

His hair was as dark as Annabelle's, and rather long, curling softly over his collar. His broad shoulders gave his open lab coat an informal air, and Dave thought instantly that he'd be perfect in the role of doorman at the Pink Building.

Berlin smiled gravely at Annabelle, rising from his chair and laying aside the calculator.

"Hello. Let me guess," he said. "Bertha's been telling you fragrantly earthy fables of life on this little asteroid."

Annabelle walked forward to shake hands with Berlin, who smiled softly as he took her hand and held it. Dave bristled at the contact and thought the tall scientist's interest in Annabelle's hand was unnecessarily prolonged.

"Sorry to interrupt your work, Dr. Berlin," Annabelle said, and she introduced herself and Dave. "You probably know that Eugene Beckworth has asked my company for whatever assistance we can give regarding the death of your partner."

"No problem. I'm here to help." He was tall, taller than Annabelle, and he smiled at her again, their eyes meeting comfortably, warm brown eyes gazing into her clear and shining green ones. "Tell me, have you been given the suicide scenario in full?"

Dave couldn't resist. "Is a frog's ass watertight?"

Berlin laughed, and Annabelle studied the way the laugh became an event in his eyes, deep brown and unguarded.

"The inimitable Bertha's been selling suicide all morning to anyone who got that electronic note from Rolly. I just let her rave. But don't think I don't appreciate Bertha and her many talents. She's easily the best secretary at the reactor, and she knows more about punctuation and spelling than us mere scientists. Why care if she loves fairy tales and puts salt on her cornflakes? I have to say that she understands almost as much physics as I do. She's one of the most valuable people here, so we give her great license."

"I take it you don't agree with Bertha that Dr. Castillo chose this unusual way to end his own life?" Annabelle asked. Dave wished she wouldn't stand so close to Berlin.

"No. Not that respect for the workplace would have prevented him. My guess is Rolly was celebrating and fell into the pool as a piece of drunken revelry. Would you like to sit down?"

Annabelle shook her head, but Dave pointedly took the seat that Berlin had vacated.

"You see, there's a bit more to that note than Bertha is aware of. It's from one of Rolly's favorite stories. Rolly only told her his dirty stories, but he used to tell me this story about a guy he knew who worked for the *Wall Street Journal*'s wire service. He used to sit all day and type stories at a hundred and thirty words per minute over the wires. That's all he did. Just type and type. According to Rolly, this guy always swore that his ship would come in one day and that he'd kiss the *Journal* good-bye with glee and abandon. Well, one day every subscriber in the nation sees this lunatic message coming over the wires: 'Free at last, free at last, Oh, God, I'm free at last.' I guess the guy's ship came in. That's what I think was in Rolly's mind, that old story. I think Rolly was either juiced or joking. He sent that note to Bertha and others after washing his insides with a bottle of illegal Cuban rum, and yo-ho-hoed into the pool."

Annabelle knew that the "Free at last" sentiment had originated in an old Negro spiritual, but she accepted the story on its merits. "Dr. Berlin," she said, "did Castillo have a ship on its way?"

"Now, there you've got me. We weren't that close. I really only paid attention when he talked science, but then

I paid very close attention indeed. His scuba friends probably know if they hit sunken treasure or something. That 'Free at last' thing could make you wonder." He wrote rapidly on a yellow legal pad on the table and tore the page off, handing it to Annabelle. "Here's the name of the dive shop where Rolly hung out. The owner would have been Rolly's co-dreamer in any get-rich-quick schemes."

Annabelle made a blowing noise with her mouth and extended her hand, palm out with the paper, in Dave's direction.

Dave looked disgusted.

"So, Castillo was a diver," Dave said. "No wonder he had so much trouble in the pool. Jesus, you guys must think we're simple. Us and everybody else."

"I know what you're thinking, but, believe me, it's unthinkable," Berlin said. "You just can't murder someone at will in the reactor. Even if you wanted to, you couldn't get past the front door, or someone would see you, or hear you. The guys in the control room said Rolly didn't even call out. That's why I think he must have been crazy out of his mind drunk. They said he was talking funny. Besides, there are so many places where it would be easier to kill a man. Why here? You can't really blame Eugene Beckworth for deciding it was an accident. I happen to believe that too. Rolly may have been the kind of guy who gets murdered—I don't have any problem with that—but you'd have to be a lunatic to kill him in the reactor building. Besides, there's absolutely nothing to suggest he was murdered. It had to be an accident. Jesus, what a mess." He ran a hand through his hair.

"Dr. Berlin, you didn't like Castillo either, did you?" Dave asked.

"Well, I didn't actively dislike Rolly." Berlin paused, looking at the desk. He looked up at Annabelle. "But I guess he was pretty hard to like. Bertha probably told you about his salacious side. I certainly respected Rolly as a scientist." He seemed to consider the matter again. "No. I didn't like him."

Dave gave the scientist a measuring look and asked, "Did Castillo often drink to excess on the job?"

"Not on the job."

"Did he usually work into the early-morning hours? I mean, was last night an aberration?" Dave asked.

"It wasn't an aberration; Rolly was here all the time. When he wasn't diving."

"He was married, wasn't he? Unhappily? It doesn't sound like he had much of a home life."

The question clearly made Berlin uncomfortable. "You should talk to his wife about that." Suddenly he grinned. "Or his secretary."

Dave smirked at the mention of the secretary. He looked at Berlin. "Dr. Berlin, have you been consulted about the disposal of Dr. Castillo's body? After all, aren't you the nuclear expert?"

"I've spoken with Dr. Beckworth, but it's not my decision. Frankly I think the Nuclear Regulatory Commission will resolve this for us, maybe as early as tomorrow." He interrupted himself with a sudden, reminiscent smile. "I can tell you the joke making the rounds this morning, though. The NRC has a rule that materials that have passed through a human body cannot be regulated—the rule was made for patients of radiotherapy, so that they could pass their urine without being licensed by the government. Well, and I hope you'll pardon the gallows humor, the suggestion has been made that we hire people to eat Rolly."

"God, that's awful," Annabelle exclaimed, but Dave bit back a spontaneous grin. Clearly working around nuclear energy had distorted some of the synaptic activity here.

Annabelle slowly strolled around the table, peering at the cluttered papers and boxes. Abruptly she stopped. "What's this lovely thing doing just lying here?"

Berlin saw that she had picked up a sparkling blue stone.

"Topaz. Irradiated topaz. It's quite safe now, Ms. Hardy-Maratos. That stone was in a group we irradiated more than two years ago, quite long enough for its small amount of radiation to dissipate. Even when we first take these little beauties out of the reactor, there's only enough radiation to make you sick as a dog for a few days. They're not deadly. The Nuclear Regulatory Commission sets hideously strict guidelines for us—we can't release those gems to their owners until they're absolutely harmless, or as harmless as anything gets. That one was given to me by the guy we did the work for."

"Where does topaz come from? I mean, where in the world?"

"Lots of places. But the best stones are from mines in Brazil and Sri Lanka."

"This was your project with Dr. Castillo? Why exactly do you irradiate the stones? What does that do?" Annabelle tried to hand the stone to Dave, but he backed away from it.

"I'll give you the condensed lecture," Berlin said, leaning his tall frame against the table. "In its natural state, topaz is usually yellow, sometimes white. The university contracts with jewelers, sometimes with mines, to irradiate the gems in the reactor. We pack the stones into aluminum cans and lower them to an irradiation point in the reactor pool. That turns them the gorgeous blue you see. Basically we knock a hole with neutrons into the lattice of the electron structure of the topaz. That alters the stones so that they absorb yellow light, and that makes them look blue. More than doubles their value. That's a London Blue you're holding. About three carats. What we did to that stone is kind of a culmination of scientific myths—the philosopher's stone, if you will."

"It's dazzlingly pretty." Annabelle held the stone up to the late-morning light streaming in through the window.

"Isn't it? The money the reactor makes for treating the stones goes directly to the university as 'service income.' What we get out of it here at the reactor is purely cerebral. For example Rolly and I were doing some experiments on the use of topaz in lasers and in infrared detectors. That's the cutting edge of topaz research. Nobody can touch what we're doing with lasers—not here in the U.S., not anywhere. This reactor is way ahead of anyone else. And Rolly was a very good physicist."

"What's so great about topaz?" Annabelle asked. "For science, I mean. Why not use, say, rubies?"

"For one thing, we don't get rubies here. Rubies would be perfect. But topaz shares a couple of qualities with rubies, and with diamonds: It's really hard and it spreads light around like a Catherine wheel. That's what you need in lasers. That's its value to us, not its blue beauty."

Annabelle handed him the topaz, with a show of reluctance.

"Mrs. Castillo hasn't been here yet, has she?" she asked. "Are her husband's personal effects still around?"

"We don't really bring that much to work. You won't even find a briefcase in the place. As you've undoubtedly noticed, the reactor is cramped, and space is worth more than, well, topaz." He gestured to a metal desk under a window. "That little desk is probably all you'll find. We don't have lockers or anything like that."

Annabelle sat and pulled out the desk's drawers, gently moving their contents. Most of the papers were covered with mathematics of a higher order than she could comprehend, all executed in a precise, tiny hand. There were a few photographs, including a framed shot of a man underwater on a coral reef, peering through a mask. Even underwater he wore extremely thick spectacles, behind a mask that looked to be especially designed to accommodate the heavy frames. Annabelle could barely see his eyes. He had been a little overweight, but Annabelle saw that his leg and arm muscles were well developed.

She held up the photo

"That's Rolly," Berlin said.

Annabelle looked closely at the photograph. It was imperfectly aligned behind the plastic cover, and she slipped the picture out of the frame. Behind it was another photo, a picture of the same bespectacled man, standing on the wooden porch of what looked like a rundown restaurant, the paint on its weathered hand-hewn shingles flaking and sun-dried, the dusty foliage of bottlebrush trees clinging against the roof. The man stood in front of a dirty window, over which hung a sign. The sign said THE ALLIGATOR HOLE CAFE.

She gestured to Dave and handed him the photo. He looked at it quickly and returned it to her. She replaced the first photograph in the frame and put it back in the drawer. She sat for a moment in thought, gazing at the underwater photograph before closing the drawer. "Dr. Berlin, was Rolly's eyesight terribly bad?"

"Pretty bad and getting worse. He was relying more and more on me and Bertha for some of the details he couldn't see. But Rolly could see fine where it really counts."

Annabelle looked an inquiry.

"Inside his head," Berlin said. "The computer you operate with the keyboard of training and imagination."

"Speaking of computers, I'm surprised you don't have any in this lab. Where could Castillo have sent that 'Free at last' note from?"

"Computers can be pretty persnickety around radiation," Berlin said. "We have an insulated computer lab across the hall, but Rolly could have signed on to any computer in the building."

Annabelle frowned. The top of Castillo's desk was covered with papers, mostly the same kind of complex computations she had seen in the drawers, the same crabbed handwriting. There was a huge aspirin bottle, almost full, and a bottle of eyedrops.

She stood. "That isn't much to leave behind as testament to a career."

SIX

"ROLLY'S WORK WASN'T THE KIND THAT SHOWS UP MUCH except as higher mathematics," Berlin said. "You know, the only humility he had, he had for his work. Some people thought he was overbearing, but I think he had an extremely clear perspective on his place in the scientific community. He used to say that we're just fleas on the raccoon's body of the universe—he never explained why he chose that animal; probably for its mask. And he was right about us fleas. That's what I sometimes find myself concluding when I stare into the reactor itself. There's so much energy—*power* is really a misleading term—feebly harvested by us frail humans looking for answers. It's pretty difficult to feel that mankind is nature's last word in the presence of the simple and grand fact of an atom's indifference to us."

"Dr. Berlin, we'd like to see the reactor," Annabelle said. "Can you arrange that?"

"I'll take you myself to the belly of the beast."

They went together down the corridor, through an immense airlock, where Berlin used a card key and spoke with an operator through a wall microphone, and up in a small elevator. They crossed a dimpled metal floor and stood by the pool, its glowing bright blue surface undisturbed by so much as a ripple.

"I could go for a dip in this pretty blue water if I got the urge," Dave said. "It really shocks me that the pool is not protected better. Or that we're not."

Only a heavy three-inch steel chain, looped across waist-high posts, stood between them and the surface of the water at their feet.

"We don't let people in here who get urges like that," Berlin said. "At least we didn't think we did."

The nuclear reactor was much simpler than Annabelle had imagined. It seemed to be a giant tub of eerily-shining blue water, with a dark circle at the bottom.

She took pictures with her EOS, concentrating on the pool, the glass-enclosed control room, and the walkway a floor above them. The tall scientist concentrated on Annabelle, following her with his eyes, clearly enjoying himself. Dave stood with his hands in his jacket pockets, staring at the pool with a disapproving frown on his face.

The operators in the control room sat at their consoles, reminding Dave of the busy intensity of air traffic controllers, monitoring their boards. If anything went wrong with the reactor, they would know it first, Berlin explained. They were affectionately known, but only by reactor personnel, he said, as the Meltdown Posse, or simply the MPs.

Dave craned his neck to gaze up at the bridge, a floor above them. Heavy chains hung even higher than the bridge, strung from huge hooks in the ceiling. His gaze traveled downward along the concrete walls, and he saw poles of varying lengths, constructed of some ultrashiny metal, stacked against the wall.

He pointed to them. "Is that the kind of thing they used to haul Rolly out?" he asked.

"The very thing," Berlin said.

Dave turned to stare into the depths of the glowing water, imagining a pulsing energy from the dark circle he could make out clearly down at the distant bottom of this blue lagoon of nuclear liquid.

"What does the water feel like?" Dave asked. "I mean, is it hot to the touch?"

"About one hundred eight degrees Fahrenheit," Berlin said. "About the temperature of a hot tub. Sometimes we joke and call this place the university reactor and spa."

"Gee, that's really funny," Dave said nastily. "You ought to go on Letterman."

"Sorry. Gallows humor."

"So you've got a gallows here, too?" Dave mumbled.

"The reactor doesn't generate as much heat as you might expect," Berlin said, by way of covering the awkwardness of Dave's bad manners. "We don't want power; we want neutrons. The core itself—you can see it if you look straight down—is only about the size of an ordinary garbage can. You're looking all the way down to below the basement. That's why we're on the second floor but the pool is actually three stories deep. If Rolly had just floated on the top of the water, he might be alive today. It's only as you go really deep into the water, quite near the core, that you encounter deadly radiation."

"How deadly?"

"Almost immediate, I would think."

When Annabelle finished shooting, the three stood

silently on the dimpled metal deck. The silence was broken by Berlin, who began to explain the throbbing blue glow of the water and, as he did so, Dave signed the highly technical explanation for Annabelle.

Clearly Berlin had not been warned by Beckworth about Annabelle's deafness, somehow escaping the president's net of control. Berlin smoothly finished his summary of the Cherenkov Effect, but there was a perceptible stiffening of his manner, an exaggerated casualness Annabelle had seen before in many people when they first became aware of her handicap. She tried not to feel the disappointment, keener now than she was prepared for. Dave, who knew her every expression well from his two years of signing with her, was touched by her sadness and felt a protective surge that almost made him hate the good-looking scientist.

"Annabelle," Dave said, knowing better than to show his reaction, "let's go see Castillo's diving platform." He gestured to the walkway overhead.

"I'll take you up to the bridge," Berlin said.

"If you don't mind, and if the rules permit, I'll take her myself," Dave said softly, eyeing Berlin steadily.

"The rules don't permit."

He showed them to the flight of stairs leading up to the top floor. They climbed the stairs slowly, Annabelle first, and she carefully scanned the steps and railing, looking for any sign that would help them understand how this prosaic piece of equipment had become a pathway to death.

At the top they stepped under the yellow police tape and onto the bridge. Annabelle slipped, and Berlin caught her by the arm.

"Watch your step," he said, mouthing the words in an exaggerated way.

But Annabelle wasn't clumsy. She stared down at the floor.

Finally she pointed to the floor near Dave's feet, to a small iridescent, metallic glimmering.

Dave extracted an envelope from his jacket pocket and turned it inside out. He knelt and rubbed the inner surface on the floor of the bridge. The paper came away yellowed and damp, and Dave raised his eyebrows at Annabelle, turning the envelope right side out, folding it, and putting it back in his pocket.

He stood and wiped off his knees. He leaned far over the iron railing and touched the cold metal of one of the five thick chains suspended from the third-floor roof and hanging in a plumb line over the second-floor pool deck. Dave righted himself on the bridge and grasped the railing. "Must have been quite a dive," he signed, considering the twenty-foot distance. "I would think a half-gainer, in the pike position, with a double somersault."

Fingerprint powder lay in a light film on the bridge railing. Annabelle wondered, with Beckworth sealing up the reactor against medical inquiry, what the police view was. Dave would have to talk with Paul Diaz at Metro-Dade. She was willing to bet that Beckworth would embrace and spread the suicide story as soon as he heard it. And if he did, that would quickly become almost unstoppable as a truth with the weight of the school behind it, unless the police turned up anything to contradict the story. She knew Paul Diaz would never participate in a less-than-thorough investigation, but the reactor itself, with its special dangers and federal regulations, might stand in the way of thoroughness, especially with the university president making up some additional rules as he went along.

Berlin had said that killing in a nuclear reactor made no sense. But to Annabelle, killing in a place that was difficult to examine with thoroughness was beginning to assume a kind of pristine and cold logic.

She leaned against the railing. "Dr. Berlin. Have the police talked to Bertha yet?" Annabelle's dark hair framed her face, falling softly against her cheeks.

He was studying her, and he was slow to respond. "What? Oh. It's more like she talked to them," he said, grinning at her, but he seemed distracted.

Dave didn't like the look on the scientist's face. He thought Berlin looked hypnotized, and Dave the Monkeyman, connoisseur of fashion and alert observer of all trends, wouldn't have worn that facial expression to a rummage sale.

SEVEN

THE SECURITY GUARD WAS NERVOUS.

He had heard that the company president was a nice lady, but it wasn't every day that she came visiting on the job. He rubbed a Kleenex over the toe of his black shoe.

From his office in the basement of the Ring Building, he could see white-coated scientists returning from lunch. He had brought his lunch, like always, but was reluctant to eat, certain that as soon as his burritos perfumed the air, she'd walk around the corner and into the office. He wished he'd brought something like peanut butter, something healthful, something without cholesterol, something responsible and American—anything but cheese burritos. He glared resentfully at the little refrigerator against the wall. He couldn't even open the door to get a soda; those were powerful burritos, purchased at Grocer King last night after he left the Alligator Hole Cafe, and there was no way he would risk walking down the hall now to the reactor canteen with such a spic lunch. Burritos had seemed so good last night.

Last night. God, he was glad that had not been his shift. Imagine being the one who missed seeing Dr. Castillo in trouble, hadn't known what was going on. Not that Terry should have seen anything. He'd followed the drill perfectly, as anyone could see from the log sheet.

The guard stood in the open doorway. She was coming down the hall.

He fidgeted, tucking in his sky-blue shirt for the fourth time, wondering what to do to look busy, authoritative, on his toes. Terry would know; he was a much better guard, macho and all. More like a cop on TV, even if he hadn't been there when Dr. Castillo had fallen into the pool.

She was wearing a pretty yellow suit, and she was smiling. Dr. Berlin and another man in a white coat were with her. And so was a guy who plainly had a gun under his jacket, a guy who didn't look like the kind of guy who would carry a gun. He wondered what kind of gun a guy like that carried. And the gun guy was waving his hands all over the place.

They stopped outside a small room called the Glove Box. They looked into it through a long, narrow window, and Dr. Berlin was showing her the place where you could stick your hands into the room through a long pair of gloves that were part of the window. The guard had always wanted to try that, but he was afraid of radiation, afraid of everything he touched in this place, especially in the inner building. But the pay was good, better than guards at hotels in Miami got. Otherwise he would have quit a long time ago. Not only was he afraid of this place, but he didn't like the people: They made cruel jokes, and they teased him about his fears. They never teased Terry.

Maybe sometime he'd put his hands inside the gloves for only a minute, just to see what it felt like to stick your hands through a window. The scientists used those window-gloves to move things around in the Glove Box sometimes. They called them pig gloves.

Inside the room on a steel table by the window was the dead guy. His clothes looked like they were still pretty wet. His glasses were hanging off his right shoulder from an elastic string. He was covered with burns, bad red burns. Radiation burns.

Wiping sweat from his brow, the guard stepped out into the hall and stood uncertainly by the door. He could hear them talking.

"As you can see," Beckworth was saying, "no doubt about it. Radiation death."

"Have you ever seen this before?" Dave asked, awed and saddened.

Berlin nodded, a shadow of something that looked like dull anger on his face.

"At Chernobyl. I was there with some of the firemen who were waiting for bone marrow transplants," he said quietly.

Dave signed Berlin's words for Annabelle.

Annabelle gazed at Rolly Castillo. He had been a small man, slightly shorter than Dave, about five foot seven, she guessed. Red burns covered what she could see of his flesh. His hair was brown and curly and lay dankly over his forehead; his body tended toward the pudgy, his clothing toward the ordinary. She put her hands in the long gloves. She awkwardly reached inside the room, lifting the dead man's thick glasses by one earpiece.

Beckworth almost grabbed her arm, then, apparently

thinking better of his gesture, stopped and put his hand in the pocket of his lab coat.

"These glasses are covered with smears," she said to Dave over her shoulder. "I wonder why anybody with such obviously poor vision wouldn't have cleaned this stuff off."

Dave glowered at her hands through the window.

"It's perfectly safe to use the gloves," Berlin said, responding to Dave's look of disapproval.

Dave stepped closer to her side to look at the glasses.

"How come he's not wearing a dosimeter?" Dave asked. He tugged sharply on his own badge, jerking the plastic triangle vigorously. "It doesn't come off easily."

Berlin looked in surprise at the dead man.

"You're right. Rolly knew better than that. Dosimeters are solely for our own protection. We all hope that our dosimeters will tell us if we've been dangerously exposed to radiation. We rely on them every day. We *like* having them read when we leave the reactor. It helps us sleep. Rolly must have been drunk."

Annabelle withdrew her hands with a shudder.

"Are you okay?" Dave looked at her pale face anxiously.

"I'm fine, Dave." She turned to Beckworth. "What's that sticking out under the body? It looks like a pair of garden shears."

"It's just a pair of scissors." Beckworth was turning his heavy ring impatiently, jerking it in an uneven rotation under his thick knuckle.

"Odd thing to carry in your back pocket," Dave said, considering Beckworth's show of restlessness before returning his gaze to the scissors handles and the corpse behind the window. "I wouldn't want to try it and cough at the same time."

The security guard looked uncomfortable. They were his scissors, the ones he had nicked on a lug nut, the ones with the ebony handles, the ugly ones Frances had brought him as a present from Honduras that had come all the way from China. But he always kept them in the canteen across the hall, to open those impossible, stupid, microwavable, smelly plastic-wrapped burritos from Grocer King.

A phone rang in the security office. The guard stepped back inside and picked up the receiver. He returned to the hall and held the receiver out.

"*Favor?* Dr. Beckworth?" he asked. "It's the NRC."

Beckworth hesitated, taking a step toward the guard. "I'll take it upstairs," he said, turning toward the elevator and gesturing for Berlin to follow him.

"Dr. Beckworth," Annabelle called out, interrupting his long strides.

He turned.

"Will you grant us access to the reactor's computer base?" she asked.

His mouth sprang open. He closed it with a snap of his teeth. "Are you out of your goddamn mind?" he demanded. He continued toward the elevator, shaking his head.

"I'll see you later," Berlin said to Annabelle, touching her elbow gently. He followed Beckworth.

"What makes that guy think he's qualified to play with your elbow?" Dave demanded in a loud voice, and he had the satisfaction of seeing Berlin's quick steps slow momentarily as he followed the university president into the elevator.

Annabelle lifted a hand in exasperation. "Dave, you're chaperoning me again," she said. "Stop it. God! You can take the boy out of the Cuban household, but you can't take the Cuban household out of the boy."

"You think I only look out for you because I'm a Cuban male. Well, let me tell you, Miss Pan-American Diplomacy, I dumped the macho lessons of my ancestors the minute they dumped me in Miami. I'll have you know that any sexism in my behavior came from American movies. As for Dr. Berlin, I merely happen to have better-than-average instincts about guys like that."

"Guys like what?"

"Guys who touch your elbow in that sickening way."

"What was so sickening about it?"

"Your dosimeter thing turned green."

She glanced involuntarily at the badge and then shot him a look of scorn.

"Let's not stand here arguing about my elbow," she signed. "We seem to have the place to ourselves. Let's talk to that sentry."

"Some sentry. He looks like he's about ten years old. If I looked like him, I'd at least try to look older."

"How?" she asked, regarding Dave curiously.

"Never mind."

After introducing themselves—a process that fascinated the guard as Dave was transformed by mere words from a thin, floridly dressed little Cuban curiosity into the Grand High Wizard of Hardy High Finance. In the presence of this wizard the guard sat with the company president in the reactor's cramped security office in the basement of the Ring Building, going over the log kept around the clock by the Hardy Security guards. Last night's record showed nothing out of the ordinary, not until the guard, a man named Terry Bodorff, had been summoned to the pool by the Meltdown Posse.

"Well, it looks to me like Berlin may be right," Dave signed. He leaned back in the chair and stretched. "I can't see how it could be anything but an accident. And that, after all, is the happy ending for everyone, isn't it? For everyone but the dead man, if we're counting him."

"I think I'll wait for the report on your envelope before I get all giddy from overwhelming relief," she said. "I don't like this whole notion of a prominent physicist taking a walk into a nuclear cauldron. No wonder the media are giving Beckworth trouble."

"Annabelle, the dead man was having a problem with his eyes. Maybe he did fall in."

"Over a railing?" Annabelle shook her head. "He was having a problem with his eyes, not with his legs." She ran a hand through her hair. "And while I'm at it, according to our own security, those stairs to the platform are cleaned every day, between four and five in the afternoon. That inner building is immaculately clean. Whatever it is that we found on that metal floor hasn't been there long enough to dry completely. And it shouldn't be there at all."

"Señorita Hardy? May I offer you a Pepsi?" The guard was clearly embarrassed by his own meager offering, but he'd rather offer her a raw lizard than mention the cheese burrito smelling up the little refrigerator.

Annabelle smiled at him but shook her head.

"Dave, if we can accept the midnight walk into the

bright and glowing blue pool—which Castillo must have been able to see, even if he couldn't see anything else—there's still the matter of that unpleasant smell on the bridge. We'll know soon enough about that. Plus what Bertha Puffo is calling the suicide note. The note just doesn't ring true with her theory of a heavenly destination on Castillo's part. The tone of that electronic note sounded more like the man was happy, going somewhere with earthly pleasures, maybe even rubbing something in on his coworkers. That note sounded more like a prank than a final farewell."

She looked thoughtful, her forehead wrinkled. "And the scuba-diving business. Castillo must have been an uncommonly qualified swimmer. He wasn't very likely to drown, not with the instincts of a diver. And why did he go straight down? It wasn't like he was wearing a diver's weight belt. There's something rotten here."

Dave nodded. "Beckworth almost came unglued from his teeth when you asked about accessing the database, didn't he? I assume you were after the origins of that suspicious suicide note?" When she nodded, Dave rubbed his jaw pensively, remembering the sound of Beckworth's teeth. "Beckworth acted like you'd asked him to turn over the secret code to the universe. As though we'd be able to understand any of their convoluted mathematics anyway. Annabelle, I'd love to give Beckworth a black eye, although I can't help thinking I'd be giving us a pretty good shiner at the same time. This place is our responsibility too. But I'm with Gilbert here." Dave gestured cordially at the guard. "I'm hungry. Let's get out of this dump. It makes my skin crawl. I can't wait to have my dosimeter read. I should be better off than you, though. At least Berlin didn't touch me."

Annabelle gave him a dirty look.

They left, and Gilbert Maria Cristiano sighed and opened the refrigerator.

The reactor personnel studiously ignored Annabelle and Dave as they returned to the ground-level floor of the Ring Building.

"Are we invisible?" Dave asked a passing white-coated woman. She flicked her eyes at him briefly, focusing in a distracted way, but continued walking without pause. "Oh. God. we're invisible. We've been erased."

Dave put his arm out and waved it in the air, apparently trying to locate his own limb. He tapped Annabelle's hand and signed to her.

"Now that I'm invisible, I just know I'm crawling with radioactivity—horny gamma rays have bred their foul offspring on my innocent flesh."

Annabelle laughed. He had made the sign for "crawl" while dragging his hand spastically over his chest.

"I don't think it works quite like that," she said. "Whatever breeding is going on here is going on in that lovely blue pool. It was beautiful, wasn't it?"

A rare contemplative mood descended over Dave's features.

"Nature's beautiful, Annabelle. And art's beautiful. And on your good days, you're beautiful. But man mucking around with nature, no matter how intelligently, twisting it into a shape so he can make a topaz sparkle—that's not beautiful. That's greed. Somewhere along the line, the very existence of this place depends on greed. You can't tell me Beckworth is trying to whitewash a haven of pure scientific curiosity. He's protecting his service income."

"I wonder if that's all he's protecting."

They arrived at Puffo's office, but the secretary had not yet returned.

"She takes long lunches," Dave signed. "I do wonder how she manages to keep herself entertained."

"Take a look," Annabelle signed, and she stood in the doorway. Dave sat at the secretary's desk, dumped her screen saver, and accessed her files, using her own password, the one he had seen when she had entered the numbers on their earlier visit. "Good thing for us I'm so sickeningly nosy," he signed.

Dave's expert fingers danced over the keyboard, and for several minutes he quickly scrolled documents across the screen. He knew he didn't have much time, so he went for the obvious. The file that caught his eye was slugged "Topaz/$," and he printed it out. He folded and stuffed it into his inner jacket pocket, logged off the computer with Puffo's password, and joined Annabelle by the door.

She had caught sight of Berlin leaving the Topaz Project lab, and she suddenly wondered if she should have combed her hair. He approached them from down the hall.

"Our little Bertha back already?" he asked.

"Nope, we're holding the fort, so you can just run along," Dave said helpfully. "Nobody will miss you. If anyone asks, we'll say you stepped out to do Eugene Beckworth's laundry. Unless you just throw it in the pool with your other gems?"

Berlin stiffened. "Who do you think you are, coming

in here and judging us all? What makes you think you understand us all so well?"

Dave flushed, caught off guard by the real passion in Berlin's voice.

Annabelle stepped forward and touched Berlin's elbow. Dave blinked, not sure if he was seeing things. Annabelle didn't touch people if she could help it.

"We're trying to understand what it must be like to work here," she said with a smile. "We just need your help."

Dave had made a recovery. "We're not trying to steal your secret formulas, Dr. Frankenstein," he said.

Berlin opened his mouth, closed it, and turned away, taking a purposeful few steps toward the lab. He stopped and pivoted, standing a few paces from them. He hesitated.

"Look," he said, directing his gaze at Annabelle. "Will you have lunch with me?"

Dave smirked, but Annabelle took his arm and gave him a meaningful pinch.

"Dave, will you take my car? I'll meet you back at the office," she said. She took her keys from her pocket and worked the convertible's key off the ring.

Dave stopped smirking, doing a spontaneous impression of Beckworth's earlier jawline exercise.

"I'll just close the lab," Berlin said, and he jogged happily down the hall.

Annabelle held out the car key and her camera to Dave with a look of inquiry. Now Dave closed his mouth with a snap of his teeth.

"Are you crazy, Annabelle? That guy's probably a murderer. Christ on a crutch, he's probably radioactive as well. And I bet he stole that topaz stone he was showing off with."

Annabelle stifled an undignified response.

"Well, I've warned you," Dave said huffily. "I'm getting out of this dosimeter palace. I wish I had gone to lunch with Bertha. At least she's making a contribution to human understanding."

He left Annabelle standing at the office door and rounded the corner to the lobby.

He came back almost immediately.

"Do you want my gun?"

She shook her head, smiling stiffly at him, and he turned away, his lips pursed, his brow furrowed, her key clutched tightly in his hand.

Annabelle waited in the quiet hall for Berlin. When he returned from the lab, he had shed his white coat, and the top three buttons of his shirt had been undone.

They drove north through the barrens of Naranja, awkwardly silent at first, Annabelle uncomfortable in Berlin's Honda Accord because she was accustomed to the more open spaces of her convertible and because she was regretting the impulse to flout Dave that had put her in this position. Berlin was uncomfortable because he did not know how to be with a woman who could not listen to him.

They drove through South Miami, the Grove, and across the Rickenbacker Causeway to Key Biscayne. The bright October afternoon was warm with breezes from the Atlantic. The green-blue waters of the shallow bay were filled with windsurfers, their vibrantly colored sails rounded by onshore breezes.

Like fat, jolly little men, Annabelle thought, like fat

bellies under tropical shirts, scudding across the bay in tubs.

Berlin saw her smile to herself out of the corner of his eye, and, without thinking, he reached over and took her hand briefly in his. She returned his smile with the full force of her own, and she was surprised by her own pleasure.

What am I doing? she thought. *I never do things like this. And with a total stranger. A handsome stranger. A stranger Dave doesn't like.*

They ate at Sundays-on-the-Bay, a waterfront patio restaurant that served boaters who docked at the bar. They shared conch fritters, criticizing them, arguing about better fritters in Key West restaurants, since they at least agreed that no mere Miami restaurant served anything but pale imitations of the island delicacy. They dipped the steaming and crunchy balls in Key Lime Mustard sauce with their fingers.

"On the dock, at Mallory Square," Annabelle said.

"You've been bedazzled by the sunsets," Berlin said. "The fritters are much better at Nick's."

They drank iced tea and praised it because it was served in the largest glasses in Miami, which they agreed was the only meaningful criterion for iced tea. They watched the boats and invented elaborate and highly criminal histories for the sailors who docked at Sundays to drink, getting smashed on piña coladas and Corona beers in the afternoon sun, stripping off their shirts and lying across the bows of their boats with their dogs or cats or birds, but, at this hour and at this bar, not with their women.

Annabelle and Berlin left the restaurant and drove the

mile or so to Crandon Beach, parking the car in the white sand lot, leaving their shoes in the car, strolling amiably to the beach. They stood side by side in the warm surf, facing the calm Atlantic.

"I love to come to the beach," Annabelle told him. "It's almost as if I can still hear the surf. I don't know if it's some weird confluence of vibrations set up by the water crashing to shore, or if it's only a sense memory that fools me, or if it's just a powerful wish—but it has a reality and a vividness for me that breaks my heart with its beauty and its power for change and variety. 'Mutability,' Shelley would have called it."

He put his hands on her shoulders, turning her gently to face him. "You break my heart," he said. "When I realized you could not hear me, there by the reactor pool, that's when it hit me that I had a million things I wanted to say to you."

"Is that what you were thinking? I thought you were deciding that I was a freak, or a sick person. Those are not uncommon reactions to the deaf."

He put his hand in her hair, blown and glistening from the salt spray. "Actually I was jealous. You and Dave—and by the way what the hell is his problem?—go into this intense little world when you sign. I felt like the handicapped one, on the outside."

"We don't mean to be exclusive. But I guess that sometimes happens among signers."

They strolled along the edge of the surf, a line of pelicans swooping along the water in the same direction. They stopped only once, when Berlin pointed to the birds and said, "They always look like pterodactyls to me."

They walked back along the shore. They sat on the

warm sand, cross-legged, knee to knee, facing each other in the afternoon sun.

"Tell me about Rolly," she said. "Why didn't you like him?"

He put his hand in the warm sand and idly drew overlapping circles with his spread fingers. "That's a hard question. I guess more than anything it was his loose mouth, the language he used, the jokes he told. He gossiped. That's unforgivable in a place as tightly packed with people as the reactor. But I'm sorry I wasn't there last night. I wish I'd been there to stop him. Can I ask you something? Something personal?"

"Sure."

"You speak so purely. You haven't been deaf all your life, have you?"

She shook her head. "No. It was gradual, spread out over my twenties. It was as if the world were turning itself down around me; first it was tones, then it was whole words. You know, it's funny. The birds were the last to go. At least they were the last living sounds for me." She turned her head to watch a pelican come to rest on the waves. "Let's talk about something else."

"How did Dave come into your life? Did you hire him?"

"My father hired him when he was a teenager. Dave started as a security guard. He's been with Hardy Security almost ten years. I taught him to sign when I took over the company," she said. "I used to be a pretty good teacher, way back in the Dark Ages."

"Okay, then, teach me, teacher," he said. "Show me how to say 'beautiful.' "

She put her right hand in front of her chin, the palm

toward her face, her fingers and thumb together. She opened the fingers and moved her hand in a circle in front of her face, clockwise, ending with her hand in the original position. She smiled encouragingly at him.

Haltingly, he mimicked her sign, then, with assurance, he pointed at her.

"Your grammar is lousy." She laughed.

"You are so beautiful," he said, touching her hair. "You are the most beautiful woman I've ever met. In my whole life. Since the day I was born."

She regarded him with interest. He meant to kiss her, she knew, but a gull screeching overhead caught his attention, his eyes followed it, and the moment was lost.

She brushed sand from her skirt and made as if to rise.

"Wait," he said, grabbing her hand. "Stay awhile. Keep talking to me. Tell me your favorite thing in sign language."

"It's a poem," she said slowly. Extending her left arm, she pointed the first two fingers of the right hand toward her left palm, moving the first finger back and forth. "Poem. It's a long poem."

"Would I know it?"

"Probably. It's 'Birches,' by Robert Frost. I don't really like the poem in English, but in sign it becomes something wonderful. You see, when a signer does the poem, she can actually make the trees move."

"Show me."

And she signed for him Frost's poem about endurance and loving the earth.

When her hands came to rest, he made the sign for "beautiful."

They walked to the car, an overdressed but oblivious couple amid the nearly naked surfers carrying their boards and towels and radios in the parking lot.

He reached to open the passenger door, but before opening it he put his hand on the roof of the car, blocking her.

"Where do you live?" he asked.

"On Poinciana Avenue in the Grove," she said. "But you can just take me to my office."

"Let's forget work for a little longer. I hate the thought of going back to the reactor. Let's go to your house."

A shadow of distress showed in her eyes, and she felt a surge of panic. "I can't go home. I have to catch up with Dave."

"What's he got against me anyway?"

"Well, he said you probably murdered Rolly."

He stared at her for a moment and then stepped back from the door.

When Berlin pulled the silver Honda to the curb outside the Pink Building, the copper pastels of Miami's hazy afternoon were throwing hot metallic highlights onto the glass, and the scudding clouds chased each other across the reflecting facade.

He turned off the ignition and shifted in his seat.

"Now, there's a display that makes me wonder why people are so freaked out by our pretty blue pool. Just look at that lightning." He pointed across her shoulder, and she turned.

Black banks of clouds had rolled up out of the west, and swollen blasts of white light seemed to squirt out of them.

Annabelle shivered a little at the black weather approaching, nudging the copper clouds out over the Atlantic. She heaved a sigh.

"I suppose we come back now to the real world, Lon. With Rolly's death there's going to be a great deal of attention centered on the reactor and your pretty blue pool. You haven't seen anything yet. Today's flurry of reporters and press releases is just the beginning. It really bothers you that people are scared of nuclear reactors, doesn't it?"

"No, they ought to be scared," he said. "What bothers me is that sometimes they're afraid of me. You know, the mad-scientist myth, the idea that I'm personally responsible for their greatest fears. Annabelle, I've devoted my life to science, but I haven't ignored history, and I firmly believe that science has no premium on damage."

"I agree," she said in her soft voice. "But I also understand the fears."

"I'm worried that you'll walk warily around me, allow me to personify those fears. Are you afraid, Annabelle?"

In the reflected copper light her face, he thought, did look worried.

"A little."

"Show me the sign for 'dangerous.' "

"Well, the sign for 'danger' is like this." She held her left hand closed in front of her chest, and stroked her right thumb upward several times on the closed fist.

"You are not in danger from this scientist, Annabelle," he said, attempting the sign. "Even for a physicist, I'm pretty human, just a man with his share of both positive and negative experiences. And I think that experience—just that, human experience—is all we have standing between us and the dead silence of the endless starry universe. Choosing our experiences wisely is the only way to own our lives."

And this time he did kiss her, softly on the lips, not touching her in any other way.

EIGHT

THE AFTERNOON HAD TURNED BLACK, AND THE LIGHTS were on in her office when she got off the elevator. The rain had started, striking against the pink glass scratchily, sounding like bare frangipani branches on a Caribbean tin roof.

Dave sat at Annabelle's marble desk, his gun in its holster on a chair, Marcel taking nervous little steps on his shoulder in response to the reverberating thunder, papers stacked tidily to his side on the cool surface of the marble.

He leaned back in the chair, a hard expression on his face.

"Hi."

"Hi."

Dave took in her appearance. "Been romping at the beach? I hope Berlin didn't try to push you in. I just have an idea that might be a habit of his. But, oh well, we all have our little quirks."

"Dave. You have no reason to say that. I know you mean well, but you are not my keeper. Or my mother."

He raised an eyebrow while ducking his head over the documents on the desk.

She gestured to the small stack of papers. "What's all that?"

Dave put his hand flat on the stack and pulled it to a spot squarely in front of him. He took the top paper and held it up, snapping it in midair.

"Item. One sheet of legal paper. On it is the name of the dive shop Rolly honored with his patronage. Jimmy Killilea's in Key Largo. I called, but the owner was out with a dive." Dave snapped the paper again, punctuating his words. "I might add that this is also a specimen of Dr. Berlin's handwriting. If this were murder, and the killer had carved his initials in Rolly's chest, I could just compare the handwriting and we could call the police. By the way, Paul Diaz called to say that if the Metro-Dade cops can help you and your dad in any way on this terrible 'suicide,' don't hesitate to call. He's satisfied it was suicide, you know. Also, not that I'm your keeper, but I dropped off your film at the lab."

He lowered the yellow sheet to an open, empty file folder on the desk.

"Dave. I'm sorry. I didn't mean that keeper remark."

He held up the next sheet, ignoring her words.

"Item. Printout of Rolly's last letter to his colleagues. What a crock. Free of what? I ask you. By the way, I checked, and Lon is short for Lawrence. That alone should be enough to keep you from getting involved with him. Lawrence Berlin? What's he got against Larry?"

"Dave, I'm not involved with him. All we did was have lunch."

"He's got a lot of nerve asking you to lunch. Plus,

Berlin? Christ in a camisole, what kind of a Nazi name is that?"

"Dave, you need to take a walk or something. Work off this fit."

"Thanks." He glanced at the window. "I love walking in lightning storms when I'm having a fit." Dave lowered the printout to the open file and held up the next paper from the stack, a ragged, dirty, and much-crumpled envelope.

"I was speaking metaphorically."

He glared at her and snapped the crumpled envelope. "Item. One envelope, belonging to me, as I can tell from the address on the outside. It certainly has my name spelled right too. But it's the contents that I find so interesting. Mind you, most of my mail is much less direct than what we find here. Human urine, plain and simple. Our faithful Edward did the analysis, and he did not say if the urine belonged at any time to a senior research scientist."

"Dave."

He placed the envelope on the stack in the file and picked up a small red booklet. "Item. A copy of 'University of the Keys Research Reactor Standards and Practices,' which I take to be the ethical code at the reactor. All sarcasm aside, Annabelle, there's no provision for drug testing or psychological screening for employment at the reactor. It's, quote, the individual's responsibility. That sits funny with me when it comes to nuclear power, but what do I know? After all, who can tell *what* I'll say when I'm having a fit?"

"Dave."

He flipped the booklet onto the file and held up three

sheets of blue paper stapled together. "Item. Hardy Security's own log for the reactor last night. It shows almost nothing, other than the fact that a certain Terry Bodorff, in your employ, can make check marks and make them with a certain crude authority. I called him: He saw nothing, heard nothing, knows nothing, and is content to be that way. His motto would be 'ignorance is bliss,' if he knew fancy words like that. He apparently did wake up out of his stupor when he was called to the reactor pool, but that only proves that he can operate a two-way radio and walk at the same time without crippling himself, which argues barely normal large-motor coordination. He has the lively thinking style of a comatose poodle. Well, we know that Rolly checked in at ten-oh-two eastern daylight time at the receptionist's desk, picked up his dosimeter badge—all this is in the receptionist's log—and took himself down to the basement to say hello to Bodorff, and went to the canteen. I hope his last meal was fabulous, which it wasn't if saying hello to Bodorff was his idea of a good time. None of this is exactly hot off the presses."

Annabelle sat down across from Dave in one of the leather chairs, crossing her legs and folding her arms.

"Dave. I wish you'd drop that thing and talk to me. You're just reciting."

"Like this?" Dave dropped the log sheet pointedly on the red booklet. He immediately grabbed another sheet. "Item. The visitors' log from yesterday, which I just mentioned. It's separate from the security log. The day receptionist goes home at five in the evening, when she's relieved by someone who doodles on the visitor's log. Anyway, you have to have a card key and a numerical code to get in the front door. The code is changed every month, rain or shine, and—I asked about this for laughs—the only people who get the codes are all the scientists, secretaries, technical staff, and administrators. Gee, what a surprise. I guess they just forgot the Miami Dolphins' backfield. The code was last changed three weeks ago. After they let themselves in, the night receptionist, name of Gayle Baker, gives them their dosimeter. If she gives them anything else, I am sure that is her business. After all, among consenting adults, who am I to cavil? But she gave Rolly his dosimeter, number three-seventeen as always, which means that his dosimeter must still be at the reactor somewhere, or else it walked out under its own steam or nuclear power—unless he handed it to Berlin when they shook hands in farewell before Rolly jumped into the drink. Just the sort of memento you give people you're really close to."

"Dave. Stop it. You can be such a snot. Listen to me."

He put the visitors' log down in the file. He lifted a finger, and the look on his face told her that he had arrived at the bombshell and was prepared to toss it. "Just so you know, Dr. Lawrence F. Berlin—and I do wonder what the *F* stands for—checked in to the reactor last night at nine-thirty. I expect he merely stopped by to see if the uranium core had exploded or anything. Just a conscientious scientist minding the furnace. He probably didn't even know old Rolly was there."

Annabelle stared at Dave.

He picked up the next sheet on his stack, a small pink memo, and avoided her eyes. "Item. WPLG called. Carly Priest wants to interview you tonight on their eleven-o'clock show, just before the weather. Beckworth told them it would be all right. He's a pearl, good old

Beckworth. Also, Nita Muldoon called from the *Miami Tribune*. As the usual spokesperson for Hardy Security, I gave her a self-serving, though highly accurate, quote. Save your newspaper tomorrow, for the Hardy Security album's Radioactive Humor section."

"Lon said . . . ," she paused, thinking. "He said he wished he had been there last night. So he could stop Rolly."

Dave regarded her from under his lowered eyebrows. He placed the pink memo in the file and reached for another. "Item. Beckworth called. He allowed as how you should phone him now that everything's straightened out and Rolly only killed himself. Suicide makes everything perfectly nice for the university. Beckworth called it 'less damage control.' I'd blame Bertha for this, except that her big mouth didn't type that stupid note in the first place." He picked up a thick sheaf of paper. "Rolly's insurance policy—accidental death clause."

"Maybe there's an explanation for Lon's visit last night," she said, but she elevated an eyebrow and shook her head.

Dave put the pink memo and the insurance policy on the file and picked up the next sheet. "Use your head. Item. The widow called. Her name's Giselle, and she wants you to take her to see the body right away. Beckworth gave her our telephone number. But wait until you hear her big agenda. She's really pissed about the suicide theory. Beckworth told her it was your idea. Oh well, you can't say he hasn't been busy. Anyway, she sounds like a nice lady, and I said we'd get back to her."

Annabelle released her arms and ran her hands through her hair. And she did a thing that Dave had seen her do before, but it always made him uncomfortable: She eliminated all expression from her face. It was just blank.

Dave put down the message from Castillo's widow and lifted a report bound in the sky-blue Hardy corporate logo folder. "Item. Our own report to the university two years ago. It includes your father's third—I repeat *third*—recommendation that security at the reactor be updated in a big way. Beckworth has apparently resisted on the score of saving university dollars. They have our Hardy Two Thousand Electronic Sentinel and so on, plus the guards, but Jacob thought a microwave fence would be a good idea, and he didn't like the lax business with the security codes. We give them the new code every month, but who they give it to is their own business. Appended to the report is an internal note from Jacob calling Beckworth a cheap old fart, which I think shows Jacob's uncanny power for tact, understatement, and final accuracy."

Annabelle's face was still blank, but Dave thought she was paying attention.

He put the report on the folder and picked up a large sheet of blue paper. "Item. The blueprint of the reactor, with our alarm system, as installed seven years ago. I'm planning to give it a trial run tonight. These things are never as amusing on paper as they are in the flesh."

He folded the blueprint and stood up to walk around the desk and place the plan under his holster. He returned to the chair.

He held up a finger. "Item. I called eight mortuaries. No sale. Not even with the blessing of the NRC, assuming we get it. Not even for cash money. Or, as Bertha would say, no fuckin' way."

He took the last item, a computer printout. "Item.

This is my favorite. It's that little document I purloined today while snooping in Bertha's deepest electronic nightmares. It's a spreadsheet. What it seems to be is a list of mines and jewelers, amounts of stones inventoried and irradiated, dates they came into the house, dates they may be released, records of movement from reactor to storage, Geiger counts, and so on. Listen to some of these names: Wimalaratne, Vavuniya, Anhinga, Pettah, Kataragama, Georgio's, Cartier. Not only exotic but eclectic. At first I thought it was a record of the Topaz Project's money, and, who knows, that could have been full of marvelous insights. I'm always intrigued by money when it comes to horseplay. But there's no money mentioned in any of the columns, despite the fact that the file was slugged 'Topaz slash dollar sign.' So understated and discreet, these scientists. But you know, Annabelle, this will bear studying in my quiet moments, perhaps before I fall asleep at night. Something bothers me about it. Something stirs a memory of something. Maybe you should take a look. You'll see that Bertha's love note at the top is particularly full of literary merit, smacking of a little dabbling in petty intramural blackmail. Strictly pathetic, to leave her poison pen lying around. I don't imagine Rolly was too scared, given the goods he had on her."

He stood up, leaned over the desk, and offered her the printout.

She reached for the paper.

At the top was Bertha's note: *Rolly. Here's the mid-October topaz inventory you were supposed to do. You miscounted, again, and your numbers are way off, again. You're lucky I don't have a big mouth. Hope you're the same. BSP.*

She studied the neat columns on the spreadsheet. She

dropped the paper in her lap and put up a hand to shade her eyes.

"I don't see it, Dave, whatever is bothering you. At least not on first acquaintance, unless you only mean the snotty note, threatening to tell on the poor half-blind scientist. I suppose you memorized this already?"

She looked up at him, and Dave nodded in a matter-of-fact way. His photographic memory was a tool as familiar to them as sign language.

Her face was no longer blank.

"Then let me keep it," Annabelle said, folding the paper and slipping it into her green handbag.

Dave came around the desk and knelt in front of her, taking her hands in his. He looked at her face. The blank look had been replaced by something he had no trouble identifying as pure unhappiness.

"Annabelle, I didn't mean to hurt you by being vicious about Lon Berlin. Forgive me? I'm such a mother hen." Marcel turned in a circle on Dave's shoulder, and pecked his ear. "Ouch. Perhaps I should have said mother superior."

She lifted her shoulders and turned away from him, biting her lip. He tugged on her hands. She reluctantly faced him.

"Annabelle. My dear Dr. Annabelle. Does he mean that much to you? Is this a Fatal Attraction thing? You just met him."

"Well, you just met him," she countered, "and you already hate him."

Dave sat back on his heels. His bird hopped to the floor, and Annabelle's mouth curved.

"No, I'm not sure I hate him," Dave said. "Maybe I'm

jealous. You and I are pretty honest with each other, Annabelle, so I'll admit I'm used to having your friendship pretty much to myself. And your chemistry with him was slopping all over the place." He flexed his shoulders and massaged his neck. "Jesus, what a place. After the body is buried—or shipped to the moon, or tossed into the Everglades, or eaten by per diem diners—I'm recommending we drop the reactor; I don't care how far back they go with your Dad. I don't like Beckworth's idea of working with us. In addition to turning down our recommendations about security, Beckworth is certainly planning to use us as puppets. It wouldn't be so bad helping him clean up this mess if we'd helped him make it." He passed a hand over his forehead. "You're right, I hate Berlin."

Annabelle patted his foot, and Marcel jumped onto her hand, startling her, and walked up her arm in a leisurely waddle.

"I have to talk to him, Dave."

"To Marcel? He's a good listener, but you won't get much feedback. Still, I suppose he's as good as your average shrink."

"I meant Berlin, you clown," she said, kicking him softly with her yellow shoe.

Dave lay back on the floor, rubbing his eyes.

He leaned up on his elbows, his palms flat on the white rug.

"What is this, my darling fathead? Even I know that just because he was there last night at the reactor doesn't necessarily make him a murderer, but at a minimum it makes him a liar. Are you a sap for danger all of a sudden?"

He lifted his hands and held the left closed against his

chest and stroked his right thumb upward several times on the closed hand.

Annabelle looked at him strangely.

"Danger," she murmured. Danger. Maybe. The past seven years of her perfect widowhood had been eminently anaesthetic, practical, and safe. Safe. The most emotionally dangerous thing she had undertaken was writing a book. And even that, even with its left-of-center conclusions regarding the historic legalization of sexism in the project of authorship, had been buttressed with ruthless research and her unassailable credentials. All of her emotions were safeguarded. Including taking Dave everywhere with her. If he chaperoned her, it was probably her own fault. She knew what he was like. And she took him everywhere. Except to bed. She did that alone. *Yes,* she *thought, I manage to get myself to bed every night. Alone.*

"Annabelle, what are you thinking? Tell me."

"I think I'll go home and change my clothes, which, as you noticed, have the beach all over them. Where are you going to be? Did you eat?"

"Yeah. I grabbed a hamburger at Fuddrucker's. Red meat—and I also skipped my aerobics class. Now, there's a modern urban afternoon for you. Anyway, I'll be here. I've got some things to do. I'll stay until I hear from you."

She stood and stretched. Marcel slid bumpily into her neck.

"Do you have my car key? Do you want me to bring you back a salad or anything?"

Dave rolled to his knees and stood. "No, thanks. We can go out later."

"Maybe we should go see the widow when I get back. You want to call her?"

He nodded, reached into the pocket of his shorts and tossed her the key. Annabelle closed the distance between them, and Marcel, his green head cocked to one side, strutted onto Dave's shoulder.

She crossed to the long antique white cabinet that stood under the window. She barely glanced at the lightning storm over Miami. As a child she had been afraid of thunder; but thunder had been one of the first sounds to fade, long before the songs of the birds—the last sounds she would ever hear—floated into the winds over Miami. She stooped, twisted the large gold key in the lock of a door in the middle of the cabinet, and pulled open the door. From a green velvet case she took her Walther TPH and checked the magazine. She stuffed the gun into her green handbag, next to the printout from Bertha Puffo's computer files.

"I won't be long," she said, and left the office.

NINE

SHE DROVE SLOWLY ON MAIN HIGHWAY THROUGH THE labyrinth of heavy traffic in Coconut Grove. The sidewalk bistros and quirky boutiques were almost obscured by the torrents of rain. Crowds of inadequately dressed people huddled into small indoor spaces, anywhere they could find room, but they carried their food and drinks with them, and their conversations. Sidewalk vendors had thrown plastic sheets over their motley canvas-and-plywood stalls and struggled with golf umbrellas that threatened to take off in the high wind. It was an easy matter to spot the tourists among the residents: Tourists dashed out into the warm rain, playing among the cars and chasing each other. The residents warned them about Florida's grim lightning statistics and huddled with their plates against the buildings.

A few blocks past the heart of the Grove, Annabelle turned left onto Poinciana Avenue, a narrow, private street that ended on Biscayne Bay. Graceful royal poinciana trees, heavy with rain, completely overhung the street. In the glow of her headlights through the slashing downpour, she saw Berlin's Honda Accord, parked midway down the block.

She felt a stab of anger and pulled her convertible behind the Honda, putting her car in park but leaving the engine running. She reached into her handbag and saw him open his door.

He ran to her car, the rain cutting across his shoulders, and she leveled the Walther at him over the door through the open window, using both hands.

"Looking for me, Dr. Berlin?"

He froze, water cascading down his face and over his broad shoulders.

"Jesus, Annabelle. Put that down. Christ Almighty, I hate guns."

"What do you want? What are you doing here?"

"I can't believe this. I'm just standing in a pouring rain, gentle as a lamb, and you pull a gun on me. Do you know how to use that thing?"

"Yes. You might even say you're in danger, Dr. Berlin."

"Annabelle, please. Put that away and talk to me."

He reached his hand toward her, and she jerked the gun at him. He took a step back.

"You want to talk to me?" she said. "That's great, because I want to talk to you. But this street is too dark and too private. I used to like that about this place, but now it makes me feel handicapped. Get in your car. Go to the end of the street and turn around. Go back out to Main Highway. I'll meet you in the parking lot behind the Coconut Grove Playhouse."

He nodded, bewilderment filling his eyes.

He returned to his car, followed her instructions, and left Poinciana.

She turned her own car when he was gone and followed him.

He was waiting for her at the theater, standing by his car. The lot was sparsely dotted with cars, dune buggies, jeeps.

She parked near his car. The rain had tapered off to a fine mist, the thunder to a faraway rumble. She got out of her car, the wet gun held at her side in her right hand.

"This is much better. What do you want to talk about?" she said. "Maybe I could show you some more sign language. Show you how to tell a few lies."

He moved toward her, shoulders hunched under his wet shirt.

"Don't even think of it," she said, raising the Walther and closing her left hand on her right. "You people from the reactor seem to have your own slant on reality. I thought scientists had cornered the market on service to truth, but I'm getting a real education today."

"What's wrong with you all of a sudden?" he asked.

"All of a sudden I found out from Dave that you were at the reactor last night, and that makes me nervous. Especially since you've apparently decided I'm so stupid you can lie to me even about the written word." She studied his dripping face. "Lon, I'm not *blind.* Our own security log showed you were at the reactor. What were you doing there? Working late with your partner?"

"You pulled a gun on me for that? I went back to use the fax machine. Believe it or not, I don't happen to have a fax at home."

"Oh, come on, Lon. That's pretty lame. What was so urgent?"

He shrugged and mumbled something.

"What?"

"My daughter's twenty-first birthday. She was born at nine forty-one, October 22, 1976. Nine forty-one p.m. Seven pounds, six ounces. Saint Barnabas Medical Center, Livingston, New Jersey. Nine forty-one p.m. I don't think I was ever happier. Nine forty-one p.m. Do you get it, Annabelle? I faxed her happy birthday from Dad. Her twenty-first birthday."

"Where'd you fax it to?"

"The Breakers Hotel in Palm Beach. That's where the party was."

"Why didn't you just go to the party?"

"Her mother didn't invite me. Look, Annabelle. I have the cover sheet and the transmission report. It's on the backseat. I save everything. I'm a pack rat. Bertha can tell you that. Anyone can tell you that. You want to see it?"

"Move away from your car. Go stand over by that pink Jeep."

She gestured with the gun. He backed away. She walked to the car, opened the driver's door, and reached inside to pull up the lock on the back door. She opened that door and, still holding the gun on him with her right hand, reached into the backseat.

The transmission report had a telephone number, call duration of thirty-one seconds, and the time the fax was dialed: Nine forty-one P.M. The thin cover sheet said, "Dr. Lon Berlin, University of the Keys, Research Reactor, To the Breakers Hotel Staff. Please deliver immediately to Jill Berlin, the ballroom. Page one of two."

She held the second sheet closer and saw the faint pink circle at the top, indicating that the page had been through a fax machine. Not every fax machine had that handy feature, but the one Berlin had used gave powerful testimony. Annabelle crumpled the papers and threw them back into his car.

"Are you satisfied?" he asked, his face haggard.

"Why did you lie to me? You said you weren't there."

"What difference could it possibly make where the hell I was? If I knew anything about Rolly, I would have told you. Or the police. I didn't even see the fucker. He wasn't in the lab. I faxed that thing from across the hall, from the computer room. That's what I really meant when I said I wished I'd been there to stop him." He ran the back of his hand over his eyes. "Besides, I wasn't ready to tell you about Jill. Not yet. I hate telling anyone I'm divorced."

Annabelle lowered her gun and expelled a long breath. He crossed the gravel to her. The gun seemed too heavy now, as if she had been holding a brick, and her right arm started to tremble. She put her left hand out to steady herself and touched his chest. She could feel his heart pounding under the Oxford cloth of his shirt.

He pulled her roughly against him and buried his face in her hair.

"You're such a strange thing—a combination of fearlessness and hesitation," he said harshly, without thinking that she could not hear him. She felt his jaw move, but decided she did not care what his words were. Instead she tried to read the communication of the embrace, as strained and uncomfortable as it was, as unfamiliar as it was to her.

They stood together for minutes. The only movement was his hand in her hair, a slow, unthinking, rhythmic closing and unclosing of his fingers.

He was the first to step back.

"Lon, what the hell were you doing at my house?"

"Just sitting there. Not wanting to go back to the reactor. I can't stand being there today. Wondering which one was your house. Nothing. I'm sorry, Annabelle. This is a rotten start."

"Let's go dry off," she said.

She drove back to Poinciana and Berlin followed, parking in the driveway at the end of the street, in front of her large two-story white stucco cottage. They walked across the wet grass to her door, but she motioned him away while she disengaged her alarm. He grimaced and stepped back, then followed her into the house.

Two cats were waiting for her, and he nearly tripped over them on the cool white tile of a graceful living room that ran the width of the house.

She crossed the room, a sparsely furnished but large area with a vaulted ceiling, a marble fireplace with logs neatly laid, a couch with flamboyant red flowers, a huge black television, books neatly arranged on the three walls. The room led into an island kitchen with white appliances, scrupulously clean, and a sheet of glass overlooking a white-painted redwood deck and the bay. He could see a vast, dark blue swimming pool and white-tile patio to the right of the deck, and clouds skidding over the bay.

She fed her cats, opening a can and shaking dry food into a bowl. "This one's Ahoy Matey," she said, pointing to a calico-and-white, and "This one's Running Shoes," pointing to a black with white paws. "So you have a daughter." He nodded gently, and she rinsed out the can and threw it into the recycling bin.

He sat on a barstool at the island, watching her.

She pointed to a bathroom off the kitchen and said, "There's plenty of towels. Make yourself at home."

She went up the stairs leading from the kitchen, lightly touching the brass rail.

He hung his soaked shirt on the shower's purple etched-glass door, left his shoes and socks on the rug, and toweled his hair. He wrapped the towel around his neck. His slacks clung to his legs, and he shook them away from his skin.

He returned to the other room, idly scanning the titles of her books, noting her fine Shakespeare collection, what he thought were probably first editions of Dickens titles, her apparent interest in French novels. He took one down and opened it, a marked-up copy of *Madame Bovary* in French. He glanced at her notes in the margins, but they were also in French. He put the book back. He saw that she owned law books, many law books, and he gave them a puzzled frown.

On a shelf near the law books were three photographs: one of Dave, holding a long cigar and wearing a tuxedo, leaning against a yacht whose red, painted name, *The Prelude,* matched the color of his bow tie; one of an older man, a very bald man, with eyes like hers; and there was a wedding photo, of a younger Annabelle, in a lacy white gown, cut extremely low over her deep bosom, and the groom, in traditional cutaway. Berlin studied the groom, a darkly handsome young man, square jaw, laughing eyes, obviously deeply in love with the stunning woman on his arm. Annabelle, too, he saw, looked blazingly happy, and he felt a prick of something like envy, or anger, that her face no longer seemed capable of that much or that kind of sheer unguarded happiness. Her face was still lovely, but there was something about her eyes, some warning, some distance.

He did not hear her come into the room.

"That's Nikki and me. He died seven years ago."

Berlin looked over his shoulder. She sat on the raised marble hearth before the fireplace and lit the fire with a long match. She wore a one-piece fiery orange swimming suit under an open hip-length scarlet robe. The muscles of her long legs looked hard and smooth and strong.

He crossed the living room and sat on the hearth next to her while she brushed and then braided her long dark hair. The fire was highlighted in her gleaming braid.

"I like to light the fire before I exercise," she said. "It's so nice to come back to. Is your daughter in school?"

"Yeah. University of Florida. Environmental Oceanography."

He followed her through the kitchen and out through sliding glass doors, his slacks clinging to his legs as he walked. The bay was gray and gloomy here, with Miami's skyline far to the left and the few towers of Key Biscayne's chic condos shimmering dimly near the horizon, but the water in her pool was lit from inside and shone royal blue against the black, painted walls of the interior surfaces. At the deep end, a black marble fountain poured its tiny stream of whispering water from the outstretched hands of a delicately sculpted mermaid kneeling on a seashell.

They stepped off the deck onto the tiled patio, and Annabelle surprised him by taking his hand as they strolled almost seventy five feet to the deep end. It was a richly original and huge pool, made either for ostentation or for serious exercise.

The mass of clouds over the bay was rolling away, out over the Atlantic.

She dropped her robe on the tile, smiled at him, and executed a perfect shallow dive. Her smooth strokes cut the water almost silently; he was mesmerized.

Ahoy Matey nudged her robe and then lay primly on it.

Berlin watched Annabelle swimming strongly in a silent, graceful crawl. The air was cool, moving. He yanked his belt open, pushed his wet trousers and shorts off, and followed her with a less efficient dive.

She was a strong swimmer, obviously conditioned and fast. He knew immediately that it would be pointless to emulate her purposeful, disciplined laps, so he turned on his back, giving himself to the water, lazily floating under the gray sky. *There's a pterodactyl*, he thought, gazing at a black streak against a sudden patch of blue opening in the west.

The water scarcely stirred around him as he drifted, so graceful and silent was her progress up and down the pool. He felt an atavistic urge to nap, to nod off in the vast, peaceful, comforting, and womblike environment. His eyes closed.

He felt her hand on his shoulder, and he slid his left arm around her waist, drawing her close to him. It was strange to him to have no use at all for all the words at his command, but it was also, in an odd way, a relief, and the years of explaining himself futilely, mapping and remapping the terrain of his heart and his mind, seemed to dissipate into a mist of memory. He wondered, suddenly, if he was being given a new chance, and then shrugged off the thought as vestigial evidence of a long-dead element of his nature that he classed with superstition and voodoo thinking. Any chance he had, he would have to make it himself.

He swam with her to the ladder, gathered her robe around his waist, and grabbed his clothing. They hurried inside, wet and chilled from the air. She threw him a dry towel from a pile on a chair and wrapped herself in another. He pulled on his trousers over wet legs and dropped her robe on the chair.

He took her wrist and led her into the living room by the fire.

"Lon, I want to ask you about something."

"Sure. What? More about my daughter?"

She shook her head and squeezed water from the braid onto her shoulder.

"No. No more questions until you bring her up yourself. It's about the reactor. Dave found a spreadsheet today. Well, actually he sort of stole it from Bertha. It's a record of all the gems coming in and going out of the reactor."

"You shouldn't have that. Topaz is one of the few totally secure things at the reactor. I'm not allowed even to tell you where we keep the stones."

"Nevertheless Dave got this report. Does Bertha keep all the records for Topaz?"

"Well, Rolly was supposed to. But his eyes were so bad, Bertha sort of stepped in to help."

"That was nice of her."

Berlin smiled at her ironic tone. "Bertha probably had her own reasons. Probably just keeping tabs on us. I'd like to see the report."

"I have it. Hold on a minute." She retrieved her handbag from the kitchen counter and brought the printout back to the living room.

She sat by the fire, next to him, watching him as he frowned over the sheet of paper. He looked troubled.

"We don't have an account called Anhinga." Berlin stood up and paced in front of the fireplace. "I've never heard of an account like that. Bertha would never do anything funny with those records. Shit. I don't understand." He stopped pacing and a thoughtful look descended over his eyes. "I'm going back to the reactor." He stretched out a hand to her. "Come with me."

"I can't. Not now. Dave's waiting for me at the office—no doubt chewing the carpet into swatches or fielding Beckworth's stupid phone calls—and we've got an appointment with the widow. What are you going to do?"

"I don't know. Maybe waste my time. Can I keep this?" he asked, refolding the spreadsheet.

She hesitated.

"I guess so."

"Is it your only copy?"

"Yes," she said, and, with a sudden and poignant realization that she was embarking on a double standard, she wondered about her own sins of omission, knowing that Dave had a perfectly good copy in his memory.

"Lon, what's your middle name?"

"Frederick," he said. "Why?"

"Just curious. It's a nice name."

"Thanks. Will I see you tomorrow?"

"Probably."

"Have dinner with me. Or breakfast. Or lunch."

"Okay, dinner. Eight o'clock at Miami Tropical Grill? Do you know it?"

He laughed.

"You make decisions quickly, don't you? Way in advance."

She looked at him.

"I can't phone people to make dates," she said simply.

A pulsing orange light flashed over the front door.

"What's that?" Berlin asked.

"Doorbell." A log dropped on the grate, and she used the poker to stir the ashes. Then she crossed the room, pulling her towel tighter, and opened the door.

A cardboard box, soaked and limp from exposure to the rain, had been deposited on the tiled walkway. She glanced quickly up the street, stooping to gaze under the dripping limbs of the poinciana trees, and she saw a dark Ford pulling around the curve to Main Highway.

Berlin came to stand beside her at the door, raising his eyebrows at the box.

The wet sides of the box seemed to swell, with little rippling bumps. She pushed at the box with her bare foot, and the cardboard gave, the side she had touched collapsing around its center. The lid sank over that side, the flap pulling away from the dark brown glue. A small, flaccid gap had opened under the glue, and, over the sticky brown residue, out crawled a three-inch palmetto bug, the giant brown Caribbean cockroach with wiggling lacy inch-long black antennae and huge wings along its hard thoracic shell, the largest cockroach in existence—and the only one that can fly.

It skittered down the box and disappeared into the wet grass.

Two others quickly followed the first, and the limp

sides of the wet box rippled and bulged in hundreds of places.

Berlin shoved Annabelle inside the house, pulled the door shut, and ran through the living room and out to the pool. He grabbed a green hose coiled against the pump house and returned to the front, jamming the hose onto a faucet and spinning the red handle. Water jetted from the hose, and he stepped toward the box with gritted teeth, aiming the powerful thin burst of water at the box.

It split apart immediately, and thousands of the huge roaches sped down the walkway in a wiggling, skittering tide of brown shells, some on their hard backs, some frantically working their long spindly legs in the gush of water over the tiles. Some of the bugs caught in the grass along the sides of the walkway and disappeared speedily into the yard. Most were blown out into the street under the relentless pressure of the water. A larger black thing sprang from under the ragged cardboard and skidded in a straight line down the walk. Berlin slowly advanced against the sliding carpet of roaches as it moved toward the street.

Even when the tiles had been clean for several minutes, Berlin kept the water steady on the walk, blowing the last shreds of the box into the street.

Carrying the hose with him, the water now aimed off into the lawn, he approached the street, brushing his arms automatically, as if the creatures had crawled backward up the jet of water.

Hundreds and hundreds of the palmetto bugs were still crawling in all directions, running randomly at first and then suddenly heading in a line for a seething brown mass of the bugs pushing and crawling over each other into a sewer drain, sensing down there the wet, still regions they always sought out. He turned the water on them with a curse and shivered as they careened and clicked against the side of the drain and dropped or flew into the sewer.

When he could see no more of the huge, shiny brown shapes, Berlin turned toward the house, where Annabelle stood frozen in the doorway, her eyes wide, her breath suspended. She looked nauseated.

Berlin waited until the roaches had all—he hoped—flown and spun and jostled each other down into the drain. He picked up a sodden piece of cardboard and shook it. A couple of roaches dropped to the street, their bodies hitting with loud clicking noises. Something else, something larger, that black thing—bounced out and skidded across the asphalt. He dropped the cardboard and crossed to the thing.

He picked it up and stood absolutely still in the middle of the street.

"What is it, Lon?" Annabelle called, watching his suddenly rigid form.

He held his hand open and walked slowly back to the house and to the open door. He held out his hand, his face flushed with anger.

Lying on the center of his palm was an audiotape, its clear plastic sleeve cracked and covered with drops of water and the sticky excrement of palmetto bugs.

The audiotape, in itself a cruel joke, bore an even crueler label: *Def Leppard: HYSTERIA.*

TEN

"THE BOX WAS COMPLETELY WET?"

Annabelle nodded, shuddering at the memory.

"Well, that gives us some information," Dave said. "Whoever brought you that little present wasn't dumb enough to let the little creatures ride in the car with him. He must have tied the box to the top of the car, and the rain soaked it. He probably meant for you to receive a dry box so you wouldn't have a clue before you opened it, but Mother Nature took a hand. Or God."

Annabelle faced him squarely, a strange glint in her eye. "You think God's taking a sudden interest in my paltry affairs?"

"I'm not saying any such thing, fathead. All I'm saying is you could have received a nice, dry package. Which you would have opened. And you would now have a house full of giant flying roaches. You got lucky."

"I don't feel lucky."

"When you go home tonight to your nice, safe, bug-free house, maybe you will."

"Maybe." She shivered. "Can you imagine packing

that box?" She rubbed the palms of her hands on the steering wheel. "I can't believe Lon's presence of mind. Spraying them down probably kept them from using their wings."

"Yeah, he's our hero, all right," Dave signed, molding sarcasm into the window of empty space before him as he went on to air-sculpt a box and added hands that shoved wriggling cockroaches into it. "Unless he was the one who packed it in the first place."

"If he packed it, he did not deliver it. He was with me."

"That, my dear, worries me more than the bugs."

The storm had completely passed, rolling east and north out to sea, and the air had a washed feel and the sky a fresh dark radiance. But the storm had also trailed a humid tumescence in its wake; it would be a sticky night.

Annabelle had parked under a globe light in the patched cement driveway of a yellow stucco house in Naranja, the cramped grounds of which had been pared and hacked and manicured into a semblance of northern landscaping—neat, geometric, anything but *Miami*. To keep even a small yard looking like this in the subtropics, Annabelle knew, took constant work, holding back the jungle that threatened to retake the city from every direction, from around every corner. And it would take an odd sort of personality to want a yard like this in casual Miami, casual because casual was only sensible for a city plunged into an environment naturally and most actively hostile to order.

"Annabelle, I'm sorry about that audiotape." He patted her hand on the steering wheel. "Very cruel thing to do."

"Very. What kind of a mind could concoct such a stunt?"

"I know it's not very fashionable to talk about pure evil and metaphysical things like that, and I won't bring up God again, but the thought I keep having is that someone *evil* wants you—us—to lay off the reactor."

"Sending me a carton of flying cockroaches is hardly the way to accomplish that," she said with acid emphasis. "It made me mad."

"Well then, maybe somebody's trying to make you mad. Have it your way."

Annabelle pulled her key from the ignition, and they got out of the LeBaron and walked up the tidy gravel walk to the double front door under the glare of an ugly system of porch lighting that made harsh, clipped shadows.

"Not a hair out of place," Dave signed. "They might as well have paved over the yard. Save a lot of trouble. Looks like the home of Mr. and Mrs. Tidy Town. I'll bet you a hundred dollars they don't have any cockroaches here."

Annabelle pushed the lighted doorbell. She had changed into white jeans and a red shirt. She noted with concern that Dave looked unusually tired or wan, or perhaps lacking his customary glow of good health and crisp, youthful resilience. Despite his having showered at the office and changed into clean black clothing, he looked dirty. It was the makeup, she decided. It looked gray against his black shirt. She hoped he would end this fashion phase soon. It seemed calculated to add the extra weight of decades to his twenty-nine years. Sometimes she couldn't tell where his deliberate eccentricities ceased and personal taste took over. She wondered if even he knew.

The door was opened by a short woman who was at

least fifty pounds overweight. Her dark brown hair was cut short, in a stylish feathery wave, probably moussed, and she wore a loose black shirt over loose gray slacks. Behind the soft fat of her face were the elegant planes of a countenance that had once been more than pretty. Her face was still appealing, but with the nostalgic appeal of a faded photograph of someone known and valued long ago, someone whose name—and the dimensions of whose personality—are just beyond recall.

"Mrs. Ruiz de Castillo?" Annabelle asked, extending her hand. "I'm Annabelle Hardy-Maratos, and this is Jorge Enamorado."

Giselle Ruiz de Castillo gave Dave's face a cold and frank appraising look before she pointedly ignored Annabelle's hand.

"So, *los mentirosos*. *Muchas gracias*. My Rolando did not kill himself."

Dave translated the widow's word for "liars" into American Sign. Even though he thought Annabelle would have no trouble reading this clearly enunciating new acquaintance, her immediate use of Spanish made Dave's gesturing hands fly into rapid motion. Annabelle could read French and German and the classical languages, but she had only limited access to Spanish beyond the few cuss words he had taught her.

The widow led them into what Annabelle thought was a sad house, filled with objects that had once belonged somewhere else, to some other time, to other people. It was a reliquary, a museum, a morgue, not a living place, and again she was reminded of a faded photograph. There were lace squares covering the arms of wicker chairs, with a supply of extra squares on a wicker easy chair that slumped in the center of its wide seat. There were china vases, a large antique coffee grinder, a doll's house—all dusted, neat, kept. Through the dining room Annabelle could see a rocking horse, freshly painted but never ridden, out by the patio, which was lighted with white globes and yellow citronella candles. The air inside the house seemed sterile, as if no cooking or smoking or perfuming or laundering were ever done on these premises. The air-conditioning was icy.

They sat on plastic-padded chairs in the dining room, around a glass table under a would-be Tiffany shade. Dave deliberately but unobtrusively put his palm flat on the table's invisible surface, leaving an exploratory smudge. Annabelle put her hands in her lap.

"Mrs. Ruiz de Castillo," Annabelle said. "I'm very sorry about your husband's death. But you've been misled. I certainly did not spread that story about Dr. Castillo committing suicide, and I certainly don't believe it."

"En español, por favor."

Now encountering the widow's mulish look of scorn, Dave realized that Mrs. Ruiz de Castillo was going to be difficult. He had seen this form of linguistic obstreperousness before. His aunts played this angry game at weddings when Anglos entered the family and at funerals when Cubans left it.

When he had spoken to this woman earlier on the telephone, they had used English, but apparently Mrs. Ruiz de Castillo was demonstrating her hostility toward Annabelle by refusing to speak her language. He would have to interpret doubly for Annabelle.

He began by repeating Annabelle's words in Spanish, and then put the widow's reply into American Sign.

"Dr. Beckworth said you told him it was suicide. And he says the Nuclear Regulatory Commission is looking into the death as a suicide." The widow paused to rub her eyes. *"Why do you say you don't believe it?"*

"Because," Annabelle said, her eyes leaving Dave's hands to regard the other woman, "we found something that makes the story compellingly unlikely." She looked at Dave. "We found fresh urine on that bridge where your husband supposedly jumped. People committing suicide don't empty their bladders first."

Mrs. Ruiz de Castillo wrinkled her nose and gave Annabelle a considering frown. *"I don't understand. Are you saying it was an accident? I still don't understand why there would be urine."*

"There's only one circumstance that I can think of to explain it," Annabelle said. "Ruling out the possibility, extremely remote I think, that your husband or somebody else was engaging in a highly unscientific stupid, crazy prank"—Mrs. Ruiz de Castillo shook her head with quick certainty as she listened to Dave's soft Spanish—"he was terrified by something and simply lost control. Or somebody did."

"Rolando never pulled a prank in his life," Mrs. Ruiz de Castillo said. *"He did not have that much imagination. And Cubans do not make jokes like that. A Cuban would not piss the floor, out of respect for his mama."* She grimaced in fastidious horror, but her look quickly metamorphosed into a sudden, soft grin of private enjoyment, knowing that Annabelle would not understand. *"Pissing on ten, that would be a Cuban joke."*

Annabelle looked uncertainly at the widow. Dave smiled to himself, but his hands flew into sign when he saw Annabelle's confusion about what he had translated. He explained, "Cuban woman are great cussers, but they'd rather cut their tongues out than take the name of God in vain. So, in Spanish, they say 'I piss on ten,' because the word for 'ten' sounds like the word for 'God.' So what she means is that pissing on God is a Cuban joke. Do not insult her by pretending you think pissing on God is funny. You have to grow up with it."

Castillo's widow had obviously seen sign language used before, enough to be comfortable around its use, and she waited until Dave had finished his explanation.

Dave held up his hands for a moment, instructing both women to be quiet. This was going to be difficult, he thought, if he not only had to translate what the widow was saying but also had to explain what she meant by her words. He heaved a sigh and waved them to continue. The widow immediately poured out a spate of Spanish.

"My husband did not make jokes. Not even Cuban jokes. But he also did not panic easily, I can tell you that. No scuba diver does. If Rolando was that scared up on the bridge, scared enough to lose control like you say, he was scared of something big and real, not something imaginary. At least I never thought Rolando had imagination. Not until today, anyway. I want to show you something I found this morning. I tried to tell Dr. Beckworth about it, but he pretended he does not understand Spanish. Mentiroso!"

She left the table and went into the adjoining kitchen.

While she was gone, Annabelle signed, "Should I assume Beckworth does speak Spanish?"

Dave shrugged. "The widow thinks he does."

She returned with a small glossy folder in her hand. She tossed it onto the glass table.

"That's two one-way plane tickets. Trans Haiti Air to Port-au-Prince. I guess Rolando had imagination, all right. He was supposed to go first flight out this morning. The tickets both have his name, and he never asked me to pack a bag."

Dave glanced sharply at her.

"Do not look at me like that, young man, like you think I am too fat for a man to take to the Caribbean, even to a toilet like Haiti. Do not look at me at all if you think my husband killed himself. He did not kill himself, not with tickets for two like that waiting for him."

Annabelle picked up the tickets. She looked at Dave. "Where did you find these, Mrs. Ruiz de Castillo?" Annabelle asked.

"With his passport in his scuba kit. There was also an immunization certificate and some chloroquinine tablets. That is for malaria. It was all hidden."

"Oh." Annabelle said, studying the other woman's defensive expression.

"Now she is looking at me. I know what you are both thinking. You are thinking, what kind of a wife searches her husband's things? I do not care what you think. So he was not planning to take me with him. That is none of your business. But"—her face flushed hotly—*"he was not planning to kill himself. Mother of God! Suicide!"*

"It certainly doesn't look that way," Annabelle said, "and I'm beginning to think the so-called suicide note may make sense after all. 'Free at last.' Do you know about that, Mrs. Ruiz de Castillo?"

"Of course I know. Rolando's secretary sent over a copy of that piece of trash. And I know that sickening story Rolando told Lon Berlin about that newspaper reporter. But Rolando

never knew anybody at a big newspaper like that. He made up that story and told it to make people think he had influence."

The note had been in English, and it occurred to Annabelle that she was now being treated to a Spanish freeze. "Mrs. Ruiz de Castillo, did your husband have any reason to commit suicide? Did he ever talk about it? Was he in good health?"

"Rolando Ruiz de Castillo was never sick a day in his life. The only problem he had was his eyes. It was cataracts. But he was getting treatment, and the doctors said he probably wouldn't get much worse. Rolando said that his partial blindness was better than the full vision of some people, because he was so smart. He was full of his own brains, Rolando, a conceited dog, but he was not morose, not suicidal."

Annabelle made a circle on the table with the edge of the tickets.

"Why Haiti, of all places? Why Haiti?" Annabelle wondered aloud, but she refrained from asking, "Why tickets for two?"

Mrs. Ruiz de Castillo's expression reflected her own—and probably very similar—questions. She shook her head.

Dave shifted in his chair.

"If you want to know what was on Rolando's mind, it wasn't suicide," Mrs. Ruiz de Castillo said, a sudden and nasty shift in her tone that Dave tried to convey on his hands. *"Rolando was only interested in women. He thought a man with a big brain was as good as a man with a big penis. They say Rolando gossiped about women, was always interested in their sex lives. I don't know the truth of that, but I heard more gossip than Rolando knew about. If he died thinking of other women, I piss on him."*

Annabelle tapped her folded hands on the table and stared into the middle distance. Dave sat by her side, now quiet and at rest, made thoughtful by the woman's heated summation of her loss. There was no grief here, he thought.

Annabelle stirred and looked up.

"Mrs. Ruiz de Castillo, what do you think happened to your husband last night?"

"I think he was murdered."

"Somebody finally said it!" Dave almost shouted, slapping the table.

"Yes," Mrs. Ruiz de Castillo said, with an approving gleam in her small eyes. *"You've heard them play with the truth at that reactor, yes? They play with it like it was their property. Do not trust them."*

Annabelle put her hand through her hair in a characteristic gesture. "Mrs. Ruiz de Castillo, is there anyone you do trust who works at the reactor? Someone you confide in, maybe who shares your views? Someone we could talk to? Someone, perhaps, who does not play with the truth?" she asked.

"No." She seemed to mean what she said, but after a slight hesitation she continued. *"If I had to trust someone, it would be Lon Berlin. He knew what Rolando was, and he does not have a big mouth."*

Annabelle could not resist throwing Dave a smug look, and he responded by frowning. Mrs. Ruiz de Castillo apparently misunderstood the quick exchange, and she rushed to embroider her statement with an explanation: *"Lon Berlin is the only one who admits there is dangerous radiation at that place, so he is not a liar. But Lon Berlin has his own problems, about which I will not speak lightly, and as long as people have their own problems, you cannot really trust anyone."*

"Is there anyone there that you particularly distrust?"

"Are you asking if I know who killed Rolando?"

"Or, if you don't know, who would be more likely than others? It had to be someone who works there."

"Please understand. I did not say that Lon Berlin did not murder Rolando. I only said, perhaps, that I would trust him. Those are two different things. There could have been something they were working on together. If Rolando screwed Lon Berlin, Lon Berlin would screw him back." Now Dave threw Annabelle a smug glance over his hands. *"You must understand Lon Berlin. He's the most capable person at the reactor. My Rolando always respected Lon. Listen to me. I say 'my Rolando.' My Rolando."* Her eyes took on a grim look. *"I do not know any more whose Rolando he was."* She leaned her cheek on her hand. *"His secretary—she might know whose Rolando he really was. But she had a knife in him. I think she's unstable."* She thought for several moments. *"Maybe she killed him."*

"Why would she want to kill him?"

"Her own reasons. Bertha always has her own reasons."

"Anyone else, Mrs. Ruiz de Castillo?" Annabelle prompted.

"I want to be a fair woman, but Eugene Beckworth did not like Rolando. The gossips say his wife was fooling around with 'My Rolando.' " She smiled acidly. *"Maybe that is whose Rolando he was. Maybe he was her Rolando."* She pushed both hands through her short hair. *"She's a diver, like Rolando. She goes by her maiden name of Prendergast."* A deep crease appeared in the pudgy flesh between her eyes.

"Maybe she killed her Rolando because he told her that her thighs were as fat as his wife's."

Dave squirmed uncomfortably in his chair.

"Oh," Annabelle said, with as much disinterest as she could manage. "Does she work at the university, too?"

"No. She has her own private practice in Coral Gables. She is a doctor of proctology."

Dave tried not to grin. After signing her words, he reached for the ticket jacket, opening it on the fold and extracting the coupons.

"Señora, if I might ask," he said, putting down the coupons distractedly to accompany his Spanish with sign, *"do you work? Do you have a job outside the home?"*

"I work in a school."

"Are you a teacher?"

"I'm the Dean of Students at the Westland School. That is mostly attendance and discipline, but I'm also the school nurse. In Cuba I was a nurse in the hospital, but here in Miami a school is more free for a nurse, you understand? I can make diagnoses and treat wounds."

So that's how she knew about the chloroquinine, Dave thought.

The wall phone in the kitchen rang, and Mrs. Ruiz de Castillo excused herself.

Dave put the airline tickets down on the table.

"Good question: Whose Rolly was he?" Dave signed. "We'll have to look at his insurance, and that accident clause."

"Particularly how much she benefits," Annabelle returned. "She's awfully adamant about making this a murder case. She had her personal roster of suspects all ready, didn't she? She's not going to collect any insurance windfall if Rolly did himself in."

"Boy, you know, people just can't please us," Dave signed. "They tell us it was an accident, we think they're dimwits. They tell us it was suicide, we think they're covering something. They tell us it was murder, we think they're greedy. I'm starting to wish Rolly was still alive so we could come down from the moral high ground."

Annabelle stared at Dave, following this reasoning to its twisted conclusion. Finally she signed, "That's a self-serving reason to wish the deceased a return from the grave."

"You're right," he signed, a look of angelic decision on his face. "We're better off morally with him dead."

Annabelle pushed her chair back to take a long look at him.

Mrs. Ruiz de Castillo came back to the table, evidently angry, but purposeful and carrying a bottle of Windex and a paper towel.

"*That was Dr. Beckworth's secretary,*" she said, wiping the table. "*I want to see my husband's body, but she said it would be better if I wait until tomorrow. Well, I have already waited a full day. Dr. Rolando Ruiz de Castillo may not have been my Rolando, but he was my husband under the law. I told the secretary that you were here, and she said that you could take me to the reactor. I am insulted.*"

Dave stared, fascinated, as she polished the table.

"*You want to go now?*" Mrs. Ruiz de Castillo demanded, the fat on her arms swinging as she leaned into the paper towel.

"Dave, I'm not sure I got all that," Annabelle said. "We're supposed to take her now?"

Dave nodded.

"Well, there's a piece of bureaucratic nincompoopery for you," Annabelle said indignantly. "Mrs. Ruiz de Castillo, I don't think all this protocol is really necessary. You can go any time you care to, and you don't need my escort, although I'd be happy to go with you. If you like, I'll have Dave call down there and get you a security pass. Our guard will let you in any time. However you want it. But I suspect you'd rather be alone."

"Thank you. I want to go alone."

"Can Dave use your phone?"

"Yes."

Dave rose to go to the kitchen phone. He pulled the reactor number from his gluey memory, dialed it, and glanced around the small kitchen while he waited for an answer. Idly, he pulled open a drawer near his hip. Neat little overlapping rows of freshly ironed napkins. This woman could give Annabelle a few lessons about her glove box. He closed the drawer. The place was hospital clean, he thought, all the surfaces shining, dustless, empty—microwave, blender, portable TV, toaster, refrigerator, dishwasher, personal computer, double oven, food processor—just an impersonal exercise in solid geometry, perfect shapes, and contours that were never used. It looked like an appliance store, Dave thought. With the toe of his black shoe, he slid open a slim drawer under the double oven. Barbecue utensils, shiny and virginal, lined up in an impeccable row, in order of length. He nudged the drawer shut.

In the dining room Mrs. Ruiz de Castillo looked searchingly at Annabelle and spoke unblushingly in perfect English.

"You have seen Rolando?"

Annabelle nodded.

"Does he look . . . is it very bad? The radiation must have disfigured him."

"It's bad. Very bad. Burns everywhere."

The widow put her head down on the table, her cheek resting on the cool glass, her hand tucked into her hair.

Dave spoke briefly into the receiver and briskly rubbed his hands together on his return.

"Annabelle. That was Bodorff himself. Remember the guy who reminds me of a poodle? The guard who was on duty last night? He's the prince of security guards. I could actually hear him clicking his heels over the phone. He asked me how he'd recognize 'the subject.' I swear that's what he said."

Annabelle eyed Dave in appreciative astonishment.

"What did you tell him?"

"I told him I'd instruct our subject to give him her real name. God, he must think he's a combination of Dick Tracy and the post office."

Suddenly the widow burst into tears. The tears rolled spasmodically into hiccups, and then into wet sobs, and then into a kind of dry choking as her head bumped the glass surface of the table. While Dave brought her a glass of water from the kitchen—taking a moment to inspect the breadbox—Annabelle thought, *Well, here comes the grief at last.* She covered the widow's pudgy hand with her hands.

Five minutes later they left the house. When Mrs. Ruiz de Castillo had shut the front door, Dave swerved off the walk to peer through the garage windows, Annabelle following. A dark Jeep Cherokee and an old white Cadillac were parked in the two-car garage. Dave wondered which one had been driven by Castillo. The Jeep, he thought, for the scuba gear. Someone had brought Rolly's car home from the reactor.

He touched Annabelle's arm, and she followed him around behind the garage. There they saw the rusted shell of an outboard motor and a basket of hard avocados. Dave offered her one, but she shook her head. He stood on tiptoe to look into the garage from another angle. The Jeep's wheels were covered with dried gray mud and black cinders.

They retraced their steps to the front of the house, and they saw the spilled rectangle of light from the front door ebb back against the house.

"She's been spying on us while we snoop," Dave signed. "Well, the house does belong to her. I wonder who her husband belonged to?"

ELEVEN

DAVE OFFERED TO DRIVE, AND ANNABELLE GRUDGINGLY accepted. She knew Dave clung with terror to the door handle when she drove at night. Freely mixing his American myths, he reacted to her speeding after dark by calling her Amelia Earhart Batman.

They drove south on U.S. 1, cutting over to Krome Avenue, taking that dark road through the redlands and Homestead on their way to the Everglades, south and west of Naranja and the reactor.

Dave turned onto a two-lane asphalt road marked as State Road 8 and, below the number, as the Anhinga Trail. He pulled the car over to the side and flipped on the convertible's windshield light. "Anhinga"—he finger-spelled it. "Anhinga. It's a bird that lives in the Everglades. That was one of the names on the spreadsheet I swiped from Bertha."

"That's the one Lon said was a bogus account."

"I wish you'd call him Dr. Berlin."

He turned off the light and pulled back onto the pavement. He watched the odometer, and, four miles down the road, he waved his hand at Annabelle. She stared into the darkness and finally spotted the velvety midnight-blue lights of the Alligator Hole Cafe, shimmering eerily to the right, hovering above the black horizon behind a distant stand of slash pines. She motioned for him to slow down.

A gravel cut appeared in their headlights, and Dave turned down the narrow lane lined with cars. He found a space between an old Ford pickup and a shiny Mercedes 500 SL convertible.

Dave could hear muted laughter and faint, tinny music from behind the slash pines, carried to them over the shallow watery fields of the Everglades, and Annabelle could smell old beer wafting across the grasses. They left the car and strolled through the humid darkness toward the distant blue lights, Dave's black shirt and slacks melting into the surroundings, Annabelle's white slacks a ghostly smear against the fabric of grass and weeds. Crickets chorused through the tall grasses from every direction with their electric music, like thousands of tiny buzz saws working at the stalky thicket, and the dry blades rustled and waved as a possum shot across the gravel ten feet in front of them. Its gray and whiskery stick of a tail disappeared into the grass, and the rustling was transferred to the other side of the road. They walked another few yards into the darkness.

The gravel came to an abrupt end, and the gleam of the blue lights—poised in the distance, suspended somewhere off in the trees—fell and spread like thin streaks of oil at their feet on the sheen of still, grassy water. An airboat concealed in the reeds on the other side of the fifteen-foot-wide arm of the river of grass was poled out from the bank, the soft splashes quickly replaced by the roar of the huge fan on the back of the flat-bottomed boat. The boat soon hit the bank they were standing on. From a perch high above the platform of the airboat, a tall black man cast a solemn gaze over them before gesturing for them to climb aboard. The solemn man's clothing, like Dave's, was all black, a partial barrier against night-biters in the great swamp, and even his thick, grizzled hair was covered with a black baseball cap, from which the visor had been removed. He shut off the fan and climbed down from the perch of the high seat poised on rusty iron spindles over the airboat's floor. Without a word he frisked both Annabelle and Dave for weapons, then climbed solemnly back to his perch.

They were rushed across the surface of the water, the boat's single headlight blazing through what looked like a high, solid wall of grass. The moist, heavy air seemed to reach out for them, despite the speed of the airboat, curling in palpable tentacles over their skin. The boat skimmed through the grass, the roar of the fan disorienting Dave, who had lost the sound of the laughter and music, and the location of the blue lights.

The island—with its central tower of slash pines—loomed suddenly out of the vast marsh, the blue lights now clearly a circle of electric bulbs strung around the roof of a two-story wood frame building on stilts, its hand-hewn pine shingles worn and black, absorbing the light almost greedily. The long, narrow porch was slung across the front of the building, and the roof's deep, blackish-blue lights flickered on splashes of jewelry and full beer glasses and teeth bared in smiles. The tinny strains of hard rock filtered onto the night air from a classic jukebox inside the place, mingling with the denser outdoor music of lubber grasshoppers and tree frogs.

The pilot folded the five-dollar bill Dave had given him and stuffed the money under his cap. Dave stepped off the boat, onto the dry land thick with a mat of crunchy roots, turning to offer his hand to Annabelle. She joined him on the edge of the alligator hole, a tight ring of willow shrubs and cocoplum acting as a natural privacy fence for the place, a roughly circular patch of more complex green growing things in the simple, endlessly meandering river of grass.

The hole had been engineered by a single alligator on the lookout for water many decades earlier. She had built a haven of access to underground caverns of water during a long dry spell; she had dug it out of the swamp by the simple process of rolling in the soft soil, over and over again, hollowing out a huge, shallow depression that was hidden among the thick cover of shrubs under the slash pines. It was an old, old abandoned winter dwelling, frozen in time under the reinforced-concrete stilts that now rose over the hole and carried the Alligator Hole Cafe and its signature blue lights into the damp air above the center of that original builder's abode.

This corner of the swamp was Mikosukee, part of the parcel of "land" ceded to those Indians when the federal government set out to supply that alligator's human contemporaries with a place to live separately, carved out on a map of that no-man's-land called the Everglades. The Alligator Hole Cafe had sprung from much the same motive power as the alligator hole itself: a knack for opportunism on the part of its surprisingly adaptable owner, as well as a need to harvest the other beings drawn to what the hole could supply that the rest of the swamp could not. For the original builder, it had been water. For the current Mikosukee owner, it was legal gambling. Annabelle and Dave had arrived at the height of the night's harvest.

They stepped through an opening in the willow shrubs and climbed the steep steps to the porch. This was the porch they had seen in the photograph of Rolly Castillo, in his desk at the reactor. And Dave thought he knew the answer to the question "Whose Rolando was he?" This was the only spot in South Florida where the customer could get the double legal jolt of a permanent crap game and total nudity in the waitresses.

None of the customers on the porch showed any curiosity toward the newcomers. The Alligator Hole was subject only to the laws its owner cared to make—like the original architect—and he made very few; customers here had nothing to fear from the outside.

Annabelle pushed open the screen door and entered the huge, smoky room, its contours and its dimensions and its unpainted wooden walls obscured by cigarette smoke and the swirling arcs of more blue neon lights pointed from the low ceiling. Immediately a fine perspiration covered her; the room was stifling.

Part of the close warmth was no doubt a function of body heat. At least a hundred bodies were sharing a room that had been intended originally for no more than a small family's minor social needs.

Naked Caucasian waitresses—naked except for dirty tennis shoes—carried trays or single drinks, their slightly bored facial expressions indicating that their completely unclothed state was as natural to them as uniforms; indeed perhaps was a kind of uniform.

Dave stood beside Annabelle, and he saw that none of the customers took advantage of those uniforms by fondling or touching or accosting the waitresses in any way. But the customers looked.

Seated around card tables, they looked. Seated at the long bar, they looked. Standing by the jukebox and dancing alone, sweat dripping from their foreheads, they looked.

And the waitresses helped them look, Dave thought. With a kind of professional detachment, they inserted their sweaty breasts between card players to put glasses of beer on the tables. They slid their sweaty rumps past the barstools, carrying their trays sideways to present the largest posterior expanse possible as they moved from the bar constructed against the right side of the room before deploying themselves among the tables. And most of them had shaved their crotches, and that, Dave thought, certainly helped the customers to look.

Torn between a desire to grab Annabelle's hand and get her out of what he knew was an improper but eye-opening experience—and an equally strong desire to absorb as much of this local color as possible on what would probably be his one and only visit to such a place—Dave hesitated.

But Annabelle was made of different stuff. She strode to the bar and pushed her way gently between two men, who, taking in her decently clad but nevertheless lush proportions, quickly stood and jostled each other in a territorial dispute over whose barstool she would be given. She reached over the bar and touched the damp sleeve of the blond bartender. He turned, and Dave could tell from his own vantage point by the entrance door that Annabelle had made a new friend. Galvanized into motion at the thought, Dave scurried to the bar and slid in next to Annabelle, putting an end to the turf dispute by waving his elbows and squeaking waspishly, "Excuse me, she's my wife."

The bartender ignored the incidental combat taking place in Annabelle's orbit and focused his attention on her.

"You've never been in here before," he said knowingly. "Come to gamble?"

"I've come for some information."

"A full house beats three of a kind, and for you the drinks are on the house." He leaned his forearms on the bar. "What more information can I give you on a hot night in the swamp?"

"I wonder if you knew a man named Rolly Castillo, if you can tell me anything about him. I think he used to come here."

"We got a TV over the bar, beautiful lady, if you're curious about Rolly. Want me to turn it on for you? All the news hens are cackling about him."

"Of course. I wasn't thinking." She flashed him a smile. "Look. My name is Annabelle." She offered her hand across the bar to shake his. "I just want to find out why Rolly hung out here. You know, was it the cards or the women? What kind of man was he?"

"You a news hen yourself?" He tucked a snakeskin-booted foot up on a shelf under the bar, and the faded denim covering his knee brushed against his elbow. He retained his moist grip on her hand and slid it over the smooth wooden surface as he shifted his arm for a more comfortable position.

"No. I have a security interest in the nuclear reactor where he worked and where he died."

"Government?"

"No."

"It goes against the grain to pass you along to a higher authority, beautiful lady, but you better talk to the boss. If you've got a business card on you, that might get you in and out faster. The boss doesn't like a lot of talk."

Annabelle thought ruefully back to the convertible parked off the Anhinga Trail. She had some cards in the glove box.

"I don't have one with me," she said. "But I'll write my name down for you on one of those order pads." She pointed to a stack behind him on a mirrored shelf.

"Well, you think up a pretty name while I go borrow a pen." He winked at her and brought his foot down with a thump on the wooden floor and released her hand. "Make it a long one. I got a thing for long names." He stepped to the end of the bar.

She unobtrusively wiped her hand on the back of her white jeans.

Dave poked her ribs. "Jesus. When he sees your name, there will be no stopping him."

One of the waitresses, a redhead with small and peachy-colored nipples, stepped to a microphone in front of the jukebox at the other side of the room. "Ladies and gentlemen." She tapped the microphone. "Is this thing on?" When a medley of shouts assured her that the mike was operating perfectly—"They can hear you down to Key Largo, honey"—she grinned in an approximation of shyness that turned Dave's usually impervious stomach.

"Ladies and gentlemen," she began again. "You got

five minutes to lose some more money and drink some more beer. Then you can all go outside for the Alligator Hole Cafe's one-of-a-kind laser light show, the best show south of the Northern Lights." Now she grinned with a wholesome cynicism that made Dave favorably reevaluate her facial equipment. "And it's the *only* thing you'll get for free tonight, barring a few bug bites."

Dave was signing this speech for Annabelle when the bartender returned.

Handing her a pen and a pad of paper, the man pointed at Dave's hands. "What's the matter with him?"

"Partial epilepsy," Dave explained, flapping his hands from the wrists. "It comes over me around nude women."

"Yeah? Well, I guess I've seen everything now." He turned to Annabelle. "He's just kidding, right?"

She shrugged. "How would I know? I've never seen the man before." She bent over the bar and began to write. But her hand slowed as it formed the letters of her first name. She thought with queasy clarity of the box of palmetto bugs. Why give her name unnecessarily? She finished writing and ripped the top sheet from the pad, holding it across the bar.

"Annabelle Beckworth, huh? University of the Keys Research Reactor," the bartender said, taking the paper and reading what she had written. "You a nuclear scientist?"

"She's a doctor of charlatanology," Dave said, apparently to himself. "If ever I've seen one."

The bartender shook his head and took the note with him as he passed through a door behind the bar.

Annabelle considered Dave as though he had

sprouted antennae. "Charlatanology? Is that what you said?"

"I only made up one word. You made up a whole identity. Annabelle, that's the only lie you've ever told in my presence."

"That's the only lie you ever *caught* me in," she corrected him, smiling.

"We ought to leave immediately. The corruption is seeping in through your pores. You're beginning to like being bad."

"It's certainly a fresh experience."

"Maybe you'd like to expand your horizons, toss off your clothes, and step up to the mike?"

She laughed. "Maybe I would."

Dave regarded the sparkling intensity of her green eyes, and suddenly he was not so sure about the tenor of the conversation. Maybe she wasn't joking. This had been a devil-may-care day even for her, he thought. First she went off on her own to lunch with a stranger—without her interpreter and even with a certain callous air of dismissal. Then she went striding up to the bartender and started flirting with him. And now she was telling easy lies. Next thing he knew, she'd be chugging down a beer, and she hated liquor. At least, he thought, scratching his head, he thought she did.

The blue lights dimmed in the room and went on again. Hands of cards were hastily played, cigarettes were smashed in ashtrays, beer glasses were gathered from tabletops, and the crowd started moving outside, to the porch and beyond, to the fringes of the dark willow shrubs and cocoplum, and to the relative relief of the softly humid fresh air.

The door behind the bar opened, and Annabelle was given a signal to come around. She quickly and discreetly signed, "Go watch the show: lasers. That's something Rolly would have been interested in," and walked behind the bar and through the door.

She followed the bartender into a small room where several quiet men stood tensely around a crap table. He held open another door, and she entered another room, another world.

The door was pulled shut behind her.

Ionizers and air filters had sucked all traces of smoke and beer and humidity from this room, leaving a pristine, featureless atmosphere, and the air-conditioning was icier than in Mrs. Rolando Ruiz de Castillo's sterile home. The air was so crisp, it seemed almost brittle to Annabelle.

She could not know it, but the air was also sucked clean of the noises from the other two rooms, and those had been replaced by the sweeping and romantic wild harmonies of Mozart's Symphony Number 17 in G Major. But she saw the profusion of small speakers spaced at intervals on shelves around the room—perhaps as many as twenty, she thought—and she surmised that she had entered a loud room, partly from the ubiquitous speakers, partly from the rapt look on the face of the massive dark-haired woman seated behind a white Parsons table in the far corner. Her eyes were closed, and a suggestion of a smile, apparently only a glimmering of the ecstasy within, hovered at the corners of her liver-colored lips.

But the woman's companion—a beautiful man, Annabelle thought—welcomed her with a cold smile and a pair of pale blue eyes, startling in their color and intensity. Henry Algagollawjiwar's irises were the color of the blue central fiery depths of Czechoslovakian opals, or of the blue limpid shallows of the waters off the Florida Keys on a particularly bright sunny day, or of the blue of early-morning shadows on the icy slopes of the Karakoram mountain range in northern Pakistan—and he knew it, because extravagant comparisons had followed Henry around the Everglades as much as he had been followed around the swamp by tourists from all over the world, tourists so smitten with those dazzling eyes that they dredged up their most decorative language from the depths of otherwise unpoetic souls.

Henry's eyes were all the more striking because his skin was very dark, red-brown and unlined, smooth and sleek. And his long black hair, braided neatly and tied with a leather thong, shone in the cold white light of the room as though it had been touched, just lightly touched, with a brush dipped in liquid platinum. He was Mikosukee, Annabelle thought, but those eyes had not been received from any denizen of the Everglades, no matter how exotic the plumage, how lost in mystery the source.

"No," he said, the cold smile curving his full lips, "my grandmother was Irish. My name is Henry Algagol-lawjiwar." He rose from the white plastic lawn chair beside the desk, towering over Annabelle, his hair brushing the pine ceiling. "I own the hole." He motioned her to another lawn chair, pulling it slightly away from the Parsons table to face his chair. "I understand you want information about Rolly Castillo."

She sat, hardly knowing what social mannerism to call upon in response to the woman behind the desk, who continued in her pose of closed-eyed and utterly beatific detachment.

"My friend is lost in Mozart," Henry said, resuming his seat by the desk. "Please don't feel you must acknowledge her existence in any way."

Annabelle glanced at the woman, and she saw the woman's meaty hand clenched over a Colt semiautomatic target pistol in her lap. Her body rippled with muscles, muscles whose kinetic force, even in repose, pushed against her simple white peasant blouse and against the thin fabric of her long, full pink cotton skirt. Annabelle, from her seat on the lawn chair, could now see the woman's legs, the enormous and thickly muscled thighs pressing out in all directions with a radiant force that made the long skirt seem, somehow, invisible and indecent. And made the gun seem small.

Annabelle wondered if the room was soundproofed and was now sorry she had come this far without Dave. These people, in their separate ways, were frightening and closed, the Mikosukee as much as the woman, for his open eyes were astonishingly bereft of emotion or any other clue to personality. They stopped her simple instinct to ask him a few questions almost as if he had held out a warning hand, or the woman had cocked the gun. So she sat silently for a moment, meeting those eyes, in an attempt to neutralize through familiarity their stifling effect on her.

"Perhaps it would be easier for you," he suggested, after returning her gaze, "if I asked you questions."

She did not believe that he was reading her mind. His anticipation of her thoughts was more likely the result of practice in confronting people who had fallen under the spell of his unique eyes and his companion's gun.

"Why don't we try that?" she said, offering a small smile.

"Very well." He sat back in the chair and extended his long legs. "Do you want to know about Castillo's gambling habits?"

"Yes."

"He gambled only moderately but rather well. My thinking is that for him it was an exercise in mathematics, nothing more. Now, would you like to know about his attentions to women in this place?"

"Yes."

"He was a beast. Full of nasty innuendo and foul language. But as far as I know—and, I would know—he never touched one of my waitresses."

Annabelle believed him that he would know. Apparently the language of his eyes was a door he could open at will and was now a persuasive instrument, and she believed him. Annabelle also glanced at the gun under the table.

"Now," he said, scrutinizing her face, "would you like to know how often he came here? He came a couple of times a week, always late."

"Thanks. Look, can she put the gun away?"

"She's not listening to us." He linked his hands together in his lap. "Perhaps you will now tell me what else you want to know about Rolly Castillo's visits to my hole."

"I want to know why he came here."

"He came to forget, like everyone else."

"To forget what?"

"His life. His wife. His unfortunate humanity."

"Did it work? Did he forget?"

"It never works. No man can shed the skin he wears to this hole."

Annabelle wondered what this man's life had been, to lead him to such a pronouncement. Did he have a life? A wife?

"Let me ask you another kind of question," she said. The film of perspiration on her arms had dried, and she rubbed her arms against the cold. "If Dr. Castillo could have forgotten his unfortunate humanity, what would have allowed him to do that?"

He sat forward slowly in his chair, bringing his hands over his knees. "That is certainly a different question. The police did not ask that one."

"The police have been here?"

"Late this afternoon."

Annabelle felt a surge of gratification. So, despite Beckworth's busy efforts and despite what Dave had been told about Metro-Dade's acceptance of Castillo's death as a suicide, someone besides herself was still turning over possibilities.

She extended her hand toward Henry. "Will you answer my question?"

"I don't know the answer."

An irrational disappointment swept over her. She had wanted some pronouncement from this man, some insight—even one he had prepared in advance—into the heart or mind of the dead man whose recent past she was trying to illumine before an eager community could darken it forever by applying the collective force of its language to his death. Suicide: that word had taken on an urgent power, and she was afraid that she would be unable to stand in the way of the authority of language once applied. A thing on four legs was a table, no matter what wood or design had gone into its substance. An accused thief was a thief, even after he had been exonerated. And a suicide, she thought, would be a suicide forever once the official language machinery of death ground out its message. No smoke without fire, no mayhem in Salem without witches, no earth without God. No bullet hole without a smoking gun.

She expelled a long breath and stood.

"Thanks for seeing me."

He stood.

"It is now my turn to ask a question of my own."

She craned her head back to read his lips.

"Go ahead," she said.

"Why do you ask these questions? You are not from the police."

She thought a moment, finally settling for a truth that would not give him a way of finding her. "Because my father asked me to."

"Who is your father?"

"A fisherman."

He extracted the paper bearing her name from the pocket of his shirt. "This is not your real name, is it?"

"No."

"Tell me, why do you look so steadily at me? Most people don't."

"Because I'm deaf, and I must read your lips to know what you are saying."

He considered her, turning his head to one side.

"Do not come back to my hole, fisherman's daughter," he said.

WEDNESDAY

If what is here on earth, in its
prodigious variety, is typical of
what is elsewhere, then the universe is a rich
and ample place. And if we, through imagination,
participate in that prodigality, conserve it,
treasure it, then we embellish ourselves.

CHET RAYMO
The Virgin and the Mousetrap

TWELVE

THE MOON WAS JUST PAST THE FULL, ITS SQUASHED-looking edge pushing against the starry blackness as it rode almost straight overhead in the clear sky.

Dave drove along Old Cutler Road, skirting the bay and winding past the outer contours of suburban Miami. It was a dangerous road, unlit, curving, intersected without warning by cross roads, but Dave maintained a consistent safe speed in the moonlight, his face showing a determined cast, and Annabelle did not protest.

But when he pulled into her driveway, she got out of the car unsteadily. She had unconsciously been pushing her foot to the floor, especially on Old Cutler's hairpin turns.

She massaged her stiff knee and glanced at the dark house and grounds. "Oh, hell. I forgot to leave a light on."

Making his gestures large in the silvery light of the moon, Dave signed, "I put your flashlight in the glove box, on the right side. I hope you haven't already made a mess in there."

She leaned over the door of the car and pushed the

button on the glove box. It sprang open downward, and she reached inside.

She jerked her hand back and jumped away from the car.

"Shit!" she yelped.

Dave vaulted across the back of the car to her side.

"What is it?" he demanded.

"I don't know," she wailed. "But it's moving."

"Don't move. No. Come with me." He grabbed her wrist roughly, and they ran to the front door. Dave typed her code into the panel by feel and snatched her house keys from her shaking fingers. He yanked the door open and flipped on a light switch.

He sent his eyes around the living room, saw her two cats nestled unconcernedly on the couch, drew a relieved breath, ran to the kitchen, rummaged in a drawer, and drew out a large black flashlight.

They returned to the car, holding hands like children, Dave casting the torch's glow before them. Gingerly he opened the passenger door and directed the beam of light at the glove box. Dangling from between the convertible's owner's manual and a stack of pink maintenance receipts, the slim body of a dusky snake was pouring itself in a wriggling stream of moonlit scales toward the floor. Dave adjusted the path of the light, and Annabelle peered over his shoulder. He jumped when she touched his shoulder.

"It's just a snake," she said.

"*Just* a snake? *Just* a snake? I wouldn't call that thing *just* a snake." He shined the light on the floor of the car.

Attempting to slither under the passenger seat, the snake was jerking itself crazily on the gray carpet.

"Oh, God," Dave said, his hair rising on end and his knees giving. "It's got two heads."

Annabelle took the light quickly from Dave's palsied hand. She knelt by the car's open door, peering in at the animal on the floor.

The snake was about two feet long, and it did have two heads. Her throat constricted, and she could not swallow. She recognized it. It was a cottonmouth, a juvenile about as thick around as her middle finger, its skin a smooth weave of black diamonds. But she had never seen one with two heads—four eyes and two lightning tongues, flicking in and out from the white, cottony linings of the two small open mouths. The little mouths were among the most venomous in existence.

"It can't go anywhere," she said, some measure of relief and a great deal of awe in her voice. "That's what all the jerking's about. The two heads want to go in different directions, and it's having a fight with itself." She put the flashlight on the seat and positioned herself firmly, digging her heels into the ground and shifting her weight for stability. She reached into the car and grasped the snake just behind its heads, clutching it firmly. With her other hand, she stabbed at the squirming length of the snake, trying to catch the wildly thrashing body. When she at last managed to trap it by sliding her forearm over the carpet and pinning the snake's body to the floor, keeping well away from the open mouths, she rolled it toward her free hand and grabbed it.

Dave backed away from her. From them.

He watched in frozen horror as Annabelle carried the snake across her yard, her hands spread and the animal heaving between them like a live wire, and toward the pool. With her elbow she switched on a light by the pump house. She elbowed open the door and tossed the snake in. She slammed the door shut.

Then, to Dave's complete astonishment, she started kicking the door, kicking it in bursts of fury. She kicked it again and again, and the sounds seemed to explode in his ears.

Dave felt his limbs unfreezing slowly. He grasped the edge of the car door, pushed it shut, limply picked up the flashlight, and walked to the house, his face still in the thrall of the fierce flush of terror that had washed over him.

Annabelle entered the house from the back, and they met in the middle, beside the fireplace.

"Call somebody," she said. "Call someone who knows about snakes. Call a herpetologist. Call a vet. Call someone to come get that freak out of my pool house. Call someone who can explain how a snake got two heads. Jesus Christ, Dave, that snake was meant to kill me. Or you. Call the police. That's it. Call nine-one-one. God Almighty!"

He went numbly to the phone on the wall beside her back door and dialed the Miami Police.

When he returned to the living room, she had started a fire over the still-warm embers. They sat beside each other on the hearth, leaning their elbows on their knees, staring across the room at the bookshelves.

Dave finally broke the silence. He turned to her and said, "Apparently someone thinks you're planning to open a Pest Supermarket. Your acquisitions budget is certainly going to be affordable."

"You know, Dave, when we first sat down here, I

actually thought of packing a bag and staying at your place tonight."

"I'd be honored. You've never done that before."

"And I'm not going to do it tonight. I won't be frightened out of my home."

"I didn't think you were frightened by that snake."

"Well, I was."

"You handled it like a pro," Dave said, the fire reflecting in his brown eyes. "I'm learning things about you tonight."

She shrugged her shoulders. "Nikki's pestiferous roommate in law school kept a Texas rat snake as a pet."

"Were you afraid of the bugs on your doorstep?"

"Terrified." She closed her eyes at the memory. "Dave, I know now that Rolly was murdered."

"Of course he was. These little attempts to force you into zookeeping prove it, as far as I'm concerned. But they won't prove it in court."

"We need to think of all the places my car was today."

"Well, that's easy. It was in the garage this morning. Then we left it in the reactor parking lot. I drove it back to the Pink Building. It was at your house when you got the bug delivery. You left it on the street when you came back to pick me up at the Pink Building." He widened his eyes. "We left it for a little while at the widow's house."

"And we left it on the Anhinga Trail," she added.

The Anhinga Trail. Dave had also left the blueprint for the nuclear reactor in the car. He looked at his watch. It was just past midnight. Perhaps he should visit the reactor as he had planned. But he did not like to leave Annabelle alone to wait for the police, and he did not relish the thought of getting back into the convertible. "The Anhinga Trail. I hope my kit is still in the car."

"Uh-oh. The blueprint?"

He nodded, pursing his lips. "I packed it in case you came along. I'd already memorized it for myself."

She leaned back against the marble face of the fireplace, fixing him with a sharp gaze. "Tell me what happened during the laser show. Did everyone stay put at the hole?"

He closed his eyes and recalled the scene. "As far as I know. It was quite dark, and the show was riveting as hell. Annabelle, it was the most awesome thing."

"Tell me about it. Tell me what you saw."

"You sure you want to hear this now? I don't want to blabber in a time of crisis."

"I hope the crisis is over." She smiled grimly. "They've certainly tested our mettle."

"I hope you don't think of me as a failure. My mettle went all rubbery. I hate snakes."

"Pooh. I think of you as my comrade-in-arms."

"It's too hot over here." Indeed, Dave's face looked flushed to her. He moved to the couch facing the fireplace, curling his legs under him. "The show was beautiful," he signed. "The guy running the lasers was almost invisible, because he was wearing black, but his face was very pale and lit from the moon. It was like a Buddha face, serene and happy and really unearthly in its perfect peace. I've never seen such a face. Sort of like he had figured out the secret of life. I wish you had seen him. Anyway there was music. Classical music. Mozart, I think. And the little Buddha-face guy fiddled with three projectors, and the most intense lights warped out all over the place. Then he concentrated them on the tall grasses, using them as a screen. He made pictures that moved in time to the music, pictures of alligators rolling around, pictures of blue herons flying, pictures of pig frogs hopping. It was extraordinary, the way he made such exact pictures on the screen of tall grass. Then he changed his style, in the wink of an eye, and his pictures turned abstract, like dancing red spirals, and kinky green double helixes, and blue cones with their ends being lopped off, slice after slice until there was nothing but a blue dot. And at the end he signed his name with a lavender flourish. It was the best light show I've ever seen. Too bad it was so short. Only about five minutes."

"How'd he sign it? What was his name?"

"Darwin. He put a pink star on both ends of the name. Be funny if that's how it's spelled on his birth certficate."

"I doubt it. But it's a great stage name." She stood and stretched. "I envy you. My experience at the cafe was a less pleasant kind of show." She paced before the fireplace, lost in thought. She looked up and caught him sneaking a peek at his watch. "Dave, this is silly. Go. I can wait for the police."

"I could go tomorrow night. But I'm afraid they'll move the corpse by then."

"Go. Please."

Dave stood and crossed to her. He put a finger tentatively on her cheek. "Wish me happy hunting."

"Happy hunting," she said with a smile.

"I'll just keep your car overnight and pick you up in

the morning," he said. "Now that you've desnaked it," he added with a shiver.

"Let's go down to Key Largo in the morning and get a look at Rolly's dive hangout."

"Fine. By the way, what kind of car does your friend Berlin drive?"

"A Honda Accord, 1994, silver gray. Why?"

"Oh, I was just wondering. But there weren't any Hondas on that lane off the Anhinga Trail. Besides, I'm trying to get a line on his character. A Honda, huh? Very un-American of him. Careful, stodgy, low-maintenance kind of guy. The kind of guy who won't put up with a lot of trips to the repair shop. Likes to hold on to his property. The jealous type. You can tell a lot about people from the cars they drive."

Annabelle glared at him. "What do you think it says about you, Jorge, that you don't even own a car?" she demanded tartly.

"Ah," he said, flicking an imaginary mote of dust from her shoulder. "I'm a deep mystery. One inscrutable son of a bitch, meaning no disrespect to my Cuban mama."

"Say good night, Jorge."

"Tally ho. Give my regards to the cops. It will make them happy to think I remembered them, what with my full schedule."

They walked out to the car. Dave made a show of looking casually under the driver's seat, but the hair on his arms prickled and his hands felt suddenly clammy. His black plastic bag was there. He unzipped it and handed her the blueprint.

He waited until she had returned to the house and

closed the door before flicking on her flashlight again and going over the car with elaborate care. He slid stiffly behind the wheel, lowering himself gently and slowly to the seat, glancing down several times before he started the engine.

THIRTEEN

DAVE DROVE SOUTH AGAIN, TO NARANJA, STAYING ON the well-lit if ugly lanes of U.S. 1, nervously checking the seat beside him from time to time, easily startled by shadows falling across the car.

He pulled the LeBaron off the road on Broad Creek Channel Cut across from the reactor, into high mondo grass, the tubular stalks whispering against the convertible. He stuck his hand circumspectly under the seat, extracted the black plastic bag, and opened it. He slipped his shoulder holster on over his black T-shirt and fastened the strap of a black nylon bag around his slim waist. He looked at the glowing numbers on his watch. 1:01.

His clean dark hair blew softly across his forehead. The breeze was pleasantly cool here, wisps of sea air.

He got out of the car and closed the door softly.

The darkly painted inner building that contained the core of the reactor was invisible against the sky, but the roof of the Ring Building stood out clearly in the glow of lights from the parking lot, like a boot box in the back of a closet in the glare of a flashlight. There were six cars in the well-lighted lot, including an old white Cadillac and a silver gray Honda.

His black tennis shoes made no sound as he crossed the pavement to the freshly mown grass around the reactor. Once on the grass, he ran, smoothly and quietly; for a moment he was visible in the lights from the parking lot, but he soon blended into the shadows hugging the walls of the Ring Building. He headed for the west side, the blueprint etched into his memory. His target was a door, one to be used only in case of emergency, one that had been opened in the reactor's thirty-year history only during annual drills; his object was the radioactive corpse.

When he reached the door, Dave stood quietly, listening, a minute by his watch. He heard nothing but the dull sawing music of crickets in the grass.

He closed his eyes, calling up a picture of the blueprint.

He ran his hand along the edge of the door, feeling with sensitive, practiced fingers for two micro-thin wires. He took a penlight from the black bag and ran it over the wires, a red one, a yellow one. He selected a couple of small tools from the bag at his waist. He sprayed white foam on the yellow wire from an inch-long cylinder, and with a tiny wire cutter, he snipped the yellow wire through the center of the foam and held his breath. No alarms yet, he thought serenely, separating the ends of the yellow wire. Contact between the severed wires would set off the alarm when the foam dried, as it would do quickly in this breeze.

He took two pieces of duct tape, precut and stuck to a Kmart customer identification card in the black bag, and taped the cut ends of the wire firmly on the door's frame, ends not touching each other.

Into the space between the door and the frame he inserted a thin, flexible strip of twenty-four-carat gold, gently and patiently probing, fractional centimeter by fractional centimeter, for the plastic filament he knew was there. In twelve minutes he had it. A breath of stale air touched his nostrils. The door was open.

There was no knob, and with the tips of his fingers he pulled the door toward him and slipped inside. It was 1:18.

He left the door infinitesimally ajar, since it would not close completely with the plastic filament disturbed. To his left was a flight of stairs. He glanced down the empty hall. He turned and ran lightly down the stairs.

The basement corridor was long and dimly lit with yellow bulbs. Señora Ruiz de Castillo stood by the window of the glove box, her hands in the pockets of her gray slacks, her forehead against the glass. *She must have been here a long time,* he thought, *and that must be Bodorff with her*. The guard in the sky-blue shirt stood behind and to the side of the woman, his hands behind his back, his spine straight, his booted feet apart. *Wyatt Earp Bodorff,* Dave thought.

The asshole had a gun in his belt. The little asshole actually had a gun. Of all the insurance pitfalls the guard could have chosen, this was one of the worst. All bets were off with Hardy Security's insurance if one of its university guards started popping off a gun. Lord only knew what the going price on a nuclear reactor is, Dave thought furiously, but it's probably more than even Annabelle has.

Deep shit, Dave thought. *Now we're in deep shit.*

Dave crept back up one step, waiting. At 1:24 Dave could hear the guard's boots rapping smartly on the linoleum floor. Soon Dave heard the sound of the elevator door. When he looked into the hall, it was empty.

Dave ran down the hall, hoping that Bodorff would interpret the scope of his duty liberally and stay glued to Señora Ruiz de Castillo for a good long while. Without shooting her. Or anyone else.

Dave glanced at the yellow and magenta warning plaque above the door to the Glove Box, the hazardous radiation sign holding fewer terrors for him than it would have held yesterday. If he could stand safely next to the pool, in the company of a scientist who knew the secrets of that pool, he could certainly stand in the same room with the man who had been found floating in it. He hoped.

He opened the door and went in, pulling it shut behind him.

The fluorescent overhead tubes had been turned off, probably by Bodorff, if Dave read his enthusiastic security guard correctly. Dave approached the corpse in the dark room, the only light the faint yellow glow from the dim bulbs in the corridor outside the glove window.

With a grim tightening of his cheek muscles, Dave put his hands on the corpse, searching the damp pockets rapidly. The dead man had been overweight, and the jeans were not only tightly fitted, they were also cold and repulsively moist. Dave extracted a small metal bottle from the jeans with some difficulty. He opened the bottle, its lidocaine label limp and beginning to fade, and smelled the nozzle. No odor.

He sprayed some of the contents into the air in a fine

mist and poked his nose into the little cloud. *Interesting,* Dave thought, *but be careful here.* Beckworth had said that trace mineral elements in Rolly's body would still be radioactive, and that certainly applied to the lidocaine, which might give off a dose of radiation. A tremor swept over Dave. It was extremely cold in the room.

The only other item Dave found on the corpse was a gray plastic key case, with a car key, another key, and a reactor security key, on which there was a smear of colorless grease. Dave replaced the spray bottle and the keys in the jeans pockets and slid his hand under the burned body.

He touched the scissors. He stepped to the head of the cold steel table, next to the wall, and pulled the blades toward him. He had to tug to make the handles clear the pocket. The scissors were greasy. Dave felt the grease, or oil, or whatever it was, between his fingers and sniffed it. He stood in thought.

Reaching past the dead man's face, Dave pulled the chain around the neck and held the spectacles by an earpiece. It was the same grease on the lenses. *I wonder what he was doing,* Dave thought, *to make such a little mess.* He wiped the spectacles on a piece of waxed paper from his bag, folding the paper carefully before tucking it into his own pants pocket. He replaced the spectacles, but had to settle for sliding the scissors under the man's hip. He could not get the scissors back into the man's tight jeans, especially not handles-first as he had found them.

The shirt was already partially out of the waistband of the jeans, and Dave pulled it all the way free, rolling it up across the cold skin, up to the neck. Dave ran his eyes over the chest, the scorched flesh, looking for marks other than the burns. There was a bruise, if his eyes did not deceive him, under the red puckered flesh of the shoulder, and scores of tiny marks on the relatively unscathed skin of the palms and fingertips.

Dave took a breath and lifted the torso a few inches off the frigid table, feeling the man's back. Rigor mortis had departed the body, and the head lolled heavily sideways against Dave's chest.

Dave gently replaced the body, pulling the shirt down over the wounded flesh. *Sorry, Rolly,* he thought, *to disturb your rest.*

With a quick glance at the ceiling and a muttered word of self-encouragement, Dave unzipped the jeans and probed the flesh of the hips and buttocks. Slipping his entire left arm under the hips, he rocked the body back and forth, and put his ear on the stomach. He could hear liquid, but not, he thought, in the lungs. He put his ear higher, on the chest and moved his arm up the dead man's spine, continuing the rocking motion. Quiet in the upper chest, but *lungs are like sponges,* Dave thought, and would absorb any water the man had breathed.

He straightened the clothing, checking the picture in his memory for the details of the dead man's appearance. On an impulse he put the spectacles on the dead face. The oily marks on the thick lenses covered the brown irises, if the glasses had set evenly on the nose. He put the spectacles back as he had found them. He blew on his own cold fingers for warmth.

Dave glanced around the room. There was a desk with a lamp. He stepped behind the desk and looked at its bare surface.

There was a small metal wastebasket with a plastic

liner under the desk. Dave pulled it out and sifted the few contents in his right hand. A paper cup, a broken paper clip, a rubber band, a gum wrapper. Dave was about to replace the basket when he noticed a piece of paper on the floor. He stooped and picked it up—a coupon for 50 cents off on any purchase of Lifestyles Condoms.

He dropped the coupon into the basket in his left hand and opened the door to a chute on the wall. CONTAMINATED AND RADIOACTIVE WASTE, it was marked.

He closed the chute's door and looked at his fingertips, slowly rubbing them together.

He quietly shoved the wastebasket back under the desk, and, when he straightened, from across the room he frowned at the door of the vault he had noted on the blueprint. He was guessing that was the gem depository.

Dave slipped silently across the small room and examined the door of the vault with his fingers. He stood for a moment, his hands pressed against the cold metal, considering.

He returned to the body and took the keys again from the pocket of the jeans.

He crossed to the vault and inserted the dead man's security card into the slot on the door and typed the month's code onto the keypad. Nothing happened. He typed in the code again. Again nothing. *Ah,* he thought, *the scientists have a few tricks they aren't sharing with the staff, or with their security firm.*

He looked at his watch. 1:44.

He replaced the key ring in the dead man's pocket.

Dave looked thoughtfully at the dead man's hands. No wedding ring, although his wife had been wearing one. *And,* Dave thought, *no dosimeter.* Nothing here to measure whatever dose of radiation the dead man had swallowed and breathed and absorbed through his skin at the core of the reactor. Nothing but the red and purple map that was his mutilated, scarred flesh.

Dave patted the dead man's rough, cold cheek in farewell and left the room, closing the door behind him without a sound. The relative warmth of the corridor's standard air-conditioning came as a relief. He rubbed his hands and nose, and paced off the distance to the security office. Thirty feet to the door. He let himself into the office and sat in the swivel chair at the desk, putting his feet up. He leaned sideways in the chair and slipped a square of plastic from his back pocket into his left hand. He took the Colt from its holster and placed it between his thighs, its 3¼-inch barrel pointed toward his knees, the stainless-steel finish warm to his right hand gripping the gun, his left hand cupped at the side of his leg. It was 1:48.

He waited.

He saw Bodorff a second before the guard saw him. *Which is only fair,* Dave thought, *since I was expecting him.*

Bodorff jerked a Smith and Wesson 422 from his belt and yanked the door open with his free hand. Dave did not move.

"Freeze," Bodorff snarled, waving the gun at him.

"I'm already frozen, you half-wit," Dave said. "It's cold in here."

"Well, get your feet off my desk."

"Christ in a catalog, make up your mind. First you tell me to freeze and now you tell me to, er, unfreeze."

"Get your hands up." The guard waggled his gun. "Who the fuck are you?" Bodorff demanded, beads of sweat standing out on his forehead.

"I am your boss, Bodorff," Dave said quietly, raising the Colt and pointing it at the guard. "Put that darling Smith and Wesson—carefully—down on the floor and explain what the hell you mean by carrying that thing while wearing a Hardy uniform, you sloppy amateur. And watch your language. Somehow profanity does not work for you."

A mean look flushed over Bodorff's features. "Oh yeah? Why should I? You're not my boss, you greasy *marielito*. How'd you know my name?"

Dave slowly raised his left hand and opened it, holding the edges of the plastic card. "Picture ID," he said. "In case you can't read," he added in a helpful spirit.

From where he stood, a few paces from Dave's feet, the guard recognized the sky-blue Hardy Security ID.

"Shit," Bodorff said, and lowered his gun.

"Put your Mattel rocket launcher on the floor," Dave reminded him, and Bodorff dropped the gun with a clatter.

Dave gracefully lowered his feet.

"Kick it over here," he said.

When Bodorff had complied, Dave shook his head mournfully.

"Really, son, I'm ever so disappointed in you for giving up your gun as though it were last week's lottery ticket. After all, I could have stolen this ID from a Hardy employee—from someone stupid. Someone, say, like you."

Bodorff looked longingly at the Smith and Wesson on the floor.

"Oh, I wouldn't dream of it," Dave said. "That little gun is like a training bra—it will only make you uncomfortable and, really, it fools no one. Believe me, I know." Dave gestured expansively with his left hand, but kept the Colt steady on the badly rattled guard. "Sit down, Bodorff. This is just for big boys, and you won't be needing your toy. Unless it's some sort of extension of your masculinity?"

The guard sat across from Dave, his hands gripping the arms of the chair, his eyes fierce.

"Now, my friend," Dave said, and his voice was glacial, "let's talk about security."

The guard shifted in the chair.

Dave shivered, still cold from the Glove Box. "My name is Jorge Enamorado. I spoke with you earlier today, and this evening from Señora Ruiz de Castillo's house. I'm a vice president of Hardy Security. Perhaps you remember my name?"

Bodorff nodded.

Dave returned the Colt to his holster. He had never taken the safety off.

"Good," Dave said. "Now, perhaps you'll be kind enough to tell me why you carry a Smith and Wesson to work. Ms. Hardy-Maratos's policy on guns is not news to you, is it?"

"Well, I," Bodorff hesitated, "well, in this line of work we . . . what I mean is . . ."

His voice trailed off.

"Just as I thought," Dave said, rubbing his ear. "You worked this shift last night. Did you have any occasion to play with your gun then?"

"I already told you—and the police—that nothing happened last night," Bodorff muttered.

"I don't feel that Dr. Ruiz de Castillo would agree with

you. By the way, did you escort the señora to her car just now?"

"Yes."

Dave smiled. "Gun anyone down on the way?"

"Of course not."

"About the 'nothing' that happened last night. Can you tell me what cars were parked in the lot when you came on duty? You came on at ten, is that right?"

"Yeah, at ten. There were the three cars that are always here, the control-room guys' cars—you know, the MPs. Dr. Berlin's car was here. My car. That's it."

"Do you know all those cars well?"

"Yeah. And they all have reactor stickers on them."

"Did you see Dr. Ruiz de Castillo's Jeep?"

"No. I guess he wasn't here when I got here. He must've got here right after me."

"Did you see Dr. Berlin himself? Did you talk to him?"

"He was up at the lab when I got here. I didn't talk to him. He was busy."

"Doing what?"

"How do I know? He was just busy."

"Well, was he jumping on a trampoline?"

"No," Bodorff said angrily. "He was sitting, looking at papers."

"What time did you see Dr. Berlin in the lab, not jumping on his trampoline?"

"Just after ten. Maybe a couple minutes after."

"Did you see Dr. Ruiz de Castillo arrive in the building?"

"No."

"He didn't come down here to say hello to you?"

"No. The police asked me that. He told Gayle—she's the receptionist—that he was going to come see me, but he never did."

"An attack of good sense, no doubt. So," Dave said, apparently to himself, "Berlin must have been in the lab when Castillo got here at ten-oh-two." He looked at Bodorff. "The guard you relieved—was his car in the lot?"

"Yeah. It was here. I didn't think you meant that one too."

Dave gave him a hurt look. "Please. I want you to tell me everything about the nothing that happened last night. The other guard would be Cristiano. Did you see him leave?"

"Yeah. I talked to him when I got down here."

"What did you talk about?"

"Nothing. You know, stuff. Like, it's hot out."

"So you saw Cristiano leave this office. You didn't actually see him leave the building, though, did you?"

Bodorff shook his head.

Dave stood and stretched. He looked at his watch. 2:02.

"You're late for your rounds, Bodorff. I do hope no one goes swimming tonight. That would look very bad. Almost unthinkably repetitious." Dave put his hand on the doorknob. "I'm going to leave you to your tasks now. One day from now—that would be Thursday, just in case you have trouble with calendars—you will bring your popgun to Ms. Hardy-Maratos and explain your views on security work. Understand? I assume you can find the Pink Building without a map?"

Bodorff nodded unhappily.

Dave stepped into the hall.

He turned back and raised an eyebrow at the guard.

"Tell me, Bodorff, do you patronize the makers of Lifestyles Condoms?"

"What?"

"What kind of condoms do you like?"

Bodorff stood up and sidestepped away from Dave.

"Trojans. For God's sake, why?"

"Oh, just a thought," Dave said airily. "Just a thought. By the way, Bodorff, don't bother to follow me. I'll let myself out."

FOURTEEN

HENRY ALGAGOLLAWJIWAR'S CAFE IN THE SWAMP WAS dark.

The outdoor lights had been shut off, and the moon floated over the Everglades like a swollen face, its eastern cheek bulging under streaks of stray wispy clouds. From the porch of the cafe, Henry gazed out over the Mikosukee Reservation and contemplated the moonspills on the open patches of water in the river of grass.

The last of the employees had left on the airboat. The churning fan was only a hum in the distance, a mechanical undercurrent in the fugue of night, a vagrant theme in the complex polyphonic arrangement of whirring voices in the great swamp.

One night was much like another in what was left of the Everglades, as though the dying swamp still wore a tough skin that repulsed the incremental pain of daily living that marked the appearances of its individual inhabitants and scarred their hides. Henry's own hide was subject to the same ravages that he had seen in the swamp's other populations when their survival needs were denied them: faces haggard, lined, dry, and filled with a dull sorrow about the eyes.

The dull sorrow, he knew, was in his own blue eyes, too, but there he had also discovered a debilitating anger, something the wretched dying animals of the swamp never showed on the endangered faces that were fading into history. Henry's only revenge against systematic white destruction of his home—more money—was being hacked out of his hide:

The topaz was as dead to him as Rolly Castillo. And he wanted the topaz. He'd never been so angry.

Henry scraped a dead apple snail off the pine railing of the porch and flicked it through the bottlebrush tree overhanging this side of the stilt house. He heard the soft splash of the hard shell about thirty feet from where he stood, past the ring of willow shrubs and into the open swamp.

Rolly Castillo had been a sneaky self-serving bastard, but Henry had never doubted that the man would bring him the topaz. Henry had known that his hold on Rolly was too firm, an immutable force, for the man to fail him. But whatever human agency had sent Rolly into that reactor pool—guilt? revenge? greed? professional enmity? sexual madness?—had taken the topaz from Henry as surely as though it had been snatched from his open hand. Henry wanted those gems. And now he would have to get them himself. If only he knew with certainty where Rolly had put them.

He leaned against the railing of the porch, rubbing his hands over his cheeks as though he could smooth away the anger that was finally writing inexorable lines of hatred into his smooth skin. From under the porch he heard footsteps crunching over the dry roots and the clumped mud of the hole.

Darwin emerged from the darkness under the house and climbed the steep steps, carrying a large leatherbound album. They went together into the empty cafe, where several yellow bulbs behind the bar still put out a jaundiced band of light across the mirrored wall. They sat next to each other on stools facing the mirror.

Henry regarded *Darwin*'s face as it hovered on the glass between the cash box and the stuffed body of a brown anole from Cuba, an aggressive lizard introduced into the swampy wilderness by immigrants who also flowed in on the tide of South Florida's rapid development, development that was killing the swamp, Henry thought—with chemicals, bad land management, and a towering, greedy appetite fit for a nest of infant snakes. Hammocks had been razed, vast arteries of the river of grass drained for condos, and wildlife destroyed by chemical pollutants and new imported species. And the tide of immigration to Florida had invaded the sawgrass marsh, cut the pine forests for timber, and stripped away huge tracts of the luxuriant, protective growth of the swamp.

Henry killed as many of the brown anoles as he could, shooting them with the Colt target pistol. He did not personally shoot the people who had brought the lizards to the Everglades. Those he was allowed legally to rob in his gambling hole.

Millions of those new residents of South Florida had arrived after fleeing the almost constant civil wars and insurgencies and coups of their Caribbean and Central American homelands. And they arrived in Miami—vowing to return home one day when their governments were free and democratic—and they put down the voracious roots that were sucking the Everglades dry.

Many years earlier, when Henry had almost died from eating mercury-contaminated fish he had caught in the open swamp, he had decided that there was nothing he could do to stop the brutal compromise and witless sacrifice of his homeland. The damage was too widespread, too pervasive, too final. But he could retaliate by contaminating the populations that had provided some of the destruction. Even though Henry did not take to shooting the invaders, he would help them to shoot each other.

It was at the Alligator Hole that Henry cut the deals that shipped arms to the most cold-bloodedly callous fighters and ruthless politicians of the tropics, and he had become a rich man by preying on their lust for the blood of their brothers. Henry supplied guns, without prejudice, to any faction, to any party, for any activity that would shed lives south of the Everglades. He had begun by joining the men who ran guns down through the Florida Keys, often loading crates into the holds of mule boats himself. Now he managed a munitions empire from his gambling den in the swamp.

And to the seat of that empire had come the man who had shown Henry how—with the right political winds—he could put a stop to further immigration. It was a pity, in a way, that the black people of Haiti would be the ones to suffer. They were already suffering. But Haitians were the one Caribbean population that Miami—in its collective and multiethnic antipathy toward blacks—had decided to resist, to turn away from its shores. Henry was going to arm the Haitian military with a weapon so fearsome it would send the suffering and innocent black residents of that island country screaming for their lives, in northbound boatloads that would make South Florida writhe in its racial hatred and finally slam the door of open immigration on everyone. The boatloads would be filled with people so badly wounded that no South Florida rationalizer could possibly claim they were merely "economic refugees" (as they always had with Haitians) and thus not entitled to the comprehensive protections given to "political refugees," some of whom were now making decisions in South Florida. If the Haitians were to be kept out by the hypocritical nigger-phobes, without finally admitting to the entrenched hypocrisy of the immigration policy that had so far separated Caribbean blacks from Central American Hispanics, then everyone would have to be kept out. Henry was going to end the distinction between economic and political refugees, and he was going to end the comfortable rationale that had made racial hatred a silent weeder in South Florida.

Henry never agonized over the horrifying probabilities—in the full spate of his fury over the dwindling defenses of the swamp—never dwelt on the moral responsibility for the harm that would be done to innocent blacks when the new weapon was introduced among them on the streets of Port-au-Prince. Henry was not a moral man; he was an angry man, desperately clutching the last shreds of his self-control. The Mikosukee had made peace with the white man, and they were now the living dead. The Seminoles had fought to the end, and they were dead.

Henry couldn't see much to choose from between the valiant, violent Seminole ghosts and his own people, now confined to a land where there was no land, cut off from jobs and schools and medical care. And dying of measles. Henry had been furious for many years.

The man who could channel that anger sat with Henry. The face in the mirror beside the stuffed anole wore a mask of habitual serenity, a peaceful and rested expression that strangely matched the anole's in its fixed, flat elongated smile. Like the lizard, *Darwin*'s face had the look of a creature that was either well rested or had no need for sleep at all. The same kind of liquid dark eyes, slightly receded into the surrounding small wrinkles of tough skin, looked back at Henry from the mirror.

The loss of the fingers and palm of his left hand had not materially affected *Darwin*'s expression of pacific calm, just as the loss had not affected his expertise with weapons. He had a gift; and the grenade that had gone off in his hand while he was constructing it had not marred or touched the tranquil thought processes that were, if not his principal vanity, then his most comforting trait. *Darwin* was a supremely happy man, having found the secret of inner harmony—absolute self-trust.

That he viewed all other humans with absolute distrust was only a practical corollary to the central fact of himself.

His distrust of the Indian, for example, was no greater than his distrust of anyone, merely a sort of standard appraisal. He did not waste time in shades of feeling, nuances of emotion. He saved his attention and thought processes, serene and elegant and precise, for the leatherbound set of delicately executed drawings he carried with him all over the world. Selling his time to Henry had not meant selling any part of himself as well, not even his attention. He designed and manufactured weapons, and that was the only contact he permitted himself with people. Even running the laser show was merely a test run for elements of his new weapon. If he entertained Henry's customers in the process, he also camouflaged his activities. Nothing was wasted.

He had brought the leather album from the shed behind the stilt house because he never left it anywhere. He certainly had no plans to share its contents with Henry.

The album contained, among the hand-drawn portraits of bombs and detection devices, *Darwin*'s best design: the thin blue-penciled lines of the intricate circuitry of a portable laser gun, more deadly even than the Belgian Five-seveN, under study now by the SAS in England, so far considered the most powerful handgun in the world. *Darwin* wasn't worried about that gun. His appreciation for his own design was in no way narcissistic. He would have approved just as heartily had it been the invention of any other specialist. But it was his. And with a serendipitous alliteration that coincided with his colossal love for orderliness, he called the weapon the Darwin Dionic Device, or the DDD.

The pumping mechanism was entirely revolutionary. The high excitation of atoms—pumping—was unmatched anywhere in the world, particularly not in such small portable systems as his device, because the significant private achievement was his adaptation of laser technology to the London Blue topaz. The gems, in the sizes he needed and with their electron lattices rearranged by irradiation, were too expensive for *Darwin* to undertake mass production of his device, but Henry had arranged to deliver the means of small scale and rapid manufacture of several hundred DDDs to arm Haitians.

Now, with the failure of the swallower to deliver the topaz, *Darwin*'s plans had been lopped off like the blue cones he had included in tonight's show. Although he longed to bring production of the DDD to fruition, he would not permit himself the distracting vice of impatience. The radioactive topaz would have to be provided somehow, but that was Henry's problem.

Darwin did not have problems.

What he had was a gun to sell. The Five-seveN would be old news on the black market once the DDD's range and penetration were known. His field test of the prototype had blazed through twelve feet of concrete at a range of half a mile. And Henry wanted the gun. Henry would have to get the topaz. Life was really very simple.

"Today," Henry said, "I will leave the hole and retrieve your topaz, little man. And then you can take it to Haiti. What your use of radiation has produced in that shed is no worse than what others have done to my homeland. But if you are going to make monsters, you won't do it anymore at my hole and with my money. The DDDs will be made in Haiti, not here."

Darwin's expression of sweet agreeableness lost a subtle shade of its habitually tenacious grip on his cheek muscles.

The door behind the bar opened.

The muscular woman trod heavily behind the bar. The spindly legs of a mosquito twined in her eyelashes, and *Darwin* looked away. The insect must have gone for her as soon as she stepped into this outer room. He did not mind the mosquito, but he found that her face had the power to nag at the edges of his serenity. The wandering hairline and the whites of her eyes and the skin around her nostrils were filled with broken blood vessels, hideous spidery blemishes, he thought, that she should have hidden decently behind makeup or a veil, and dark glasses. Really, such blemishes were intrusive, a bold sort of thrusting disease she should have kept to herself behind some screening device, or the closed door of the backroom.

But Sabriya Agha was not a considerate woman. She had that pushing sensitivity *Darwin* associated with all female athletes. At 175 pounds of powerful and disciplined muscle, Sabriya was a formidable athlete. A former softball star at the University of Miami, she was fast, perfectly coordinated, and mean. She stuffed a couple of sticks of Wrigley's spearmint chewing gum into her mouth and returned *Darwin*'s scrutiny across the bar.

She stood, her back to the mirror, and with an excruciating and slow twist, she cracked her vertebrae. To *Darwin*, it sounded as if she had started from below her thick waist and had set off a chain reaction that traveled up to her bulging neck.

She dropped a folded newspaper onto the bar.

"It's like the topaz melted into thin air," she said to Henry. "Have you seen this?" She pointed to a story above the fold on the break page, the *Miami Tribune*'s local section.

Henry glanced at the paper. It was the early edition, the edition that sometimes made its way out to the hole with a customer. Apparently this copy of the Wednesday edition had been left behind tonight by one of the late arrivals. Henry picked up the paper.

The headline ran over the story and photo Sabriya had indicated: SAFETY FACTOR QUESTIONED IN REACTOR SUICIDE.

The photo was a long shot of the reactor. The story was set in a gray-shaded box.

> The apparent suicide of a prominent scientist in the early hours of Tuesday has raised grave questions concerning design safety and plant management at the nuclear research reactor in Naranja, about 12 miles south of Miami.
>
> The body of Rolando Ruiz de Castillo, Ph.D., was dragged from "the pool," a three-story cylinder of water that acts as primary cooling system for the nuclear reactions generated by the enriched uranium core at the University of the Keys facility.
>
> Dade County officials say that the death of Ruiz de Castillo highlights concerns they have had for years regarding safety regulations at the reactor.
>
> "You always have to worry about nuclear energy when it's practically in your backyard," said Xavier Vicario, county manager.
>
> "But I find it difficult to fathom, even in the safest of scenarios, that one of their own people could use that facility to drown himself," Vicario added.
>
> University president Eugene Beckworth defended the safety record of the reactor, saying, "In thirty years of operation, that reactor hasn't had so much as a minor accident—and it's been truly said of suicides that, if they're serious, they'll find a way. You can't blame the reactor for the irresponsible actions of a disturbed individual."
>
> Coworkers say that Ruiz de Castillo left behind a note in the computer database at the reactor, and that the note strongly suggests that the scientist intended to

take his own life by jumping into the pool. Beckworth would not comment on the wording of Ruiz de Castillo's note.

A spokesperson for the Nuclear Regulatory Commission (NRC) in Washington, D.C., said that the agency would conduct an investigation into the incident, starting today, and that the investigation would include research into the final disposition of the body of the deceased.

In addition to the NRC investigation, the university has undertaken its own in-house inquiry, under the auspices of Hardy Security and Electronics, Inc., the Miami-based security giant owned by Annabelle Hardy-Maratos, daughter of Jacob Michael Hardy, the popular philanthropist and founder of Miami's Ecology Coalition.

Neither Hardy nor his daughter could be reached for comment, but a spokesman for the security company said that the resources of that company would be made available to the university in investigating the background of the apparent suicide.

"We can do nothing on the scale or with the scientific authority of the NRC," said Jorge Enamorado, a vice president of Hardy. "But we can and certainly will act as facilitators for the school's own enlightened efforts to deal with the aftermath of this tragedy."

Morticians in Miami have expressed reluctance to handle Ruiz de Castillo's remains.

"We just don't know about the effect of the radioactivity, and we're scared," said James T. Williams, president of the Morticians Society of South Florida and owner of Sunnyvale Funeral Home at 9575 Kendall Drive.

According to Enamorado, the body is being held at the reactor, pending the NRC's findings.

Ruiz de Castillo is survived by his widow, Giselle Ruiz de Castillo.

Henry lowered the newspaper to the bar. "There is nothing here of importance that we did not already know." Henry reached across the bar and plucked the mosquito from Sabriya's lashes and smashed it between his fingers. She did not flinch. "I see no reason to concern ourselves over Rolly Castillo any longer. The pinch he felt was manifestly enough to force him into making the ultimate gesture. But that's his problem, or was. Our problem is the topaz. It's either still at the reactor or he put it someplace else. A place that should not be too hard to find." Henry punctuated these last words by tapping the bar with his long forefinger.

"It is not impossible that he meant to keep the gems for himself after all," Sabriya suggested. "If so, he could have hidden them where we'll never find them."

Henry frowned, rubbing his lip, "I don't think he could have found a buyer as silent and invisible as I am."

"Let's hope he made this easy for us," Sabriya said, making wet, smacking noises with her gum. "I sure as hell don't want to go to the reactor."

FIFTEEN

THE LITTLE PARADE MARCHED UP ANNABELLE'S WALKWAY at nine o'clock. The bright and already-hot sun sparkled off three pairs of well-shined black shoes—one pair being elegant flats from the women's shoe department at Saks—as two blue-shirted security guards followed Dave to the door. The guards carried grocery bags.

Dave rang the doorbell, which would set off the flashing light in her living room and one upstairs in her bedroom. He waited patiently, leaning back against the white stucco wall with his arms around the squirming animal he carried against his chest. Dave was enjoying the eighty-four-degree warmth of the morning. He wore lime-green Bermuda shorts and an olive-green T-shirt he had bought from what he called "the commando catalogs" that arrived daily at their offices in the Pink Building. This one had come from Universal Cavalry, "world's finest military and adventure equipment." On the front was pictured a sniper, lying in tall grass, rifle at the ready. It said, "If you run, you'll only die tired."

Annabelle opened the door, and Dave walked into the coolness of her living room.

"I thought you might need a kinder, gentler zoo delivery boy today," he announced, holding out the gray kitten.

Annabelle put out her hand and jerked it back. She did not want a kitten. The two cats already living with her had both been gifts from Dave, but they represented only a fraction of the cats he had tried to foist on her over the past two years. A particularly fecund cat occupied the woods behind Dave's apartment complex and seemed to crank out enormous litters at a miraculous rate. And Dave, his tender heart impervious to her repeated and insistent lies that she was thinking of getting a dog, wasted no opportunity to attempt another infestation of her house.

"This little fellow will be just the thing to take your mind off the nasty specimens someone keeps sending you," Dave said, adroitly avoiding her eyes. He gestured to the guards. "Take those cat groceries into the kitchen." The two men tramped through the living room past Annabelle. "And since you won't be able to settle Hotspur in yourself today—he has a Shakespeare name, you see, so he'll be right at home here—I've brought along some cat-sitters." Now he met her eyes. "And"—he drew a great breath, in preparation for delivering the clinching argument—"with the way things have been going here, I thought it would be a good idea to install a couple of guards on the property. The kitten will keep them busy. Take a deep breath before you say no. This litter has seven other little furballs that I'll have to give away, and I don't have that many friends. In fact I . . . well, never mind that."

"Dave . . ."

"You won't regret this," he declared happily, and placed the kitten on the cool tile floor. It promptly squatted, without conscious irony, and created a small yellow puddle on the floor.

"See what I mean?" Dave said, nodding to himself, apparently pleased with his forethought. "The guards can get busy right away. By the way, their names are Tony and George. They already had names when I picked them up, or they would be out of Shakespeare too. Annabelle, you've got that 'no way' look on your face."

"Hotspur can stay today, but I can't keep him."

Dave lowered his eyes. She had used the kitten's name. It had been a stroke of genius on his part to name the cat. Now she was stuck with it. And the guards were inside the house without an argument. Two birds, one stone.

Annabelle shook her head and turned to go to the kitchen.

Dave whistled, but she kept walking.

Her dress, vibrant orange swirls on a deep red background, left her tanned back exposed down to her waist, without so much as a strap to interrupt that vision of healthy skin. The full skirt swished around her knees provocatively, and Dave wished fervently that they were merely going to Key Largo as planned, without the diversionary trip he now proposed to lay out for her. He did not want Berlin to see this dress. It would just complicate things.

Dave followed her to the kitchen, where she was putting a cup into the dishwasher, having stepped around the guards. She looked up at him, her hair falling over her shoulders. *She's so pretty,* Dave thought.

"Change of plans, my dear," he signed. "Beckworth called to say there's a meeting with the NRC he wants us to be present at. I've alerted Arantxa, who thinks she's the secretary for all seasons and is getting very uppity. She actually sassed me on the phone. She'll meet us at the reactor."

"Arantxa, the pearl of great price," Annabelle said.

"What's that from?"

"The gospel according to Matthew," she answered, "Or *The Scarlet Letter*, take your pick. Hawthorne, of course, was quoting, but the context is nice. Hester's child, Pearl, was something like Arantxa, innocent and original but very much her own woman."

Annabelle's secretary had mastered a system called real-time stenography, using a twenty-three-key computerized stenotype machine and her own system of shorthand. Arantxa could capture up to two hundred sixty spoken words per minute, with a 98 percent accuracy rate. The words would be printed out on the screen of a laptop computer for Annabelle, only seconds after the words had been uttered. The technology had been pioneered in courtrooms so that deaf people could participate fully in their trials, but Arantxa had adapted her own symbol system to the technology, and she often worked with Annabelle in situations where many speakers, speaking from many directions, would be contributing.

"I think I have a picture of this meeting before it even happens," Annabelle said. "A bunch of suits from Washington coming to wave their paperwork around and make disapproving bureaucratic faces."

"As long as they don't wave snakes, they can make any faces they like, as far as I'm concerned. Before we go, I'd better tell you about my adventures last night."

She raised an eyebrow. "Not more snakes, I hope?"

"Not if you don't count Bodorff."

"That guard? The Dick Tracy guard?"

"He's more like Wyatt Earp, I've decided. More on him in a minute. I won't bore you with the details of how I broke in. Suffice it to say that Jacob was right, as usual. Their security is a brontosaurus. Highlights go as follows: The corpse is still unburied and a reproach to the reactor that employed him. Odd stuff in that Glove Box room, Annabelle. You remember that oily shit on his glasses?"

She nodded.

"Well, it was on his keys, too, and on those scissors. And on the door to a waste chute. I brought back a sample for our lab. He also had a bottle of lidocaine in his pocket."

Annabelle looked a question.

"It numbs. Dentists use it, for example. It really has no effect unless you spray it on the mucous membranes," Dave said.

"Could that have something to do with his cold?" Annabelle asked.

"I doubt it. It would be overkill, if you'll pardon the expression, for something like a sore throat. Also, I tried his key in the vault down there—our number code did not work, which I suppose is reasonable, given the value of the jewels, if I'm right about the jewels being in that vault. Also, and don't laugh, I found a coupon for Lifestyles Condoms. Makes you think, doesn't it?"

Annabelle smiled.

Dave now turned to the guards. "You guys better go outside for a minute." He led them out to the pool area and shut the door. A stern look had descended over his features as he faced Annabelle. "You may have to fire Bodorff, although I hate to make it look like we've found a scapegoat. He was the security guard on duty when Rolly died, but that's not the problem. Last night he was packing a heater on the job, a Smith and Wesson toy. If I didn't want to set you off on a feminist diatribe, I'd call it a girly gun."

Annabelle frowned.

"Yes. Bad news. I told him to come to the office tomorrow to explain himself to you. I imagine you will be a revelation to him, especially if you wear that dress. No doubt he'll tell you all about what a dangerous line of work he's in. He will also tell you that Berlin was still there after Rolly arrived, after ten." Dave held up a cautioning finger. "I am only reporting. Beyond that, he knows nothing. And I mean nothing. Encounters like that make me worry about my fellow man. By the way, I asked, and he uses Trojans. Apparently not his coupon."

"I'll bet he really warmed up to you when you asked him that," Annabelle said with a half smile.

"He looked at me like he was Luke Skywalker and I was Darth Vader's pulmonary therapist." Annabelle scratched her head and narrowed her eyes at this twist of a movie allusion, but Dave sailed on through the sea of his reflections. "But enough of Bodorff—the real gem, so to speak, is yet to come. When I left Bodorff to tend to his light saber, I slipped upstairs into the computer database station. I had some time to kill, and I was all dressed up in my cat-burglar uniform, so I thought I might as well catburgle, no offense to Hotspur. Annabelle, I'm making you an accessory after the fact by telling you this, but I sort of strolled around in the bowels of the database, using a system of homegrown commands that I think you would find mildly amusing."

Annabelle simulated a shocked look.

"Well, how could I resist, with Beckworth's mind so closed to sharing the toys in his sandbox? Anyway, I played around in Rolly's account, and I found—listen carefully now—that Rolly used the database on the fatal night to send electronic mail, all right, but he sent one note, and only one, at ten thirty-one p.m. And he sent forty more at eleven fifty-nine p.m., or at least his account sent them. But he can't have been anywhere near a computer terminal at eleven fifty-nine. The operators in the control room opened the airlock for him a minute or so after midnight."

Annabelle crossed her arms. "Then someone else was using his computer account."

"Yes. But, but, but—people are usually pretty careful about their passwords. I only caught Bertha's because I'm an accomplished sneaking low-down dirty professional snoop. Most people can't pick up a password that fast just from seeing fingers on a keyboard. And I was lucky."

"Dave, you make a lot of your own luck."

"Maybe," he said, rubbing his ear.

"A Cuban cat in the computer system," Annabelle mused aloud, an element of dawning wonder in her voice. "My goodness. Hotspur would be proud to learn the trade from you." She patted his hand where it rested on the counter. "So if Rolly sent one message at ten thirty-one, then only one of those 'free at last' notes that the reactor staff got could have come from him. Who did Rolly send that one to?"

"Account number six-seven-four-one-six-four. That's Bertha's password."

"Golly," Annabelle said.

"Golly indeed. So her version of the note is legitimate; at least it appears to be the only one Rolly could have sent himself."

"So who sent the others at eleven fifty-nine?"

"My guess would be Bertha, since she was the only one who had received Rolly's note earlier. And God only knows why she did it. By the way, what time did your friend Berlin say he left the reactor?"

"He didn't say. But why would he have Rolly's password?"

"That's what I asked myself, so it must be a good question. Since I didn't have a good answer, I ambled over to the reception area, thinking I'd chat with the dosimeter woman about the weather and all and who *she's* been sleeping with, when I was inspired by a thought. What if, like poor Rolly—and now our little friend Hotspur—she occasionally needed to empty her bladder? She was drinking coffee like mad, so I figured it was only a matter of time, and I holed up in that office Beckworth took us to, watching her from the doorway. I had only a ten-minute wait before nature yodeled to her and off she went.

So I left. I simply and merely and openly walked out the front door. Imagine my relief when the portal monitor did not let out a squeak—I'd been awfully intimate with that radioactive corpse. Then I sat in the car and thought it over; it makes perfect sense: They cannot with any conscience do anything at all to make it difficult to escape that place. See my drift? They have to make it tough to get in, right? But what if the reactor did go critical sometime? I think it's like the airlock Berlin showed us on the way to the core—getting out is easy. It *has* to be at a nuclear reactor."

Annabelle was thoughtful. "Getting out of the locked room is child's play, then. If Rolly did have company on that bridge, we only have to worry about how he, or she, got in. And you got in without a key."

"Ah, but I did have a key. I had the blueprint and my tools."

"So you did." She softly kicked the dishwasher door closed and started the machine. She leaned against the door. "You want to know how a snake acquires two heads?"

"Is this a riddle?"

"No. I got a report from Dr. Leonora Hughes this morning on my computer. She's a professor at the University of Florida's College of Veterinary Medicine, and she responded to a query I put up on my electronic bulletin board last night. I printed out her response." Annabelle drew a folded sheet of paper from the pocket of her dress. She spread the paper open on the counter, and Dave leaned on his elbows to read it.

The note said, *It sounds like you've got Siamese twins. They are extremely rare in the snake world, and collectors might pay as much as $10,000 for the juvenile you found. Breeders have tried with only haphazard and minimal success to create them in quantity. The most promising new work looks like the stuff they're doing in Oak Ridge, Tennessee, near the National Laboratory (that's where the Manhattan Project got started, before it was moved to Los Alamos), but most of us in* *the field think the breeders are not so much mastering new techniques as capitalizing on the effects of old or serendipitous radiation. I'd like to see your specimen.*

Dave pushed the note across the counter to Annabelle. "Where are the twins now? Or should I say, where is the twins?"

"Gone. The police vet took them—it."

"Nice." Dave drummed his fingers on the counter. "Nuclear breeding." He pushed his fingers down flat on the counter, struck by a sudden thought. "Somebody would pay ten thousand dollars for that fright?"

"Dave, I had a professor in graduate school who used to say that for every weird thing, there are at least twenty-two people who do it."

"What was the course—Abnormal Psychology?"

She grinned. "Shakespeare. Well, shall we go meet the nuclear feds? It might be fun to watch them turn up the heat on Beckworth and see him fry."

"Perhaps we can even ask them for their recipe."

SIXTEEN

THE WINDOWLESS CONFERENCE ROOM IN THE RING building was lined with potted silk palm trees and plastic philodendrons that Dave thought had come from Kmart's sale center. A huge bulletin board covered one wall, with red letters strung above candid photos of reactor personnel. The letters spelled out OUR NUCLEAR FAMILY.

When he and Annabelle had entered the room, she spent several minutes gazing at the photos. Rolly had figured prominently in the "family," if the numerical instance of his representation in the bulletin board's photos reflected his actual impact on lives at the facility. There was only one photo of Rolly and his secretary together, a photo of the scientist holding the woman's hand over a deep open box of glittering blue stones and grinning madly, as if he were threatening to shove her hand down into the shimmering, radioactive blue stones. Many of the photos had a similar theme: reactor personnel making light of the quotidian dangers that were part of their working world.

A couple of photos of Rolly and Lon Berlin stood out from the others by virtue of their serious tone. These were candid studies of two men working together: sometimes the intensity of their shared probing into the microcosmos of the atom showed in a kind of fanatical concentration; sometimes their apparently mutual coldness showed in a kind of stiffness in their bodies.

Annabelle felt a warm hand on her back, and she turned. Metro-Dade Homicide Captain Paul Diaz smiled at her and led her to a corner of the room, with Dave at his heels.

"I heard about your snake," he said. The smile was gone, and his dark eyes snapped with anger.

"Paul, I don't know where that snake came from, but I've been told it could be a product of something called serendipitous radiation, which I think means unpredicted or escaped radiation. But it didn't have to come from here. Even in my business, we use radiation—microwave fences and so on."

"Maybe. I may be a little behind on all the science here, but there's one thing that you don't have to be a scientist or a mathematician to figure out. The talk all over the nightclubs in Naranja is Rolly Castillo's gambling debts. We also talked to a waitress from that Everglades club, and she says he was in up to his neck. Guys in debt for playing games usually know some pretty heavy types—maybe the type who sends anonymous snakes." He put a hand on her shoulder. "And Rolly Castillo wouldn't be the first man who took suicide as a way of avoiding his creditors."

Annabelle gaped at him. So Henry, blue-eyed Alligator Hole Henry, had lied to her about the gambling. Had offered the lie on a plate, without her even asking.

Diaz tightened his grip on her shoulder. "Annabelle, why the surprise? Do you know something I don't?"

"I think we should pool our information, Paul, but I'm on my way to Key Largo. Can I have Dave call you later?"

He frowned at her. "I think I can tolerate him on the phone. At least I won't have to look at that T-shirt." He turned and walked to the other end of the room, and she followed his progress, trying not to laugh.

"What's the matter with my shirt?" Dave wondered aloud.

Diaz stood at the periphery of the gathering, still frowning.

Four men in dark blue suits sat along one side of two Formica-topped tables that had been pushed together in the center of the room. Beckworth and two other men in white lab coats sat across from them, and Annabelle and Dave took seats at the head of the double table, with Arantxa seated away from the table and behind her employer. The stenotype machine was on a desk beside Arantxa, and a laptop computer was on the table before Annabelle. Diaz lowered himself into a deep leather chair with arms at the other end of the double table, glancing suspiciously around at the other, plainer chairs, obviously not relishing being put in the seat of honor. All participants wore the gray plastic dosimeter badges.

A reel-to-reel audiotape recorder was running on a sideboard under OUR NUCLEAR FAMILY, behind the university president, and a young man wearing a lab coat stood quietly beside the equipment.

Beckworth introduced the suits as commissioners from the NRC and recited their names from a list on the table before him. The ranking commissioner, Christopher Neary, a blond man in his early thirties, had ogled Annabelle in the corridor as she entered the conference room, and he had made a point of gaping ostentatiously at her exposed back.

Dave signed the introductions, which had already appeared on the computer screen, but he added, after Neary's name, "Hormone Man."

"Despite the fact that we have all agreed that Dr. Castillo died by his own hand," Beckworth said with a rigid smile, "Captain Diaz is here officially to observe these proceedings. That is, of course, perfectly in keeping with the reactor's own policy of candor in all things regarding this tragedy. Before we commence, I would like to make you all known to Billy Elmore, here by my side." He patted the white sleeve of the man on his right. "Dr. Elmore runs this reactor with an iron glove, and I must say he can take credit for a tight ship."

Elmore looked embarrassed. His white lab coat covered a poorly fitting brown suit. His thick brown hair curled wispily over large ears, but the poorly matched toupee on the top of his head reminded Dave of cruel jokes he had made in high school when the principal had sported a similarly ill-disguised hairpiece. Dave had capitalized on any excuse to visit the front office: "Is this where I have *to pay* my library fine?" he would ask. "Is this where I come *to pay* for prom tickets?" Not that Dave had ever attended a prom—although he had once rented a green tuxedo on the off chance that he could find some pretty girl as a necessary adjunct to the tux, some game girl who was undaunted by his reputation for rudeness and hideously accurate impressions of people who crossed him, some girl like the young Audrey Hepburn who would see promising royalty under his then froggy exterior. When no such girl came forward, he had made himself a nuisance about the prom tickets, fascinated by his first encounter with a hairpiece.

"We tried to speak with you yesterday, Dr. Elmore," Neary said, "but we were told you were not available."

"Doctor Elmore had been up all night with the, uh, disturbance," Beckworth said before Elmore could open his mouth. "I gave him permission to go home and get some sleep."

"Are you that short on sleep, Dr. Elmore?" Neary asked with peremptory zeal. "Surely an emergency of this nature would dictate your presence here on the job."

Elmore's reply arrived as a surprisingly twangy and slow-going drawl. "I had an asthma attack yesterday. No one is more regretful about that than I am."

Indeed Dave now noticed a Ventolin inhaler clutched in Elmore's right hand, which was resting lightly on the table.

"I can submit a note from my physician if the commission would like," Elmore offered.

"No thanks," Neary said sarcastically. "We have enough paperwork as it is." He ignored Elmore's hurt expression, perhaps, Dave thought, did not even see it, so quickly did he dive his head over the stack of papers in front of him.

"We have your written report on the events of Tuesday morning. As far as the commission is concerned, you and your staff in containment did everything well within safe guidelines, and that's our main, indeed our only, mission here. The NRC has no moral or ethical mandate about how you do your job, so long as you do it safely."

"Well, that's certainly reasonable." Beckworth beamed.

Neary glanced across at the university president.

"It's not reasonable," Neary said unemotionally. "It's the law." Beckworth's frigid smile seemed to thaw across his suddenly flaccid lips.

Under the table, Dave quickly drew his fingers into a fist and his elbow back toward his side, in the athlete's gesture that signified deep agreement with a referee over a disputed call. "Yes!" he breathed, lowering his gaze to the table.

Beckworth bent a basilisk stare on Dave's shining brown hair.

"The questions we hope to resolve this morning," Neary continued, "are those regarding safety procedures here—and we have found them perfectly within the guidelines on our tour both this morning and on other recent visits. And of course the disposal of the body."

"Wait a minute," Dave interjected, looking up from the table. "What about access to the containment pool? Are you saying that's safe?"

Neary consulted the legal pad on the table in front of him.

"Are you the security guy?"

Dave sat forward in his chair.

"Yeah, I'm the security guy. And seated next to me is the security gal," Dave said, ice in his voice. "Those are our official titles, if you're keeping a record. So?"

"So, we have prepared a memo to the university indicating certain lapses on your company's part, certain areas where we think security could be augmented rather significantly," Neary said. "Dr. Beckworth is in agreement with us. We met on the matter early this morning."

"That's great," Annabelle said, putting her hand over Dave's under the table. "If you'll be kind enough to supply us with a copy of that memo, we'll include your recommendations with the report we've already made independently to the university—three times—not only agreeing with your conclusions, but anticipating them."

Surprise now showed on Neary's face. "You already have it in the can on the lax security here?"

"We'll mail you the report," Annabelle said.

"That's very interesting," Neary said, directing a piercing look at Beckworth, who was drawing lines on a notepad, his head tilted, his eyes cast down. Neary shrugged and pointed his pen at Annabelle. "We have your company's security log for the night of Dr. Ruiz de Castillo's death. It seems in order. We'll add to today's record the report of the operator who witnessed the fall," Neary said. He turned to the young black man at Beckworth's right. "You're Phillip Koetzle?"

The control room operator nodded.

"Tell us briefly what you saw," Neary said. "We already have your written statement."

Koetzle took a breath. "It wasn't much. I answered the page from the airlock and asked who it was. I heard Rolly say his name, although he sounded strange, like he had a bad cold. But it was definitely Rolly. I released the airlock door, and he came up in the elevator."

Neary interrupted the operator's narration. "Did you admit anyone else to the containment building that night? What about the other two operators?"

Koetzle shook his head once. "Nobody else came up that night. And I know that the other MPs didn't let anyone in. We were together all night, and when Rolly came up, it was in the middle of our shift—nobody even went for a Coke."

Neary put his hands together on the table, interlocking his fingers to make an *X* of his hands. "So what happened after you released the airlock for Dr. Castillo?"

"I saw Rolly get off the elevator; in fact I think I waved to him, but I'm not sure I remember that. Then, maybe three, maybe four minutes later, I saw him fall through the air, out of the side of my vision. I heard—and the other two ops heard it—a splash and a kind of thud; I guess he hit the side going in. Maybe twenty seconds later we had the hook out and were grappling for him. He was in pretty deep, and it took a while."

Neary interrupted again. "Tell us how long 'a while' is."

"Four minutes. No longer. Then we pulled him out and put him on the deck. By taking turns, we all three had our suits on by then."

"Contamination suits?"

"Yeah."

Dave looked thoughtful.

Annabelle looked up from the computer screen. "Can you tell us if Dr. Ruiz de Castillo was struggling at any point. I mean, when he fell, or in the pool?"

"I can't really tell you much about the fall, it happened so fast," Koetzle said. "I guess the fall was straight and smooth, like a line drawn downward in my peripheral vision. But he never struggled in the water. I was the first one out there, and he wasn't moving at all—not on his own, just with the drift of the water."

"Was Castillo alone when he came through the airlock and into the containment building?" Neary asked.

"As far as I know," Koetzle said. "You're supposed to tell us if you're bringing someone up. He didn't say anything about anyone, and I didn't see anyone else."

"Thank you," Neary said. He took a Xeroxed page from a notebook under the stack of papers. "This is a copy of the suicide note. Everybody here got one of these?"

"Not everyone," Elmore said. "We're pretty sure it went to forty-one people. Just the people with computer accounts."

"What does that mean? For the record today," Neary explained, as if he were going through the motions, having heard this piece of reactor business already.

"Those of us who need computers, scientists and secretaries and administrators and so on, have 'accounts,' a number and a running tally of computer use," Elmore said. "They're not really accounts, not for paying purposes. Just record keeping."

"Okay. So everyone with a computer account got one of these. I frankly don't know what it could be except a suicide note," Neary said, "although that's not really the commission's business. I will say that a suicide here cannot be held as an instance of unsafe practices. That would be like condemning the Brooklyn Bridge because some lunatic chose to jump off it."

Annabelle gestured at the paper Neary was holding. "May I see that?" she asked.

Neary passed it to her, and Annabelle sat back in her chair, frowning at the note.

"What's the matter? You haven't seen it before?" Neary asked.

Dave poked Annabelle, and she looked up to read the screen.

"I've seen it," Annabelle said, barely loud enough to be heard. Dave looked closely at her, wondering what had triggered her curiosity.

"Whose account did this copy of the note come from?" she asked.

"Dr. Lon Berlin's," Neary replied. "Now we come to the matter of the body. It's still reading on the Geiger counter, but the level is extremely low, and we think that the half-lives are such that by Friday you can safely dispose of the remains. The NRC can recommend here, but the university ultimately takes responsibility for the body on Friday. If you do anything with it before Friday, our responsibility will be to slap you with a fine and probably some sanctions."

Beckworth wriggled in his chair. "We won't act before Friday," he said uncomfortably, in a loud voice.

"See that you don't," Neary said. "We know that you'll run into a public relations nightmare if you're thinking of a land burial. A land burial would be perfectly safe, however. But we know all about public relations, so in a spirit of purely professional amity, we have a couple of suggestions, nothing official. Burn it, or bury it at sea. Friday, no sooner." Neary cleared his throat. "Of course you'll consult the widow," Neary said, almost parenthetically. "Now, in conclusion, I'd like to make it clear that the commission's jurisdiction does not extend to investigating the cause or causes of this situation, but we do find the note from Dr. Ruiz de Castillo compelling as it suggests suicide. I believe

Captain Diaz has a statement to make. Keep the tape running."

Paul Diaz had seen a great deal of death, and much more bureaucratic machinery in dealing with it, but this meeting had chilled even his jaded heart. That iceberg from the NRC gave him the shivers. "Metro-Dade Homicide has made a thorough investigation of this death, and we concur with the NRC. We're signing off on death by suicide. In the absence of evidence of foul play, and there is no such evidence, and in the absence of anything to make an accident seem likely, we're satisfied that we need not pursue this matter further. I would like to add, however," and here Diaz bent a meaningful look at Neary, "for the record today, that the police express their condolences to the widow and to Dr. Castillo's colleagues. It was a horrible tragedy."

"Of course," Neary said. "That goes without saying."

"I have a question for the captain," Annabelle said, her eyes on the computer screen.

"Go ahead," Neary said, and he abruptly smiled at her across the table. "Ms. Hardy-Maratos, feel free."

"Paul, what do you think about that urine on the bridge on the third floor? You guys are too good to have missed that."

"Annabelle, we're troubled by it, I guess like you," Diaz said. "But, we've got nothing but zeroes on everything else—like nobody with Castillo, like no sign of a struggle—so we've reluctantly concluded that the doctor wet his pants. It happens."

Neary swept his eyes around the table comprehensively. "Is that all? Does anyone have anything to add?"

There was silence.

"Then we'll need an office with a computer and a printer," Neary said to Elmore. "We'll write this up for you, and we'll prepare a release for the media."

Neary stood, and his three fellow commissioners stood also.

Neary looked at Dave, who had taken the copied memo from Annabelle. "You can keep that copy of the memo," Neary said. "We have others."

"No thanks," Dave said, tossing the paper at him. "I have enough paperwork as it is."

Neary snatched the memo off the table with a cold look. He turned and left the room, his colleagues following. Diaz stayed seated, chatting with Beckworth and Elmore.

As Arantxa gathered her equipment, Annabelle kissed her on the cheek. "*Mis orejas,*" Annabelle said, smiling at her secretary, and pivoting when Dave touched her arm.

"Boy, do we have to talk," Dave signed. "What stung you?"

"The suicide note."

"I can't wait." He made a sweeping gesture, an ironic flourish culled from Fred Astaire's stock, and she preceded him out of the conference room.

She walked with Dave toward the computer room across from the Topaz lab. Behind them Neary called out, "Ms. Hardy-Maratos. One minute, please."

Dave, usually conscious of his obligation to be Annabelle's ears when possible, omitted to mention to her Neary's call, thinking that contributing to the commissioner's emotional stress level through the inconvenience of making him run to catch up might possibly be a moral or ethical victory not within the scope of the NRC.

When Neary did reach them, he put his hand on Annabelle's naked back with a touch of familiarity that almost made Dave grind his teeth.

Annabelle stopped, reading Neary's lips.

"Ms. Hardy-Maratos, I'd like to see that report from your office about the reactor's lax security. I'll be available in about twenty minutes. Will you join me back here?"

"Why?" Dave asked sweetly. "Are you coming apart?"

Neary glared at Dave. "Butt out, Dick Tracy," he snarled.

"Commissioner Neary," Annabelle said in her soft voice, "Mr. Tracy and I have work to do. If you can't wait for us to mail our report, call my office and give my secretary your fax number." She turned away, but as an afterthought faced Neary again. "May I have that memo after all?" she asked.

Neary reached into his jacket pocket and extracted the folded memo. He handed it to her mutely.

Dave took Annabelle's elbow tenderly and theatrically in his grasp and led her into the computer room, closing the door behind him with a snap. They sat next to each other at a terminal, while Dave logged on, using Bertha's password. He pulled up the directory of her electronic mail. Facing Annabelle and pointing at the screen, Dave said, "What have you got?"

"I think I know for sure who sent those forty messages at eleven fifty-nine."

"Who?"

"The best secretary at the reactor."

Dave wrinkled his forehead. "Yeah, she's the most likely one to have Rolly's password, but what makes you grin like that?"

"Am I grinning?" Annabelle grinned. "Dave, whoever sent the forty notes corrected the punctuation from the original."

"What?"

"Look at the one in Bertha's computer memory," Annabelle directed.

Dave used the keyboard to call up the memo: *I'm free at last, I'm free at last, Oh, God, I'm free at last. rrc.*

"That's the one that Rolly must have sent at ten thirty-one, the original. We know the one to Bertha's account went out first," Dave said. "What's wrong with the punctuation?"

Annabelle held out the memo that had come from Lon Berlin's computer mailbox. Dave smoothed it out flat on the table. He read: *I'm free at last; I'm free at last; Oh, God, I'm free at last. rrc.*

"Bertha's copy has commas where the one from Lon's computer has semicolons," Annabelle said. "The copy Neary had, the one that came from Lon's account, reads, 'I'm free at last semicolon I'm free at last semicolon Oh comma God comma I'm free at last period.' And then the initials. 'I'm free at last' is an independent clause, which should take a semicolon, or a period. Bertha knows her stuff. The later messages are all grammatically correct."

"Wow," Dave said. "She must have read her mail from home that night, because she sure didn't read it here at the reactor. The log doesn't show her on the premises." He rubbed his ear. "She didn't have much time to decide what to do. To make it go out on Rolly's account, she'd have to retype it after logging on with his password. She must have corrected the punctuation subconsciously. And, at eleven fifty-nine, she must have just hit the 'all' button when she was prompted to give the address of the recipients. If she waited any later than midnight, the other forty notes would have a date different from the one she got. Everybody getting that note in the electronic mail—their indexes would show only the date, the first seven characters and Rolly's initials. It's like the system we use. The individual indexes do not give the time the message was sent, but they give the date. Bertha did not care to risk simply destroying the one she got, the ten thirty-one note, because, as anybody with common sense knows, they have a record of transactions in the database itself. Nice, very nice."

"See?" Annabelle said, pressing keys to return to the index of mail in Bertha's file. "Next to each numbered message are the first seven characters of the piece of mail. Like here," she said, pointing to the first one, which said, *Bert: p.*, "Each space counts as a character." Annabelle scrolled down the index, stopping at the nineteenth item.

"Here's the suicide note," she said. " 'Free at'—the computer doesn't care how the message is punctuated. You could punctuate a message with asterisks or square-root signs—what do they call those? Radicals? What the computer does care about is which account sent the note. See? Next to Rolly's note will always be Rolly's initials, the seven characters, the date. Hah! But not the time!" Annabelle looked at the index. "I wonder why she's still keeping the note. Perhaps because it was the only genuine one."

"Well," Dave temporized, "we'll have to find out if anyone else here is a punctuation freak—as much as you and her—but I'll bet a hundred bucks you've got her." He frowned. "But now we have to figure out why she did it."

Annabelle rested her hands on the keyboard, lost in thought for a moment. "Rolly typed that message to her. On his account. Nobody could erase the transaction from the database. When Bertha received the note, she sent it to everyone else so that it would not appear—ever, anywhere—that she was the only one who knew what he was up to, or that she had any special knowledge about Rolly's plans at all. Dave." There was excitement in her voice. "When Bertha saw that note in her electronic mail, she thought Rolly was leaving. Really leaving. Leaving the reactor. Free at last. I think she knew he was skipping out." Now Annabelle fairly crowed, "No way is this a suicide note. Rolly sent it to Bertha, and Bertha only. It's a personal note. He was getting free of something she knew about." Annabelle's eyes grew wide. "Dave, the gambling debts."

"Even I might go to Haiti if I had gambling debts I couldn't pay."

"If I'm right, and Bertha understood that note all along, and then Rolly ended up in the pool, she might have believed Rolly changed his mind and killed himself over his troubles. So she may not really be a liar."

"No," Dave said with a look of disgust. "She's just a trickster, playing around with other people's secrets. Such nice friendly, open folks they have working here," Dave said. "Maybe when I'm sick of working for you, I'll apply for a job here as an arsonist or a pickpocket."

Annabelle scowled. "Know what, Dave? I just realized something. At eleven fifty-nine Bertha was busy—frantic probably—getting this note to everyone. At least we know she wasn't murdering anyone. This is her alibi."

The door opened behind them.

Lon Berlin gazed at Annabelle's back. The reflection on the terminal screen of the opening door caused her to turn. She smiled.

"Are we still on for tonight? The Tropical Grill?" he asked.

"Whoops," she said, looking at her watch, which said 11:25. "We're off to a late start for Key Largo. I don't know when we'll be back. Probably too late for dinner."

Dave smiled happily, his lips pursed, nodding in agreement.

"Why don't I meet you down there?" Berlin suggested. "I know a great place in Islamorada."

"That's a good idea," she said, standing and smoothing her skirt. "You still want to try for eight o'clock?"

"Eight o'clock's fine. Can I pick you up somewhere?"

"How about the dive shop you told us about? Killilea's."

"I'll be there at eight," Berlin said. He glanced at Dave, who sat so still he appeared to have been stuffed. "Annabelle, can I speak to you alone for a minute?"

"Don't mind me," Dave muttered. "I was just going anyway." He logged off the computer and stepped into the hall, closing the door behind him with such slow deliberation that it was almost as definitive a gesture as a good slam.

"Annabelle," Berlin said, putting his hands on her arms, "that is the most stunning dress on the planet. You are the loveliest woman on the planet. Are you even from this planet? I will not be able to concentrate all afternoon, and I meant to keep looking into that spreadsheet Dave found. Ah, the smile you are now wearing is a fitting match for that dress. You look radiant, and I hope it was something I said."

"Yes, it was something you said," she admitted. "But it's also something Dave and I just figured out. I feel the small satisfaction of eking out progress in increments of rational application. Science, Dr. Berlin."

"What have you and Dave figured out?"

"My dear Dr. Berlin," she said, running a finger along the open collar of his shirt, "the nature of the red herring."

SEVENTEEN

ON THE WAY TO KEY LARGO DAVE HAD SAT BESIDE ANNA-belle in gloomy silence, listlessly counting mile markers. Not even Annabelle could turn this crappy road into a death-defying spin on the edge of eternity. Dave found himself glancing from time to time at her as she steered the convertible down the straight confines of the claustrophobic stretches of U.S. 1 in the upper Keys. She looked antsy.

By twelve thirty they had crossed the drawbridge that took them into Monroe County and the Conch Republic, so named when the Florida Keys had "seceded" from the United States in the early 1980s in a mock rebellion that was nonetheless genuinely furious, even given its purely symbolic nature. The citizens of the Keys were outraged over a new drug-enforcement policy that enabled their cars to be searched, without a warrant, without even probable cause—by police looking for drugs—when they crossed onto mainland Florida to do their shopping or attend a ball game.

Dave thought the mile markers measured intensity of

commitment to the gentle ideals of the new republic—which seemed to consist mainly of drinking rum and relaxing and fishing—as much as they measured distance. The farther they got from Miami, the keener became the burning civic duties: diving into a piña colada and allowing the gentle rays of the warm sun to hypnotize the enlightened citizen into a serene acceptance of his fellow travelers in the republic.

People who traveled regularly in the Conch Republic—that warm and friendly chain of coral islands that stretches south and west of mainland Florida into the Gulf of Mexico and culminates in Key West, the spiritual home and capital of the republic—used the mile markers on U.S. 1 as their reference points and as their barometers of personal tension. Mile-marker zero stands at the southernmost point of Key West, the island city where many had found absolute zero on the tension scale, a coincidence of space and mind that had turned the town into a magnet both for exhausted people and for bums of all descriptions.

Annabelle had pulled the red convertible off U.S. 1 just past mile marker 104 on Key Largo, site of the Caribbean Club, which claimed to be the location where the Bogart/Bacall classic noir film *Key Largo* had been made. The truth of that claim mattered to film and geography buffs—and to Dave the Monkeyman, who had received his education in Americana from its films—but it hardly mattered in the republic, where fantasy was supposed to merge with reality, where the powder-blue waters looked bluer and better than the retouched photos sold in the Keys, where a Beach Boys song about mythical Kokomo was as powerful as planning and zoning commissions, where a Jimmy Buffett tune was the creed, and where islanders repeated apocryphal-sounding true stories about tourists who came for the weekend and stayed for the rest of their lives.

Mile marker 104 was also the local address for the Ugly Pelican, which since the forties has been a fisherman's bar, seedy, dark, and comfortable. The bar still flourished among a certain older segment of islanders, but the Ugly Pelican had added a terraced restaurant overlooking the Gulf and serving the kind of food that Dave called nouvelle healthy. Annabelle had never much liked the place when it had been home exclusively to hard-drinking fishermen—her father for one—but she had grown fond of the new open-air Terrace Grill, with its already-legendary slow waiters and its unmatched views of the Gulf. The celebrated slow service was part of the mystique of the Ugly Pelican; in fact, with 104 miles yet to go before reaching *mañana*-land, the Nirvana of Key West, diners here had no choice but to sample the slower rhythms of the Keys, to turn their frenetic minds and bodies over to these tropical-shirted manipulators of the space-time continuum.

Dave, however, was a hard case, and he was growing increasingly irritated by the frequent and prolonged disappearances of their waiter.

"God, I wonder if they make the waiters here take IQ tests," Dave signed. "How long can it take to find out what the soup of the day is? And don't you think that's the sort of thing the waiter would just know?"

Annabelle sighed, sliding down in her lawn chair and closing her eyes, her legs stretched out and her ankles crossed, her elbows resting on the arms of the canvas chair, her head back against the cushion.

"Dave, I always forget how impossible you are in this restaurant."

"Well, it's very unfair of you to close your eyes like that—you can't tell when I'm complaining about anything." Dave cracked his knuckles and looked toward the kitchen, apparently undismayed at losing his audience. "And I ordered iced tea hours ago." He held his watch to his ear and shook the timepiece. "My watch must be broken. According to its lying face, we've only been here twenty-five minutes." He slewed around in his chair again. "Ah, here comes Einstein now."

The waiter, wearing a black shirt with rows of pink flamingos, stopped to adjust an arrangement of red ixora flowers on a neighboring table, then ambled rather aimlessly to Dave's side.

"Avocado peppercorn, with a garnish of nasturtium petals," he drawled. "It comes with warm lemon-dill bread and zucchini spears."

"No wonder you couldn't remember all that," Dave said scathingly. He tapped Annabelle's bare arm. She opened her eyes lazily.

"Have the soup, my dear," he signed. "It's chicken barley with whole wheat toast."

"Whatever," she murmured lazily, and closed her eyes again, savoring the breeze blowing steadily in from the Gulf.

Dave ordered the avocado soup for them both, and the waiter departed. A ceiling fan clacked softly overhead.

"I wish I smoked cigarettes," Dave said to himself. "I need a nervous habit."

He rose from the chair and strolled to the salmon-colored stucco half-wall, leaning his elbows on its pleasantly rough ledge. Between him and the water was a jungle of yellow and red crotons, growing with lush abandon among the deep-green sea grape hugging the gentle slope of the island. A couple of jet skiers disturbed the limpid water, and a huge yellow butterfly floated among the crotons. Otherwise his vista had a mattelike, static quality. But Dave's thoughts were busy.

The NRC and the Metro-Dade cops and the university have all convinced themselves that Castillo threw himself from the bridge into the reactor pool, he thought. *I don't believe that, and Annabelle doesn't believe that. From the operator's description, I don't think Castillo was even conscious when he went into the pool. And I don't believe any scientist, especially one who fancied himself with women, would choose to make his final exit via an extremely painful and disfiguring atomic furnace.*

I seem to not *believe and* not *think a number of things—that's very negative. What do I have that's positive?*

For one thing, Rolly and Bertha seem to have traded salvos in a war of nerves over sloppy record keeping on his part and sleeping around on hers. And his farewell message to her was an announcement that he was free of something, maybe the gambling debts, meaning that he had found a way to get his hands on some money. What else? Bertha, in an excess of guilt and self-involved contravention of the cause of justice, had made a copy of the message and sent it to everyone over his initials, apparently in an attempt to cover her own knowledge of what she thought was his imminent escape from the scene. Or her involvement in any other of his peccadilloes.

And providentially, and probably with blind innocence, she had provided herself with an ironclad alibi.

As for Rolly's peccadilloes, what in the hell was he doing with oil or grease all over himself? What had he been doing with those big scissors? Where was his dosimeter, dosimeter number 317? Had he been having an affair with the university president's wife? Why was he planning a one-way visit to Haiti, of all the places in the world? If he had put his hands on some money, why not Paris? Or Rio? Or anywhere but the squalor and dangers of Port-au-Prince?

And what was Lon Berlin really doing at the reactor that night? He had told Annabelle that story, probably true, about his daughter's birthday, but faxing hadn't taken him all night, and he had still been there when Rolly arrived.

Dave heard the waiter clinking dishes at the table, and he turned. Annabelle was sitting up, watching Einstein place huge blue soup bowls on white plates—and that's when Dave made the connection. Blue bowls. Blue. Blue.

He almost hopped to the table.

He grabbed Annabelle's wrist and shook it. She widened her green eyes, startled.

"Christ in a cardigan, the topaz! Rolly going to Haiti has something to do with all that radioactive topaz, not with his stupid marriage. We've been staring into a smokescreen. This whole death-suicide-accident-tragedy hocus-pocus, dare-we-call-it-murder, has something to do with those pretty blue baubles."

Annabelle dropped her spoon, so brisk was Dave's jiggling of her wrist. "Dave," she breathed. "Okay. I get it. But . . ."

"You need not point out that I can't explain what the hell this means. You may simply congratulate me on making the connection," Dave said, dropping her wrist and seating himself.

She gazed at the table for a long moment.

"Dave, listen to this," she said, gesturing with her spoon, which she had retrieved from the table. "Say you're a scientist. Say you work with that beautiful topaz every day. What do you think about all those lovely blue stones?"

Without hesitation Dave said, "Stealing them."

He sipped his soup. "Without a question. Stealing them. Anybody would, like bank tellers who touch money all day. But thinking about it doesn't mean you do it." He waved a crust of lemon-dill bread in a random gesture toward the Gulf. "Necessarily."

"Well, say you're a scientist who has thought about stealing the stones, and say you're also a scientist whose accounting procedures are irregular."

"I might be acting on my greedy thoughts if I were such a scientist," Dave said, a thoughtful look on his face. "But what if I do steal them? Wouldn't I be the first one suspected? And here's another good one, as long as I'm at it: Where do I unload the stones? I can't just have a yard sale or put up a stall at the local flea market. Probably wouldn't get a good price for them, if you know what I mean. This soup is excellent."

Annabelle sipped the soup absently. "Let's say you're a scientist whose yard sales have been a flop. What do you try next?" She broke a crust of bread from the loaf. "Let's say I actually have a list of people who deal in topaz—mines and jewelers, a list like the one in Bertha's computer. Know what I might try?"

Dave lowered his spoon slowly to his bowl. "You

might try making a deal with someone on that list. Especially if some gambling types had you by the balls." He closed his mouth, clipping off that last word. "Or whatever."

Annabelle smiled. "I might just try to sell those pretty stones. That topaz, after all, is much more valuable after it's been treated. Those scientists are creating value. There might be a deal there."

"There's one thing wrong with this brilliant theory, Annabelle," Dave said, his disappointment clearly written on his face. "There aren't any stones missing."

"Oh, yeah? Maybe Bertha had some thoughts to the contrary. Maybe that's what she meant in her snotty note about his numbers being off. And remember that spreadsheet?"

Dave nodded.

"Well, remember that Lon told me the reactor has no account called Anhinga," she said triumphantly. "What if that's a dummy account holding the topaz to be swiped? What if it holds stones Rolly siphoned from legitimate accounts?—Dave, *new* accounts, because nobody would know about stones missing from them for years, because it takes years for the reactor to release irradiated topaz."

Dave sat back in his chair, nibbling on bread. He closed his eyes, picturing the numbers on the spreadsheet. He opened his eyes and sat quietly for a moment, gazing across the Gulf, nodding.

"What if Rolly was a thief?" Dave rubbed his ear. "What if Rolly stole millions in stones? How could he possibly get radioactive stones past that portal monitor? And who would push him into the reactor pool over such a theft?"

"Maybe he was pushed because he was stealing the topaz, or maybe he was pushed *for* the topaz." She paused, watching a yellow butterfly hovering over a red nasturtium petal in her soup. "But, you know, it is possible that a theft of highly radioactive topaz, fresh from the pool, could provide an awfully good motive for murder, even for someone who didn't want the stones."

"Motive for whom?"

"Well, Lon Berlin, for one," she said. "Don't look at me like that, Dave. I'm only thinking out loud. He wouldn't stand for a partner who was compromising his own project and his own integrity. And there's Beckworth. A senior research scientist and tenured faculty member stealing on the university's turf and from the university's service-income records? Beckworth might actually breathe fire for that."

"Oh, God, I hope it's Beckworth," Dave said gleefully.

"It could be Elmore. His asthmatic absence from the reactor on reckoning day might mask a multitude of sins."

"Sins? I wonder if you're getting religion." One of his rare philosophical moods descended over Dave. "As a lapsed Catholic, especially a lapsed Cuban Catholic, I can tell you that I sometimes worry that religion will get me first. I never feel really free."

A pelican swooped across the powder-blue water, skimming a long line on the surface.

"Dave, Rolly must have been some wily mathematician."

"You know, Annabelle, you have a really suspicious mind, even a criminal mind. And have you noticed that, unlike the widow, whose list of suspects includes two women, yours includes only men? You may be a girl chauvinist pig."

She snorted. "Let's pay the bill and get out of here, that is, if we can get the waiter to make a return visit sometime today."

"I'll bet you a hundred dollars I can make him appear immediately."

"That's crazy. He won't be back for at least another twenty minutes."

"Wanna bet?"

"I don't want to take your money, Dave."

"Is it a bet?"

"You're on. But he has to be here within fifteen seconds." She consulted her watch. "Go."

Dave picked up his empty soup bowl and dashed it onto the concrete floor. The crockery shattered in a spectacular explosion of sounds that rent the soft stillness of the air.

"Oops," he said. "So careless. Oh, dear, oh, dear, I'm so ashamed."

Their waiter and a couple of busboys hurried to their table.

"*La cuenta, por favor,*" Dave said. "The lady will pay."

Annabelle glared at Dave.

"I'll get you for this," she said.

EIGHTEEN

THEY LEFT THE UGLY PELICAN, BUT BEFORE THEY RE-sumed their drive, they checked the convertible for wildlife. The only foreign presence was a golden butterfly on the warm red hood of the car.

Jimmy Killilea's dive shop was just a few yards south of mile marker 100. The familiar red and white dive flag was painted on the white stucco northern wall of the shop; PRO DIVE CENTER was lettered across the flag in black. Annabelle parked the convertible next to a dark Ford Taurus and got out, tossing her sunglasses onto the hot and dusty dashboard.

She stood under a sign hanging over the door from thick ropes. It said,

KILLILEA'S OF THE KEYS
WHERE THE $MART $NORKEL
PADI TRAINING PROGRAM
DIVE THE REEF

Under her feet was a mat with a woven straw parody of *American Gothic*, the farmer holding a pair of fins and his wife holding a mask. Above the couple's heads it said, "If we're not home, we've gone diving."

Dave tapped the mat with the toe of his shoe.

"Very tasteful," he signed. "I'm thinking of buying one for my office."

Annabelle twisted the knob on the door and walked into the shop. The seashell chimes that clinked upon her entrance were lost on Annabelle, but Dave gave them a glance.

The shop's merchandise was scanty, with very little diving gear for sale, but cameras and reef maps were amply supplied, along with books for experienced underwater photographers and advanced divers. Posters lined the wooden walls, posters of dive sites in Australia, Hawaii, the Keys, the Caribbean, Micronesia, and the "hot" wreck dives off New Jersey's coast. Under a stenciled banner reading EXCITING NEW SCENERY FOR WORLD-CLASS DIVERS, two posters in exotic color were tacked to the wall.

"Look at these," Dave signed, but Annabelle was already walking over to the scenes from Sri Lanka. In the pictures men in loincloths sat on the ends of wooden poles in shallow water, and the captions said "Stilt Fishing on the South Coast" and "Stilt Fishers—an Ancient Economy Above the New."

"Sure looks uncomfortable," Dave said.

A tall blond woman, tall enough to play for the Miami Heat, Dave thought, lifted a swing counter gate and stepped into the front of the shop. She was wearing loose-fitting shorts and a super-large white sweatshirt, but her rippling muscles were poorly disguised. She was perfectly tan, with improbable muscles—steroidy, like a lifeguard on a cruise liner, Dave thought. Or a doorman at the Pink Building.

"Hi there," she said. "You guys interested in foreign dives? I can get you just about anything, anywhere."

"Excuse my ignorance," Dave said, "but I never heard of Sri Lanka being a hot dive."

"Oh, that's pretty new," she said. "I just got those posters in. That's a dive site mainly for the U.S. Geological Survey and for the Sri Lanka National Aquatic Resources Agency, so far. But a lot of pro divers I know are really excited about Sri Lanka—they've discovered incredible mineral sands—monazite and uranium, thorium too. And the copper deposits produce a really weird color. I've got photos, if you want to see them."

"Uranium?" Dave asked.

"Sure. Those are some pretty special diving conditions. I'm one of the few civilians who's dived those sands, but there will soon be a lot more, I can tell you that."

"I'll just bet," Dave said, his eyes large. "My goodness gracious. I've forgotten why we're here."

Annabelle put out her hand and said, "You'll have to excuse my friend Dave; he's a little gun-shy about uranium."

The two tall women shook hands, Annabelle finding it necessary to bend her neck back in order to make eye contact with this giant.

"I'm Annabelle. We're looking for the owner, Jimmy Killilea."

The blond woman smiled, showing perfect white teeth.

"I'm Jimmy. Yeah, I know, everyone expects a man.

It's my mom's fault for hanging 'Jemima' on me at birth. What can I do for you guys?"

"Is there any uranium around Haiti?" Dave asked.

"There ain't nothing worth nothing in Haiti, man." Killilea smiled and led them to several short wooden crates, placed on end by the counter. On the wall were three framed certificates, indicating that Jimmy Killilea was an instructor with rating from the National Association of Underwater Instructors, the Neptune Association of Scuba Educators, and the National Association of Scuba Educators.

"This okay?"

"This is just dandy," Dave said.

Annabelle rarely felt dwarfed by other women, but the shop's owner towered over her. Annabelle sat down, craning her neck to keep her eyes on the woman's face. The woman seemed to sense Annabelle's perspective, and sat, leaning back against the wall, her long legs stretched out in front of her.

"We'd like to talk to you about Rolando Ruiz de Castillo," Annabelle said. "We're looking into his death on behalf of the university. I understand you were his dive partner."

"Yes, I was," she said, and a look of what appeared to be genuine sadness spread over her face. "Rolly was one of the best divers in the world. Absolutely cool, totally dependable. Many times I've trusted my life to him. That's really bullshit what happened at the reactor."

"How do you mean?" Annabelle asked. "By the way, I'm quite deaf, but I read lips very well, so if you'll just face me when you speak, I'll be able to keep up."

"No problem. I can actually do some sign if you like,"

she said, signing her offer. "It's really useful on dives. You'd be surprised how many handicapped people get into scuba diving. It's a freer world down there for a lot of them, if they know what they're doing. Maybe you know something about that."

"A little," Annabelle signed. "What's 'bullshit' about the events at the reactor?"

"That suicide baloney. I would have known if Rolly was like that. You guys dive together?"

Annabelle nodded.

"Well, then you know what I mean about knowing your partner," Killilea said. "You get to know your partner's character pretty well on dives, especially their impulses, and suicide is an impulsive action, I think. Besides, Rolly was in top spirits. The best mood he's been in for a while. Like a weight had been lifted off his shoulders."

Dave looked at Annabelle and then at Killilea.

"Have the police talked to you?" he asked.

"Yeah. But I don't know if they listened."

"What did you tell them?" Annabelle asked.

"That I'd last seen Rolly on Sunday, on a dive to Pickles Reef. That's about it. Also that he seemed in good spirits and good health. That he didn't commit suicide. Just like I told you."

"Pickles Reef?" Dave asked. "Isn't that kind of an amateur dive?"

"Yeah. That was a little strange for Rolly, such a shallow dive. It's only about sixteen or twenty feet, so I wasn't much interested in going down with him. I just took him out in the boat. Rolly didn't need a partner at only twenty feet with almost no current."

"That was the day before he died. Was there anything

unusual about Sunday's dive, other than the place?" Annabelle asked.

"Not really. It was a night dive because I couldn't leave the shop earlier. But it was purely routine otherwise. Just a dive."

"What could have possessed him to dive Pickles Reef?" Dave asked. "Is there a new wreck or something?"

"There's just those old barrels down there," Killilea said. "Since his death I've thought about what Rolly might have been interested in. People say they look like pickle barrels, and I guess they do. The barrels were sunk a long time ago, and they're covered with new coral and so on. But there's no pickles. Rolly knew all that. He didn't even take a camera. Just a light. Those barrels are just full of mortar that was on its way years ago to the forts in Key West and the Dry Tortugas. It's about two miles south of Molasses Reef—from the air that reef looks like spilled molasses—which is probably the most dived reef in the world. Pickles is just a curiosity, not all that popular. But maybe Rolly just wanted some variety. My other boat is out there right now, over Pickles. In fact with a diver who knew Rolly a little from a couple of dives. They came down together once or twice."

"Could you take us out there?" Annabelle asked. "I'd like to see the site of Rolly's last pleasure trip."

Killilea considered Annabelle, studying her eyes and the set of her mouth. "Do you think he killed himself?" she asked.

"No. I think that's bullshit too," Annabelle said emphatically.

"Then I'll take you out. You guys got gear?"

"In the car," Annabelle said.

"One more question," Dave said. "Do you have any ideas about why anybody would have killed Rolly?"

Jimmy shrugged. "Rolly had a life like anybody. Life. The Job. The Wife. He had all the usual crap. The police asked me the same question. So did a woman from the *Miami Herald*. But my motto is, Don't answer questions with more than you know, and don't ask questions if it's none of your business."

Annabelle put her hands together in her lap and looked around the shop. A ceiling fan rotated overhead.

"Did Rolly ever talk about his wife?" Dave asked. "Unless it's none of my business."

Killilea shook her head. "No problem. You guys are okay. Yeah, he talked about her some. She was a neatness freak. His house was practically sterile, he said." Killilea smiled in reminiscence. "She tried diving once, but she didn't like the ocean—said it was too messy. I don't guess, though, that was the only thing wrong with their marriage. I guess she thought some other stuff was messy too." She smiled again. "You asked."

"Can I be blunt?" Annabelle said.

"Are you going to ask about whether he was having an affair with that Dr. Prendergast woman, the school president's wife?" Killilea reached her right arm over the counter and pulled a photograph from where it had been taped to a drawer. She handed it to Annabelle.

Dave looked over Annabelle's shoulder. The picture showed Castillo with his arm around a rather horsy brunette, with teased hair and long nails. They were standing in front of the shop. Annabelle turned it over to look at the date: *Sept. 15, 1997.*

"The police asked me about this," Killilea said, "and

the easiest way to answer was show them that snap. I guess there's no secret about it. And this way, showing this picture, I don't have to answer with more than I know."

Dave took the photograph from Annabelle and walked over to the door to get more light. When he returned to the counter, he handed the picture back to Killilea.

"What can you tell us beyond the photo's obvious message?" Dave asked. "What did you tell the police?"

"Just the truth. He showed her a good time on Molasses Reef on a couple of dives. And then he porked her. He told me he didn't respect her as a diver, though."

"Maybe she was the woman scorned," Dave mused aloud. "Well, I certainly wouldn't respect her either."

"God, Dave," Annabelle gasped. "You're such a prude. Since when are you the Moral Police?"

"Oh, I'm a recent self-appointee to the force," he replied. "Did you get a good look at that picture?"

Trying to hide a grin, Killilea handed the picture back to Annabelle. She held it at an angle to eliminate the glare on the glossy surface.

"Oh," Annabelle said.

High on the side of Dr. Prendergast's fleshy left buttock, exposed and cupped by Castillo's hand, was a dainty oil drawing of a Christ figure with outspread arms. A Key Largo house painter had developed a lucrative side-trade among tourists eager for his body paintings, but this imitation of the statue of Christ of the Abyss—a nine-foot-tall bronze structure standing on a concrete pedestal in twenty-five feet of Key Largo's blue waters—was not among the artist's standard work, according to Killilea.

The tiny oil drawing struck Annabelle as both well done and suggestive of the couple's relationship. Or suggestive of what the woman had hoped the relationship would be. The underwater location of the Christ of the Abyss was a frequent site for divers' weddings, and of lovers' pledges.

"Jesus isn't so strange for a proctologist's butt, really," Dave said, with cheery but completely feigned large-mindedness. "Perhaps she is a faith healer."

NINETEEN

THE SUN GLIMMERED IN A SOFT WHITE HAZINESS through the crystal-crisp blue water above them and made Annabelle think of the throbbing blue glow of the reactor's pool as she scanned the surface briefly before following the downline after Dave. Killilea's boat, the *Virgin Spirit,* loomed above them over the north limit of Pickles Reef, poised to eclipse the sun.

Dave waited for her on the floor of the ocean, about twelve feet deep. He signed "south," gestured with his compass, and kicked his fins. Annabelle swam at her leisure beside him, holding back her more powerful kick to stay by his side. It was difficult to smile with a regulator in her mouth, but Dave saw the smile in her shining green eyes when he glanced occasionally at her.

He would never perfectly understand her world, a world without sound, a world without music, a world without the infinite variations of tone that comprised his own corner of the universe. She did not even have a radio in her house, where he had a CD player and Tom Petty and the Heartbreakers. She had lights, where he had a doorbell. She depended on her other senses in unusual ways, where he mostly took his for granted. But down here, even though there was a kind of subtle music to the deep, a music denied to her, he thought he could penetrate her silent cosmos briefly, without the thousands of sensual interruptions of the surface. He felt close to her.

They swam together, almost kick for kick, stopping to examine the scattered, crusted barrels, the homey detritus of military transport ships. The barrels were obviously undisturbed, lying at rest on the white and gray sand in the shallow valleys carved between the coral structures by shifting currents and relentless time. The reef was crowded with vibrant darting hues, flashy darting fish, especially the gaudy parrot fish and the dainty blue snappers with their yellow tails.

"I will not order fish for dinner tonight," Annabelle signed, when they paused to allow a school of glass minnows to sweep before them around a garden of elkhorn coral. A moon jellyfish floated ethereally between them like an undulating nylon window.

They resumed their journey over the barrels, Dave following the course set by Annabelle. She was an expert diver, thoroughly at home, he thought; perhaps she could even forget her handicap here for a time, here in this colorful world that stimulated the eyes and touched the heart. Since they never spoke of her handicap, except as it became a logistical matter concerning them both, Dave was usually on his own when it came to estimating the impact of her loss on Annabelle's emotional world.

Annabelle and Dave swam over the barrels, their pink exposure jackets blending into the communities of colors on the reef. A swarm of glassy sweepers dappled Annabelle's jacket with perfect silhouettes as the silvery fish crossed over the reef above them in the ice-candy-blue water.

Annabelle swept her arms by her sides, gently stopping her forward movement, and the fish shadows slid on without her. She reached for Dave's arm, but he had stopped too. Ahead of them, perhaps by forty feet, a man and a woman were struggling near some of the long-submerged barrels. Several of the barrels were lying on their sides, open and leaking thick black clouds.

The man had his hands full, for the woman, a muscular woman, was obviously an inexperienced diver—alternately puffing on her regulator and holding her breath. But she was also a determined woman, and she was hacking at a barrel, wielding an ugly Tulsa spike knife with strength and skill. The man, who looked to be in superior physical condition, stayed out of range of her plunging knife, but he managed to stalk her somehow like a second self, monitoring her equipment, her situation, ready to take her up—she was in distress, and it was only a matter of time before he would be forced to act.

Suddenly the lid of the barrel popped off, sinking slowly to her feet, and the woman plunged her hands inside, groping wildly.

Annabelle pulled Dave's arm, drawing him through a thick coral archway and into the shadows of that living architecture.

"It's the Alligator Hole owner," she signed. "And the woman in his office."

Dave's eyes were large behind his mask. "She's as big as a truck. An ugly truck."

Signing to Dave to stay where he was, Annabelle

swam behind a spur of the coral forest and approached the struggling couple from the east. From about ten feet off, through a jagged aperture in a wall of coral, Annabelle caught a glimpse of the woman's wild eyes, splotched with angry red behind her mask, which was already partially filled with water.

Finally, the man put his hand over the woman's face from behind and skillfully yanked her regulator from her mouth; in a convulsive movement she dropped the knife. With powerful leg strokes the man began to drag the struggling woman to the surface.

When they were far above her, the woman's frantic movements creating a veiling turbulence in the water, Annabelle swam to the scene of the destruction. Four barrels had been opened, and black ooze seeped and floated from them, forming a dark, dense, waving river in the pale blue water.

Annabelle stuck her gloved hand inside the barrel the woman had opened last. There was nothing but rotted mortar and slime, nothing inside to account for that frenzied search. A fifth barrel lay nearby in this cluster. Annabelle took her own knife from its strap on her inner ankle and approached the barrel. Its lid had been opened recently, she could tell, for the coral encrustation had been neatly cut along the rim. She examined the other opened barrels. They appeared to have suffered only the messy attack of a few moments earlier; none of them showed the tidy seam drawn along the rim of the fifth barrel.

She scanned the water for Dave, at length spotting him overhead, swimming in the shadow of a dive boat on the surface. She turned her attention back to the barrel lying on its side. There was a small graphite *C* sketched on the barrel. She slipped the point of her knife under the lid along the cut seam, pushing down on the haft. The lid popped off in her hand, and she placed it gently down on the sand. She put her hands on the side of the barrel and set it upright. There, resting against the wooden side of the barrel was a plastic sandwich bag holding six blue stones that glittered even here, nearly twenty feet below the surface. She lifted the bag, stunned for a moment, unable to think.

Topaz. It was topaz.

Recovering her wits, she searched the open barrel carefully, digging in the ooze, but apparently the one sandwich bag was the only item of recent vintage. Black muck surrounded her in the water.

With the plastic bag in her left hand, both arms along her sides, Annabelle kicked slowly and evenly, parallel with the ocean floor, moving over and carefully surveying the barrels scattered about the reef. None of them showed the even, cut seam of the barrel she had opened, or the graphite *C*. She gazed around and considered the nature of the coral formations around the site. They were arranged in a loosely organized, unusual diamond shape. An easy spot to identify, she thought, once one knew where to look. She glanced at her watch.

Dave swam into view. She held out the plastic bag, and he reached for it in surprise, astonishment in his wide eyes. He held the bag at arm's length.

Annabelle signed, "Look what Rolly bequeathed to the reef. I think this bag's all there is. I checked the other barrels. At least as well as I could without bringing in a crew."

A silver, flickering wall of French grunts glided by,

and Dave inserted the bag playfully among the fish, dividing the school into two streams, which flowed together once again on the other side of his hand.

"I love the rules down here," he signed. "What a sensible world."

Annabelle gazed at the topaz in his hand amid the school of grunts. "What are we going to do with those?" she signed. "Do we care if Jimmy sees them?"

He considered the stones. "Better not, even if she doesn't ask questions about what's none of her business," he signed, and stuffed the plastic bag into his trunks. He glanced down at the resulting lumpy bulge. "Maybe she'll think I'm John Merrick."

"I can't remember who he was."

"You should watch more movies. He was the Elephant Man."

He and Annabelle checked the compass and headed north, toward the boat.

TWENTY

DAVE HOPPED LIGHTLY ONTO THE PIER AND WAITED FOR annabelle to toss him the stern line. He slipped the looped rope around a metal fastening, and Killilea shut off the engine. She had parked beside her other boat, the *Virgin Queen*, the one that had taken Henry and the woman out to Pickles Reef. The *Queen*'s pilot sat on the dock, swinging his tanned legs angrily. There was no sign of his recent passengers.

Annabelle glanced at the pilot as she handed up her gear to Dave. He reached to help her onto the pier. Killilea vaulted the distance from the stern, landing softly on the concrete dock. She squatted beside the pilot, and they exchanged some quick words. When they had finished, Killilea slapped him playfully on his thick arm. He stood and returned to the *Queen*. Killilea leaned into the *Virgin Spirit* to haul out Dave's oxygen tank.

"They took off right after he brought her up," she said, lifting out the tank. "Henry got her up in plenty of time, and she's okay. She shouldn't have been down there in the first place. I'm surprised at Henry for allowing it."

"She must have been hell-bent on something, to try," Dave said. "Does your pilot know where they went?"

"Sort of. After the woman reamed out my pilot for telling her she didn't belong in the water, she hit him. Fucking hit him." Killilea laughed out loud, throwing her head back. "Fucking slapped him upside his head. *Big* mistake. She said she was sorry, that it was just a reaction to her panic, but he doesn't have to take that shit. He let out the throttle and gave them the ride of their lives, back to Key Largo. They're probably bruised, and I'll bet she's throwing up. They were going to try another dive shop to get a boat to take them back out there." Killilea smiled.

"It ain't gonna happen that way, though," she said. "That woman should never have slapped my pilot—he got right on the radio and spread the word around. Those two creeps will be wasting their time driving around this afternoon looking for another pilot. What exactly happened down there on the reef?"

"Mostly just a lot of flailing around, and not knowing how to breathe with the regulator," Dave said. "I thought you said that guy dived with Rolly."

"He did. I just assumed the woman was okay too. Anyway, it just shows that nobody—I mean nobody—should be down there without training. I don't care who they're with. Or how big they are." She shook her head, her eyes shining with glee. "Stupid bitch."

They walked across the highway, carrying the tanks, and Killilea unlocked the shop while Annabelle and Dave stowed their gear in the backseat of the convertible.

"I followed them up," Dave signed, "when Henry was dragging the ugly woman to the surface. I swear, Annabelle, she looks like a female version of the Incredible

Hulk, only not as cute and not as green. Anyway, I surfaced behind the stern and eavesdropped. He was yelling at her to calm down. I heard him say something about gems, about trying again."

"They knew exactly where to look," Annabelle signed. "Or almost exactly."

"Yeah. Annabelle, at least we confirmed one of our nasty suspicions."

She nodded.

"There *is* topaz missing from the reactor," he said, "even if it's only six stones."

"Well, those two seem to be as curious as we are. I looked those barrels over carefully, and I don't think there's anything else down there." She ran her hands through her wet hair. "Dave, this could be a golden opportunity to go back to the Alligator Hole Cafe. To see their livestock."

After using Killilea's backrooms to shower and change, they left the shop. The small parking lot was empty, except for the convertible, and traffic on U.S. 1 was light. The late-afternoon sun cast deep shadows on the powdery white gravel as they crossed to the car.

"What about your date?" Dave asked. As soon as the words were out of his mouth, he could have bitten his tongue.

"Oh, my God," Annabelle exclaimed. "I forgot that. Go back in and call Berlin. Tell him to meet us at that gravel cut off the Anhinga Trail. Make it seven o'clock."

Mumbling to himself, Dave went in to use the phone. When he returned to the parking lot, he signed, "I hope he gets sick of you jerking him around like this."

They drove north, crossing back into Dade County

just after four o'clock. At Martha's Bait Shop west of Homestead, they stopped to rent a small aluminum canoe and bought some rope to lash it across the back of the convertible. Dave left a fifty-dollar deposit for the boat and bought a couple of Cokes.

The Anhinga Trail was deserted at this hour, and when they spotted the gravel cut and turned off the road, the narrow lane was deserted too. Annabelle drove the car deep into the tall grass. She unlocked the glove box and took out their guns, handing Dave's Colt to him without a word. She slipped her Walther into the deep pocket of her dress.

They carried the canoe and its one paddle to the much-worn muddy spot where the airboat had picked them up the night before and lowered their canoe into the still water. Dave took Annabelle's flashlight from the back pocket of his lime-green shorts and placed it on the floor of the vessel. He stepped into the canoe and sat, grasping a root protruding from the bank to steady the boat while Annabelle climbed in.

He slewed around in the forward seat. "It all looks so different in this light. I may not remember how to get there."

"You'll remember."

He pushed away from the bank and into the river of grass. A fierce look of squinting concentration on his face, he shifted the paddle from his left to his right in smooth, silent strokes. They were accompanied by the knobby spines of occasional alligators, and Annabelle spotted a rare wood stork in the highest limbs of a towering slash pine. Dave once pushed back on the paddle to stop their forward motion in the water. He beckoned over his shoulder to Annabelle. The prehistoric shape of an anhinga was emerging in a black cascade of dripping, matted feathers from the grassy water directly before them. It rose, spreading its dark wings and twisting its long neck around to present its beady brown eyes to them, its sharp yellow beak pointed at them like a knife. The bird dragged itself out of the water and heaved its soaked and heavy wings onto the bank on their right. The anhinga would be there for hours, preening and drying its wet feathers before it could fly again.

They continued through the swamp, Dave steering roughly for the island of slash pines. The water track meandered, and Dave was often forced to look over his shoulder to keep his bearings, but at last they saw the pine shingles and roof of the cafe rising from the swamp ahead of them. He put his hand out and grabbed the crunchy mat of roots under the willow shrub ring, and Annabelle jumped onto the shore. She held the canoe while Dave hopped out, and she dragged the light aluminum shell up onto the bank.

The stilt house appeared to be empty. Nothing disturbed the stillness of the clearing or the silence inside the building. Dave made a quick sign to her that he heard nothing alarming.

He crept slowly up the stairs, and Annabelle stepped into the deep shadows under the house, into the center of the alligator hole.

Now she could see the outlines of a shed behind the house, partly shielded by tall grass and cocoplum. She crossed the hole, approaching the shed, walking carefully over the treacherous, wildly uneven floor of the dry hole.

She stepped up onto the surrounding matted floor of the island, toward the shed.

She walked through the grasses, brushing them aside as she went. She reached out and touched the pine door. It was warm from the slanting rays of the late-afternoon sun. A huge iron padlock hung securely through the slot over the iron staple in the hasp. With the butt of her gun she hammered at the hinged end. Damp pine chips flew out from the old door, and soon the hasp slipped from the clammy wood. She gripped the hasp and gave it a vicious yank, her teeth gritted. The hasp fell drunkenly against the frame of the door, its hinged end swinging free from a rusted nail. She pulled the door open.

It was dank and dark inside, and a cloud of humid air seemed poised inside the door.

She stooped to peer inside, into the only patch of light in the shed, a ragged yellow pool that fell through a crack on the western wall where a couple of the damp boards had separated. She could see the sharp, rectangular outlines of what she thought must be the laser-show equipment Dave had described to her. And closer to the door, in a small fog of sour smells, she could see the blue glint of steel mesh. Behind the mesh, in slow, rippling torpor, skinny and satin-smooth coils threw back the meager yellow daylight that filtered spottily onto the moving puddle of their lethargically twining bodies.

Balancing herself by putting her gun hand on the rough pine frame of the door, she leaned into the shed, trying to sort out the wiggling mass and count the heads. Two of the young cottonmouths were Siamese twins.

Pushing back from the shed, she stood and stretched her arms overhead, wondering at this bizarre juxtaposition of a new technology and an old, old terror. She suddenly caught the acrid smell of cordite and whirled around, snapping off the safety of her gun.

A spurt of brown dust had risen sharply from the dried mud at her feet. A bullet hole gaped in the skull of an enormous cottonmouth stretched toward her along the path she herself had made through the grasses. Dave stood twenty-five paces away from her, his gun held in both hands and aimed at her feet. She thought a wisp of smoke issued from the barrel of the Colt.

"Don't fucking move," he said, his voice shaking. "I don't know if I killed it."

She stared numbly down at the vast and solid length of the snake. "It's dead," she managed to whisper.

Slowly Dave lowered his gun. He sank to his haunches and dropped his sweating brow on his forearms, trembling. Annabelle now noticed, with a numb detachment that made it seem that she was watching a movie, that Dave's shirt was plastered to his thin and heaving sides with sweat.

He stood and came toward her. He pushed the snake's body off the path with repeated shoves from the toe of his shiny black shoe.

"When you stood up, it went for you," he said. "I had only a second to fire." Sweat rolled down his cheeks. "Jesus Christ, Annabelle, I could have killed you."

She took his hand, and they walked back under the stilt house toward the canoe, their guns dangling at their sides.

At the water's edge, she looked back at the cafe.

"It's got an alarm system," Dave signed. "The kind

with an electrical field. I did not touch it. As soon as I saw what it was, I came to find you."

"Thank you," she said simply, but as if from a great distance.

Dave rowed them back through the swamp, Annabelle holding the flashlight over his shoulder. Their progress was sure now, even in the deepening shadows of the gloom rapidly falling over the Everglades. By the time they reached the water end of the gravel cut, it was fully dark, and the moon was a swollen disk rolling up from the eastern sky, its flattened edge seeming to push against the adamant blackness of the bowl of the heavens.

They walked to the car, the gravel crunching underfoot.

Dave reached into the car and turned on the headlights. He tossed his gun onto the backseat. Annabelle threw hers in beside his gun. They moved to the front of the vehicle and stood in the light.

"The Mikosukee knew where to look for the topaz," Annabelle said. "And he's got baby cottonmouths at his hole. There was a cage full of them in the shed."

"Yeah. But why would the Indian kill Rolly?" Dave pulled his shirt up and over his head. He shook it out and used it to wipe his face. "Annabelle, I've been thinking. Even if Rolly was cooking the project's gem accounts, and even if he'd already set up a deal to market his wares—to the Indian, maybe—he still had to get the blue buggers past that portal monitor. You always have to come back to that portal monitor. I don't know what the hell this jump into the reactor pool was all about, unless maybe Rolly meant to jump out a window with the gems and simply mistook his direction when he went into the pool."

"It would certainly fit well with what we know of his eyesight," she said, smiling feebly. Headlights arced across the gravel cut as Berlin's Honda pulled off the highway.

"Here comes your Nazi friend," Dave signed, his hands taking on an eerie yellow tinge in the headlights, the muscles of his face tightening.

Berlin parked next to the convertible, leaving his headlights on. He opened the door and swung his legs out of the car, an angry look on his face.

"He looks like he just got a call from Joe Goebbels, saying the gas ovens are on *der fritz*," Dave said with deliberate enunciation and malicious force.

Annabelle stared at Dave, shocked by the hard glint in his dark eyes. This was not his usual disapproving look. She stepped around her car and touched Berlin's shoulder.

"What's wrong, Lon?" she asked, scanning his angry face.

"Annabelle," Berlin squeezed her hand roughly. "You're not going to believe this, but there's about a half million dollars' worth of topaz missing from the reactor. Radioactive topaz. Newly baked. I discovered the loss myself this afternoon. Whoever has it could be in great danger from the radiation." Berlin put his elbows on his knees and rubbed his temples with his fingers. "I don't know what to do anymore," he declared bitterly.

Annabelle stooped and took his hands away from his face.

"Lon, how did you track this so quickly?" she asked.

"I put the whole damn collection through the robot—our project has a robot. It's really just a pair of metal arms, but it's smart and can sort and count the stones. And I had some help—I used that spreadsheet as a map. I can't even start to believe this, much less figure out where they could be. They have to be somewhere in the reactor—the portal monitor would have gone off big-time—they're the hottest stones we have." He gave her an ironic look. "*Had.*"

"Who else knows about this?" Dave asked, his eyes flinty.

"Nobody yet," Berlin said, "but I've got to tell someone soon. I don't even know whom to tell, if I should go to the police or Beckworth or what. Or the NRC."

Dave stood in thought. "Berlin," he said, "what's the number code for the vault in the glove box?"

"What? I can't tell you that!" Berlin got out of the car and closed the door. "Wait a minute. How do you know about the vault?"

"Give me a break, Berlin," Dave said, curving his lips with nasty scorn. "Hardy does the security out there. We can't do that without a blueprint. That vault is the only place you could store the topaz. Besides," he added offhandedly, studying his knuckles in the headlights, "that room is where you put all your radioactive shit, *pendejo*."

Berlin clenched his fists and took a step toward Dave.

"I ought to hurt you, you little monkey," Berlin snarled.

"Could you, I wonder?" Dave asked, seeming to consider.

"Yeah. I'm a lot bigger than you are." Berlin loomed over Dave.

Since he had shot the snake back at the alligator hole, Dave's spiraling wrathful energy had been aching for an outlet, and this scientist, apparently, was a token gift to Dave from a repentant cosmos.

"Su madre." Dave sneered. "Don't let that stop you—I know a lot more moves. *Me cago en tí.*"

Berlin's right arm twitched. "You started on me the minute we met," Berlin said, and he backed Dave up against the car by flattening his palm on the smaller man's bare chest. "Are you jealous? Is that it, you little fuck?"

"No jodas, hombre de ciencia." Dave spat, and he moved in, aiming a lightning punch at Berlin's left kidney.

Berlin doubled over in surprise and shooting pain.

"Hell," Annabelle said, uncertain of the words they had exchanged, but furious about their grossly obvious body language. Disgusted by this mutual display of macho belligerence, Annabelle reached into the Honda and leaned sharply on the horn.

Both men jumped. They gawked at her from their stiffly held positions.

"You're acting like a pair of tomcats, pissing all over each other and yowling at the moon," she said, acid in her voice. "I ought to toss you some hunks of raw meat. God, sometimes men make me sick."

Berlin stood tensely.

"Me too," Dave allowed sheepishly, relaxing his wiry body.

Annabelle could not resist a small smile.

Berlin straightened slowly.

"Tell Dave the code," she urged.

"What's he going to do with it?" Berlin asked warily, his hand on his back, the dull pain now blossoming out from the sharp stab of the kidney punch.

"What do you think I'm going to do with it?" Dave snapped. "I'm gonna hot-wire your portal monitor, *pendejo*, and return these." He jammed his hand into the pocket of his shorts and tossed the plastic bag at Berlin.

Berlin was slow to react, stunned and disbelieving, and he missed Dave's throw. The bag thumped to the white gravel at his feet, the stones twinkling green, like emeralds, in the yellow headlights.

TWENTY-ONE

"ANNABELLE, CAN YOU CUSS IN SIGN LANGUAGE?"

"Can I, or can anybody?" she asked.

"Anybody, I guess," Berlin said.

They sat across from each other at a weathered redwood picnic table outside Manny Garcia's Dive Inn, a rundown but renowned drive-in seafood restaurant near the bay in Homestead, where they had stopped for a quick meal before heading north to follow Dave to the reactor. Dave had left the Anhinga Trail alone in Annabelle's convertible. In the dark and in the emotionally heated atmosphere, he had forgotten both his shirt and the rented canoe, and their last sight of him had been a pair of thin, naked, very tan shoulders sticking up above the gray upholstery.

"Of course," she said. "Sign is a language, full and complete, including what I consider the necessary blue spectrum. It can be funny to watch when two signers get mad at each other. They start inching farther and farther from each other, the madder they get, because they need more and more room to use larger foul language. It's analogous to raised voices. But when I'm really angry, there's just no substitute for English." She sensed that Berlin wished to avoid topics concerning Dave and the reactor and topaz and Rolly Castillo, and she was relieved to provide something safe. She looked sheepishly across the table at him.

"If this were a full confession, Father Berlin, I'd admit that I can also cuss in four other languages, but English is definitely my best. I've read studies that show most Americans who wouldn't touch a foreign-language class at least know some foreign cuss words. But English is probably the best language in the world for cussing—we have synonyms for everything and great explosive, resonating consonants. I get terrific feedback in my mouth just from forming the shapes of the sounds and from the vibrations. The resources of English can be a shattering linguistic pleasure when you really need them. When you cuss in sign, you have to rely on the strength of feeling in the gesture, really to get the most out of it."

"I feel like cussing," Berlin said. "My plan was to sweep you off your feet, seduce you with fine cuisine, a full moon, generous amounts of wine—all this carefully designed to put you in the mood to go to bed with me." He gestured comprehensively at the parking lot. "Instead I fill you with cholesterol and seat you by a trash can. On the other hand," he said, leering at her, "the moon is undoubtedly full."

The moon was just past the full, but she did not contradict him. "Do you think your plan would have worked?" she asked, tilting her head to one side and sipping white wine from a styrofoam cup.

"Well," he said thoughtfully, but with a broad grin, "if

it hadn't, I'd at least have had a satisfying meal. I like plans that give me only winning options."

"Little stories that only have happy, happier, or happiest endings?"

"Something like that. I like to win. Why be miserable?"

He kissed the palm of her hand, stood, gathered their trash, and stuffed the remains of the meal into a Dumpster. She stood and tossed her cup into the trash.

They strolled to his car, parked in darkness at the edge of the lot, under a Washington palm tree. He was about to open her door when she surprised him by taking his hand and tugging it.

"Let's walk," she said. "We have to get out of this habit of conducting our relationship in parking lots. First it was at the playhouse in the Grove, then on the Anhinga Trail, now here. What difference will a few moments make before we have to face the aftermath of Rolly Castillo's unhappy little plan again?"

"You think he had a plan?" Berlin said.

"Somebody did."

They left the parking lot and turned down a quiet lane leading east to the bay. The bloated moon cast a platinum suggestion of paleness into the shadows, hinting that, in the gloom, clear shapes and sharply defined things still had their existence, despite the sorcery of night's blurry disarray. At the foot of the lane they stopped, on the edge of the sinuous disk of the gray, salty cosmos that bled into the starry horizon.

Berlin put his hands on her shoulders, turning her gently to face him. He leaned back against the bole of a coconut palm and lifted his face slightly to submit to the moon's radiant translation.

Annabelle studied his features curiously.

"Listen," he said. "Listen carefully. I want you to understand everything I say to you."

He slid his hands from her shoulders, down the smooth skin of her bare back. He flattened his palms on her waist, pressing her to him, against his abdomen. He moved strong hands to her wrists and lifted her arms to his shoulders.

He kissed her softly, firmly on the lips, his hands shifting to her sides, to her rib cage, under her breasts.

Again he raised his face to the moonlight, and she saw the shadow of the new growth of beard on his lean face, and she saw the tired lines around his eyes, but she also saw the fierce light in his brown eyes that spoke of reserve energy, a tremendous personal force that transcended the physical. She remembered what Giselle Ruiz de Castillo had said about him.

He was capable.

TWENTY-TWO

FROM MANNY'S THE DRIVE TO NARANJA TOOK ONLY TEN minutes.

They planned to stop at the Castillo house. Earlier Berlin had promised Beckworth—after many impatient but evasive objections had failed—to stop in at a long-overdue meeting between the reactor brass and the widow. Finally, after almost two full days, they would be openly discussing with Mrs. Ruiz de Castillo the touchy topic of the dead scientist's scarred remains.

When he had been informed of the hastily arranged gathering, Berlin had tried every excuse he could think of to get out of the meeting, impatient to leave for the Anhinga Trail, but Beckworth had insisted, demanding to be told what could possibly be of greater importance than the reputation of the reactor. He had demanded to be told where Berlin was planning to spend the evening. He had demanded to know, his gray eyes flaring, if Berlin would be seeing Ms. Hardy-Maratos. He had informed Berlin that scientists at the reactor must at all times conduct themselves with decorum and in the right company politically.

Beckworth had demanded to know if Berlin thought everyone at the reactor had been blind when he had driven off to lunch with that woman. He had insisted that it was Berlin's duty to be the one employee at the reactor that the school could count on. Through thick and thin. He had made Berlin feel sick.

That conversation nagged at Berlin as he drove toward Naranja.

Annabelle glanced often and impatiently at her watch, wondering what Dave was finding at the reactor in the topaz vault, wishing he could be present at this meeting to interpret for her, wishing she could skip the meeting altogether and get on to the reactor. The stress was showing on Berlin, too, she thought. He rubbed his eyes frequently as he drove, not sleepily but from strain.

Four cars were parked along the grass in front of the Castillo house. Berlin pulled in behind a vintage Mercedes, shutting off his lights with a tired motion and slumping back in his seat. He turned his head on the cushion to look at Annabelle.

"You're so pretty," he said. "I don't want to go inside and look at those ugly, bickering people."

She touched the scratchy plane of his jaw with a fingertip. "Why do you have to be here?" she asked. "Can't they resolve this without you? Or at least bicker without you?"

"Maybe. But Beckworth would have my hide. I would have risked it, too, if I were plying you with wine. But, now, well, I should be here. Yeah, they could have done this without me—that's Elmore's Mercedes in front of us," he said. "Billy knows as much about nuclear management and half-lives as I do. Probably more. But—and this is much more important than Beckworth's stupid insistence—sometimes I can handle Giselle. She's got a wild temper under that veneer of civilized prudery and fanatical neatness, especially now. She's fraying at the edges a bit under the special circumstances of Rolly's death."

"Who else will we have to look at or bicker with?" Annabelle asked.

"Bertha. The Beckworths."

"Why is Bertha here? What does she know about radioactive bodies?"

"Don't underestimate what Bertha knows. She knows all our secrets, scientific and otherwise. But she'll take minutes, or some version of a record. Beckworth is careful about stuff like that. Covers his ass, or so he thinks. Frankly sometimes I think he exposes his ass with his addiction to paperwork. My motto is Never put anything in writing."

"But I thought you were the Xerox addict," she said, bemused. "Doesn't that mean you do your share of writing?"

He smiled crookedly. "The rare family fax and carefully phrased scientific articles. I never allow glimpses of my ass on those. I even hate signing checks." He sighed. "Shall we get this over with?"

She hesitated.

"Lon?"

He looked at her, surprised at the worried tone.

"Nothing." She looked out the car window. "It's just that I hate these situations. I get fatigued when I have to try to cope with more than a few nonsigners. I've grown very dependent on Dave in situations like this."

"Can you read shorthand? You could sit by Bertha."

She shook her head.

"Then sit by me. I'll try to help you." He reached into the backseat and grabbed a notebook. "I hope you can read my writing. This will be sort of cool, and it's bound to raise gossip. Might as well get some fun out of this."

She touched the door handle, poised to leave the car, but he dropped the notebook on his lap and reached for her. He kissed her urgently, his hands in her hair, which had curled riotously from her dive on Pickles Reef.

This kiss was different, bruising and deep, far from the civilized sensuality of their previous embraces. He stretched his legs across the floor and pulled her on top of him, moving his hips under her.

The door of the Castillo house opened, light flooding out onto the manicured grounds. Giselle Ruiz de Castillo stood in the doorway, gazing across at the Honda.

"Shit," Berlin said.

Annabelle sat up, short of breath. "God, I feel like a teenager," she said.

The widow waved at the car, and Berlin hoped that her scrutiny had been rewarded only with recognition of his car, which was blessedly in the shadow of an orchid tree.

From the door pocket of the car he extracted a plastic hairbrush and handed it to Annabelle. She dashed it through her hair, got out of the car, and dropped the brush back on the seat. She walked toward the house, surreptitiously rubbing her mouth. Berlin's long strides allowed him to reach her side before she stepped onto the graveled drive.

"It's about time you got here, Lon Berlin," Giselle Ruiz de Castillo said, holding out her arms and using his full name, a formality of endearment she reserved only for him. He leaned down to squeeze the short woman and kissed her loudly on both cheeks.

"I'm so sorry, Giselle," he said. "I miss Rolly."

Her fat arms returned the pressure of his embrace, and she let him go. She smoothed the fabric of her oversized blue blouse.

"You should have been here sooner, *chiquita,*" she scolded him gruffly. "Already inside those *gansos* are hissing at each other."

"I know, Giselle. I know. I'm sorry. But at least when they're hissing, they're not biting."

She regarded Annabelle, who stood beside them, assessing that daring backless dress, shamelessly wrinkled. "I wasn't expecting you, miss," the widow said matter-of-factly and turned to go into her house, completely at ease with English and with letting Annabelle know it.

Annabelle made a face and followed her. Berlin closed the door behind him when he stepped into the living room.

Eugene Beckworth and his wife, Rachel Prendergast, sat on the green-and-white-striped rattan couch, both with legs crossed and arms folded. Billy Elmore perched on a striped ottoman across from them, wearily patting his toupee. A man in a black suit stood in the middle of the living room, seemingly oblivious of their entrance, his hands joined behind his back. Bertha Puffo sat apart from the group, in the dining room at the glass table where Dave and Annabelle had sat the day before. Her hand held a pen and was poised over a notebook. She was dressed in shorts and a T-shirt.

"I think everybody here knows everybody else," Mrs.

Ruiz de Castillo said, "except for James Williams from the funeral home," and she turned her hand over in the direction of the man standing alone in the center of the room. He was not invited to sit. He inclined his head gently toward Berlin and Annabelle.

"Now we can talk," the widow said, nodding sideways at the latecomers. She took Berlin's hand and said, "Sit by me, Lon Berlin." She sank into an overstuffed green chair, and he sat on its lace-covered arm. She slapped his thigh with a resounding smack, and he jumped up. She removed the lace rectangle, and he resumed his seat.

Annabelle dropped resignedly onto the space left at the end of the couch by Beckworth and his wife. She hoped from this vantage point either to maximize opportunities to read lips or, failing that, to be least in the way.

Rachel Prendergast glanced at Annabelle under long, mascaraed lashes, and Annabelle suddenly felt self-conscious, as if her bruised lips must be fiery red and puffy.

The president's wife wore a low-cut black tank top tucked into pink deck pants. Her sandaled foot tapped on the tiled floor, and Annabelle regarded the red toenails, her mind's eye traveling the distance up that twitching leg to a memory of a tiny and sacrilegious oil painting on the woman's vulgar rump. Annabelle hid a smile, and, looking up, was surprised to see Berlin carrying a chair from the dining room. He put the chair at the end of the couch and sat, his notebook open, his gold Cross pen poised over a sheet of paper.

Annabelle beamed a smile that took his breath, and a quick vision of the front seat of his Honda flitted into his distracted mind. He wrote, *Disappearing ink, because I never put anything in writing.*

"I guess you all know poor Miss Hardy-Maratos is deaf," Giselle Ruiz de Castillo said. "Lon Berlin is going to do his best to help her out."

Bertha smiled sourly to herself at the table.

"Well, now, that's a nice thing, Lon," Rachel Prendergast purred. "Whoever heard of you going out of your way to help somebody?"

He wrote, *She's being a BITCH, as usual.* He wrote *bitch* in lavish, giant letters, the notebook angled so that Prendergast could see them from where she sat.

"Lon, darling, your playmate must be blind as well as deaf if you have to write that large," she cooed, a malicious spark in her dark eyes.

"You stop that shit," the widow said to Prendergast, scooting forward in her chair, an effort that pulled the other lace cover off. She replaced the cover with care as she spoke. "*Eso es pura mierda.* I won't have you talking shit in my house."

Beckworth frowned at his wife. "I think we can all be businesslike about this. It's getting late, and we've all been under a great strain."

Elmore shifted on the ottoman. "It's down to an open-water burial or burning. Burning is much cheaper and easier."

Berlin wrote, *E: burn body, cheaper.*

Giselle Ruiz de Castillo flew out of her chair with surprising speed and agility, and with a fiery red flushing into her jiggling cheeks. "Burn him? Burn him? Isn't he already burned? You want to burn him some more? You want to burn Rolly? What is he to you? You're monsters. You don't even mean decent cremation—you mean burn like a lab animal." She grabbed a pink vase with *Fiorenze* painted on its rim and hurled it behind her into the dining room in a smooth underhand motion. Pieces of crockery burst around Bertha Puffo's feet, and she held them in the air, otherwise unperturbed, as though this outburst were part of a pattern familiar to her.

Berlin now lay the pen on the notebook and spoke soothingly to the widow, but he looked at Annabelle. "Giselle, I happen to agree with you, but Billy is only trying to cover the options the NRC gave us. That's Billy's job. I think the appropriate thing to do is give Rolly a whopping fine burial at sea, with full pomp and circumstance. The works. Rolly lived half his life in the water, Giselle, and I think he'd like being put to bed there."

Giselle Ruiz de Castillo glared, her massive breast heaving, waiting for a challenge from Elmore. None came. He fingered his toupee nervously, but said nothing.

Beckworth put his hand on his wife's knee. She shifted, and his hand fell limply at his side.

"Giselle?" Beckworth said. "What do you think about burial at sea?"

She glared at him. "I like what Lon Berlin said," the widow stated between her teeth. "Rolly would like what Lon Berlin said."

Beckworth cocked his head at the funeral director. "Is there any problem with burial at sea?" he asked.

"No, sir. As long as the widow signs the release form, which I have all filled out and ready," Williams said.

Berlin picked up his pen and wrote, *Cadaver guy: sea burial OK if G signs paper.*

"Does anyone have a problem with this?" Beckworth asked.

Giselle postured like a major-league manager bellying

up to an umpire. "Who should have a problem but me?" Her words came out as an explosive yelp. "You can all get out of my house, with your problems. I can sign a paper without you having your problems. Rolly was my husband. He didn't like any of you anyway. Especially you, Prendergast. Get out. Everybody get out."

"Lon Berlin, you can stay," Giselle Ruiz de Castillo said. "Everybody else get out. You're making a mess of my house with your problems."

Williams coughed discreetly and slipped a folded paper from an inside pocket.

She grabbed it and stormed to the dining room table, kicking the crockery shards aside, yanking the pen from Bertha's grip and signing her name to the document. She brandished the paper. "Get out now."

Bertha closed her notebook and rose from the padded chair.

Beckworth, his wife, and Elmore filed to the door, which Elmore opened. Williams collected the paper from the widow and glided silently to the door.

"We'll have a hearse at the reactor Friday morning at ten," he said, slipping outside.

"Can I use your john, Giselle?" Bertha asked, heading from the dining room to the bedroom that opened from it.

"Okay, but use the towels under the window."

Berlin wrote, *Bertha has to pee. Hearse to reactor Friday. Meeting adjourned. Wanna go steady?*

TWENTY-THREE

ONE OF THE GRAY PLASTIC BOXES HAD SEVERAL LARGE smudges of that same oil. A couple of the others had slight traces. Dave frowned.

He stirred his yellow-gloved hand in an open box, marveling at the glittering blue stones. These are only pieces of the earth, he said to himself. Just chunks of the planet.

If Berlin was right, and half a million bucks in topaz was missing from the vault, this was quite a colossal stash that was left. There were at least fifty full boxes of the gems. Expensive chunks of the planet. Millions and millions of dollars of blue and shiny chunks of the planet Earth.

Dave selected a large stone from the top of the shimmering blue heap of treasures and stashed it in the coin pocket of his green shorts. *What a beautiful planet,* he thought. He shivered.

But how in the world had Rolly sneaked even six of these little beauties past that portal monitor?

I'll give Marcel his freedom if this little exercise in futility gets me anywhere. I'll bet that I can't get even this one lousy stone out of the building without getting caught—without making the portal monitor wake from its mechanical snooze. Still, I think a playful fate has plans of its own for that stubborn bird, and there can't be any harm in trying. Unless I get arrested as a jewel thief.

He restored the boxes to the slots where he had found them and left the vault, clanging the heavy steel door shut. Berlin's number code had worked like a charm, and Dave had found the pattern of oil to be complete. But what did it mean? Where had it come from? Rolly had lidocaine in his pocket, not a jar of oil.

Rolly. Poor old Rolly. Dave crossed to the steel table and regarded the corpse sadly. *Paisano.* A Cuban. A brother.

Dave patted the cold left cheek, and the head lolled grotesquely toward him. The staring eyes seemed to take in Dave's green waistband and the gooseflesh on his cold, bare abdomen. The fluorescent bulb overhead glared on the burned right ear—this was more light than on Dave's last visit to Rolly. Where could there be an oil source on a corpse that had only a bottle of lidocaine in its pocket? Dave looked at the head. Ear wax? Of course not. Didn't feel the same at all. Nevertheless, Dave stooped over the table, rising on his toes to peer inside the ear.

There was a puncture mark, a tiny dimple in the unburned skin of the ear canal. Ugh. What was that thing?

It had to be a needle mark. Was Rolly doing some weird drug? More than ever, Dave wished Beckworth had ordered a comprehensive autopsy. But what kind of drug did you put in your ear?

Dave tried to straighten the head on the steel table with his gloved hand, but gravity had overcome inertia finally, and the head was newly positioned to stay, to gaze futilely at this cold room, waist-high, until whatever new force finally disposed of Rolly.

A shadow fell across the table. Dave looked up.

Bodorff stood at the window, a tentative smile on his face. Dave winked, and that human concession seemed to animate the guard, whose posture became more nearly vertical and his shoulders more horizontal. Dave shook his head. The things, the little things that can make a day. Dave pulled the glove off and tossed it to the desk. He left the room, turning off the light as he went.

"So how're things in the shooting gallery?" Dave asked politely, closing the door to the Glove Box.

"Aw, come on, Mr. Enamorado, don't talk like that."

"Don't? How do you want me to talk? Like the Marl boro man? Like Charles Bronson? I'm tired and hungry, Bodorff, and I'm afraid that what you hear is what you get. Tough beans."

Clearly out of his depth, Bodorff nonetheless persisted.

"You want a cup of coffee, Mr. Enamorado? I just made some fresh."

"I'm beginning to think you have unplumbed depths, Bodorff. I'd love a cup. You don't happen to have any blackened redfish hidden up your sleeve, do you?" Dave had not attended to his growling stomach since the Ugly Pelican's avocado soup and the Coke on the Anhinga Trail.

The guard shook his head.

"Oh, well. Not to be greedy, Bodorff. Coffee would be just fine. In fact it would be a lifesaver."

They walked together down the hall to the security office, and Dave could smell the aroma of a very fine coffee.

"What is that divine fragance?"

"It's stuff Gilbert brings in from home. I think it's Honduran. His sister sends it to him. She's always sending him stuff."

They drank the coffee in the office, Dave sitting cross-legged and limber, Indian style on the desk, Bodorff on a chair he had turned around backward, straddling it.

"You got an extra shirt, Bodorff?"

The guard stood and crossed to a file cabinet, opened a drawer with a metallic squeak, and pulled out a wrinkled uniform shirt. He handed it to Dave. "Sorry about the wrinkles."

"These are wrinkles of the gods," Dave said, shrugging himself into the shirt. "I'm freezing." He glanced down at the sky-blue shirt. "It's been a long time since I wore one of these."

"You used to be a guard?"

"Are you writing my biography, Bodorff?"

"Sorry."

"You just get here?" Dave asked as he buttoned the shirt.

"Nah. About an hour ago. Quiet night."

"Bodorff, do you ever get to see the gems they keep in that vault? The pretty blue gems? I find I am much moved by their beauty tonight."

"Dr. Castillo showed me a couple of times. They sure are pretty."

"Do you always work the night shift?"

"Yeah."

"Then Dr. Castillo showed you the topaz at night? What was he doing with the topaz when he showed you?"

"Just showing me, man. He was proud of it. Then he'd lock it up like he was putting his baby to bed."

"Do you ever tell your friends about the pretty blue stones? You know, just the guys over a beer?"

"No way, man. That stuff is total security—big-boy shit."

"I see," Dave said, putting down his empty mug. "I must be going now, Bodorff. Thanks for the java and the wrinkles." Dave unfolded his legs and jumped off the desk. He sauntered into the hall, tucking in the wrinkled uniform shirt. "See you tomorrow at the office." Abruptly he stepped back into the office. "Bodorff, if that portal monitor upstairs went off, would you hear it down here?"

"Yeah, it beeps here in the office. I never heard it, but I guess that's good, right?"

"Yeah. I guess so."

Dave thought it was impossible to steal topaz from the reactor building, unless someone used the emergency door, and nobody but Dave had used that door in a long time. And anybody using the door without Dave's special knowledge would set off a different kind of alarm.

Dave departed on his impossible errand to steal one blue stone, heading for the elevator. He glanced into the darkened Glove Box as he passed. *Sleep well*, paisano.

He rode the elevator to the first floor.

He walked toward the lobby, hands dug into his pockets, head down, deep in thought about the uses of the earth. And he was caught off guard.

The receptionist was standing by the door, actually in the portal monitor, with her hands up. Outside the door, visible at the outlines of the paper witch, armed with Uzis and aiming them at the woman's head, were two people wearing black ski masks. But Dave knew one of them immediately, from the evidence of the eyes glaring through the holes in the stretched knit fabric. Even underwater, even from a distance, the Indian's unusual blue eyes had been unforgettable, and as for the woman, now that he registered her clearly, her muscular frame was as good as if she had handed Dave her driver's license.

And she had an ugly rigidity about her ugly muscles. She spotted Dave and trained the gun on him. He raised his hands in the international posture of submission, cursing himself for the deep introspective interlude that had led him into this ambush.

The receptionist lowered her arms in obedience to the Indian's gestures and opened the outer door with shaking hands. The Indian shoved her back into the lobby and came through the portal monitor. The big woman followed, carrying a small roll of copper wire.

To Dave's utter consternation, deep resentment, and loss of breath, she pushed him down and sat on him. His wrists and ankles were quickly and professionally and painfully trussed in the wire, which she snipped with wire cutters that sliced viciously.

"Christ cum laude." Dave gasped when she twisted the wire already biting into his wrists. "That hurts."

"Shut up, you fuck, or I'll show you how it feels on your tongue," she snapped through a thick wad of chewing gum. She flipped him onto his side, like a freshly landed tuna.

Dave subsided into silence, watching the woman.

The Indian took the roll of wire and bound the receptionist, but she had fainted upon being pushed and had thus escaped Dave's feelings of abject abasement. Not, he thought, that fainting was a better feeling.

The woman pushed her face, reeking of spearmint, into his.

"Where's the body?" she demanded.

"What body?" he asked innocently.

She sat back on Dave's knees and slapped his face with the butt end of the gun. "Where's the body, asshole?"

"It's upstairs," Dave whimpered dramatically. "Please don't hurt me, lady."

"Where?"

Dave thought quickly. He would send her to the most heavily protected place in the facility. "On the second floor. You go down this hall," he twisted his neck to nod his head in the direction of the corridor, "and you get into the airlock. Then you go to the second floor. But you can't open the airlock without a key."

"I've got a key," she said, waving the Uzi.

She and the Indian ran down the hall.

Dave closed his eyes, thinking hard.

He opened his eyes.

He inched slowly on his side toward the portal monitor, several feet in front of him.

The wire was tight, and his progress frustrating. He gained ground, but seemed to lose it immediately, sliding on the linoleum, the only measure of his effort being the downward progress of the elastic waistband of his green shorts. He now wished that he was still without a shirt, for the wrinkled material of the borrowed uniform shirt slipped on the polished linoleum.

He rolled onto his stomach and used his chin to drag himself forward along the linoleum floor. And his chin exerted enough traction for a pulling motion that worked him toward the portal.

His head passed the portal, and he kept pulling with his chin, spikes of pain running into his jaw and along the back of his neck.

He heard the burst of gunfire. The woman had used her key on the airlock.

More gunfire. The second airlock door.

His shoulders passed the portal. He pulled along the rubber mat on the portal ramp, the treads biting into his chin, his breath coming in strangled gulps that made him cough. He could feel skin ripping away from his face. His shirt mopped the trail of blood his chin was leaving on the floor.

At last he pulled and shoved his waist into the portal. Nothing happened.

"Please," he begged through gritted teeth, and his chin and jaw throbbed with pain. Sweat stung his eyes and his bleeding chin. "Please don't let this be another pathetic waste of money on useless high-tech bullshit."

He gave a wrenching tug with his mutilated chin, lurched forward, and the portal's computer set off its alarms.

The single chunk of the planet in his coin pocket had done it.

He lay on the floor, turning over on his side, listening to the raucous, welcome music of the alarm. *Come on, Wyatt. Don't fail me now.*

He watched the paper witch flapping against the outer glass door and counted off seconds. In twenty-eight seconds he heard the solid clomp of wood-heeled cowboy boots running on the linoleum. He almost cried with gratitude.

Without a single stupid question, Bodorff cut Dave's wire bonds with a Swiss army knife and helped him to his feet.

"I love you, Bodorff," Dave said, kissing the guard on the cheek. "Give me your gun." A drop of Dave's blood stained the sky-blue of the guard's shirt.

"Mr. Enamorado, I don't have my gun."

"Of course you have your gun. Guys like you don't listen to guys like me," Dave shouted, hopping up and down in adrenaline forged anxiety. *"Cristo en la cubeta!"*

Bodorff tugged the Smith and Wesson from his pocket, and Dave grabbed it.

"Call the police, my prince," he shouted, and raced down the hall.

The airlock stood gaping open, both doors slid partially into the thick concrete of the surrounding walls. The card-key panel was now a jagged hole. Cartridge shells looked like dead roaches on the floor. Dave held the gun in both hands and advanced into the open space between the Ring Building and the containment facility. He listened. The quiet rang in his ears.

He stepped cautiously forward into containment.

He slipped out of his flats and crept toward the elevator on bare feet. They must have taken the car up to the second floor, he thought. He leaped for the spiral of stairs, and ascended two steps at a time, silent and rapid, like a gecko lizard on a window screen.

Dave had sent them to the second floor. He would make for the third-floor bridge—Rolly's bridge—to gain the advantage of invisibility and perhaps the advantage of a good, unobstructed shot. All he had was his knowledge of the reactor. They had Uzis.

TWENTY-FOUR

BERLIN STOPPED THE CAR AT THE DOOR. HE COULD HEAR the portal monitor. He'd never heard this particular model before, but that's what it had to be.

He jumped out of the car and ran to the door, fumbling for his card key, punching in the code. Annabelle dashed from the car and grabbed his arm.

"What?" she demanded.

"The portal monitor," he said, pushing the door open.

Then they saw the guard, standing in the well of the receptionist's desk, gesturing as he spoke into the telephone. The receptionist was on the floor, bound with wire and moaning.

The guard caught a glimpse of them and clawed at his pocket.

"Shit," he said, remembering where his gun was.

"Where's Dave?" Annabelle demanded, a sick feeling in the pit of her stomach.

Bodorff had belatedly recognized Dr. Berlin.

The guard pointed to the hall. "I don't know if he

went up or down," the guard said. "Whoever did this has some serious firepower. Sounded like machine guns."

Before Berlin could react, Annabelle was off down the corridor, heading for the steps to the basement.

He finally caught up with her outside the Glove Box, out of breath. The hall was as quiet as a hospital ward at three in the morning.

"I was sure he'd be here," she said.

"Stay here, Annabelle," he said. "Stay absolutely here. Don't move." He breathed deeply and exhaled slowly. "This is really scary, and I don't want you to move. Get under a table and hide. I have to go to the reactor. What if they do something to the reactor? Jesus Christ! Don't move from here."

He turned and ran to the elevator, jabbing the button frantically. He hurried inside, and the door closed behind him.

"Oh, sure," she thought. "I'll just find a table to hide under. That's a brilliant idea."

She ran for the stairs, raced back through the lobby, waved to Bodorff, who was snipping the wires on the receptionist's ankles, and left the building. Her long strides took her rapidly to where Dave had parked the convertible against the wall of the Ring Building. She leaned into the backseat and seized her Walther and Dave's Colt.

She returned to the lobby and grabbed the guard by the collar. "Do you know how to use this?" she asked, shoving the Colt in his hand.

"No, ma'am," he said.

"Christ in a casserole," she exclaimed, borrowing one of Dave's phrases along with his gun. "Come with me and pretend you do." She put her index finger on the Colt's butt end. "If you have to shoot, you have to push this thing here to make it fire. See? Just pulling the trigger alone won't do anything. You've probably got seven shots—six in the magazine, one in the barrel. Got that?" Then she remembered the cottonmouth. "No. Five in the magazine, one in the barrel."

"Yes, ma'am," he shouted eagerly, blissfully unaware that she could not hear him and happily palming the Colt that Dave had held on him only the night before.

They took the route Dave had taken, through the devastated airlock, and up the spiral stairs, Annabelle pausing only to glance at Dave's shoes and hurriedly shed her own.

When she stepped barefoot out onto the dimpled metal of the second floor, everything appeared to be normal. The three operators sat at their consoles in the glassed control room, their backs to her, apparently intent on their gauges, bent over the board with blinking lights. Berlin stood at the glass wall, facing out of the control room, his face expressionless. There was no sign of Dave, or of anyone else. She paused there, level with the last step, feeling the warmth of the guard's breath on the back of her legs. He had not yet emerged into the pool's cavernous chamber.

The rigidity of Berlin's stance puzzled her.

She was not aware that she had held her breath until she expelled it slowly when she saw him move his hands from his sides. He closed his left fist over his lean stomach, and stroked his right thumb upward on the closed fist.

Everything was not normal.

That was the sign for danger.

With her left hand behind her, she signaled the guard to stay back, praying he would understand her frantic gesture. Her heart hammering in her chest, she stepped toward the control room. She walked slowly, her eyes on Berlin, her peripheral vision charged for any movement, the gun at her side. The pool glowed warmly to her right.

The blue brightness flickered in cold reflections along the motionless steel chains hanging in the still, clean air over the pool. The long metal retrieval poles stacked against the concrete walls surrounding the pool glistened blue and dead gray.

Berlin subtly repeated the gesture, stroking his thumb on his fist, but not moving in any other way. She stopped.

She turned her head slowly and caught the blue flash of a metal pole as it swished through the air behind her. She ducked, and the pole cut through the air over her head, missing her by centimeters. Before she could bring her gun to bear, the woman was on her, and Annabelle was crushed to the floor under that enormous weight, her gun squirting out of her hand and across the floor, splashing into the pool. It was the Mozart woman, the woman from the reef.

Bodorff watched from his place of concealment on the stairs, his eyes just above the level of this peculiar theater's floor, like the prompter in the footlight box on a Broadway stage.

The woman grabbed Annabelle's hair and twisted, jerking her head sideways. Annabelle yelped and reached for the woman's mask, jabbing her thumb through the eye hole and into one of those scarlet-splashed orbs, kicking her legs futilely while the woman leaned on her with all her weight, exuding a powerful dose of spearmint.

Berlin was marched out of the control room, the Indian's Uzi digging into his back. The Indian removed his ski mask to contemplate the women on the floor.

Berlin watched helplessly as Annabelle struggled with the much stronger woman. Somehow Annabelle managed to shift, and the two women rolled on the metal floor, their legs flailing; thick legs throbbing with cables of muscle flashed by, entangled with long smooth legs; a dirty pink skirt twisted with the fiery red of Annabelle's dress.

Again the muscled woman emerged on top. She leaned on Annabelle's neck with one hand, and Berlin could hear the stifled gasp of breath. He took an involuntary step toward the women, but the Indian shoved the cold end of the Uzi into his kidney, and he stopped.

The masked woman, now thoroughly enraged, snatched a gleaming blade from a sheath at her waist. She stuck the point over Annabelle's heaving breast, and the combat was over. Annabelle lay on the cold floor, her green eyes huge and angry, but she lay still, trying to breathe. The other woman held the knife steady.

"Where's the body?" she demanded. "Don't fuck with me anymore. We want the body." She removed her fist from Annabelle's throat.

"Tell her where it is," the Indian said with quiet authority. "She likes killing people."

The woman's thick hand twisted the grip on the knife handle.

Berlin opened his mouth to tell them what they wanted to know, to bellow out Rolly's location in the basement room, his eyes on the woman's long knife. The knife glowed blue in the pool's reflection, and Berlin's heart felt crushed in his chest by the petrifying weight of icy terror.

An unearthly squeal exploded overhead, and a stainless steel chain swung through the air, straining in a metallic scream from its hook in the ceiling and smashing Dave into the Indian's shoulder. The Uzi skidded across the floor into the pool, and the Indian tumbled to his knees.

Dave dropped lightly to his feet and shoved the Smith and Wesson into the long braid at the back of the man's head.

"Tell the madwoman to drop the knife," Dave snarled. "Or I'll drill you, *coño*. I can't miss at point-blank range."

A ghastly smile crossed the Indian's face, and a flicker of rage leaped in his uncanny blue eyes. "You tell her, Tarzan," he said, with stunning scorn for this small assailant.

Dave shoved the gun harder into the Indian's hair. "Tell her to drop the knife. Or I'll blow your goddamn brains out through your nostrils."

The Indian turned his head slightly. "Sabriya, perhaps you'll be good enough to comply with this man's wishes."

"Fuck you, Henry," she said. "And fuck the Cuban shrimp with the gun. He can only kill you once. I can hurt this lovely lady a thousand times. Cuban shrimp, *you* drop the gun."

She pressed the knife against Annabelle's flesh, and a ruby droplet welled up on the smooth tan skin. Dave hesitated, withdrawing the gun slowly from the Indian's braid and throwing an agonized look at Annabelle.

The muscled woman smiled behind her mask, wrinkling the fabric into a travesty of enjoyment. "Make up your mind, you greasy spic. What the hell, I think I'll just kill her for practice."

Annabelle turned her head. The pool was only inches from the woman's knee. She groaned sickly, and the woman drew back on the knife reflexively.

In a flash Annabelle pulled her knees up and rolled with all her strength toward the pool. The other woman's weight carried them together with a resounding splash into the hot water.

With a powerful kick, Annabelle freed herself from the woman's grip and lunged up, over the side, pulling herself, dripping, onto the metal deck.

The woman's masked head bobbed as she flapped her arms spastically and reached for the side. Annabelle grabbed the mask, tossed it away into the water, and reached for the woman's hair. She dunked her head under the water, holding her down.

She hauled her up by her hair, but the woman was still struggling.

Annabelle dunked her again and held her under until a stream of bubbles burst to the surface. She hauled her up again. The woman was unconscious. Annabelle clutched the limp arms and dragged her onto the deck up to her elbows, barely aware that Berlin was at her side, pulling on the woman's hips. Together they beached her on the floor. A gray lump of gum bobbed on the surging blue water beside the slowly sinking ski mask.

Annabelle's arms were shaking violently as she put her palms flat on the floor and knelt over the woman on all fours, her red dress clinging to her heaving rib cage, wisps of steam rising from the fabric.

"What should I do?" Annabelle whispered, tears streaming down her face. "Am I going to die like Rolly?"

Berlin wrapped his arms around her tenderly and helped her stand. "No way. A quick shower, and you'll be fine. You were miles from the core," he said.

She did not comprehend a word, but his actions spoke volumes to her as he ruthlessly stripped her dress from her shaking body and tossed it on the floor. He yanked off his shirt, popping off the buttons in all directions, and held it in front of her, gesturing for her to shed her panties.

Henry Algagollawjiwar had been in many tight places, and this he rapidly assessed as a moment given by fate into his hands. He dropped suddenly from his knees to the floor and, in one smooth movement, pulled Dave's feet out from under him. Dave went crashing to the floor, his elbow cracking with a sharp and sickening noise on the metal. Henry grabbed the little Smith and Wesson and leaped to his feet.

Dave bit back a gasp. His lower left arm stuck out at a sort of Picasso angle, as Dave thought of it in a moment of extraordinarily poignant clarity.

Henry backed toward the spiral stairs.

"My sincere compliments, fisherman's daughter," he said with a glimmer of white teeth and a faint bow in Annabelle's direction.

He turned, and a spurt of red flashed from the stairwell.

Henry stared in magnificent disbelief at the welter of flesh that had been his right hand. A flood of gore and one loose bloody finger slopped over into his sleeve. The Smith and Wesson had been blown away.

Bodorff stood on the third step from the top, booted feet apart, his hands gripping Dave's Colt with peculiar authority.

He yelled, "Freeze, asshole," in perfectly clipped and threatening tones, as though he had been rehearsing the moment all his life.

THURSDAY

We are all survival machines.

RICHARD DAWKINS
The Selfish Gene

TWENTY-FIVE

ANNABELLE SAT ON A STOOL IN THE TOPAZ PROJECT LAB, clad in the borrowed garments Berlin had rounded up after she had been thrust into a shower: the white lab coat and bright yellow anti-contamination trousers hung on her slim frame, and she had found a safety pin in Bertha Puffo's desk to keep the coat closed over her breasts. She had retrieved her sandals from the floor near the damaged airlock. Her damp hair was shiny and smelling of industrial-strength soap.

Metro-Dade Homicide Captain Paul Diaz stood across from her, his elbows on the paper-strewn table, his old blue jeans full of homey grass stains and patches. They were his gardening pants, the first thing he had grabbed when the call had come from the Metro-Dade dispatcher. His Colt Diamondback revolver was stuck in his jeans pocket.

The facility was crawling with cops—uniforms and plainclothes—and commissioners from the NRC, and civil defense officials, and fire rescue workers. The lab was a temporary island of quiet and calm in a sea of official business by the emergency teams of Miami—and a boiling sea of hysteria by Beckworth and Elmore.

"I wish you'd talk Dave into going to the hospital, Annabelle," Diaz said. "He's a stubborn Cuban hothead, and a broken bone's a tricky thing."

"He hates hospitals," she said, "and besides, I think he's embarrassed. After the paramedics put him in that sling, he ran into the university's president. Beckworth had the bad judgment to ask him, in what Dave described as a booming John Wayne voice, 'What the hell happened to you, son?' " Annabelle smiled. "And then Dave screamed, 'I slipped and fell, okay? Why is everyone suddenly interested in writing my biography?' " She laughed softly. "Paul, I'll see if I can persuade him to allow my doctor to look at him. That's the best I can do."

"Okay. You know best."

"Paul, Dave really has nothing to be embarrassed about. But you know how he is."

"Yeah, he has a hero complex. Thinks he's a cross between James Bond and Peter Pan." Diaz made a soaring, fluttering gesture with his hand and rolled his eyes.

Annabelle laughed out loud.

Diaz chuckled and leaned over the table to squeeze her shoulder briefly. "That stunt he pulled on the swinging chain must have been something to see."

Annabelle nodded, yielding to the impulse of a deep yawn, stretching her arms luxuriously. "Sorry, Paul. I didn't mean to yawn in your face. What have you got on those beasts who tore this place apart?"

"The Indian is so clean, you could eat your dinner off his record," Diaz said. "The man's got a pretty good reputation in this town. That place of his in the Everglades has never even been cited. The FBI has been trying to link him to gunrunning in the Keys for years, but they've never been able to touch him. The Bureau and other federal types have also been looking into an operation he's a silent partner in down in Port-au-Prince, another gambling club that may be supplying the military with popguns. They may get something on that, but our relationship with Haiti is so fucked up right now that I think they're wasting their time. And despite Metro-Dade's fondness for you, we can't even charge him with having freak snakes on his property."

Diaz thumped his fist on the table. "But the assault charges tonight will at least give his lawyer some work, and I think"—here Diaz crossed his fingers—"the DA will go as high as attempted murder. We've got the woman dead to rights on trying to kill you, and the Indian's at least an accessory. The woman's name is Sabriya Agha. Maybe you heard of her?"

Annabelle shook her head.

"She played softball at the University of Miami on the 1988 National Champs. Maybe you were still in New Haven then. Agha was really something. Batted four fifty-nine. Awesome to watch her. She had a swing like Rod Carew and a temper like Billy Martin. She was a fighter then, roughed up a couple opposing players, but she got school discipline for that. She does have a consistent record since then—served a couple months in Correction on an assault in Orlando, got off on a couple of other assaults in Miami. When Dade County's through with her, there's an outstanding warrant in Broward, another assault." Diaz rubbed his sleepy eyes and looked at his watch. "The Broward sheriff's office is going to have to sit on their thumbs and wait until we see how big and how long we can make our charges."

Annabelle shrugged, stretching her aching muscles.

"What time is it, Paul?" she asked, after an automatic glance at her bare wrist. Berlin had thrown her watch down a chute in the containment building.

"Three o'clock."

Beckworth stormed through the open door, his face red and his gestures twitching. "Annabelle, thanks to your rash and misguided actions, this reactor is going to have to shut down," he roared.

"Shut down?" she asked. She blinked her sleepy eyes. "Completely?"

"The NRC won't let us operate without that airlock," he said, advancing on her at the table.

Annabelle was bone tired, and she clenched her fists in her lap. "Beckworth," she said, her voice low and clear. "Jorge Enamorado and I risked our lives for the precious reactor tonight. Why don't you just get the goddamnned airlock fixed?"

Beckworth sputtered. He worked his mouth, producing only a sort of flapping gobble, an absence of even the formal linguistic parameters of gibberish. A line around his mouth went through shades of red, achieving finally a stable maroon shadow.

An extremely young woman officer, with short red hair the color of Mexican tile and wearing the tan-and-brown Metro-Dade uniform, came to the door of the lab and paused on the threshold, glancing first at Beckworth curiously and then at Diaz expectantly. Annabelle signaled to Diaz, and he turned.

"Captain, there's another situation here in Naranja,

and the duty sergeant said I should find you," the red-headed cop said.

"Well, what is it?" Diaz asked impatiently.

"It's a suicide, sir. A jumper, Captain—woman named Bertha Puffo. That eight-story condo on Naranja Lakes."

TWENTY-SIX

THE ONE-BEDROOM CONDO UNIT WAS DEPRESSINGLY cluttered, the kind of clutter that flaunted its owner's personal habits. Butt ends of Tareyton Light cigarettes floated in dirty coffee mugs. A toothbrush, the bristles a faded orange from too many bloody attacks on the gums, lay on the kitchen counter among the dishes. Lipsticked Kleenex was stuffed into a tall metallic iced-tea glass, like a hybrid carnation in a sewer pipe. On top of the TV, a newspaper—opened to the crossword puzzle, which was half finished and apparently abandoned—flapped gently in the occasional gusty breeze from the sliding doors open onto the tiny balcony facing east over a parking lot and fields of mondo grass. A pair of earrings soaked in a saucer of alcohol, a visible signpost to a probable infected lobe. The television was on, tuned to the Weather Channel, and a peppy meteorologist was rendering "Tropical Update," complete with satellite pictures of a wave developing off the coast of Africa.

The police had finished photographing the apartment

and searching it for the silent, informative physical presences that offer testimony on sudden death.

"Christ in a conga line, you should see the crud in the shower," Dave called from the bathroom, a tiny closet of mildew and warm odors off the bedroom. He walked into the living room carrying a red plastic portable radio in his right hand. His left arm was tucked into a gray polyester sling, and the lines of pain etched around his eyes belied the cheeriness of his scorn for Bertha Puffo's housekeeping.

"This is the dumbest thing I've ever seen, Annabelle," he announced, holding out the radio for her inspection. "This is a solar radio, which I found in the shower. Well, guess what? There's no window in the shower. This radio's about as useful as an electric handbag."

Annabelle nodded vaguely, hardly aware of his find and his sunny, determined voyeurism.

Diaz plucked the radio from Dave's hand with an impatient and tired sigh. "Dammit, Dave. Would you stop touching things? You're acting like a little kid in a doctor's office." Diaz put the radio down on a card table covered with scraps of thread and fabric. An old Singer sewing machine stood on the table, its needle poised on the seam of a dress-in-progress.

"Jeez," Dave said, fingering the yellow paisley silk held down by the needle, "no wonder she jumped. I wouldn't wear this to a dogfight."

"Get your hands off that," Diaz snapped.

"You know, Paul," Dave said, "you get a trifle surly just before dawn. Fabric doesn't hold fingerprints, anyway."

"No, but it holds other marks, you stupid sap." Diaz

turned to Annabelle, sleepily considering the white lab coat that had slipped from her shoulder, exposing the smooth line of her neck, the soft shadow in the hollow over her collarbone. "Annabelle," Diaz said, putting his big hand on her warm shoulder.

She was seated at a small walnut desk beside the sliding doors, staring at the terminal screen of Bertha's personal computer, an old Tandy 1000 HX. The screen was on, showing white letters on a blue field, the prize exhibit of this gloomy collection of tawdry testaments to the last minutes of Bertha's life.

Annabelle looked up dreamily from the screen, still lost in thought, her green eyes focused on some distant image.

"Annabelle, we're gonna close this up and go home," Diaz said. He considered her faraway look and glanced at the computer screen. "There's not much doubt about the note," he said gently, pulling up a dinette chair with a green and rose needlepoint seat. "The keyboard shows only Puffo's fingerprints, and that note couldn't get onto the screen without somebody touching the keys. It wasn't even saved into memory—I saved it myself before I let the fingerprinters loose. If somebody other than the deceased had typed the note with gloves, Puffo's own fingerprints would have been smudged. But they're nice and clear and fresh and definite. They're hers, Annabelle. And only hers."

Annabelle nodded glumly. There was something about the note, but Paul was surely right about the prints. His expert had done an on-the-spot comparison between the prints on the keys and the dead woman's fingers before the body had been taken away from its bloody resting-place on the cement eight floors below the balcony.

"Are you planning to leave this machine turned on?" she asked.

"Everything stays the way it is," Diaz replied. "I'll seal the apartment and come back when I can see past the little angora sweaters on my eyeballs." He rubbed his eyes vigorously. "If it makes you feel any better, at least this time we've ordered a full autopsy. I sure feel better knowing the coroner's not getting any sleep either."

She smiled, a fatigued and half-hearted effort.

Dave stepped onto the balcony and peered over the pale orange concrete wall that formed the railing. Directly below him, eight stories down, three uniformed officers stood guard around the area roped off by the police when the paramedics had taken the body away in an ambulance. Dave could see the bright lines of chalk on the pavement, the outline of the broken body. It looked almost like a teacup with a shattered handle. The harsh artificial glare of white light from the parking lot was garish against the gray pavement, an umbrella of impersonal forces gathered to illuminate this new tragedy.

The pattern of chalk reflected the tortuous position of the woman's arms upon impact. She had been found lying facedown, her features crushed, her knees gathered under her stomach, her left arm under her body. Perhaps she had been trying to cushion the fall with that arm, Dave thought, shaking his head. And with her knees.

Dave tentatively touched his own left arm with the fingers of his right, surreptitiously moving the sling aside. His arm hurt like hell, and the puffy flesh showed red over a sharp bump below the elbow. His jaw muscles ached, big scabs had begun to form under the growing shadow of the stubble on his face, a tiny burn graced his hip, and he thought he had aged forty years when Annabelle had gone into the pool. His interest in Bertha's possessions, and in her death, was completely feigned: He wanted to take Annabelle home and forget this ghastly night. And then he'd go home, to sleep a sleep of exhaustion, after one little unfinished chore. But he wouldn't tell Annabelle about that. He wouldn't tell anyone.

Annabelle rose from the desk chair, taking a final glance at the suicide note on the screen: *I'm really sorry about everything. If Rolly Only Could See me die now. Bertha Susan Puffo.*

Dave moved inside the apartment to stand beside Annabelle, reaching up slightly to place his good right arm gently around her slumping shoulders. He read the text aloud.

"It doesn't improve upon reading," he said to Diaz. "Has an odd sound."

"Yeah, well, I never read a suicide note that sounded good," Diaz said.

"Boy, you'd think these reactor people were all going for a Pulitzer prize for autobiography," Dave said snidely, but wincing when he moved his arm. "The way they all write notes all the time about their slightest mood swings reminds me of Shirley MacLaine and Dennis Rodman. Rolly and Bertha. Rolly and Bertha."

"Take Annabelle home," Diaz said gently, giving Dave a nudge. "And, Dave, you need some sleep too."

The two men looked at Annabelle's abstracted face. She was making no attempt to participate in their conversation. There was nothing of her customary energy for full understanding of her surroundings. She was simply staring at the computer screen.

The silence grew. A new load of cubes dropped suddenly into the icemaker in Puffo's refrigerator, and the noise sounded to Dave like someone stumbling in the messy kitchen.

Annabelle twitched the sleeve of Diaz's denim shirt.

"Paul," she said, "I don't think you should go home quite yet."

"Why not?"

"Because you're going to have to get some judge out of bed and get a search warrant issued," she said apologetically.

"What for?"

Her face was drawn, gray shadows under her green eyes.

"I know who murdered Bertha," she said unambiguously. "And Rolly."

TWENTY-SEVEN

THIS WAS A TEST, A SPIRITUAL CROSSROADS, A *hadj* FOR a twentieth-century man in search of his lost soul.

The seeds of a violent and corrosive anger had taken root in what he had thought was his arid emotional soil, and *Darwin* was faced with a setback to the progress he had attained toward serene union with the bodiless, unsentimental, cold heart of the cosmos. But he was fighting his anger, fighting through the discipline of meditation. Proper concentration and the subsequent letting go, however, were eluding him.

Darwin knew that Henry had badly miscalculated from the start, and it had been the thick, blinding mists of anger that had betrayed Henry. In his blindness he had mistaken the rather insipid hardware of reactor security for callous unconcern; and he had mistaken those corporate warriors for amateurish children. They *were* amateurs, but they were not children. When *Darwin* had seen the .45-caliber hole drilled through Mango's dusky skull, he had known that she had been sent to grass by a marksman of consummate skill and uncommon sangfroid.

No. Not children. Without them, Henry's simple plan would have worked. Like most of Henry's enterprises, the raid on the reactor had been ingeniously simple, a lightning strike to get in and out without the complex machinery of personnel and materiel that a larger movement would have entailed. But *Darwin* had been against it from the start. He had argued for snatching the body from whatever vehicle ultimately carried the remains of the swallower to their final rest. But Henry, anxious over the possibility that the frightened university would burn the body, had bluntly resisted any course but the one that ran straight to the reactor. And that anxiety—like all emotions—had been an anarchic force leading to failure.

But not for *Darwin*. He was going to get the topaz. The DDD would leap from the obscurity of his leather album and into a permanent place in the coldly practical line of weapons that had begun with the first man who had staved off the oppression of instant emotions by learning to take the time and forethought necessary to explode lead through a tube. If it had not been for weapon design, *Darwin*'s rapidly advancing spiritual quest might have died prematurely. The flawed grenade that had taken most of his left hand might have sent him reeling into despair. Instead he had schooled himself to interpret that accident as a warning, a cosmic reminder that impermanence was the natural state of emotional and physical man, and that even a hand was only a physical possession. Baggage.

He had since then kept his business successful and

his spiritual quest alive by limiting his physical needs to the essential. Like the topaz.

But what *Darwin* needed now was a newspaper. At a quarter to six in the morning, in the still darkness, the final edition of the *Miami Tribune* was lying in double plastic bags on lawns all over the city and its suburbs.

He stopped his rented Mustang convertible and stepped daintily onto a dewy lawn on Tiger Tail Avenue in the Grove. He slid the wrappers off the newspaper on the lawn and dropped them back onto the St. Augustine grass, thoughtfully flipping the paper out of its folds.

Darwin had categorized most American newspapers as lacking mature distance and restraint. And this particular newspaper compared unfavorably with the king of junk emotion, *America Today*—with perhaps even less restraint.

He had not found much restraint in Miami at all, with its welter of languages, its tumultuous tropical flora, its unlicensed drivers, its laissez-faire attitude toward guns, its nerve. He would have hated life in Miami if he allowed himself such emotions.

He stood contemplatively on one foot, the other slung behind him on the toe of its polished brown loafer, and he read with mild interest the story under the front-page banner headline.

The headline—and, really, the whole paper looked like a comic book, with all the color boxes and the tiny photos stuck in every bit of white space—screamed from its strip under the nameplate. The headline read, FORMER UM SLUGGER, MIKOSUKEE SIDEKICK STORM REACTOR.

Darwin flicked a gnat fastidiously from the *c* in

reactor and walked slowly to the Mustang, reading and thinking about the piece:

> Armed with machine guns, a former star catcher for the Lady Hurricanes and a well-known Mikosukee nightclub owner blew their way into the nuclear research reactor in Naranja early this morning, injuring five people and damaging the reactor before they were subdued by private security forces.
>
> Witnesses say that two masked persons carrying automatic weapons forced their way into the research facility, owned and operated by the University of the Keys, and overpowered university personnel.
>
> "It was a nightmare, like out of a Schwarzenegger movie," said Gayle Baker, the night receptionist.
>
> "They tied me up with wire," she said. "And I thought they were going to kill me with their bare hands."
>
> Baker said that alarms at the facility did not sound until they were triggered by security personnel.
>
> According to Metro-Dade police, the persons who broke into the reactor and assaulted its staff are Sabriya Agha, who led the 1988 Lady Hurricanes to the national softball championship, and Henry G. Algagollawjiwar, a Mikosukee Indian who owns the Alligator Hole Cafe, a nude gambling club on the Mikosukee Reservation in the Everglades west of Homestead.
>
> Police said that Agha and Algagollawjiwar shot out an airlock that divides the reactor itself from an outer research and office structure called the Ring Building.
>
> A security guard on duty at the reactor said that the

pair made their way to the actual core of the reactor, where he disarmed them after a firefight.

Both Agha and Algagollawjiwar are in police custody, following treatment at the scene for wounds received in the fight.

Charges are pending.

Among the injured were Baker, three technicians, and an unarmed security official who was visiting the plant, according to the security guard. The technicians were hospitalized for observation at Homestead Hospital.

A sixth person, Annabelle Hardy-Maratos, who owns Hardy Security and Electronics, Inc., located on South Bayshore Drive in Coconut Grove, suffered minor radiation contamination, according to police. She was treated at the scene in a special shower apparatus.

University officials could not be reached for comment on the nature and extent of damage to the nuclear plant.

Civil defense officials said that no plans for an evacuation of surrounding neighborhoods has been implemented.

The reactor was the scene early this week of the dramatic suicide of Rolando Ruiz de Castillo, Ph.D., a senior research scientist employed by the university. He apparently fell to his death into the containment pool that houses the uranium core of the reactor, according to police.

Darwin folded the paper neatly and tossed it onto the front seat of the Mustang.

The story had been accompanied by a photograph of

a Hispanic-looking man in shorts and a guard's shirt. He was sitting on a stretcher, flanked by two female paramedics in uniform. A second man, in full uniform, stood behind the patient, his hand on the wounded man's right shoulder. The cutline read: *Jorge Enamorado, wounded in the gunfight, receives first aid at the scene, while reactor security guard extends a hand in comfort after the ordeal.*

"Darwin" opened the door and sank into the cushioned velour opulence of the car's interior. He pushed a much-thumbed purple spiral notebook from the breast pocket of his white shirt with the stub of his left hand—it was in this unassuming and very private volume that he recorded the often surprising and profound results of his meditations—and flipped the curling pages to a short list of addresses and telephone numbers he had culled this morning from the White Pages. With a ballpoint pen, he crossed out *Hardy Systems, Alhambra Drive.* The newspaper had given him the information he needed. He wanted the one on South Bayshore.

He tucked the notebook back into his pocket and attempted to start the car. It struggled to turn over, conked out, and then displayed on its dashboard in yellow pictures and text the news that the engine had not gone on. His serene face revealed nothing of his thoughts as he pulled the key out of the ignition and started the process all over. With the same results.

Not so much as a twitch marred the smooth tranquillity of his facial muscles as he opened a cardboard carton on the passenger's seat and lifted out a boxy and curiously lightweight gadget. It was about the size of a tall portable CD player, with a front panel bristling with level gauges and knobs.

With his customary unruffled composure, he lifted the device and slipped out of the car. He placed the device on the hood and donned a pair of protective goggles. He picked up the boxy contraption, turned, and aimed the gadget into the car at the vehicle identification number on the dashboard of the Mustang. He activated several switches, rapidly and with practiced dexterity. A bright flash and a loud thud disturbed the morning stillness, and a pencil-thin ribbon of white light emerged from the box. *Darwin* held the contraption steady, and soon nothing was left of the identification number but a fine powder. Then he carried the device to the back of the car, and, with the same flash and thud, he vaporized the license plate.

He flipped switches on the panel. With prim care he placed the device on the trunk. With the thumb and forefinger of his right hand he slipped a square of silver polyester from his back pocket and shook out its folds. He tucked his device into the polyester bag, hung the goggles from his back pocket, lifted the silver bag over his right shoulder, and strolled off down the street, heading east toward South Bayshore Drive with a mantra on his tongue and a sweet smile on his happy face.

The car would take days to trace. It was not good for the soul to become attached to unnecessary material things. Baggage.

TWENTY-EIGHT

DAVE'S FACE WAS DRAWN, AND PUFFY UNDER THE drooping eyes, as he stopped the red convertible at the gate of the Pink Building's garage. He could barely summon the strength to drag the plastic key from his pocket, lean over the door, and open the iron gate. As he drove up the ramp, the first long rays of the rising sun hit his rearview mirror, and he did not see the little man who slipped into the garage behind him like a moving beige shadow.

Dave parked in Annabelle's reserved space and stumbled out of the car. He trudged to the elevator. When the door opened, he walked inside, pressed the button for Penthouse, and leaned his aching head against the wall of the elevator car.

The elevator rose.

He stepped out onto the thick carpet of the top floor and opened the door to the suite with his key. He barely glanced at Annabelle's door, moving down the hall to his own office. The elevator door closed, and the indicator light showed that the elevator was going down again.

Dave entered his office.

Rosy light filtered in through the blinds on his east window. Marcel's cage was draped neatly with green burlap; no doubt Arantxa had covered him when she had left last night. He pulled the cover off, and Marcel emitted a sleepy squawk. Dave sank into his chair and peered glumly at the bird through the copper bars of the cage.

"Marcel, you've been a disappointment in the talking department, but you never shat on my shoulder. An action that speaks louder than words, little buddy."

Dave cleared his throat, wincing at the pain in his neck muscles.

"But, feathered friend, a promise is a promise, and you have a whole new life in front of you. And just remember, there are some people you *should* shit on."

Dave stood, pushing his chair back with his knees. He fished a sparkling blue stone from the coin pocket of his shorts and tossed it onto the cherry wood of his desk.

With a lump in his already aching throat he opened the door of the cage. Marcel leaped for his hand and waddled up Dave's arm until he was facing backward on the man's shoulder. He leaned contentedly against Dave's ear.

Dave closed the little wire door, hoisted the cage, and plodded slowly back down the hall, the weight on his good right arm difficult to balance because of the sling confining his left. The elevator door opened immediately, and Dave stepped in, on his way down and out to Parrot Jungle, to fulfill his promise to the bird before he allowed himself the luxury of sleep.

The door closed on the man and his bird, and a beige shadow seemed to ooze along the wall.

The shadow emerged into the open hall, wearing a latex glove on its right hand.

Darwin coaxed the lock on Annabelle's door to give up its mechanical secrets with the ease of rolling a marble down a hill. He slipped inside and closed the door behind him.

On the magnificent marble desk was a neat stack of papers. *Darwin* sat in Annabelle's chair and began a detailed study of the documents. He took his time—sometimes reading an item twice, sometimes three times—scrutinizing the papers by the hot orange light of the rising sun streaking through the windows behind him.

He found no evidence at all that these people were looking for his topaz, the topaz the dead swallower had failed to bring in. None of these documents even hinted at the existence of the topaz. Were these corporate vigilantes children after all?

Closing his eyes, and with a disciplined square gesture, he swept the papers to the floor. He trod on them unthinkingly, like sand on a beach, and he crossed to the cabinet under the windows.

He pulled files out one by one, eliminating them efficiently from consideration before tossing their contents on the rug. He moved from section to section of the cabinet, working left to right, leaving nothing untouched in his thorough examination. When he had finished, after some forty-five minutes, the sea of documents had spread over the floor, engulfing the stack from the desk, and the sun was well up in the dull blue sky.

Darwin glanced around the room. A graceful white couch occupied the north wall, under an oil painting of tiny fish in a blue sea and on a blue sky. He admired the painting with tepid detachment and an eye on the sun's progress. The painting was just touched on its upper left corner by the rays of the sun, which turned two of the fish green.

He knelt by the couch and poked his right hand under its frame. A good, solid wooden frame. From a deep pocket in his khaki trousers, he plucked a small plastic box, about the size of a tin of throat lozenges. It was a device containing a carefully measured dose of clear gelatin, and he activated it by pressing a thin lever on its plastic front. He peeled a strip of paper from the adhesive bar on the back of the tiny object and reached under the couch, attaching the device to the wooden frame.

He stood and left the room, closing the door and restoring the tumblers on the lock to their original position, bothering with this nicety because of the device he had planted under the couch. He wanted no untimely curiosity, or drafts.

The hallway was still dark, and after the growing brightness of the big office, he found it necessary to grope along the walls to find his way.

Suddenly he stopped, an unfamiliar sensation of consternation flooding his veins. There in a small office, on a loveseat, her dramatic profile outlined by the invading rays of the yellow sun striping its fiery presence through the blinds, was the most beautiful woman *Darwin* had ever seen. She appeared to be asleep, so still and peaceful was her posture. Desire stirred in him.

Without a sound *Darwin* readied the laser and hung the rubber strap of his goggles around his forehead. He took careful aim through the open door and fired. The flash of light illuminated the hall in sharp relief, and the beam vaporized her head. The lovely profile no longer interfered with his vision of the morning light. He had forgotten to cover his eyes with the protective goggles, but he felt fine, and he regarded this lapse as an unplanned but successful field test of the weapon's many properties for controlled environmental manipulation. It was ready to be tested more widely, once he had the topaz.

Darwin, his equanimity unimpaired and his incipient desire quashed, packed up his spartan array of equipment, and left the premises the way he had come in.

TWENTY-NINE

"CHRIST IN A CRASH HELMET!"

Dave gaped at the remains of Ethel the Rockette, the life-size doll that had adorned his office with the unchanging and brilliant smile on her china face. A fine white powder had settled on her spangled shoulders, the only residue of the smile that had vanished with her head.

They stood together in the doorway to Dave's office, their faces stunned, their volition suddenly extinguished.

"Dave," Annabelle whispered, awestruck by the space where the doll's head had been, "it's as though Ethel's head just evaporated. Poof."

"Me cago en Dios," Dave said, hiding his face from Annabelle, his voice tight. "Two companions in one day."

"What?"

"Nothing." He took a slow step toward the headless doll and stirred a finger in the dust on her black costume. His finger came away white. "Annabelle, I'd rather have seen a cottonmouth in my desk chair than this."

"The person who did this *is* a cottonmouth," she said

hotly. "Dave, I'm so sorry about Ethel." Struck by a sudden fear, she said, "Oh my God, Dave, where's Marcel?"

Dave looked uncomfortable. "Don't worry about Marcel. He's in a safe place."

Annabelle put her hands in her hair and stared at the ceiling. Dave watched her as she nodded her head, apparently conducting an inner dialogue with herself. She suddenly dropped her hands and transferred her gaze to the remains of the doll. "Dave. Guess what. The Mikosukee didn't do this. The muscle woman didn't do this. They're both in police custody. So who did? And with what? You can't just make a china head go *poof* by waving a wand. I may begin to believe in magic. Next thing you know I'll be drinking levitation tonic."

"I'll share it with you."

He opened a humidor on the top of his desk and extracted a long Cuban cigar. He stuck the cigar in his mouth without conducting his usual elaborate ritual of sniffing the tobacco and snipping the end. He surveyed his office with sad eyes. Satisfied that nothing else had been damaged, he took Annabelle's elbow and led her down the hall to her own office.

Dave opened the door of her office with his key, which he found he had to jiggle in order to roll the oddly unresponsive tumblers of the lock. He abruptly sucked in a deep, sighing breath. Papers were strewn around the office, and the cabinet doors were hanging open. But nothing had, like Ethel's head, simply vanished. In Annabelle's office the damage seemed to consist of wholesale vandalism, but no magic disappearances.

With uncalculated grace Annabelle collapsed to a sitting position on the threshold, dropping her face into her hands. The white button-down shirt she wore tied at her waist hiked up her back, and the ends of the red scarf she had threaded through the belt loops of a pair of jeans trailed on the carpet. She had dropped the red tennis shoes she had been carrying in her hand. She sat up and then lay back on the hall carpet, eyeing the ceiling vacantly.

"What more can happen to us, Dave?" she asked in a hollow voice. "Of course, with only two hours of sleep, I may not know if I'm dreaming or not. Maybe this isn't happening at all."

"Stay where you are," he signed, making his gestures in the air over her face. He stepped gingerly into the office.

Dave had slept for only one hour, but he had spent an indulgent twenty minutes in his shower, the water running over his abused body in welcome warmth, and he felt restored, or at least not as lousy as he had at dawn. And dressing with care often had the power to awaken his adrenaline, so he had cooperated with his own chemical starter by arraying himself in a black dress shirt, white satin bow tie, white suspenders, and black knee-length shorts. He sported a large spray of red-orange hibiscus blossoms on the gray sling. His scraped chin seemed to pulse with a dull red life of its own.

He tiptoed across the carpet in his black flats, making a circuit of the office, scanning the scattered papers. He dropped to his knees and crawled under the desk, angling himself along on the edge of his good right forearm, crooking his right hand to hold the long cigar off the carpet, craning his neck, and holding his broken arm painfully against his black shirt.

He emerged, checked to see that Annabelle had not risen to watch his maneuvers, rolled his eyes toward the ceiling, and let out a long and loud hiss of agony. *"God! That hurts!"*

Arantxa appeared at the office door, clucking at Annabelle in Spanish and helping her to her feet. She regarded Dave's sling and fiery chin with a kind of compact and peevish horror. "Mr. Dave, what have you been doing to hurt yourself like that?" she demanded, sounding to Dave like a baby-sitter interrupted on the phone.

"Ice-dancing lessons," he said curtly, sticking the cigar in the corner of his mouth. "It was the triple axel that got me. What the hell happened in here?"

Arantxa shrugged her shoulders. "I don't know, Mr. Dave. It was like this when I got in, just like a hurricane blew in"—she made a sweeping gesture to the right with her chubby arm. "And blew out"—she swept her arm back to her side. "Ice dancing is very beautiful."

Annabelle walked slowly around her desk on bare feet and slumped into her chair, swiveling dejectedly from side to side.

Dave eyed Arantxa over his cigar. "Did you call the police?"

"No, Mr. Dave. How do I know you didn't do this yourself?" she asked in an apparent spirit of honesty, but with a kind of singsong exasperation and a sigh, and turned to the door. "Maybe you were looking for something. I don't know with you, Mr. Dave." She stepped into the hall and was gone.

Dave was appalled, and his aching jaw throbbed in protest when he opened his mouth. "How do I know you didn't do this yourself?" he mimicked, in a close approximation of Arantxa's monotone, the cigar bobbing in his mouth. He yanked the cigar from his mouth, cleared his throat, and raised his voice. "Mark my words, Arantxa, you've put too many quarters in the sass machine."

He popped the cigar between his teeth and whirled to face Annabelle. The force of his turn caused the sling to jet away from his body. A spasm crossed his face, and he ducked his head. The muscles of his face writhed. When he looked up again, his features were composed in a tight debonair mask and the cigar was balanced elegantly between the long fingers of his right hand. He elevated one eyebrow at the pitying look he encountered on Annabelle's face.

"Dave, I know your arm hurts. I can see by your eyes," she said. "There's no reason for you to be embarrassed over a broken arm. I'm beginning to think you'd prefer to have been shot."

"It doesn't hurt that much." He indicated the sling with a careless wave of his cigar. "I'm only wearing this because it gives me an intense, soulful air, like the young Meryl Streep. Like when she was wearing that heart-rending cardigan in *The Deer Hunter*. Do you want me to call the police?"

"There doesn't seem to be any real damage beyond poor Ethel and papers thrown everywhere. Besides, what can the police do? If there's so much as a stray fingerprint in this place, I'll be shocked." She left the chair to lie down on the couch. "Paul didn't take me home until almost seven." She covered her mouth and yawned. "The real damage, Dave, is your arm, only you're too stubborn to get it taken care of properly."

"Yeah." He sat on the floor next to her.

"People damage. That's what this is all about."

Dave studied her profile. That blank look was creeping back over her face—that expressionless mask she sometimes erected as a barrier against even the intrusions of friends. He touched her cheek tentatively with the tips of his long fingers and pushed gently. "Stop that, Annabelle." He put his hand up in the sign for "stop."

A corner of her mouth turned up crookedly. "At least we're almost at the end of this tunnel of horrors," she said. "Now that Paul's got that search warrant. At least I hope we are."

"Have you heard from him yet?"

She shook her head.

An elderly man wearing a bright, sky-blue lab coat stepped into the doorway of the office, gaping at the jumbled papers and at his prone employer. The starched coat crackled against his blue jeans as he paced a few feet into the room.

"Good morning, Edward," Dave said. "Nice coat."

The man in the blue coat grinned. "It's one of the new ones Mr. Hardy ordered," he said. "My wife says it's very becoming."

Dave winced. "That coat looks like it came off the sickbay set of an old *Star Trek* episode. It's cheesy. Edward, is it polyester?"

"Gosh, I don't know."

"What the hell use are you as a chemist, then?" Dave asked.

"Well, for one thing, I can tell you about that oil now."

Dave nudged Annabelle's hip. She raised herself on her elbows.

Edward cleared his throat and looked straight into her luminous green eyes, pronouncing his words precisely. "It's dimethylpolysiloxane," he said.

"Oh, yeah?" Dave asked, sketching a circle with his cigar. "Is that like levitation tonic? What the hell are you talking about?"

"Silicone oil, Dave, almost pure silicone oil."

"So?" Dave asked, sticking the cigar back in his mouth. "What's that?"

"It's used as a lubricant, like in hand lotions."

"But," Dave said, "I take it this particular stuff wasn't a hand lotion. You said 'almost pure.' "

"Well, it's got cornstarch mixed in."

"This isn't *Wheel of Fortune*, Edward," Dave said. "You can just spell it out for us. We don't want to buy a vowel."

"I've never heard of this particular mixture being used on anything but a condom," Edward said.

Dave tightened his lips around the cigar and narrowed his eyes. "Perhaps a Lifestyles condom?"

"It doesn't matter. They all use the same stuff."

"Edward, thank you," Dave said, turning his head to one side and considering the older man's familiar face as if seeing it for the first time. "I wonder if it would affect someone's sex life to know all the stuff you know. Perhaps that is why you have avoided analyzing that coat."

Annabelle sat up on the couch as the chemist left, stifling a smile.

"Condoms," she mused. "So Rolly was playing with condoms that night."

Dave toyed with the narrow skirt of the couch's upholstery, fingering the rich white brocade, his even white teeth sunk in the cigar. "I don't imagine for one minute that Rolly was using condoms as they were intended," Dave signed with some awkwardness, the sling interfering with his eloquence. "For him to get that silicone oil in as many places and in as much quantity as he did, he must have been using more than one condom. Many more than one. Are you thinking what I'm thinking? I'm not thinking that Old Unfaithful Rolly had gotten amazingly lucky that night."

"Dave, I'm thinking he was bagging topaz, like those cocaine smugglers who swallow the stuff in condoms."

"Swallow," Dave said excitedly. "Annabelle, we know where the missing topaz is!"

"Yeah, and so did those maniacs last night. Remember? All they wanted was 'the body.' " She closed her hands together over her stomach. "The Alligator Hole. The gambling debts. That bogus account called Anhinga." Her eyes glittered. "Dave, that was Rolly's deal."

"But what about those stones we found on Pickles Reef?"

"Perhaps, my dear Watson," Annabelle said, "those stones were a test. To see if he could do it."

"A dress rehearsal."

"My God, what an incredible personal risk. Dave, that must be something to see—swallowing a half million dollars in hot rocks. Rolly submitted himself to great physical damage to get out from under his debts."

"Those burns on his fingertips!" Dave made a face. "He didn't get those from the pool. The radioactive topaz must have nipped his fingers like Jack Frost. Like the burn on my hip."

"But swallowing half a million in stones. That must have hurt like the very dickens."

Dave nodded, touching his stinging throat tentatively. "That's where the lidocaine comes in, my dear."

"Oh," she said wonderingly. "To numb the throat. That's why he sounded funny to the operators."

"And now we know how he was going to get the stuff past the portal monitor—a gastrointestinal suitcase." Dave pulled the cigar out of his mouth and glared at it. "We put the strangest things in our mouths, Annabelle."

Again they were interrupted by company at the door. Terry Bodorff stood there, a censorious look on his face and his arms akimbo. Behind one of his arms crouched Gilbert Maria Cristiano, peering through the space between the arm and Bodorff's stiff body. Cristiano wore the sky-blue Hardy Security uniform shirt, but Bodorff wore a tight white T-shirt, its sleeves rolled up onto his shoulders.

"Good morning, Miss Maratos-Hardy," Cristiano said, eyeing Dave's flower-spangled sling uncertainly. Bodorff eyed the ransacked room.

"Ah, Gilbert Cristiano, the *nice* guard," Dave murmured, a sardonic gleam flickering in his eyes. "How kind of you to escort Bodorff, the hero of Naranja. At least according to what he himself has been telling the media. Disarmed the terrorists singlehandedly after a firefight, huh, Bodorff? That what you said?" Dave snorted. "Dishanded one terrorist without a single fight is more like it."

"Excuse me?" Cristiano said.

"Never mind that," Annabelle said hastily. "What can we do for you, Mr. Cristiano? We'd invite you in, but things are at sixes and sevens in here." She waved her arm to indicate the chaos of papers.

"Excuse me?" Cristiano said.

Annabelle rose wearily to her feet and walked to the door. "I'm sorry, Mr. Cristiano. What brought you here this morning?"

"I've come to confess about Dr. Castillo," he bleated, his dark face turning crimson.

"What?" Bodorff snarled, and his hand went to Dave's Colt, which was tucked into his belt.

Annabelle touched her forehead with the heel of her hand. "Mr. Bodorff." Both syllables of his last name seemed to be wrenched from the deepest part of her being. "What an unusual habit you're becoming for us. Give me the gun."

He blinked rapidly and handed her the Colt, barrel first and pointed at her chest, his finger on the trigger. Because she knew the gun's safety features, Annabelle did not flinch, but she glanced over her shoulder at Dave with a look that said she was in the presence of a great and far-reaching stupidity. And she knew that Dave had just received a jolt of energy to fuel his anti-Bodorff fetish.

But Dave surprised her.

"Barrel first, Bodorff? Hallelujah, it's a miracle." Dave sat on the floor, open-mouthed, much moved at this evidence of how utterly at the mercy of dumb luck Henry Algagollawjiwar had been to receive his comeuppance at the hands of this guard who had shot him with a gun whose components might as well have been fabricated from the stuff of cartoons, so little did the guard treat them as pieces of a dangerous reality, so little did he understand their significance.

"And to think this is our hero." Dave sighed, and launched into clumsy sign, hampered by the sling. "The man who singlehandedly subdued a real-life gunman. Annabelle, I mean it. I now believe in God again. It had to be an act of God that Bodorff actually hit the Indian when he aimed at him. Makes you think, doesn't it?" Dave pointed the cigar at Bodorff. "You are a prophet in disguise, a 1990s Elijah. Where's your chariot? I'll go dust it for you."

Annabelle held the gun at her side. "Mr. Bodorff, you did uncommonly fine work last night. I believe you prevented the escape of a very dangerous man. And you may have saved our lives. Because of the enormous debt I feel, I will not ask you for your resignation." Bodorff's jaw dropped. "I may even send you a nice little bonus. But if you ever again carry a gun while in my employ, I will summarily fire you. I won't wait for an explanation. Do you understand?"

Bodorff nodded, his eyes hooded, his face flushed.

Annabelle turned to the other guard. "Now, Mr. Cristiano, what is this confession all about?" she asked gently.

"I think I'm in a lot of trouble, Miss," he said. "But I got to tell you the truth, you're such a nice lady. Those scissors, the scissors in Dr. Castillo's jeans?"

"Yes?"

"Those are my scissors," he said miserably. "I didn't put them there in the Glove Box, but those are my scissors."

"Where did you put them?" she asked.

"I always put them on the nail by the Coke machine in the canteen," he said. "Dr. Castillo must have borrowed them or something. But I'm not talking bad about him. It's okay if people borrow them." He cast a significant look at Bodorff. "As long as they put them back."

"Mr. Cristiano, you don't have anything to worry about," she said reassuringly. "But I'm glad you told us this. It will help us understand what happened to Dr. Castillo. You're an honest man."

Cristiano coughed. "And I got something else to tell you."

Annabelle waited, giving him an encouraging smile.

"I got to tell you that I can't work for you anymore. The president of the university gave me this." His hand trembled as he held out a folded piece of paper. "I'm sorry, miss."

Annabelle took the paper, spread it open, and read the terse contents. Cristiano had been fired for insubordination.

"What did you do to make this happen?" she asked, raising her eyes from the paper.

"Nothing." Cristiano lowered his eyes. "I just told him something."

"What did you tell him?"

Cristiano hesitated, and then the words came tumbling out. "He told me to get into a radiation suit because I had to help with the temporary repairs to the airlock. So I told him to fuck off. I'm scared of radiation."

Dave slapped his hand on the floor. "You told Beckworth to fuck off?"

Cristiano nodded miserably.

Annabelle smiled broadly. "Mr. Cristiano, how would you like a security job here? In this building?"

Cristiano blushed furiously. His head bowed. He nodded, his eyes seeing only the floor and her bare feet.

But Bodorff, his hands in his pockets, rocked back and forth on his heels, a speculative look on his face. Surely it wasn't this easy to get moved uptown? The look of deep, ponderous thought intensified on his features.

THIRTY

"THANK YOU BOTH FOR WHAT YOU HAVE DONE FOR Hardy Security," Annabelle said, offering her hand first to Cristiano, who touched it quickly, and then to Bodorff, who held it and squeezed it and poured so much meaning into it that she imagined it had swollen under his eager treatment, and she raised her eyebrows. Bodorff executed a brief salute and said, "I gotta get going; I'll take Cristiano's shift today."

Then, with an unpremeditated and completely unintentional reversal of Dave's religious experience, Bodorff opened his left hand and dropped five bullets into Annabelle's hand. "I emptied the clip," he said. He retreated down the hall with Cristiano.

"That *son* of a bitch," Dave shouted, grabbing the deep pile of the carpet and yanking.

Annabelle laughed. She strolled back across the room and flopped onto the couch. She dropped the Colt on the floor next to Dave. "Here's your gun."

"I'll have to have it fumigated," he said disgustedly.

"Dave, what was Rolly doing with Cristiano's scissors?"

Dave contemplated the end of his cigar. He raised his eyes to Annabelle. "Cutting something. I don't want you to think I'm, like, this big expert on condoms, because I'm not. But it would make them a lot easier to swallow if you cut those neck things off."

"I guess they'll have to cut Rolly open now, and we'll know," she said. "It's what Beckworth should have done in the first place. Do you think this is the last we'll see of Bodorff?"

Dave snorted.

"Rampant pests like him don't go away that easily, not that I'm ungrateful to the pest," he said. "Annabelle, now that we're alone," he glanced at the doorway, "what gave the killer away?"

"Sorry, Dave," she said, "I didn't catch that."

He repeated his words in sign.

Annabelle closed her eyes, her face looking as if the memory pained her. When she opened her eyes, she had a pensive, melancholy expression. "Dave, everything just came together in Bertha's note. It was so clear."

The phone on her desk rang. Dave gestured to it impatiently and hopped up, stuffing the cigar in the corner of his mouth.

"Ms. Hardy-Maratos's office," he said into the mouthpiece, the bobbing cigar punctuating his words. "Jorge Enamorado speaking."

He listened for almost three minutes, contributing nothing but keen attention. He cradled the phone in the crook of his shoulder, looked for a piece of paper in vain on her desk, snatched a document randomly from the floor, and jotted down some words while he listened.

When he hung up, he slapped the paper and turned to Annabelle. He made the sign for "Bingo."

"That was Paul Diaz," he said. "They found dosimeter number three seventeen. In the cabinet with the cleaning supplies. Inside a box labeled sulfuric acid. And Paul's got an arrest warrant."

She executed a grim little smile, clearly taking no pleasure in having been right.

Dave stood and left the office. When he returned after several minutes, he carried a small bottle of clear liquid. "Sulfuric acid, according to Edward, has many uses. When I asked him what its effect on topaz would be, he said that it can break down the resistance of the crystalline structure of topaz. That means it can help you break big topaz stones into little ones. It's a chemical Rolly might easily have been storing. Especially if he was going to have a problem swallowing the big stones."

Annabelle sighed. "Then that's why the box was so suggestive to Bertha. Why she must have been interested in it."

"Just tell me about the note first. We'll get to the sulfuric-acid box."

"Well, there we were, in Bertha's messy little apartment," she said, shifting onto her side, "and I started thinking about things being so messy, after Rolly's death, I mean. Messy for the reactor, messy for us, messy for Giselle, messy for Beckworth, messy for Lon, messy for Elmore, messy even for that Prendergast piranha. And I was sitting there, staring at the terminal screen, and I saw the message so clearly."

"Annabelle," Dave interjected. "There's nothing wrong with my eyesight, or with Paul's, for that matter. We both saw the message clearly."

"No, Dave, you both saw the note. What I saw was the message," she said gently.

"What?"

"Give me a piece of paper," she said.

He grabbed a sheet from the floor.

She took a pen from her pocket and wrote on the paper he had given her. She handed it to him.

"See?"

She had written, "I'm really sorry about everything. If Rolly Only Could See me die now. Bertha Susan Puffo."

"See the letters she capitalized, Dave?"

Dave looked at the paper.

"I,R,O,C,S." he said.

"IROCS," she pronounced it. "International Race of Champions. The Car. Who drives IROCS, Dave? According to Bertha's notion of ethnic humor?"

"Cubans."

"Dave, when I saw that—and we know she was a super-careful typist; those capital letters didn't just happen—I knew she had left a message for us. So the message is, 'Cubans me die now.' Her murderer was a Cuban."

"Hell, I'm a Cuban," he said.

"Just listen. I remember thinking the timing of Bertha's murder was interesting, following that meeting at Giselle's house. What, I asked myself, had happened at that meeting? Aside from a stupid little spat between Lon and that Prendergast woman, nothing. Except that they decided on burial at sea. Except that Giselle signed a paper. Except that Bertha asked to use the bathroom. Giselle's bathroom. Giselle's a Cuban. So I figured maybe Bertha found something in there that Giselle didn't want her to find, something that gave Bertha enough of an idea to confront Giselle. Bertha was the last to leave. Bertha found something. And what was the one thing that only Rolly's murderer could have? That should have been on the body?"

"Dosimeter three-seventeen," Dave said.

Silence filled the room.

Annabelle lay back on the couch.

Dave restlessly moved his legs across the carpet. The scattered papers crinkled noisily. He sat still, pricked by a thought. He rose to his knees and started pawing through the papers, tossing them around him in a blur. A few came to roost on Annabelle's face, and she elevated herself on an elbow, watching Dave's frantic search with a puzzled expression.

At last he grabbed a thick, triple-folded document.

"Aha!" he said gleefully.

He sat with his legs spread and opened the document, scanning the pages quickly.

"Here it is," he said, looking up. "A copy of Rolly's life insurance policy. I never got a chance to read it."

Annabelle waited in silence.

Dave stopped reading and met her eyes. "If he suffers a, quote, nuclear-related death by accident or misadventure, unquote, she gets two million dollars," he said. "I guess that's why she didn't just stick him in the microwave. She must have found the plane ticket earlier than she said—he was going to leave her. No wonder she was so pissed about the suicide theory. It was costing her two million in insurance dollars."

The phone rang. Dave drew a long sigh and crawled awkwardly to the desk, reaching up for the receiver. "Ms. Hardy-Maratos's office. Jorge Enamorado speaking."

Again Dave listened for several minutes. He hung up. "Bertha's autopsy results," he said. "That was Diaz. Big surprise. The fall killed her."

"But how did Giselle get her cooperation?" Annabelle asked. "How did she get her to type a bogus suicide note and vault over the balcony? For that matter, how did she get Rolly to be such a lamb to the slaughter?"

"Annabelle, Diaz said the only suspicious mark on Bertha's body was a small puncture inside the ear." He paused and took his cigar from his mouth, considering the brown cylinder as though it were a long-forgotten page from a particularly depressing diary. He looked up at Annabelle. "Rolly had a mark like that. I wondered if he had an exciting new drug habit, the kind that gives Miami's criminals such bad public relations."

"A needle. Giselle's a nurse," Annabelle said thoughtfully. "Call Paul back and ask if they found a syringe in the house when they found the dosimeter."

Dave had a dull, disgusted look. "He already told me the inventory. They bagged a big fat syringe, the opaque kind you get in a pet store for feeding baby animals. That's what he thought it was at first. But this one was accompanied by a great big needle that fits it to a tee. But the fun part is that they found the needle inside a pair of—get this—anticontamination gloves. Those yellow things like the suits, the kind I wore to handle the topaz, the kind of pants you wore last night. That's why Paul mentioned it. I guess Giselle's little motivator was pretty scary. Nice weapon."

"Did they test the syringe?"

"Yeah. Paul wasn't going to mention the syringe, except for the fact that it was in the yellow gloves. Know why? You wanna know the really chilling part? You wanna know what they found in the syringe?"

Annabelle raised her eyebrows.

"Good old honest tap water," he said. "Plain old fucking tap juice. Giselle must have scared the pants off Rolly and Bertha with those gloves, and it was good old fucking plain old ordinary tap fucking water all the time. I bet she told them it was some weird radioactive killer secretion straight from the bowels of a uranium Godzilla."

"Scared the pants off? I guess that explains the urine on the bridge," Annabelle said, shaking her head.

"Maybe. Rolly was the one stuffing that radiation down his gullet. Maybe it was resting on top of his bladder."

Annabelle rubbed her eyes. "He was taking terrible chances with his body." She frowned at her fingers. "I didn't show you, but there was a letter *C* marked on that barrel with the topaz on the reef. It was in graphite, pretty recent. It must have stood for Castillo. What an irony—he signed away his life with a letter on a barrel." She drummed her fingers on the side of the couch and sat up. "Dave. There's one other thing I have to talk with you about. Our lab delivered my photos, the ones I took Tuesday." A solemn look had descended over her face, and he wobbled to the couch on his knees, the cigar now sloppily gnawed and wet.

"What is it, *amiga*?"

"Giselle had to get into the reactor before she could kill her husband."

"So?" Dave rubbed his ear. "Oh. I see what you mean."

"Dave, nobody just walks into that building. You need a security key." She paused. "Or an Uzi."

"Or somebody to let you in," he said, plucking at the fabric of the couch.

"Exactly," she said. "And there's only one person who could have let Giselle in. My photos show that none of the operators in the control room could leave without abandoning a whole instrument panel, or without the others knowing. And Bodorff certainly didn't let her in. And the receptionist didn't do it. I seem to have a number of excellent shots of the one person who could have let her in."

"Your Nazi friend."

"My Nazi friend," she echoed grimly.

Dave put his hand to his chin unthinkingly and winced from the unexpected pain. He dropped his hand quickly as though he had scalded himself and grasped the bottom edge of the couch in recoil from the stinging sensation on his chin. The cigar rolled under the couch. He reached under the flap of fabric, and his fingers touched the plastic box.

"Hello, what's this?" he said, pulling the device and the cigar out, and holding them before his face.

His eyes grew large, and he put the little box down with agonizing and slow deliberation on the soft carpet. Laying his finger across his lips, he grabbed Annabelle's hand and eased her off the couch, hardly daring to breathe. He pulled her to the door, holding her right hand in his. At the door, with a hissed intake of breath, he shot out his wounded left arm and grabbed the handle of the fire alarm. The ceiling sprinklers poured out hard jets of water instantly, and bells clanged all over the top floor. They could see people running for the exits, including Arantxa, her chubby legs churning on the hall carpet.

Dave grabbed Annabelle and, disobeying all the posted warnings, he summoned the elevator. The door opened immediately, he punched the button for the first floor, and he dragged Annabelle inside and threw her against the far wall, shielding her with his body.

The door closed, and the car shot down seventeen floors, but the blast sounded to Dave as if the bomb had been inside the elevator shaft, and the shock waves hurtled them to the floor of the elevator car. Debris rained on the roof of the car as it ground to a halt. Despite the powerful blast seventeen floors above them, the polished brass door slid open smoothly, rolling across its well-oiled bearings, at the lobby of the Pink Building.

The doorman stared inside at them as they huddled together.

Annabelle loosened her grip on Dave's injured arm and stood shakily. The doorman hovered solicitously and helped her from the car.

Dave saw them standing together in the tiled lobby, and, behind them, through the transparent rosy slabs of the lobby wall, he could see falling dust, debris, and an occasional thick shard of pink glass. Papers and scraps of blueprints fluttered down through the sunny morning. Sirens blared in the distance.

"Well. Aren't you going to help me up too?" Dave demanded.

The doorman gave him a withering look, but reached

inside the elevator to touch the Open Door button. Dave, however, apparently found this gesture inadequate.

He scorched the doorman with a burning look of contempt. "You're just mad because you can't think of a comeback to my little limerick."

The doorman pursed his handsome lips and cocked his head to listen to the approaching sirens. He glanced across the lobby and out through the pink glass. The debris was falling less densely now. The lobby seemed safe enough. Annabelle was staring at the falling pink shards and blueprints, as though in a trance. The doorman glanced back at Dave, who provided the final goad by leering at him smugly.

The doorman removed his perfectly tanned and manicured finger from the elevator button and stepped back.

The door slid closed.

THIRTY-ONE

THE WATER SPARKLED AND TUMBLED INTO THE PEARLY black marble shell from the little mermaid's hands, like a shower of ice splinters in the dazzling late-afternoon sun.

Dave was asleep on a lounge chair, nestled into plump, flowered cushions. His head was cradled on his right arm; his broken left arm was resting on his stomach in a pristine white cast. His gentle snores shook his thin chest from time to time, and Annabelle watched him from the kitchen window, feeling an almost fiendish smugness about the painkillers she and her father had persuaded their physician to administer over Dave's eloquent and probably loud protests. With an unexpected pang she wished to know the sound of Dave's voice. She glanced down at the warm soapy water in the sink and drew out the last teacup, scrubbing its thin gold rim pensively with her fingers.

Jacob Hardy had returned early and with great commotion from the bonefishing tournament, having read the article in the *Miami Tribune* about the fight at the reactor.

Jacob, in the full cry of his fury and fear, had been ready to thrash his pilot to make greater speed than the tearing twenty-eight knots that had finally brought his sportfishing boat to Dinner Key Marina.

It was from there, as Jacob was tossing the bowline to his first mate, that he saw a section of the top floor of the Pink Building seem to bulge and lift into the clear blue sky. And he heard the deep, reverberating boom of the explosion. Jacob had done and felt many things in the course of a thoroughly well-lived fifty-nine years, but the cold constriction he experienced in his solar plexus was a startling new sensation to him. He went numb, and he thought his heart had stopped.

He had run across the docks and through City Hall Plaza to the office building, his mind blank, his eyes scanning the jagged outlines of the top floor, his long and powerful legs carrying him at a speed he would not have thought possible. He vaulted over the backs of cars weaving crazily on South Bayshore, weaving as their drivers slid to the curbs at the sound of sirens in the distance, weaving to avoid the glass on the street, weaving to get a better look at the storm of paper raining down the south wall of the Pink Building. He had shouldered his way through the small but burgeoning crowd and leaped up the shallow stairs to the lobby, to see Annabelle, apparently unhurt, conversing animatedly with one of those spectacularly healthy doormen.

In that moment Jacob was certain his heart had stopped. His tanned skin was covered in gooseflesh, and he bowed his head in dizzy relief, bending over his trembling knees.

Jacob had insisted on removing Annabelle from the

scene, bellowing at the Miami Police that the cops could damn well interview his daughter in her home. They had received a police escort to his daughter's bayside villa on Poinciana—"as we damn well ought to."

When the whole story had finally come pouring out, over hot tea and turkey sandwiches around Annabelle's island kitchen, Jacob laid the blame for the entire series of dangerous incidents on University of the Keys president Eugene W. Beckworth.

"I told you he was no good," Jacob said.

They had given statements to the Miami Police regarding the bombing, but those statements were necessarily short. Annabelle and Dave knew nothing that would even suggest a suspect. They were asked to repeat several times their tale of the big doll's missing head. And they were asked many times about their own security on the eighteenth floor. Dave—tired of defending the company against charges of inadequate security and suffering agonies of thrilling pain in his left arm—lost his temper.

"If you think our record is so terrible," he shouted, "I'd like to know what you make of the murder statistics in this city you're all so busy protecting. Christ in a crime wave! You make it sound like we *advertised* for a bomber to come up and redecorate the penthouse."

Jacob silently applauded Dave's outburst. Dave was the same right-thinking man Jacob had lifted out of the anonymous ranks of Hardy security guards. Jacob prided himself on judging character. But not even Jacob was prepared for the highlights of the story they were now telling. Dave had shot a snake, broken a bone, and plucked Annabelle from an explosive doom. Jacob could not bring himself to demonstrate his gratitude openly, but when the police had departed, his quiet discussion with the doctor had been forceful and to the point: "Do what you can to knock him out. He's too thick-headed to take a pain-killer."

Annabelle, who would never know how her own contributions to the solution of the reactor murder had been dismissed by her father in favor of casting a masculine coloration over the story, smiled at the doctor encouragingly.

And so Dave slept in the warm afternoon sun, Hotspur the Shakespearean kitten ensconced on his lap. Annabelle dried the last cup and wiped her hands, leaning on the edge of the sink in thought. The damage to the Pink Building seemed to her remote, and unimportant. Injuries to her staff had been minor, for Dave's alarm had been instantly obeyed. The most seriously wounded was Arantxa, who now lay asleep upstairs in Annabelle's guest room, her back and hips having been treated for cuts and abrasions from the flying wreckage of her employer's office.

The damage to the Pink Building, however, was extensive, and estimates on repairs would have to wait until she could summon emotional energy for anything outside her own home.

She glanced now at Dave and felt a novel sensation of completeness that he was whole and in her care. She would let him sleep and sleep until he lost that green tinge to his face. Let murders and murderers and bombers and jewel thieves and poisonous reptiles take over the city—she didn't care.

In the window she saw the reflection of the light flashing in the living room behind her. The doorbell.

She ignored it. She folded the towel and put the clean dishes into cupboards. But she did not want to sleep. She intended to get a book and sit outside with Dave. The light flashed insistently.

She could not think of a single person she would want to see. Jacob had returned to his boat. She barely knew her neighbors. She was not expecting anyone. Even Dave's kitten guards had been dismissed. She crossed to the bookshelves, running her fingers over titles. She stopped and considered the photographs: her father, Dave, her younger self, Nikki. For the first time the wave of longing that usually engulfed her when she saw this picture refused to be conjured up. The man in the picture seemed like a stranger to her. She was idly puzzled by this absence of feeling. Perhaps her physical exhaustion was reflected in her emotional responses; perhaps one kind of numbness bred another.

The flashing light now intruded itself on her tired eyes like a stinging dash of salty water. She would have no peace until she put an end to it.

She went to the door and looked through the peep-hole. She would not be taken by surprise again by strangers delivering packages.

Lon Berlin stood on the step, a worried look on his face—his handsome face, she thought. She rested her forehead against the smooth, cool surface of the door. *Go away*, she thought. *Just go away*.

She sighed, deactivated the alarm, released the lock on the door, and pulled it open. Sunlight flooded into the room.

He put out his hand to touch her arm, and she stepped back.

"I heard on the radio," he said. "Are you okay?"

"I'm fine."

He smiled uncertainly and put out his hand again.

"Don't touch me," she said evenly.

"You're hurt, Annabelle," he seemed to conclude. "The explosion hurt you?"

"No, I'm not hurt."

"Then what's all this sudden shyness?" He stepped over the doorsill. "Can you understand what I'm saying, Annabelle?"

"You never asked me that before," she said blandly. "Of course I understand you. Maybe better than you think."

"Why are you acting like this? I'm not some stranger."

"What do you want here?"

"I thought I wanted to see you, to see if you were hurt. Now I want to know what's going on with you."

"Nothing," she said wearily. "Absolutely nothing. You'd be shocked at the indifference. The real nothingness."

He advanced into the room, and she backed away again, unafraid but unwilling to suffer his touch.

"What the hell are you talking about?" he said, shaking his head.

"I'm talking about Rolly and you."

The dark expression on his lean face lifted. "Oh. I know. God, Annabelle," he said, putting his hands out toward her. "The nightmare is over. Giselle's been arrested. You don't have to think about that anymore. It's over."

"Just how smug are you?" she demanded. "Get your

hands away from me. Do you think I don't know what you did?"

"I think that explosion must have hurt you more than you're admitting to yourself. Or to me. What do you imagine you are talking about?"

"I'm talking about murder. It doesn't matter if you didn't actually help Giselle throw Rolly into that sea of fire you call the reactor. You're still a murderer." She put out her hand as if to erect a barrier.

"Have you gone mad? You know why I was at the reactor that night. You saw the fax yourself."

"I saw the fax." She blew a puff of air out through her mouth and glanced toward the kitchen. When she looked at him again, she saw that he had followed her gaze. "In fact I happen to know that you actually sent it, because this morning I sent a fax to the Breakers Hotel myself, asking them if they got your fax. Unlike you, Dr. Berlin, I have a fax machine right here in my home. Many deaf people do."

He shrugged in relief. "Well, there you are. I wish you had simply taken my word, but at least you know my story is true. You checked it out yourself."

"Yeah. I checked it out." She backed up a step toward the bookshelves. "And when they faxed their response—that they had indeed received a note from you—I faxed another question."

"What?"

"I asked them if they had *delivered* your fax."

He shifted his weight and looked at the floor.

"Dr. Berlin, I guess I don't have to tell you what their answer was."

He shook his head. He raised his eyes to hers, and the

look of despair on his face was plain and crystallized in the hard muscles of his cheeks. He rubbed the back of his left hand over his jaw.

"They said they never delivered your fax because there was no Jill Berlin at the hotel. There was no party that night."

Annabelle's voice was soft and tired.

He nodded. "What made you doubt me, Annabelle?"

"You really want to know? You want to hear this?"

"Yes," he whispered.

"It was several things," she said, ragged edges of exhaustion in her voice. "Your friendship with Giselle. Your feelings for Rolly. Your intimate knowledge of the comings and goings of the topaz. You, of all people, had to have known that the pathways of those stones had been diverted. Plus, that supposed party at the Breakers would have been held on a Monday night, in the middle of the semester, a couple hundred miles from the University of Florida. Even the best partyers don't usually go to such lengths. This whole party thing has always had a bad smell." She pursed her lips and nodded to herself. "And, Dr. Berlin, Dave didn't like you."

He glanced sharply at the photographs on the bookshelves.

"Why did you do it, Dr. Berlin? Why?"

"Because," he said on a quick breath, "because Rolly was going to screw everything up, everything. Because he was stealing the reactor blind. Because he was going to take all my work and get rich—my work, Annabelle. Rolly was too fucking blind to be of any use to the project. I was covering for him more and more. I don't know how he was going to sell the stones, but he was rolling topaz into that phony Anhinga storage account from new accounts—accounts we couldn't release for years, accounts he was going to stick me with when he left. Oh, I knew he was leaving. Giselle told me about the plane tickets. But I didn't kill him, Annabelle. You've got to believe me. Giselle killed Rolly. I only let her in. She asked me how she could scare him, and I told her how. That's all I did. I told her how to scare him. I didn't know she was going to kill him. You can't blame me for the murder."

She felt briefly nauseated by his pleading. She strained to glance toward the kitchen from the corner of her eye.

"Annabelle, I didn't kill him. But day after day we handled all those jewels, and the thought of him getting rich from the beauty I had created was killing me. Killing me. Don't you understand? Why shouldn't I be rich? Haven't you ever, even once, wanted to take something that wasn't yours? You've probably never been exposed to the painful temptation I was exposed to day after day. The Topaz Project is a unique phenomenon. How do you control yourself in the presence of such abominable temptation?"

Annabelle felt the sick, limp pull of a tepid pity.

"Dr. Berlin, that's an old, old whore you're flirting with. An old, old argument. You don't occupy a special perch above the rest of us, Dr. Berlin. We're supposed to control ourselves. Some things are just wrong. It's that simple."

He jerked his head impatiently. "Oh, sure, it's simple." He flung the words at her. "God, how moralistic you are. As though this frightfully cold cosmos operated on moral laws."

"I don't know about the cosmos," she said dully. "I only know a little about this earth."

"You just don't understand. You don't know what it's like to want something that bad."

She blinked at him, anger flaring at last in her eyes. "Oh *yes* I do. I'm living a life, too."

"Annabelle," he took a step toward her. "What are you going to do? If you're thinking I had anything to do with that explosion, you're wrong. I've done nothing to you."

"I know," she said, now trying to raise her voice, "because I know all of your movements since last night. You couldn't have planted a bomb in my office. Neither could Giselle. The police have been watching her."

"That's a relief, at least. Annabelle, can't we just go on from where we were? Or make a new beginning? My feelings for you are strong, genuine. Give me a chance. Please," he said, taking another step toward her, "can't you try to understand? I'm not a bad man. I'm sorry about Rolly, I really am. I swear to God."

"Get out of my house before I call the police. I'm going to have to call them anyway, but I'd rather not have you arrested on my property."

His expression shifted, seemed to ripple oddly before her tired eyes. "I don't have a choice here, Annabelle, because I'm not going to jail for something that wasn't my fault anyway." His voice was harsh, and beads of sweat were standing on his forehead. "Rolly started this. Can't you see what a monster he was?" His shoulder twitched. "Don't move away from me."

She edged along the bookcase, but he darted his arm out and grabbed her hair in a fierce twisting motion. She cried out, and he jerked her hair harder.

"Dammit, Annabelle, this is so stupid. We're good together. I don't want to hurt you like this."

She slashed her open left hand up against his jaw with all of her strength, and he gasped, his grip on her hair shuddering loose. She tore away, stumbling across the room. He lunged and tackled her around the knees. They went down and rolled together toward the fireplace. His arms were locked around her lower body, and she flailed at him with her fists.

He released her legs and, in a wild rush, dived for her arms. She tried to wriggle away, but he caught her left wrist, yanking on it until she felt her shoulder pop. She saw him look quickly toward the fireplace. The poker was just out of his reach. He pulled on her arm as he inched toward the hearth, breathing heavily. She kicked his shin and gave a desperate jerk on her arm. She slipped out of his clutch and leaped to her feet, her breath coming in ragged hisses.

He stood slowly, out of breath but with the poker in his hand. His eyes were wild, but he managed to gasp out, "Please. Don't do this to me."

She sidestepped to the bookshelves, her eyes on his, warily.

"What the hell," he said, flexing his shoulders. The poker swung loosely from his hand. "Somebody else is after you, Annabelle. I've got a free hand to kill you. And no one will ever suspect me. They'll all think this is another bomb thing. I've got a ticket, a free ticket."

"You're not going to kill me."

"What's to stop me?" He walked slowly toward her.

She said nothing, waiting for him, their eyes locked.

She let him come nearer, the poker swinging lightly at

his side from his lowered hand. She braced her hands against the bookshelves.

He took her chin in his extended fingers, stroking upward along the line of her jaw.

"You're so beautiful, my dear. So beautiful." His eyes traveled from her jaw to the curve of her ear. "There's nothing to stop me. Nothing and no one to stop me."

With a measured coldness she turned her head and looked with smiling deliberation toward the kitchen.

He jerked his head in the direction of her gaze.

She swung a first edition of *David Copperfield* and cracked the end of its stiff spine on his throbbing temple.

He wobbled. His knees gave. He crumpled leadenly at her feet.

With trembling hands she stooped and picked up the old book, which had fallen open to the first page, and read the opening sentence with startled recognition:

Whether I shall turn out to be the hero of my own life, or whether that station will be held by anybody else, these pages must show

She pressed the volume against her cheek. The book felt cold against her heated skin.

"I beat the dickens out of him," she whispered, profound surprise written on her tired face.

FRIDAY

Cosmologists were already interested
in any extra particles that might
exist in the universe, because they are always
on the lookout for the "missing mass" needed
to make the universe closed.

JOHN GRIBBIN
In Search of Schrödinger's Cat

THIRTY-TWO

"YOU KNOW, ANNABELLE, WE SHOULD JUST TURN IN OUR guns and permits and carry our library cards for protection. We'd be a lot safer."

"Dickens might not have worked against that cottonmouth you shot, not at twenty-five paces. He's more of a point-blank author."

Dave was sitting on a pink leather barstool in the aft lounge, the motoryacht's cruising speed of sixteen knots ruffling his brown hair. He sipped Cuban coffee from a dainty porcelain thimble of a cup, its powerful caffeine slam making larger cups the sole province of the seriously macho, or the uninitiated.

He swung his legs, which, dangling from the baggy purple shorts he considered appropriate for a funeral, looked thin and childlike. The collar of his purple polo shirt was turned up, revealing the snap on the back of his yellow cotton bow tie. He called it an "automatic" tie, but Annabelle knew he was covering considerable mortification that his broken arm had made it impossible for him to tie what he called a "real" bow tie. His black flats, however, were flawlessly polished and glinted in the pastel glow of sunlight entering the lounge through its tinted green portholes.

He wore a yellow silk sling, having discovered that his cast could be used as an occasion for a variety of fashion statements, and Annabelle was certain that before the cast was removed, she would see it adorned in as many eloquent ways as he could invent.

"I never got around to reading *David Copperfield,*" he confessed. "Maybe I'll borrow your copy and read it aloud to Marcel. Christ in Congress, he's such a freeloader, Annabelle. I offer him the whole world, and he turns up back on my doorstep like a Jehovah's Witness."

Annabelle smiled. Marcel's return had injected Dave's face with a fugitive pride, but he kept up a steady stream of verbal abuse—directed against what he portrayed as the parrot's parasitic attachment to free meals and rent-free living—that only highlighted his fascination with the Prodigal Parrot's Homecoming.

"You know, I must have been clipping something else all these months," Dave mused, his legs swinging nonchalantly. "I thought it was his wings."

"You clipped him yourself?" Annabelle was shocked. "Dave, you could have crippled him."

He grinned smugly. "Well, I didn't. I guess I just have a natural knack for it," he said with palpably false modesty and a Cary Grant flourish of his left hand. "Marcel can fly like a goddamnned stealth bomber."

Annabelle glanced over Dave's shoulder and out the porthole, her gaze caught by a bright red cigarette boat crossing their wake at fantastic speed, the sun glinting off the heavy chrome of its pointed bow. The pilot was a small man, a man who stood serenely at the wheel, taking the crashing bumps without seeming to notice. His mirrored sunglasses jumped on his tranquil face with each pounding lunge of the fast boat, but his bright orange baseball cap appeared to be glued to his head.

"Dave, look at that guy," she said, twitching his sleeve. "Hasn't he got a great face? I mean, he looks so happy."

Dave pivoted on the stool and studied the man she was pointing to. "Yeah, I see what you mean. Like something untouched by life. I wonder what his secret is." Dave swiveled back to face the main salon and the people milling around there, talking and eating chicken *croquetas* and vegetables with their coffee. "That guy reminds me of someone. Maybe it's just that his smile looks like a lizard I saw somewhere." Dave frowned.

Beckworth and his wife stood by the buffet—she looking bored and chewing celery, he looking sick. The yacht's smooth cruising speed, and the open doors and windows, should have eliminated seasickness as a factor for the funeral party, but Beckworth had that yellow tinge around the mouth that signaled a seafarer already in acute distress, or getting there quickly.

Elmore and his wife sat on canvas chairs near the door of the salon. He was chatting in a desultory monotone with the NRC's Neary. Mrs. Elmore was keeping a watchful eye on Rachel Prendergast across the main salon. Elmore nervously and repeatedly checked his perfectly combed hairpiece, obviously worried about the effect of salt spray and the breeze on the man-made fibers.

"Annabelle." Dave stopped swinging his legs and alertly regarded Elmore's finicky attentions to the hairpiece. "Who's going *to pay* for this shindig? Are you putting this on the university's bill?"

"Nah," she said, regarding her shapely, unpolished fingernails. "I want to do this for Rolly, Dave. I can't explain why."

"You don't have to explain anything, my poppet. It's your yacht."

Annabelle put a hand on Dave's cheek, careful to avoid the scabby souvenirs of the portal monitor. "Jorge Enamorado, you are a noble guy. 'A friend may well be reckoned the masterpiece of Nature.' "

"Ha! I recognize that one," he said triumphantly, wallowing in his pleasure at finally catching her on her own turf. "Ralph Waldo Emerson himself—the Transcendental Pete Rose. Well, well. 'It's a long worm that never turns.' " His face gradually took on a serious cast. He sketched quotation marks in the air: " 'For every thing you have missed, you have gained something else.' " He repeated the quotation marks with a flourish. "Annabelle, I hope you take that to heart when you remember that Nazi slob Lon Berlin. That was Emerson again. My favorite piece of Anglo literature is 'Self-Reliance.' "

"I don't know what I've gained," she said, smiling naughtily. "But I know what I didn't lose."

"Are you being dirty?" Dave opened his eyes in fascinated speculation.

"Wouldn't you like to know, you world-class prude?"

He cleared his throat, hastily changing the subject.

"Annabelle, do you realize what an employment vacuum they've got at the reactor? Two scientists, a security guard, and a secretary."

"Speaking of the reactor, Dave," Annabelle said, a

foreboding frown in her green eyes, "Beckworth wants to talk to us about what he called 'our status.' "

"I hope you told him where he could stick our status."

"Dave, we've still got four months to go on our contract with the university. I can't tell him to stick it."

Dave eyed Annabelle. "Cristiano did."

"Well, he's a better man than I am." She grinned. "Let's circulate. Beckworth looks too sick to bother us now."

They strolled together through the salon, speaking briefly and on neutral topics with Neary and Elmore. Dave moved on to speak, with the ease of shared troubles, to Gayle Baker, the reactor's night receptionist. She showed him her wrists, which still bore the red circles imprinted on her flesh by the wires that had bound her. She studied the green and brown bruises girding his scabs, and she commented on their bond of suffering and asked for his phone number. Dave followed Annabelle past the dining room and the galley and into the wheelhouse. They climbed the ladder to the sundeck, Dave primly going first, out of consideration for the voluminous folds of her long and swirling fuchsia skirt. At the top he reached down to take her hand and help her onto the white fiberglass deck. Her yellow shoes made tapping noises as she ambled to the rail with Dave.

Receding in the northwest was the glimmering squat skyline of Miami Beach, the city of Miami lost in the hazy afternoon behind the beach. The Art Deco hotels and the high-rise condos of Miami Beach were barely a suggestion of geometric regularity against the coast. The blue Atlantic stretched behind the yacht like a plate with a few white crumbs on its rim.

"There's that guy again," Dave said, pointing to the choppy water south of the wake of the yacht. The seventy-six-foot *Prelude* drew a long double white line in the water, and the red cigarette boat's thinner line paralleled the yacht's. Dave stepped quickly across to the pilot's console and spoke briefly with Mark Goodlove, Annabelle's heavily muscled Bahamian pilot.

Dave returned to her side with Goodlove's binoculars. He trained them on the cigarette boat with his right hand, slowly moving the focus wheel with his index finger. He studied the smaller boat's pilot for a few moments and handed the glasses to Annabelle, shaking his head as he tried to call that face out of the files of his photographic memory.

She saw scuba gear in a backseat, and a silver-wrapped package on the seat next to the little pilot. She took time to peruse the lower half of the man's face, which was tranquil, almost surreal in its overt contentment. The upper part of his face was obscured by the sunglasses and the visor of the orange cap. She lowered the binoculars.

"You know, Dave, I'd like to meet that guy. What an intriguing face. I wonder what he's doing all the way out here. He can't be meaning to dive. He's all alone."

"He's certainly got diving gear," Dave signed, turning to face southeast toward the pine box lashed across the bow of the *Prelude* in simple state. "I swear I've seen that man before. Someplace where the light was different." He shrugged and looked down at the cast on his arm. "Oh, well. Goodlove says we'll be in international waters in five minutes. I feel bad that we don't have a man of God on board. Or holy woman."

Annabelle shaded her eyes with her hand. The coffin was flanked by two tall sailors, women who had worked on the *Prelude* since Annabelle had owned the boat. The sailors stood at respectful ease, their white uniforms gleaming in the sun.

"I think this will be okay, Dave. A much more spectacular funeral than Rolly would have had if we had not been in the picture." A cloud darkened her expression. "I guess we should realize how lucky we are to be in the picture."

Elmore's toupee appeared at the top of the ladder. He climbed onto the sundeck, his brown three-piece suit incongruous among the more casually dressed experienced sailors. Beckworth puffed up the ladder behind him, his blue seersucker jacket damp on his back, his heavily moussed brown hair sticking up from his scalp in two stiff tufts.

"Beckworth looks like a huge bleached roach," Dave signed. The two university officials walked toward Annabelle and Dave, Elmore hesitantly, Beckworth lurching, his weight appearing comically suspended from his thick shoulders. The yellow glow around his lips was now a creamy gray.

Annabelle had not spoken with Beckworth since shortly after the surgery on Rolly Castillo's body had been completed at the reactor early that morning. The pathologists had removed twenty-one very cold and sloppy condoms from the cadaver, condoms filled with irradiated London Blue Topaz.

Beckworth had then clearly been nursing a fierce resentment against both Annabelle and Dave, blaming them for the bath of publicity the reactor was undergoing in the media.

"You were supposed to control this, public relations–wise," he had shouted at her. "You were supposed to shield us from this sort of public poking in the entrails. Instead you seem to delight in talking to the press and shoving irresponsible accusations at our people. What the hell kind of security is that?"

Beckworth had said he found it particularly galling that Lon Berlin was being questioned by the police, especially after he'd "been wining and dining Annabelle."

Annabelle had pointedly kept her mouth shut. She had turned on her heel and left the reactor basement, choosing to wait in the Sunnyvale limo for the cortege to start.

Now Beckworth seemed prepared to froth at his gray lips.

"I want a word with you, young woman." He panted, his cheeks shivering. He stood wobbling on the center of the sundeck. "I've got something to say to you about damages. Oh, God," he moaned as the contents of his stomach seemed to shift in response to the turmoil in his inner ears. He steadied himself with an effort. "Ms. Hardy-Maratos, your company will be hearing something from university counsel tomorrow morning," he said, gulping.

Annabelle looked at Dave. He elevated one eyebrow fantastically, as if that eyebrow were a caterpillar arching its back, a creature capable of movement independent of Dave's already animated face.

She stepped forward on steady legs and put her face near Beckworth's. His breath nearly made her reel.

"A proper autopsy in the first place would have spared you some of this grief," she said icily.

The gray in his face mixed with flushing red, producing a putrid old-rose color that reminded Dave of spoiled salmon.

Beckworth drew himself up to his full height.

"You won't get away with twisting the blame around to me," he stated with a kind of final certitude. "The university has bought and paid for you, little lady. You answer to me."

He plucked at his belt, hitching up his trousers, and nodded his head at her several times for emphasis.

She faced him squarely and directed a clear gaze into his eyes.

"Fuck off, little man," she said without heat or apparent rancor, but with precisely clipped syllables. "In fact *get* off. I bought and paid for this boat, and you answer to me."

Annabelle raised her bare arm and extended crooked fingers in signal to the two crew members at the bow. They left their post at the coffin and took up position behind Annabelle.

She motioned to the *Prelude*'s dinghy, a fifteen-foot Boston Whaler named *The Lewd,* attached by chains to the sundeck. The sailors quickly removed the chains. A gigantic iron hook attached to the end of a hydroelectric davit raised the dinghy from the deck and carried it to the side of the yacht, where one of the sailors suspended it by the simple expedient of pushing the button on the electric control panel of the davit. The sailors resumed their stance behind Annabelle.

"Get this man off the *Prelude,*" she ordered.

The sailors took his arms and marched him, shocked and protesting weakly, to the side of the yacht.

"Just a minute," Annabelle said. She turned to her pilot.

Beckworth caught her hesitation, a glint of gloating anticipation in his eyes. She didn't have the nerve.

"Are we in international waters yet?" Annabelle asked.

The pilot showed no emotion on his lustrous dark face, but his brown eyes twinkled.

"Aye, Captain."

She signaled to the sailors, and they lifted Beckworth into the dinghy by expert hands twisted into his seersucker coat and cotton trousers. The dinghy was lowered into the sea by the davit, the chain spooling out, with hardly a splash to mark contact with the deep.

"Let her go," Annabelle ordered. The davit chain was released. Beckworth stood shakily in the dinghy, bent at the knees to keep from capsizing, pounding his fists in the air.

Without a backward glance Annabelle walked to the bow, to stand by the coffin, gazing out to the east. They sailed on, the midnight-blue water slapping against the hull of the yacht.

Goodlove throttled down the engine when the boat was thirteen miles off the mainland. The boat idled in neutral. The sailors went below to inform the other passengers that their destination had been reached.

When all fourteen passengers had assembled in silence on the sundeck, standing in uneven rows on the white fiberglass floor, Annabelle spoke, her soft voice carrying on the clipping breeze that ruffled her hair and tugged the corners of the Cuban flag Dave held in his right hand.

"I don't know if anyone here is actually mourning Dr. Rolando Ruiz de Castillo," she said. "This won't be a religious moment. I can't do that for Rolly. But I'd like to quote briefly from one of the meditations of John Donne, a seventeenth-century poet." She paused, a salt mist in her eyes as she caught sight of a purplish line on the horizon that might have been Miami. " 'No man is an island, entire of itself; every man is a piece of the continent, a part of the main. If a clod be washed away by the sea, Europe is the less, as well as if a promontory were, as well as if a manor of thy friend's or of thine own were. Any man's death diminishes me, because I am involved in mankind; and therefore never send to know for whom the bell tolls, it tolls for thee.' "

The ship's bell chimed dolorously four times.

Dave unfurled the flag in his right hand, lifting it into the breeze, and Annabelle helped him cover the coffin with the silky red, white, and blue fabric. The two sailors pushed the pine box to the edge of the bow. They lifted the end of the box. And the body, zipped into a harshly white, weighted cotton bag, slipped out through a hinged panel and dropped into the sea.

The box was lowered back into its first position, and Annabelle folded the flag.

Goodlove throttled forward and turned the yacht north and west, for Miami.

The cigarette boat, hovering about four hundred yards to the south, plowed its way to the spot where the body had been jettisoned.

A red and white dive flag was raised over the little

boat, and the slim pennant snapped in the lively southwest breeze. The lone seaman's face was placid, his perpetual smile having given the lips a look of sweet fixity, like a Madonna's ceramic serenity.

He donned the air tanks, in no hurry.

This was deep water. But he had all the time in the world. Time to examine the depths, time to realign his own spiritual position in the cosmos, time to relocate his lost soul.

And the silence out here was very conducive to meditation.